ANIMATED BAGGAGE

by

Hilary Shepherd

HONNO MODERN FICTION

First published by Honno

'Ailsa Craig', Heol y Cawl, Dinas Powys,

Wales, CF64 4AH

1 2 3 4 5 6 7 8 9 10

ISBN 978-1-906784-31-7

Published with the financial support of the Welsh Books Council.

Cover design: James Fleming at Gigantic

Printed in Wales by Gomer

ANIMATED BAGGAGE

In memory of Soheir

who died too soon

Walberswick, England
Monday May 16, 1988

It's a fantastic day for it, she thought, watching the group of bright figures clustered round the distant dinghy on the shingle. She listened with half an ear to the squabbling voices of children in the other room (no major crisis erupting yet) and cut four slices of bread. She slid them under the grill and looked up again at the bright scene framed by the kitchen window. The sky was scraped clean and a brisk breeze chopped at the tidal race of the river. A red sail inched its way up the mast of the dinghy. She reached over and switched on the radio.

'...for today, Monday 16 of May.
A bomb explosion in the Sudanese capital, Khartoum, has killed seven people. The explosion happened last night at the Acropole Hotel, a popular meeting place for foreign aid workers. A simultaneous machine gun attack on the nearby Sudan Club left a number of people wounded. An extremist Islamic group is believed to be responsible.'

She stood in the middle of the kitchen staring distractedly at the radio and didn't notice Catrin sobbing until the small girl was hanging round her left leg, thumb stuffed in mouth. Even Catrin might pick up on the familiar names. Bee snapped down the off-switch.

Danny's voice said from behind her, 'What's that smell of something burning?' He peered owlishly from the doorway. 'Mum! The toast's on fire!'

1

She yanked the pan out from under the grill. Four flaming sheets of black cardboard curled and smoked and Catrin wailed 'Now there isn't any bleklist for me and I *so* hungry!'

''You're always hungry,' Danny said unfeelingly. 'Anyway Mum can make some more. Can't you, Mum.'

What should she do? Damn her parents for being too mean to put a phone in.

From the public call box on the village green she telephoned the Foreign Office while the children played on the swings. She waited for her call to be put through, the phone swallowing her money greedily. Through the glass she could see Danny bouncing Catrin and Kit up and down on the see-saw but their excited squeals were snatched away by the wind and she could hardly hear them. Any minute now he was going to topple them both off. She opened the stiff, salt-stained door and yelled at him to be careful. A matter-of-fact woman's voice was speaking into her right ear: the Foreign Office could not release any details yet but if she wanted to phone later they might have more information this evening.

Gee thanks. She rang directory enquiries, watching Adam as he sat dreaming by himself on one of the swings with his teddy tucked under one arm. She wrote down the number. On the see-saw, excitement was rising to fever-pitch. She pushed open the door of the call box with one foot: 'Danny! Be careful!' The BBC answered, another distant voice, unable to tell her any more than had been broadcast on the news. She rang Kay but was told she was out of the office. She decided, without much thought, that it would be wiser not to ring their parents, and anyway all her change was used up.

Her world had been turned upside down and there was no one she could tell.

On the beach it was warm in the sun for mid-May, in spite of the wind. She sat on a rug in the shelter of the sand dunes and stared out to sea while the children played their usual endless games. In the clear sunlight the North Sea was the deepest of blues. The tide dragged slowly backwards leaving a flat, hard fringe of glistening sand. Time sagging away. How long before she could try phoning again? Catrin tripped and fell but Kit pulled her up, kindly for once, and helped her fill her bucket back up with sand.

A touch on her shoulder – she turned sharply, squinting up against the sun.

Kay leaned down and kissed her cheek. She peered anxiously into Bee's face but the children were already launching themselves across the sand. 'In a minute! Give me two minutes talking to your mum in peace and then I'll come and be a proper aunty.' She looked at Bee again and raised her eyebrows.

Bee shook her head the merest fraction. She cleared her throat. 'I tried to phone you. Why aren't you in London?' The children were drifting back down the beach to their sandcastle. Danny had returned to his private corner in the hollow of a sand dune, and his book.

Kay sat down beside her on the rug, shoulder to shoulder, looking out over the dark blue sea. 'They gave me compassionate leave. I'm afraid I did lay it on a bit but I thought you might not have heard. You have though, haven't you. Did you hear it on the news?'

She nodded, watching Danny, but he was too far away to overhear so long as they kept their voices low. 'I've been phoning the Foreign Office all day but it's like getting blood out of a stone.' She turned to Kay in sudden alarm. 'Is that why you're here? Do you know something?'

'No, no,' Kay said soothingly. 'Only what was on the news. I just wanted to be with you.' She took hold of Bee's hand and squeezed it.

'Did you come straight here?' Bee asked after a bit. It was the only safe thing she could think of saying with the children possibly in earshot.

'I called in on the Aged Ps on the way but only very briefly. Just in case you'd rung them, really. Ma of course was offended that you hadn't. She was doing her prancing filly act. You know what she's like in a crisis.' She put on her mimicking-Ma voice, '*Well, she can't possibly think of going back there now!*' Pa was so moved he put his newspaper down *and* took off his specs. It happened too late for there to be anything in this morning's paper, by the way.'

'Have you heard any names?'

'No, but there was a bit more on the news just as I got here. A British family of four killed, two of them young children. But no details about the others yet.'

Bee looked at her sharply, then looked away, saying nothing. They sat for a moment or two in silence. Kay said suddenly, 'Charles *wouldn't* have been there, would he?'

'I don't know. I just don't know.'

She didn't make a sound. She didn't move. But she felt as if she were suddenly imploding. In a moment Kay was on her knees on the rug, holding her tight. Bee shook violently, frightening herself as well as her sister, more than if she had cried out loud.

After a while she recovered enough to detach herself from Kay's arms and look anxiously towards the children. But they played on, and Danny read his book, as if no shadow had passed across them.

Chapter 1

Three gunshots: bullets ricocheting off the walls of the stairwell and sending up little spurts of dust. One of the men collapsed and slid down the stairs, leaving a bloody trail behind him.

'I thought you said this was family viewing,' Maggie said coldly.

He shrugged. 'Gets the violence over and done with before the title goes up,' he said, lying through his teeth since he couldn't remember what the bloody film was about.

'Get the hell outa here!' the wounded man shouted at his companion. An interesting spurt of bright blood came out of his mouth.

'Right, that's enough!' Maggie snapped. She marched over to the set and ejected the video, ignoring the howls of protest from the gaggle of children seated on the floor. 'We'll have to watch *Cocoon* instead,' she said. To another chorus of protest.

He watched with mild interest, sitting with his beer like a man watching squirrels in a park. Two days back and the Unicef Family had swallowed him whole. Five adults and a motley assortment of kids, and not one of them (mercifully)

5

his. He sat back with his beer enjoying the fact. Maggie dropped the offending video on his lap on the way back to her chair. He sneaked a look at the title. Never heard of it! He must have picked up the wrong one. She went on shooting him dark looks from her corner as the film started. He raised one eyebrow. She looked even better when she was cross, her face all taut and her eyes flashing.

The others settled down to watch the film and he let his mind wander. What did Maggie see in Will? Why are generators always so infernally noisy? It was surprisingly good to be back. Another Khartoum Sunday.

Later, as they sat round the table over the remains of the meal, he caught Maggie's eye across the table. He grinned but she shot him a vitriolic look.

Then she charged. 'I don't understand you, Charles! When Bee and the kids aren't around you seem to duck all responsibility as if you'd never had children yourself.' She gave him a penetrating stare. 'You wouldn't let your own kids watch a violent film like that, would you?'

He wasn't going to admit he'd brought the wrong film. Besides, something in her attack was strangely arousing. He raised his eyebrows.

'It's as if you switch back to being a bachelor,' she persisted, making bachelorhood sound like a crime. 'Is that how you feel? Footloose and fancy-free as soon as you're on your own?'

'Don't go on, Maggie love,' Will remonstrated mildly. 'There's got to be *some* compensation for being here on your own without your family.'

But she was really gunning for Charles this afternoon. 'It hardly seems fair. Here you are, swanning about as if you're a free agent and poor old Bee back in England struggling on her own with four young children!'

'Give me a chance, Mags. I couldn't force them to come back with me. And I was with them until five days ago.'

'How long have you got to suffer on your own then, Charles?' Will asked.

'She's coming out with the kids at the end of the month. Three weeks and six days,' he said, looking at Maggie to see if the precision of his maths had made an impression, but she had turned away from the table to supervise Sam blowing his nose. Leaning over to stuff Will's hankie back in his trouser pocket, she said, 'Could you remind her about the books she said she'd bring for Zahara?' And he assumed he was off the hook until she added, 'Assuming you *do* ever communicate with her.'

'Zara? Zara who?' asked Will.

'Oh you know who Zahara is, Will! The Zahara who runs the school our two little darlings go to?'

'What books?' asked Charles.

'She wants books and some equipment – Bee said that if she's got any space she'll bring some of the books with her now, and we'll bring the rest out when we come back in October. Zahara's very grateful. She only set up the school three or four years ago, I think. We're really pleased with it, aren't we Will?'

Dick, their genial American host, brought more cans of beer from the fridge and handed them round the table. 'How long are you going to be in Khartoum?' he asked Charles.

'I'm due to go down to El Obeid on Tuesday. *Insha'allah*. If Sudan Air is flying.'

'I wish I was!' Dick said wistfully. 'We hate living in Khartoum, Alice and me. It's filthy and it stinks. And it's damned hot!'

'And you've got air conditioning,' Charles said. 'And there's the American Club *and* the Sudan Club. You can play squash and tennis and go swimming whenever you want. And there's even a pizza takeaway in the Meridian, and Friday brunches in the Hilton. You've got a few compensations.'

Will looked up, interested. 'Would you rather live in Khartoum then, Charles?'

'No, but I do think you lot have an exaggerated idea of how wonderful life is anywhere else. Believe me, there are lots of compensations in Khartoum – don't take them for granted!'

Maggie snorted. 'Huh! That would be something, taking Khartoum for granted!'

He parked the borrowed Unicef truck on the street outside the Acropole Hotel, among the other battered pick-ups. Inside the building the air was hot and stale. He greeted the night watchman and began to climb the stone stairs.

Halfway up, at the first landing, the light was on in the hotel office. He could see George Pagoulatus was still there at his desk. Behind him an American was talking on the phone with his back to the room, a journalist phoning in copy about food security with the phone clamped to one ear and his finger jammed in the other, struggling with a bad line. Charles could hear every word as he climbed on up the stairs. All the same, for a moment he wished that it was him on the phone, talking to Bee. But Bee was at End Point and out of reach.

The lounge was brightly lit and full of people. Some talking earnestly, some laughing uproariously. All nationalities but most of them white. Above them the blue haze of cigarette smoke resisted the ceiling fans. He crossed the room towards the table where the newspapers were kept, looking out for someone to talk to. He didn't have the energy to start from scratch with a stranger tonight. Nor to talk shop: he spotted Dietrich and Tomas deep in conversation in the corner and beat a hasty retreat. Get two Unicef employees in one place and the conversation will run on nothing but Unicef. It was a kind of natural law. But he'd had enough of that for one evening. He went back down the stairs and across to the annexe.

His sandals echoed flatly in the empty stairwell. At the top of the stairs he turned the key in the old-fashioned door and went into the shuttered room. His open cases stood on the rack and on the floor, clothes and papers spewing out of them. He knew how Bee would tut if she saw them but in her absence they could spew sadly away. He thought of what Maggie had said, about him and bachelorhood. How little she knew.

He'd been out all day and the room was suffocating. He turned on the fan and opened the shutters wide. A cold shower refreshed him briefly but the heat soaked straight back into his skin. For a while he stood by the window in the dark, dressed only in his damp towel, trying to catch a bit of breeze. He switched on the bedside light and took his book out of his bag. He was just settling himself on the hard, cotton-filled mattress when the power went off.

'Shit! Welcome back to the Sudan!' His voice sounded strange in the darkness.

Now that there was no possibility of reading he was irretrievably awake. He waited for the generator to come on, but it didn't. Above him, the fan drifted listlessly to an invisible halt.

Saaid grasped him by both hands and they went through the long formulae of greetings. The Arabic felt rusty on his tongue from lack of use. Only when they had established that Bee and the children (and sundry grandparents besides) were all thoroughly well could they fetch the luggage and load it into the pick-up, and even then Saaid kept stopping to clap him

9

on the shoulder, laughing and welcoming him again. It was nice to have been missed.

He stood for a moment by the truck before climbing into the passenger seat, looking around him and smelling Northern Kordofan again after the arid desert air of Khartoum. Saaid laughed at him, understanding.

'What's all this?' he asked Saaid, gesturing at the two Mig fighters which crouched like ominous black birds on the tarmac apron, just below the control tower of El Obeid's small airport.

Saaid shrugged. 'The government's jumpy,' he said. 'You know how it is – the rains come in the Nuba mountains and the SPLA gets busy again. There's been bad fighting south of Wau.' They climbed into the cab of the pick-up, Charles in the passenger seat.

'Have the Migs been flying?' He stared at them, thinking they were terrifying enough when they were parked up and empty.

'They go out most days. They're very noisy, you can't miss them!'

They drove into town. The glare of the early morning sun striking off the low zinc roofs of the houses made his eyes ache even behind his sunglasses. He felt suddenly tired, as if he had been away for years, not weeks. Though nothing looked any different except that all the gardens were visibly struggling in the heat, suggesting the water supply may have been more than usually erratic.

'Water's not good,' Saaid said, just as he was thinking it. 'The town reserves are enough for ninety days only. Ninety days! If it doesn't rain, what will happen? Even now, in my district, we only get water for one hour in the evening. Sometimes not at all.'

10

Charles was silent. A niggling, selfish worry started clawing its unwanted way into his consciousness. If things were that bad now and if it didn't rain, would Bee and the kids be able to come back at the end of the month? That was only four weeks away.

They drew up in the street outside the Unicef office and the staff came out to greet him. Aziz, looking as languidly skeletal as ever, began hassling him about water pumps before he'd even got through the front door. 'In a minute, in a minute!' he said, laughing. He looked round the office, observing the small changes. Halima had moved her desk. There were some new maps on the wall showing hand-pump installations. Otherwise everything looked reassuringly familiar, until the phone rang and made him jump. Aziz answered it calmly.

Halima laughed at his expression. 'It works now. Sometimes,' she said in English.

'It works?'

She shrugged. 'Sometimes it does. For five minutes. Ten minutes, yesterday.'

It would be a blessed relief not to be enslaved to the radio for every bit of contact with the Khartoum office. He asked cautiously, 'And the electricity?'

She made the familiar rocking gesture with her hand. '*Nus nus*. Some days not so bad, some days not so good. But the water is bad.'

'Saaid said. Have you got problems at home too?'

'Most days we can fill a barrel.' She turned and glowered at the *gafir*, who had come sidling into the room behind them. 'What do you want?'

Yusuf ignored her, bowing to Charles with his usual grin. A funny little fellow, Yusuf, with his matted hair sticking up all over his head, always grinning. Even had he still possessed his

11

front teeth his grin would have looked disreputable. Charles said in Arabic, 'Yusuf! What can I do for you?'

'Worthy sir, I am needing new *jelabiya*. I can no longer carry out my duties in this old one.'

Charles looked at him, nonplussed. He didn't look any worse than usual.

Yusuf added, a gleam in his eye, 'Sir, I am to be married soon. To a young wife. I must look responsible in my job now.'

Charles congratulated him, hoping his surprise wasn't visible: Yusuf must be fifty at least. Poor girl, I hope she knows what she's getting, he was thinking as he turned to Halima. She was sorting papers on her desk, pointedly ignoring Yusuf. 'How much to buy a *jelabiya*, Halima?' he asked in English.

She shrugged reluctantly. 'Thirty pounds?'

He pulled out his wallet and counted out three limp Sudanese notes. Yusuf tucked them quickly into his pocket. Halima observed pointedly in English, 'Now Idris will want one too.'

'We'll cross that bridge when we come to it,' he said lightly. 'At least we've only got two *gafirs*.' He smiled at her, his best, most mollifying smile. 'I'd better go – I need to get my stuff over to the house.'

It was really hot now. The sun was high enough to strike with the power that made him think of darkness, not of light: it seemed to leach the colour from everything, even the sky. The house, sitting squat in its generous garden at the corner of two streets, looked very shabby in the relentless glare as they pulled up outside, and the bougainvillea by the garden gate was limp.

Saaid helped him lift his cases and boxes from the back of the truck. The *gafir* came out of the shadows of the front verandah, his bald head gleaming in the sun. For the

12

umpteenth time that day Charles went through the long ritual of greetings.

The front door shuddered and creaked stiffly open. He hated going into the house alone. They should be with him, the children excitedly running ahead. Instead the house lay still and lifeless, a covering of dust on everything in spite of the closed windows and shutters. He picked up one of the children's books from where it had been left on the *angareb*. The gritty dust made it feel dirty. The sight of the children's toys in the baskets and Bee's painting things neatly stacked on the table shouted their absence. He hurried across the room and unlocked the inner door onto the side verandah. Here, where the net walls had let the dust storms do their worst, the fine sand lay so thickly that the tiled floor was no longer black and white. It was strange to see the long expanse of the verandah empty, all the usual clutter of their existence carefully packed away in the locked inner rooms. A gecko, disturbed by his entry, ran across the floor and up the stained wall. He could clearly see its footprints and the snake-mark of its tail left behind in the dust.

The garden gate creaked and a tall, gaunt figure came striding into the compound, wrapped in the blue chiffon of a faded *thobe*. Fatouma! By what intuition or sorcery or invisible communication system had she known so quickly that he was back? He went out to meet her gratefully, and she greeted him with unusual enthusiasm, as if she were genuinely pleased to see him. He gestured at the forlorn house, at the inhospitable dust that smelled stale and was so unpleasant to the touch, but she was already taking off her *thobe*. She folded it carefully and placed it on a chair. A few minutes later she was sweeping vigorously and great clouds of dust retreated in front of her, revealing the black and white of the floor. He went to the kitchen and began boiling pans of water to fill the filters so that he might have drinking water by nightfall.

Zahara Hassan Mohammed, child of troubled stock, looked at her own four daughters and observed how easily their one quarter of Englishness sat on their shoulders. It had never been that simple for her, she had never been certain of the benefits of being English, and besides, it wasn't English, it was Welsh, but nobody here could deal with that and she had long ago stopped correcting anyone, even herself. Half the advantage, double the trouble, she said. Hybrid vigour, her husband Ibrahim always replied, kissing her on the end of her Celtic nose. Mongrel! she countered ruefully, tugging at her frizzy hair. But her daughters seemed proud of their mixed blood, moving with ease between the different dimensions of their inheritance, speaking English at school, Arabic at home, always calling her 'Mummy' just as Ibrahim was always 'Abu' so that one word or the other stuck up like a little signpost in both languages. They had made their own stab at consistency. And besides, the consistencies for them were greater than they had been for her.

On the wall in their living room there was a photograph of herself and Ibrahim on their wedding day. Their western-style wedding – his dark suit and bow tie, her white wedding dress. Like every part of Zahara's life, her wedding was in duplicate: a western wedding with one set of photographs, and a traditional Sudanese wedding with a different set. And she had two names, as did her sister and her three brothers. To her mother she was Sandra and on the trips to the UK as a child, to what her mother always called 'home', she was Sandra to everyone, but at home in the Sudan she was Zahara to everybody except her mother. She answered to either without

14

even thinking about it. This was the pattern of her childhood: speaking in Arabic to her father, in English to her mother. Answering to two names; living between two worlds.

She was sitting in the office with Josie. It was Thursday, the end of the week. The office was small and cramped and their two desks were crammed in side by side, a cascade of papers on the desktops, and books and files on sagging shelves on the wall. Josie's big, scruffy bag sat in the middle of the floor with folders jammed into it and a headscarf spilling out. Zahara's neat little Italian leather bag, very old now and scuffed, sat meekly on the chair at her desk. Zahara was sitting on the floor making a list of the books which were stacked in tall piles in one corner, while Josie sat slumped in the chair at her desk, limp and dishevelled.

'Can't we leave this till Saturday?' Josie asked, her American accent even flatter than usual because she was hot and cross. 'It's been a long day! A long week, come to that.'

'You go home, Josie. I can do this on my own. I said I'd have it done a week ago.'

'Does it matter?'

She shrugged. 'Probably not. But Maggie Smith said she would be writing to a friend of hers – she thought this Bee lady might be able to bring an extra box of books back for us, if she can get a message to her in time.'

'Can't we just send for them ourselves? Wouldn't that be quicker and easier?'

'Josie, we've been through all this,' she said wearily. 'I can't, because I'm a Sudanese citizen so I'd have to pay import fees and you know how ridiculous those are. And you can't because you're not supposed to be here at all.'

'Oh yeah, quite so,' Josie said glumly. 'I always forget about the import fees.' She watched Zahara for a while in silence. Outside, the girls' voices rose and fell from the playground where they were playing on the slide. 'She's gone to a lot of trouble, that Maggie Smith, hasn't she? I hope she isn't expecting a discount on the school fees.'

'I'm sure she isn't,' Zahara said distractedly, writing down another title on the pad on her knee. 'Actually, she's been very supportive. I told you what she said, didn't I? That she's so pleased to have found a school that tries to be as broad in its approach as we do? And she likes the way we concentrate on the three Rs.'

'I wonder, will she still be thinking the same way when the kids get to be eight and ten instead of four and six? That's when we need to hang on to them, if we're going to grow this school.'

'I don't suppose they'll still be here when Sam and Cathy are ten and eight. They never stay long, do they, these expats? Except for you, of course,' she added, looking up at Josie fondly. 'You've been here for ever!'

'Humph, I'm not that old.'

Zahara chuckled. 'I was thinking I might invite Maggie and her husband to come to the river house one Friday for *fatur*, as a thank you. I just have to okay it with Abu first. Would you be able to come, do you think?'

'I might, but don't count me in. You know how it is.'

Actually, I don't, she thought, looking up at Josie who was twirling a long lock of greying hair between her fingers and holding it up to inspect the split ends. Josie's life was a silent mystery, even after all these years. And she was getting harder and harder to pin down out of school hours. She hadn't been to Abu's house now for many, many Fridays.

'How is your dad?' Josie asked. 'Erudite as ever?'

16

'He says he's learned more since he retired than he learned in the whole of his life up till then. Actually I think he just means he loves having the time to read about the world outside medicine.'

'That's fine and dandy so long as he can remember what he's read,' Josie said gloomily. 'These days, as soon as I shut the book I forget what was in it. It's worrying me, you know. It's not just new things. I seem to be forgetting things I've known for so long I thought they were carved on my brain. Charlotte asked me this morning what Alexander the Great's horse was called and I couldn't for the life of me remember.'

'Bucephalus,' said Zahara, half not listening as she wrote her list.

'I know – I remembered in the middle of lunch. But it's frightening. I'm wondering if it's more than just the menopause. Zahara! You're not listening!" She nudged Zahara with her foot. "I'm saying something important!'

Zahara tore her attention away from the books. She frowned suddenly. 'Are you saying you're afraid you might be going senile?'

Josie sat up. 'No. Just batty. Go back to what you're doing, I didn't mean to interrupt.' She wound her hair into an untidy knot on the top of her head and fixed it in place with a pencil as she looked down into Zahara's anxious, upturned face. 'You know, you've got freckles! I never noticed that before!'

'Haven't you? I've always had them.' She rubbed her nose self-consciously. 'It's my mongrel blood showing through.' She put her hand on Josie's broad knee. 'I don't think you should worry, Josie. We all forget things – even Abu does. I forget things all the time. You know we all do. It's the heat. It's the rains not coming. It's difficult at the moment, for everybody. It isn't just you being forgetful.'

Josie gave a sceptical humph, but she patted Zahara's hand fondly. 'I'm going off home for a cold shower. Yo'all should go home, it's getting late.' She stood up and peered through the little bit of the window that wasn't taken up by the noisy air conditioning box. In the playground of the American Club, where they rented three rooms for their school, Zahara's four daughters were playing on the slide, silhouetted against the sun that was setting beyond the line of bare, dusty trees. Behind the girls, Josie could see club members making their way along the path for a game of tennis or a swim after work. The rainstorm last week had long ago dried to nothing and the air was rosy with dust. The girls' dark heads were haloed by the sun and their voices chirruped as they talked and laughed together, a contained little clan of four. Josie, amazed as always by the way these four played together without storms and tantrums, turned back into the room where Zahara was bent again to her task. *But of course, it is a family characteristic,* she thought. 'Go home, Zahara! Your lovely Ibrahim will be tiring of waiting for you!'

'My lovely Ibrahim is taking an evening class – we shan't be seeing him till very late.'

෴

Her mother was an English Rose. That's official because Abu says so, though really of course she was Welsh. But *English Rose* is what Abu says. When he tells the story, their mother is the brightest thing he sees when he first arrives at the hospital in Cardiff in the middle of winter. Cardiff is grey and wet. The hospital and all of the houses smell of boiled cabbage and disinfectant. But there is this lovely young woman who makes him think of full-blown roses, in the English summer to which

18

he has not yet been introduced so that he has to imagine it to take his mind off all the rain. But Abu, you were in Wales! they always say, when he tells them this story. And he replies, It was all the same to me. The rain, he says, going back to his story, and then the dreadful snow. Snow, Abu? they exclaim, wonderingly. It has never snowed for them when they have been in Cardiff. I hadn't been introduced to your mother either, he says, which is the next bit of the story. But you know these English girls – (or Welsh girls, he adds with a wink) – being introduced doesn't seem to matter. And I already knew her name: everybody called her Doris, she was never known as Miss Pugh.

Doris, the name Grandma Pugh had saddled her with. The hated name. Why don't you just change it? Zahara had asked once. Nothing is ever that simple, her mother said, darkly.

In her mother's story, she is the young nurse, their father is Hassan the handsome black doctor from the country nobody knows anything about, except that it is very hot and sandy, and General Gordon met his grizzly end there long ago. From the start, everything about Hassan bowls Doris over, from the gap between his brilliantly white front teeth to the way he says her name. Dor-ees. And he is impressed by her neat, efficient nursing – he tells her so. He is the most courteous man she has ever met and by far the most exciting. He tells her many things, about tents and camels, and the enormity of the night sky in the desert. And how his father owns many head of cattle, and sheep and goats, and fine racing camels, and a white donkey for his father to ride into town on when they are staying at their big house with many rooms in Omdurman, which is the old city next to Khartoum. And she hears the hunger of homesickness in his voice, and that he is lonely, and then her heart is quite lost. How can she protect him from the

19

brutal dullness of a Cardiff winter, the wind damp off the sea? He does not even know about scarves and gloves and vests and woolly socks. She takes him in hand. He comes from an important family; she can hear that they are wealthy even if he never says so outright. Doris' father was a steam-engine fireman and he died a long time ago, leaving her mother to bring them up alone, her and her older sister. They have never had any money but Hassan doesn't mind any of that, he accepts her as she is. He calls her his Flower of the Desert.

This is the story Doris tells Zahara when Zahara is little, and Abu tells her his stories, and when they are in England, at Aunty Audrey's house in Surrey, Aunty Audrey tells her more stories than her mother tells because she is the keeper of family history in Grandma Pugh's family, just as Zahara is in Abu's. She stores all the stories away and tells them over and over to Saadiya, who is two years younger than her, to Nazmul too, when he is old enough. But by the time her brother Ali is old enough to listen the stories have got complicated: a different storyline is beginning to overlay the old one. Or maybe it is just that she is getting older and things no longer look quite the same.

Chapter 2

Meetings. Macro politics, micro politics. Between the different government departments. Between the aid agencies and the government. Between the agencies. Within Unicef itself. And finally, in his own backyard, domestic politics as Malik the *gafir* asked for a new *jelabiya*, having heard that Yusuf and Idris at the office had both received one. So many religious holidays coming up, Malik said, looking Charles in the eye. Challenging him to suggest that he is a lesser *gafir* than the Unicef office *gafirs*. And Charles, dipping into his dwindling private pot of Sudanese currency, wondered how much longer the Khartoum office would delay sending down his salary, or would he have to borrow money from the office to pay his own household bills?

He was in the office by six every morning, Fridays and Sundays too, though they were supposed to be his days off. His attention was pulled in many directions at once: a workshop on handicrafts aimed at generating earning power for women; plans for building latrines; immunisation projects; the installation of water pumps. He was the figurehead people came to when they were trying to get something done. The one they complained to when things went wrong. He was pushed to the very edge of his abilities, keeping all the balls in the air, keeping as many people as possible as happy as he judged it was legitimate for them to be. Pushing here, resisting there. Sometimes he found himself fighting the very people with whom he should have been working. Often he felt that the Khartoum office was where all the important things were happening, that he and his colleagues in the three regional offices were left out on the edges of the tide, too easily forgotten. Three regional offices! In a country as vast and needy as this one, and as difficult to travel about in. Surely, he thought, if an aid agency is measured by the aid it delivers, it must be the regional offices that are the hub of the activity, not the remote and distant capital? But reality was little people on ladders struggling to get to the top. They stayed in the centre, too afraid, he thought (outsider that he was), to risk stagnating in the provinces.

So he made his own small rebellions. On the radio, by letter, occasionally (when it was working) on the phone, he pushed and pulled, trying to make his voice heard in the Khartoum office. Hoping that in that way he might make a difference in the real world.

Still the rains had not come. In El Obeid storms rumbled and threatened nearly every day, but there was only one rainstorm and that was half-hearted and quickly over. In Dilling, a mere two hours drive away on the road south towards the Nuba mountains, it rained heavily every day and last week they had got stuck in the mud there for over an hour. Thirty miles north of El Obeid, in the market town of Bara, it hadn't rained at all.

The landscape was demarcated too, as sharply as if the town had been set down on a geological dividing line. In El Obeid and to the south the earth was red, to the north it was white. Looking back he would always remember: *this* was south of El Obeid (red earth, acacia scrub, villages set amongst trees, greenness and grass in the rainy season), *that* was north (white sand, naked villages, sand dunes, his memories all in patterns of black and white).

He went north to Bara to visit the new wood-lots.

They drove on roads which were no more than a scattering of vehicle tracks across an open, undulating landscape, the pale sand glaring in the sun, dotted with scrub thorn and the occasional swollen bulk of the massive *tibeldi* trees, which were sacred and therefore protected. Today, as it happened, marked twelve full months since the day that Bee had first arrived with the children in El Obeid. At the end of this month he would have been in his post for sixteen months. *No other life seems real any more*, he was thinking as Saaid swerved off to the right onto an even vaguer track. They rounded a clump of thorn and three camels looked down on them from their browsing, blinking their slow, heavy-lidded blink as Charles, from the passenger seat, looked up at their heads swaying above him. A gangly camel calf, very new, stepped unsteadily from behind one of the camels.

'Eh, *walad!* shouted Saaid gleefully as he swerved to avoid it.

Boy, Charles thought, chuckling and holding on hard as they bumped over the stony ground. Of course Saaid would instinctively identify everything as male, even a camel calf.

How small a life without camels would be, after this!

A few minutes later they left the scrub behind. That was always how you knew you were approaching a village, he thought, each one swimming in its own dry puddle of bare sand. They raced their shadow over the hard, bright ground.

The powerful sun should make it summer but it was strange how this harsh and leafless landscape always made him think of winter. All the shades were a variation on white or black: the caustic sunlight plunging into the centre of each

23

tree, glinted black on thorn, grey on shiny bark, or beating dazzling white on the paleness of the sand. The only colour was the vivid daubs the women made, wrapped in the long veils of their *thobes*. As they drove up to the huts a woman rode past on a donkey, swathed in brilliant red. Three more women strode across the sand furled in different shades of blue. It was a searingly beautiful landscape that made him wish he could paint. But Bee, who was the painter, found the harshness stultifying. 'I think I need water to paint,' she said. And she didn't mean water colours. She meant she needed the colours of a sky that reflected water, and the vibrancy of moisture trapped in leaf and soil. She needed the depths of colour in the ocean and in the sky above it. He looked at the startling landscape around him, thinking of this, and felt a small frisson of irritation.

The first two wood-lots had failed completely. Rats, locusts, desiccation – the seedlings were nothing but pathetic little sticks in the sand. But in the third wood-lot nearly all the seedlings had survived. His spirits lifted as he looked round him at the tiny sprouting plants and the enthusiastic faces of the women who crowded with them into the nursery. They were all talking at once, the shrill, strident voices of women who work all day in wide open spaces. So full of spirit and of hope that they made him feel like a pauper, a mere supplier of funds. A voyeur not an activist. Which made their gratefulness seem singularly unearned and inappropriate.

He looked at Saaid, walking along the paths between the beds, adding his forthright views to the discussion on how to deal with the plague of gerbils. He wondered if so utterly urban a creature as Saaid felt equally humbled in the shadow of these women, or did he, having been used to this world from childhood (and besides, being a man), see all this as ordinary and merely the way the world is?

It was clear he had to make a decision. He already knew what the answer must be. The rains would surely come, but they had not come yet, and there were some years when they failed to come in any quantity. In the whole of July there had been only ten millimetres of rain in the town and the reservoirs were nearly empty. Bee was due to bring the children in five days time but for the last three days there had been no water in the house tank at all. He went to the Post Office and sent the telegram he'd been praying would not prove necessary: *DELAY COMING NO WATER WILL WRITE EXPLAINING LOVE YOU*. As he came out of the post office there was a ponderous roar from the outskirts of the town: the Mig fighters on their daily sortie. That put him in his place.

Two days later Ugandan John looked at the tank and announced that his problem was a faulty inlet valve which could be replaced immediately. That same evening there was water in the tank. As soon as the tank began dripping again, through all its many little leaks, the myriad birds returned. They perched on the metal girders on which the tank was mounted and drank from the falling trickles. Charles was home early because it was a Friday and the office was officially shut. He stood in his empty house, watching the birds from behind the screen of the insect netting, and wondered if he had been too hasty sending the telegram. It was raining so near to the town but when the rain was as localised as this only some of the outlying *hafirs* and reservoirs were being filled. His head knew he had acted for the best but his heart was rebelling. He couldn't wait without them forever, whether it rained or not. They would have to manage somehow. The house was so quiet. The expanses of bare floor seemed crudely naked without the children's clutter. Some days he went all day without a proper conversation with anyone. (Office talk didn't count as conversation: in the office he was never a private person.)

He went into the sitting room and sat in one of the easy chairs with his book but his concentration kept wandering. Had she been relieved when she got his telegram? To be spared a little longer in her beloved Suffolk, as if she'd been given a reprieve. Would the children start to forget him? They were so young. A month is a long time for a child, six weeks would feel like for ever. He was banking on it ending up being no more; he hoped it might be less. He could hardly remember them, not properly. When he tried to, the memory wouldn't quite come. The feel of their little limbs under his hands, the pressure of their confidence as they nestled hotly against him: the effort it required to remember these things made the children seem unreal as if they were somebody else's memory, not his own.

Later the wind got up, and when he went out into the garden at dusk to speak to Malik he saw a great dark curtain across the sky, marching up out of the south. The colour of wickedness, hook-winged like a vulture, the brown stain stretched from one side of the horizon to the other. A searing wind blew out from under it, like a vicious draught from under a door. The wind had a stale smell, the smell of stillness, the smell of dust. A *haboob*, a dust storm. He hurried indoors to shut all the windows, even though it was so hot.

All the same, when the *haboob* struck, the dust got in everywhere. Too fine to be visible, but it was in his hair, in his nostrils, his ears, on every surface that he touched.

And then, quite suddenly, it passed. The air cleared, the sky was high and blue with its habitual pre-dusk serenity, and all the storm clouds – and the dark, barred rain visibly falling – lay somewhere away to the east of the town. *Somebody else is happy tonight,* he thought, looking at it sadly, *somebody is hopeful they might plant tomorrow.*

After his solitary supper, making the most of the power being on, he wrote a report on the computer. The irony couldn't escape him: no proper water supply, intermittent electricity, no phone, but they did own a computer. (Good move, that, though Bee had thought it a waste of money.) He typed with one finger while the wind hustled and tugged through the windows, which were open again to the hot night, making the round paper lightshade swing like a crazy moon. Somewhere a metal gate was banging over and over. In the station the trains were screaming their usual frenetic evening ritual. In the bare park across the road, the karate club practised its nightly routine to a chorus of grunts and shouts.

Strange how rain threatening and not falling makes you feel so tense: the build up of expectation, the emptiness of postponed relief. The trains scream for passengers but do not leave, the young men practise for battle but war does not quite come. The gate bangs, and the house is empty. Where are they? Not here, not here.

The old Vauxhall sputtered ominously as if at any moment it might breathe its last and Zahara prayed her usual silent prayer: *don't give up on us! Not yet, please: keep going just a little bit longer.*

It was Friday and they were driving out to her father's house as they always did on Fridays. 'I hope we're not going to get stuck,' she said out loud. It was not a nice day in the city: a *haboob* of the heavy, windless kind was wrapping Khartoum in a blanket of rosy grit. It would be like a London smog were it not for the heat, and the sun above them (invisible in the haze) glinting oddly on the roofs and bonnets of all the cars on the busy road.

'You're too anxious,' Ibrahim said, looking at her anxiously. She knew that he worried about her. She worried about herself. Why couldn't she just be a happy person? It would be so much simpler. 'You should have faith,' he added, just as the car spluttered to a halt near the roundabout on the edge of Souk Two. They had gone no more than three blocks from home.

The girls chorused 'Oooh!' from the back seat, and Aasha, the smallest, wriggled in the front seat with Zahara, wanting to be allowed to get out and help her Abu fix the car. 'I can,' she said, gazing earnestly up at her mother.

'Shh,' said Zahara, worrying that the food in the boot would spoil in the heat if they didn't keep moving.

Ibrahim fiddled about for a while on the far side of the dusty red bonnet. A few minutes later he dropped the bonnet back down and grinned at them triumphantly through the dirty windscreen.

'Have you mended it, Abu?' Aasha sounded disappointed. How could her beloved father have achieved such a momentous thing without her input?

'Nothing serious,' he said as he jumped back into the car. 'Just a loose plug.'

Zahara held her breath as he turned the ignition. The car fired hesitantly, then faded. On the second attempt the engine fired into throaty life. Aasha clapped her hands excitedly. '*Alhamdulilah!*' she squeaked, and her big sisters in the back seat laughed indulgently.

A yellow taxi passed them. As they pulled onto the roundabout the taxi was turning right ahead of them. Suddenly its passenger door fell off into the road. They saw the surprised face of the large European man as he sat there in his seat, abruptly exposed. The children squealed with delight.

'Did you see the big *khawaja's* face?' Yasmina giggled.

'You see?' Ibrahim said, 'We aren't the worst car on the road, not by a long way.' But Zahara was anxiously instructing the girls to lock their doors in the back. She held on tight to Aasha.

'He was a very fat *khawaja*,' Aasha said seriously. 'Perhaps his fat pushed the door off.'

❧

Zahara remembers being eight years old. Grandma Pugh and Mrs Jones from next door are sitting one in each armchair, two pairs of feet planted firmly on the carpet, slightly pigeon-toed in their sensible shoes. Four sturdy legs clad in sensible stockings. Under tweed skirts, a glimpse of pink, brushed-cotton bloomers. Mrs Jones is chuckling as Nazmul and Ali tumble like kittens on the carpet. Even Grandma Pugh cracks the ghost of a smile.

'They're not *really* black,' says Mrs Jones. 'More like coffee-coloured.'

Grandma Pugh grunts. 'I've told her! I said, 'You'd best stop at four, they're getting darker as you go on.'

Behind the sofa, where they are playing with their dolls, Saadiya looks at Zahara, her eyes big and round. At school in Khartoum Zahara is often taken for a Syrian. In Cardiff she has been taken for Italian. But it is true that nobody ever thinks that Saadiya is Syrian. Or Nazmul or Ali.

Their dolls are lined up along the back of the sofa: three pale, blonde-haired plastic dolls and one shiny black bakelite one. The dolls look different, somehow, from how they looked a few minutes ago.

Later when Mummy is tucking them up in bed Saadiya blurts out what Grandma Pugh said. 'Grandma is a stupid old cow,' says Mummy. 'She's never forgiven me for marrying Abu.'

Ali stands in front of Grandma Pugh as she sits in her armchair. He says in Arabic, Grandma Pugh's legs are like *tibeldi* trees. Mummy says (as she always does in Wales and in England), 'Speak in English, James, it's rude to speak in Arabic when you're in Wales.' Which is funny, Zahara thinks, because why aren't they speaking in Welsh then, and Grandma Pugh as well? But when she asks, Mummy says, 'Don't be cheeky, Sandra.'

Why is it different in Wales and England from in the Sudan? wonders Zahara. Mummy doesn't speak much Arabic so in the Sudan she still speaks English. But Ali is dutifully translating himself: 'Grandma's legs,' he says but she interrupts loudly so that Grandma Pugh won't hear what he is saying and Nazmul barges sideways into Ali and knocks him down on the carpet for a play-fight. 'Boys! Boys!' says Mummy crossly, but Grandma Pugh only laughs.

Fancy that, thinks Zahara. *Perhaps Mummy doesn't know that tibeldi trees are what she calls baobabs?*

Now she is nine years old. They are at Grandma Pugh's house again, but this time it is Christmas night, and their stockings are still empty. They are slotted into Grandma Pugh's house like sardines in a tin: Nazmul and Ali are in the rarely used front room downstairs with their two cousins, in sleeping bags. Nazmul is on the hard, old-fashioned sofa because he's the oldest, the other three on the floor between the sofa and the fireplace. Ali is afraid of the bone herons on the mantelpiece, which the ghost of Grandpa Pugh brought back from Egypt, long, long ago in the First World War. The clock on the mantelpiece whirrs and mutters and he thinks it is the herons. There is a laughing Negro head as well. Grandpa Pugh was Cosmopolitan. That is what Mummy said when Nazmul asked why he had brought these things all the way back to Cardiff. They sell herons like that in the market in Khartoum, they ought to be familiar, but in Grandma Pugh's house they are only menacing. 'I thought Grandma Pugh didn't like blacks,' Nazmul said, looking at the Laughing Negro, but Mummy said Grandpa was different. And anyway, she added, Grandma was more tolerant of ornaments than she was of people.

There had been enough larking about when the boys went to bed to silence any old heron. Mummy said James wouldn't mind the herons any more, not after he had spent a night with them.

In Wales nobody knows their Arabic names. And in England they don't either. England is where Aunty Audrey lives now. They spend most of their holidays at Aunty Audrey's.

Sometimes in Wales and in England they get homesick for Abu.

She is sharing a bed with Saadiya in the tiny box room upstairs, but at this particular moment she is paused in the doorway on her way to the toilet, wondering how few steps she can take to get to the bathroom because the lino is very cold on her bare feet. Grandma Pugh is snoring in the big bedroom at the back, next to the bathroom whose particular antiseptic smell stands for Grandma Pugh's house when Zahara thinks about it back home in Khartoum. That and the sea-green back scrubber shaped like a fish that swims for ever, minus its tail, along the edge of the scarred, cast-iron bath.

She is about to take her giant steps across the lino, careful not to wake Grandma Pugh, when Mummy's voice comes suddenly from just at her elbow, behind the door of the front room where she and Aunty Audrey are sharing the double bed. Uncle David should be in the bed with Aunty Audrey but he is on duty this Christmas so he isn't here, and Mummy said that she and Aunty Audrey can have their bit of fun too and a chance to giggle together just like her and Saadiya. For old times' sake, she said. But she isn't giggling now, she is croaking, like someone who is crying when they shouldn't be. 'I can't stand it any more, Auds,' she says, just the other side of the wooden door at Zahara's left shoulder. 'He refuses point blank to come back. He seems to expect me to put up with living there for the rest of my life! He could so easily get a job here if he chose to. That's what hurts the most! His refusing to do something for me after all I've done for him. I really don't know how much longer I can go on!'

And then Aunty Audrey's voice, gently murmuring. Zahara, frozen in mid-leap, has a sudden, awful vision that Grandma Pugh's house might end up being forever and not just for a few nights once a year.

I'd rather live with Aunty Audrey, she thinks. Then we could ride the ponies every day.

She had cleared the table and washed up. The girls were down on the swings, in the shade at the front of the house: she could hear their happy voices drifting up. Ibrahim was reading an old copy of the *New Statesman* in the lounge. Her father was among his books. She did her usual mental tick list: all present and correct, all reasonably happy. A pity Jamil and Mastura had not turned up, but at least the *haboob* had lifted. It was a passable afternoon, if hot. *If only the rains would come,* she thought, taking a cup of tea to her father.

He looked up as she opened the door and smiled. She noticed how white his hair was going at the temples, though it was still thick. The lines in his face were etched very deep now. He looked tired.

'My good daughter,' he said, patting her arm as she put the cup down carefully among his papers on the crowded desk.

'You have two good daughters,' she said.

'Yes, but only one that I see every Friday. You are very good to your old Abu, Zahara.'

He put his arm round her and pulled her to him. She stroked the top of his head. 'Is it lonely for you, Abu? With only two children left in Khartoum? It used to be so very noisy in this house!'

'And still is when your four are here.' He let go of her and picked up his cup. 'Actually it is you that I am worried about. Any word yet on Ibrahim's job?'

She shook her head. Ibrahim had been teaching at the university for ten years but always on a temporary contract. There had been talk of it being made permanent but nothing was ever done about it. She knew Ibrahim was afraid his post might disappear altogether, as so many had, though he didn't talk about it much.

'Are you making ends meet, Zahara?'

She smiled reassuringly and ducked the question. 'We really must find you another house-girl, Abu. It's getting terribly dusty in here.'

'It is, but I don't really want one, you know. Nobody could replace Old Faatma. Poor old Faatma. Did I tell you her son came to see me?'

'Yes you did. You do need somebody, though. During the week when we're not here – I'd be so much happier if I knew you weren't completely on your own. And that you were eating properly.'

'Oh but I do. I do. What you leave behind you on a Friday lasts me nearly till the next time we meet.'

She looked at him suspiciously. 'That's just what I mean! You need more than left-overs!'

'You always leave me plenty of food. Thinking of which...' He opened the drawer of his desk and took out some banknotes. 'Here, for next Friday.'

She didn't protest. She never did. He gave her more than she ever spent on him, and that was part of their unspoken arrangement, by which he helped ease their difficult domestic finances a little. Soaring inflation, fixed wages – and the school barely paying its way yet (though she was sure that it would, given time).

'Would you mind, Abu, if I invited some people to *fatur* one Friday soon?'

'But of course. This is your home too, Zahara. Who are they? Friends?'

'Well, Josie for one, if she comes. But she never does these days. She's got problems at home, I think, but she doesn't talk about it.'

'I am sorry to hear that,' Hassan said. 'I've always been especially fond of Josie.'

She smiled. 'I know you have, Abu. And it's mutual. But these other people – the two children were enrolled in the school a while ago but I don't really know the parents, we've only met a few times. I think you'll like them, though. Will and Maggie. They seem nice. Will is very serious. He works for Unicef. Primary health care, so you'd have lots to talk about. I'm not sure what Maggie does apart from look after the children, but she's very kind. I'd like to get to know her better, but actually the reason for asking them is as a thank you. Maggie's been so helpful, promising to get books and teaching materials for us when she goes back to England on leave. She's asked a friend of hers to bring some back for us this month. I'd invite them home for a meal but you know what it's like in the flat, it's so small. I don't really like inviting people there.'

He squeezed her hand to tell her she didn't need to explain. 'Anyway,' she said, 'they would like to meet you. And to see this house. I don't suppose they've been anywhere quite like it. But I will wait until I've found you a house-girl. We do need to have a good clean-up.' She ran her finger along the edge of his desk and held it up. He looked at it and shrugged. 'Oh Abu! You never notice anything unless it's in the pages of a book!'

She picked up the paperweight on his desk. Such a heavy thing, familiar as if it had been in his study for ever, though she remembered quite clearly the day he had bought it, in a small town on the Nile when she was about ten. She laughed, holding it up and pointing to the perfect apex of the small brass pyramid: 'Is that artistic licence, do you suppose? Or wishful thinking?'

He grunted. 'They've renovated some of them now, you know. Since we were there. A team of German archaeologists, I believe. It might have been artistic licence at the time that paperweight was made but it is probably what they look like now. Or some of them. I hope they haven't spoiled them. We ought to go and see – your girls don't know their own heritage!'

She laughed, remembering this had been his complaint when they were children.

She is ten years old and she is running, across flat sand that gleams like a plate. Ahead of them, the big *jebel* is square and black against the pale sky. They are running to get warm. It is early morning. When they run back, their mother is standing by the truck with the new baby in her arms, hidden in a woollen shawl. Her face is hidden by her big hat. Just her mouth visible below the black shadow of the hat, a thin line across a pale space.

A week ago Abu had picked up Zahara's school book and said, What's this? It was her history book. They were doing the the Norman Conquest. What about Sudanese history? he asked, and she was confused, not knowing what he meant. So now they are driving north of Khartoum, going in search of their own history, he says, and they still don't know what he means. Their mother, tired with the new baby, is silent and cross. It is December and they left Khartoum in the bitter dark just as the pre-dawn muezzin was sounding, but the sun has risen now and their bones are warming up again. If Mummy would run she might feel better too, but she stands by the truck with the baby and waits.

The fragments of mica in the sand are winking and flashing. The ground is as flat and level as if it's been ironed. Abu calls them back to the truck: they have a long way to go yet, he says.

Hours later, they stop in the shade of an acacia tree to eat *fatur* of bread and the hard Syrian cheese which is made like a thick plait and dotted with onion seeds. Nazmul says the seeds are dead ants and Saadiya picks them all out. The truck driver has set the meal out on a red cloth on the sand. He shares it with them, and afterwards he clears it away.

She is disappointed. It *is* a temple, she can see that, but it is very small. She had expected something bigger. 'Look at the stones!' commands Abu. 'Think: how did they lift them up there?' She looks up the side of the wall, which is made of blocks as if a child has carefully piled them one on top of the other, except that each stone is so big it is impossible to think of ordinary men lifting them. And down the side of the wall, zig-zagging from side to side of the stone, they have carved a long snake. Nazmul is very excited by the snake but Abu is hurrying them back into the truck. 'We must keep going,' he says.

They drive until the sun goes over its peak and begins to soften a little, to a place beside the railway, which they recognise because they have seen these strange mounds from the train when they go in the special railway carriage for Abu to dispense medicine to the villagers. What does he want to show them? There is nothing here, not even a village. He is smiling. 'Do you know what those are?' he asks, pointing to the hillocks. It is a test. 'Termite hills?' suggests Nazmul but only for something to say. Abu says, 'Those are spoil heaps. They are two thousand years old. Do you know what a spoil heap is?' Nazmul shakes his head and Abu says, 'The slag heaps you see when you go to Grandma Pugh's in Cardiff – those are spoil heaps. But these,' – and he waves his arm proudly, as if these funny little hills belong to him – 'these are so old that the Prophet Jesus wasn't even born when they were made. And they're not from mining coal – they're from smelting iron. This place where we're standing was the first great iron-founding centre in the world. Think what that means when you think of England now! A great civilisation existed here one thousand and eight hundred years before England's industrial revolution. These people even ruled Egypt for a while; they ruled as far north as the Mediterranean. Come, I will show you.'

Zahara is thinking, All this way just to look at rubbish heaps? But she doesn't want to hurt his feelings. They go through a little gate in a fence. A man in a grubby *jelabiya* asks them all to sign their names in a book. She writes her name carefully, and offers to write Ali's for him because he's too little,

37

but he wants to write it himself, in big untidy letters. Saadiya writes her name and then Nazmul writes his. Abu writes his full name, and then their mother's, and the baby's. They have taken a whole page just for their family!

Inside the fence, the ground is covered in stones and lumps of rock. Here and there, the cut-off stump of a pillar. This is familiar. She has seen places like this in England. 'It's like Verulamium!' she says, pleased because she is very fond of the Romans. The *gafir* explains this was a city once: these were the villas and the streets. She looks at the low-lying rubble and begins to see there are patterns: vague squares and grids, made by the stumps of pillars cut off at knee height and the ribbons of walls. The sand stretches over the spaces in between now, like a carpet which you might turn back to reveal old floors. 'This was a very wealthy city,' says Abu. 'A centre for trade from as far away as China. Traders coming all that way, to buy precious things and sell spices.'

Later, they sit outside the Rest House in the windy, desert darkness, wrapped in blankets. The moon is like a big ice ball and it is glinting on the back of the camel that creaks its way round and round in the corner of the compound, driving the wooden thing which Abu says is crushing *simsim* for oil. 'Sesame,' he says to Mummy in English, but even Mummy knows that *simsim* is sesame. It is the *gafir's* camel. The *gafir* lives here all on his own with just his camel, opening the Rest House when people come. Now he is sitting with them on the rickety *angarebs* under the full moon and he is talking to make up for all the times he has no one but his camel to talk to. She cannot understand him. His Arabic is very strange, and anyway he hasn't got any teeth.

Abu is sitting wrapped in one blanket with Nazmul, she and Saadiya are wrapped in another, but Saadiya is shivering so hard that Zahara can hear her teeth chattering. 'Come,' says Abu when he too hears Saadiya's teeth. 'Come and sit closer.' And they edge up against him, Saadiya in the middle like the filling in a sandwich, leaning against his right arm while Nazmul peeps out from under his left. Mummy is inside the Rest House with the baby and Ali. She said it was too cold for the little ones and Ali had a tantrum because he didn't like being called a little one like the baby. Now he has gone quiet. She would quite like to be in bed too, the wind is so very cold, but it is exciting to be up still and sitting with Abu and the driver and the *gafir,* no other people anywhere, just them, and the camel, and the stars. Perhaps there is nobody left in the world but them.

She has never seen so many stars. The sky is stuffed with them. If you don't quite look properly they seem to whirl about, as if you can see the spinning of the earth.

'Abu, Abu! A shooting star!' Nazmul's voice comes out in a squeak. She didn't see it; she was looking at the way the moon is shining on the *gafir's* bald head when he takes his turban off to scratch it. He looks funny without his turban; his head seems much too small. Then he plonks the turban back on, like Grandma Pugh's hat, the one she keeps for going to church in.

'I want to see a shooting star!' says Saadiya. 'Then you'd better keep looking,' said Abu. He is big and warm and they nestle against him like chicks under a mother hen. 'Do you get chickens in the desert?' she asks, but Abu doesn't hear her. He is listening to the driver telling a story about a shooting star he saw once that was as big as an orange, flaring through the sky to land far away in front of him as he drove from El Obeid to En Nuhud. He would see where it hit the earth, he thought, but he drove and drove and got to En Nuhud without seeing any sign of it. *Could a shooting star hit the earth?*

She looks up at Abu. His face is in shadow, just his teeth glinting as he smiles. She can see the gap between his front teeth. He tickles her cheek with one finger, reassuringly, and shakes his head, just very slightly, so that only she can see.

The next morning they are up before the sun and driving fast over the stony sand, the sky behind them showing a bar of red. Then the whole world glows orange-red as the sun heaves itself slowly over the horizon.

They don't see them at first. Just a long ridge rising out of soft sand, with a row of bumps along the skyline. It is Nazmul who guesses first. 'Pyramids?' he says, uncertainly. The timing is perfect: as they drive up to the bottom of the slope the sun's rays catch the line of little broken-topped pyramids. There are lots of them, all along the ridge.

'Why are they that funny shape?' asks Saadiya.

'Because,' Abu says, 'when the Turks came in the nineteenth century they had an Italian called Ferlini with them and he knocked the top off every single one looking for burial treasure.' Nazmul sits up. Treasure? 'Actually,' Abu says, 'the Meroites buried their dead a long way underground. The pyramids were only a kind of gravestone on the top but Ferlini didn't know that.'

'Did he find any treasure?' Nazmul asks.

'Only in one, but that was enough to make him try the rest. And even from the one he made a fortune.' Nazmul is so excited that Abu laughs. 'Anything interesting has long since been carried away,' he says. But they are all eager now, tumbling out of the truck to touch the ancient stones. This is what History feels like. At any moment a bit of pot or a piece of tile might emerge from the sand after a thousand years of working its way back to the surface. They scrabble about hopefully. Even Mummy looks happy today, sitting with baby Jamil on her lap in the back seat of the truck.

40

After the pyramids, when the sun has been up for a long time and the air is hot, there is another temple, with stone rams so perfect that you can run your fingers round the whorls of their carved fleeces. Below the temple, camels and donkeys are still being watered at the ancient well, which was in use long ago when the temple was built. The camels lower their heavy heads to drink from the leather waterskins, which skinny boys are filling from the well. The camels have velvety muzzles and when you see them up close their long-lashed eyes are gentle. They make her want to pat them. The herdsman, seeing her movement towards the camel's flank, laughs and says something to her father.

'He says that camel kicks as well as bites,' says Abu, and Zahara jumps back hastily.

Later, in a town by the Nile, Abu buys a little brass pyramid from a shop. They are going to have fish and chips. 'Sudanese fish and chips,' says Abu, 'the best in the world.' But Mummy is worried about them catching germs. The restaurant is a tin shack, and the fish – Abu says – was flicking its tail that very morning in the river. The man comes over when he sees Mummy and flicks a dirty cloth over the table. Mummy looks as if she might be going to be sick. She turns her face away and won't look at any of them. But when the man comes back with the fish, which is fried in batter just like proper fish and chips in Cardiff, he has a newspaper under his arm which he spreads on the metal table before putting the big pieces of fish down. Then he comes back with a hot pan and ladles chips straight onto the newspaper. He tells them to eat. And gestures again to Mummy, when he thinks she has not heard him, that perhaps she is deaf.

It is the best fish and chips they have ever tasted. Now they know the Sudan has everything: scenery, history, and fish and chips too.

Chapter 3

At five thirty in the morning he was knocking on the door of Toby and Sandy's compound. It was still dark, the early morning muezzin was sounding from the nearby mosque. He had to hammer on the metal door for some time before there was any response. They emerged at last, bleary-eyed. 'Too much partying last night?' he asked, laughing, as they climbed into the Land Cruiser like two old men. He jumped into the driving seat. Two religious festivals in one week and all the offices closed: it was the perfect time to go down to Kadugli on a social visit but he couldn't do such a long journey alone so he'd suggested a short bachelor expedition.

The two VSO lads were ready and waiting when they got to their house on the other side of the *souk*, but they looked just as bleary as Toby and Sandy. They had all been at the same party. Charles felt crisp and grown up beside them as he drove out of El Obeid on the Dilling road. The sun came up gentle, cradling the landscape. Dozy birds, not yet quite awake in the half-light of dawn, lifted off the road in gusts as they approached. He drove fast along the newly graded dirt road and breathed in deeply as he looked from side to side at the rosy landscape, listening with only half an ear to the desultory note-sharing of his fellow passengers. The strength of Toby's home-brewed *kerkedeh* wine and their four varying degrees of hangover seemed to be all the others were interested in just now. *Look at that!* he thought as they passed the little *jebel* where he sometimes took the kids to fly their kites: the crags and crannies of the rocks along its spine were etched in stark relief by the horizontal rays of the sun, and to the west of the *jebel* its tumbled shadow was so precise that every rock and crevice of its bony spine seemed to be separately visible. *If Bee could see that!* he thought. But if Bee were here, he wouldn't be where he was now. Five hours driving to Kadugli, twenty-four hours with Dave, his Unicef colleague in the Kadugli office (supposedly a social visit but of course they would talk shop all the time, because that's what you do), and then five hours driving back again: it would hardly be enough to lure Bee into dragging four children out for a run.

It occurred to him, as he watched the early morning lift itself up, that she usually saw this landscape in a very narrow window of time, mostly in the late afternoon, and crowded by four tired, hungry children.

He wished he could carry back with him a share of all the wonderful things he saw as he travelled about, like small offerings to lay at her feet, but in the face of all this strange, searing beauty he felt he had no gift for description. If only he could somehow lend her his eyes! He looked about him, thinking of the letter he would write later. But after a while the words in his head dried up and his mind went blank. If she could get out more, he thought lamely, and without the kids, maybe she would see it differently.

The sun rose and paled. And the conversation in the Land Cruiser rose and then subsided again, and they travelled mostly in silence, each locked deep in his own thoughts. The first faint flush of green – on the ground and in the trees – was seeping in at the edges of all the dry-season yellows and browns. Autumn colours predominated still, the reds, the

43

golds and the yellows. It smelled like autumn, too, and it struck him suddenly that the word for rainy season was *kharif*, which translated as autumn, when logically you'd think it should be spring – the season of renewal and things growing, not of death and hibernation.

A hornbill heaved itself off the red dirt of the road and flapped heavily into the scrub trees. A few miles later a group of monkeys crossed the road a hundred yards ahead of the Land Cruiser, pausing halfway across to look at them in alarm before scurrying off out of sight. At Kor Sungikai they crossed the newly opened military bridge over the dry *wadi*. At Dibeibat they bumped across the railway line. Two hours after leaving El Obeid they stopped in Dilling for breakfast in the *souk*, Afterwards, Toby took over the driving.

From Dilling to Kadugli the road was tarmac, but it was so studded with snaking heat eruptions and pot holes that most of the time they drove along the verge, dodging back onto the metalled surface only where the sand was soft, or where a dry *wadi* passed under the road. Swerving on and off the road and bouncing so hard you could hit your head on the roof if you weren't careful, it wasn't a journey you could sleep through. *But who would want to*, he thought, steadying himself in the passenger seat. The sun was glaring now and one by one they put on their sunglasses.

We look like the bloody Mafia, he thought.

As they drove south the landscape was shifting in character. The scrub got thicker and the *jebels* more frequent: heathery pink or lilac blue in distant silhouette, with a tendency to arrange themselves pleasingly at the ends of long stretches of the yellow road. The shrub trees crowded in on the road now, like a vast empty garden. They passed sparse settlements, picturesque clusters of circular huts with a date palm or two,

44

and thatch the same colour as the surroundings, topped by a crescent cow horn. The air was full of the heady, fleeting scent of flowering trees. That smell of the rainy season which could make a hardened man weep with homesickness years later.

They began to meet the Baggara on the road. Big herds of cattle and flocks of sheep and goats passed by on their slow progress northwards towards El Obeid, following the rains and the new grass. Men and boys, some with a new-born lamb under one arm, standing to attention at the side of the road to watch the Land Cruiser pass, their grins as white as their *jelabiyas* and as bright as the blades of the long spears in their hands. One old man was carrying an ancient musket.

'Serious business, defending these herds,' said Toby. 'You don't see the rifles and Kalashnikovs but they'd get them out in a jiffy if they thought anybody was about to steal an animal. Or a woman, I s'pose.'

'Where do they hide the Kalashnikovs? They're not that easy to hide,' one of the VSOs said, his tone sceptical.

'Among all those pots and baskets loaded on the bulls, I guess. Or with the women in those tents perched on top of the camels.'

They passed another vast herd, fanning out through the thorn trees on both sides of the road, sliding northwards like shadows through the dappled shade, the camels rolling easy, the cattle gliding brilliant as jewels in shades of red and white, of tan and of black, their coats sleek as velvet with good grazing. The big bells hanging from their necks chimed with the rhythm of their walking. Here and there a woman rode through the herd perched on the family bed, upturned like a raft and strapped across the back of a bull or a camel, and hung with pots and pans. Occasionally a camel passed carrying a tented litter, rocking and creaking. The draped tents were decorated with leather tassels and cowry shells and they looked like something ancient and majestic. Biblical, even. They rode alone these women, rocking gracefully, or sometimes with one elegant, braceleted arm casually encircling a small child seated beside them while with the other hand they guided the camel by a single rope through its muzzle.

'Do you think only the beautiful ones get to ride in those things?' Sandy asked. The women stared down at them as they glided past and drew their *thobes* loosely across their mouths, half-hiding their faces but not their smiling eyes. And looked back over their shoulders as they rocked away, still smiling. Inside the bumping Land Cruiser the five men watched Mafia-like from behind the blank lenses of their sunglasses and smiled back their pale, impersonal smiles, passing southwards in a cloud of red dust. Sandy said 'I've never understood how you can control a camel with just that bit of string.' Nobody answered him. It was curiously silencing, this witness of ancient passage.

This is how I could imagine the Garden of Eden, thought Charles. With prosperous cattle following the rain and the air full of the perfume of flowers. And the fleeting, mutual pleasure of unreachable women passing unavailable men.

Calvin Dare, pseudo Jesus Christ (or possibly Clint Eastwood), all-American action-man now reincarnated as head of Unicef in Khartoum, came to El Obeid to organise a special trip to Babanussa and Meiram for government officials and aid agency representatives, of whom (since he was doing the organising) Unicef was the most visible. Represented by himself, of course, and his resident acolyte in the region, i.e.

Charles. His lesser intention being (as Charles was quite well aware) to scrutinise said acolyte. The El Obeid office was fast becoming the gateway to the south for the passage of aid in the wake of SPLA rebel activity and the re-emergence of famine. But in any case, ever since he had arrived in post in April, Calvin had been scrutinising Charles. 'Hey!' he said whenever they met in Khartoum, slapping Charles on the back in avuncular fashion (though he was not so very much older), 'how's it going down there?' And Charles, who always thought this made Calvin sound like an overly enthusiastic clap doctor, would look into those sharp blue eyes and know he was being assessed. He could never tell how he was measuring up. But now, in the excitement of arranging a major visit complete with special train and military escort to go down into the troubled lands of Southern Kordofan, Calvin was mercifully distracted. He had the minister to butter up, after all.

The train crawled painfully slowly over the hot damp plains. This far south it had been raining for several weeks. Water lay in sheets on either side of the railway and the air was humid with rampant growth. Ironic, he thought, that it wasn't drought that was the cause of famine here: in the rainy season, every year, the SPLA pushed the conflict northwards as fast as it could, a tide of refugees pushed inevitably in front like lines of flood-wrack.

They didn't reach Meiram until just before nightfall. The town was not much more than a collection of small huts and mud-brick houses, and a half-constructed grain-store, but the population was swollen with a large influx of southerners, whose numbers were increasing every day. Unicef was asking for permission to construct an airstrip in Meiram so that they could use their small plane to fly in grain close to the refugee camps.

Calvin looked (Charles thought as he followed behind him) superbly rakish in his red neckerchief and check cowboy shirt, walking beside the minister. The sun beat down on Calvin's bare head, his dark Jesus-curls. He was gesticulating to the right and to the left, talking animatedly to the impassive, sweating minister. The minister was wearing a black suit. Snippets of the conversation drifted back to Charles as he followed in their wake. Once, Calvin stopped and addressed him directly, asking him for facts and figures.

There's a book in this, he was thinking. *One day, when I'm no longer here.*

It was growing dark and their military escort was getting more and more jumpy. He looked at their weapons, at their tense faces. It didn't make for relaxing chat; made him want to look over his shoulder the whole time. It was a relief when they were shepherded out of the open, into one of the larger mud-brick houses.

The room was crammed with people. It was hot and humid, mosquito-haunted, taut with strident voices. Hurricane lamps threw faces into crude relief and cast strange shadows on the stained walls that had once been painted spearmint green. The village chief mumbled an introduction and for a few moments there was wary silence. Then one lone voice asked a question and the floodgates opened. What is going to be done for us, the townspeople asked over and over with grim insistence, while the refugees scarcely said a word. He watched their gaunt, anxious faces. He could feel how frightened they were, he could see how desperately exposed and vulnerable they felt in this small town where nobody wanted them. It was obvious that all that the refugees wanted was to get out of Meiram and head north, to the safety of the large communities of southerners in Khartoum. They couldn't understand the authorities' reluctance to let them go.

'We can clear an airstrip,' Calvin was saying. His American-settler self was taut with excited energy as he sat there in the lamplight, his red kerchief pulled loose at his neck. He sat with one leg crossed over the other knee, grasping his smart leather boot at the ankle with one hand while with the other he articulated patterns in the air. After each sentence he paused, looking at his boot, while the sentence was translated. He looked only a little sweaty. Charles pushed the damp hair off his own forehead and wondered how he did it. 'I will need ten good men,' Calvin said, and Charles thought, *Christ, he'll be calling up the bloody cavalry next!* Such a shame his every word had to be translated.

'What about the security situation?' argued one of the army officers. 'You will need a military escort for any movement of grain, even if you manage to make an airstrip the plane can land on. If you seek to push further south you will need more than that: as it is, we can only allow trains to go south to Aweil if a temporary ceasefire is arranged with the SPLA.'

'Then we'd better arrange one,' Calvin said calmly.

'The government is anxious to do all it can,' said the minister. 'For all our people.'

Smarmy bugger, thought Charles.

And the townsmen said, 'We are also your people! We are poor, we too are in need. Why do these incomers deserve more than us? All our grain is imported and costly. Why should cheap grain come in for them and not for us?'

He looked at Calvin with interest, wondering what he would reply. The translator was still translating. Another man cut in, 'The traders will lose out! This aid grain will destroy local markets, it will undercut investments already made!' The man who said it was plump and fierce. *I'd bet my arse he's a merchant*, Charles thought, but the man didn't declare himself.

Did Calvin realise how inevitable it was that grain would leak out of the system? How else would the refugees buy the other basics like the cooking oil that they would need if they were to turn the grain into a meal, unless they traded some of the grain first? It was an old, old argument – should relief go only to refugees and never to the indigenous inhabitants, or should it go to both – but these people were not to know that. This was immediate, and it was happening to them, and that was all they cared about. The detail would be worried about by distant officials. The ordinary people would do what they could with whatever came to hand. And the merchants would do well out of it because merchants always do. He watched the angry faces as he listened hard to what was being said. It was difficult to follow the rapid twists of the argument and the varying accents but the mounting tension didn't need to be deciphered, it was palpable.

Hours later the meeting drew to an awkward, unsettled conclusion. He went back to the train with Calvin and the other officials. They lay down on the wooden benches (Calvin in his pioneering boots, the minister in his dark suit) and slept uneasily, eaten by mosquitoes. The darkness was total. Not a light showed, from the train or from the houses. The only sound was the urgent revving of the frogs all round them and the occasional bark of a dog. He lay for a long time without sleeping, listening to the frogs and the sonorous snores of his companions, his head crowded with the restless images of faces. He was haunted by their fierceness: the anger of survival, group pitted against group. They circled in his head like a relentless motif. The turbulence of the townspeople, believing themselves threatened, and the strange, anxious passivity of the watching faces of the southerners, so still that only their eyes moved from side to side as they listened helplessly, their fate precariously balanced in the collective hands of a loose community of strangers.

Back in El Obeid, he cooked a meal while Calvin stalked his bookshelves. It was the first proper meal they'd had for two days. There was an inevitable camaraderie in being together, just the two of them in the lamp-lit house, whatever he privately thought of the red kerchief and the pioneering boots. The smell of frying meat, the domestic trivia of drinking water arrangements and questions about what books he read in his spare time – these details were like symptoms of potential friendship.

A light breeze stirred the darkness and rattled the papery bougainvillea against the insect netting. It felt fresh and pleasant after the humidity of Meiram, but here too the frogs were sonorous as if they could sense the rain was coming.

Calvin came in from the sitting room with a book in his hand. 'Let's get this straight, right. You're on sabbatical?'

'Secondment.'

'Okay, secondment then. And from the University of Cambridge?'

'East Anglia. It's in Norwich. Not that far from Cambridge,' he explained, as if it was relevant.

'For two years?'

Charles nodded, concentrating on his onions.

'And then what?' Calvin demanded.

'Back to old academia.'

The onions spat in the frying pan, the frogs chorused in the darkness.

'Professor, are you?'

'No. Lecturer. And I do research. Our Department does research for third parties like the World Bank and the

International Labour Organisation, that sort of thing. I'd been working on and off in the Sudan for six or seven years when Unicef offered me this post. They hadn't managed to find anybody else, that's why they were happy to take me on secondment.'

'Pays more, does it, academia?'

The same old myth! He stirred the onions irritably and turned down the heat. 'No. As it happens, very much the opposite.'

'Uh huh.' Calvin peered into the frying pan. 'Smells good.' He subjected Charles to another of his penetrating stares. 'You know, you should consider making a career of this life. You've got the potential.'

Charles inclined his head, wondering if this was a proposal or merely a compliment.

'That apron suits you,' said Calvin, and disappeared back into the sitting room.

Over the meal they talked business. There was a lot to discuss. Should they concentrate purely on food aid, or try to do something more sophisticated by taking health care in on the back of food relief? What should they do about the persistent rumours of slavery? What about this nagging issue, so eloquently raised in the meeting, of balancing the needs of indigenous versus displaced populations? The dim light bulb overhead swung gently in the warm night wind as they sat at the table. A cat yowled somewhere in the dark garden. Charles noticed how, in the time they'd been away, the dust had made the black and white floor tiles red again, showing up his and Calvin's footprints tracking this way and that.

'Happily married, are you?' Calvin asked suddenly.

He looked up, startled. Calvin was doing the stare again, so he gazed back steadily, wanting to say, None of your bloody business! But he didn't want to wrong-foot himself. He wanted to say, *Very*, but that sounded suspiciously over the top. So he just said 'Yes.'

'Where is she, then?'

'They were booked to come back at the end of July but I had to tell them to delay coming – the town water supplies are nearly exhausted. Until it rains here, it's better if they don't come.' He held Calvin's gaze.

'I've only met your wife once. I suggested that you might think of getting your kids a donkey. Shirley and I did that in Botswana and the kids just loved it. You know what your wife said?'

'No,' Charles said, holding his breath.

'She said one donkey at a time was quite enough, thank you, and she had four donkey foals to deal with as well.'

Under the exuberant moustache there was just the hint of a smile. Charles breathed out again with relief.

'A sound marriage is a necessary basis for a life out here. I mean, this is on the verge of classifying as a hardship post.' Calvin looked about him almost with distaste and Charles wanted to leap to the defence of their shabby verandah, of their funny old house, of El Obeid. Calvin went on, 'But a good marriage can make all the difference.'

He wanted to say, *It's not a pre-requisite, is it?* But he might muddy the waters and make Calvin think things were other than they were. He missed Bee's voice suddenly. Throaty, low-pitched, a touch sardonic. Her favourable comments were generous when they came but usually hard-won. He was not inclined to explain her to anyone, least of all to Calvin Dare.

'I like to see people in their home environments. I'm a better judge of people when I can put them in context.' Calvin was eyeing him sternly. 'I think you're sound. You could go far. Will you really want to go back to that academic job in sixteen

53

months time? Swap all this real world action for your ivory tower again? I'll tell you straight, Charles – I would see that as a loss to Unicef. You're intelligent, you know the country well, you speak the language. And you're not afraid to challenge your colleagues, or officials either, when you think it necessary. I'm not easily impressed, but I have been impressed by what I've seen these last few days. But I am looking for a five-year commitment. There's no way you can settle for less in a country like this. It takes two years to find your way in, three years more to make it work. I'm laying it on the line here, Charles. If you want it, there's a permanent post waiting for you. But I do need that five-year commitment.' Calvin pushed the novel he'd been reading across the table: 'I picked this up off your shelves. Have you read it?' Charles shook his head. 'Wouldn't bother if I were you. I've just skimmed through the first chapter. Not worth reading.'

In the morning, as he drove back from seeing Calvin safely onto the Unicef plane, he watched the Twin Otter rising jerkily, a silver dot in the sky above him. He knew exactly what would be happening on that plane right now: Calvin Dare, rising through thermals in the same way he aspired to rise through the echelons of Unicef, would be planning how he might build on his success with the minister yesterday. And now and then, for light relief, his thoughts would wander to speculating how he might persuade Charles to make that five-year commitment.

Chapter 4

Zahara sat in the kitchen with her cup of tea watching Nura ironing listlessly at the table. She was much too pretty, this girl. They needed somebody practical and hard-working, not a flighty young thing, but, as Abu said, they could hardly have denied her a job on the grounds of being pretty.

She looked at Nura's slender neck, the braided hair swept up to a knot high on the back of her head. Nura sensed her looking and put one hand to her forehead, an elegant gesture denoting weariness, Zahara supposed. Or the headache she'd complained of earlier.

It was not the prettiness that was disturbing her, Zahara decided. It was the sly look Nura slid in her direction before putting her hand to her head, as if she was checking that Zahara was looking. It was the haphazardness with which she went about her chores, even though she must know Zahara would be watching her closely this first week. Above all, it was the ease with which Nura had divulged her ambition to find a job in a *khawaja* household and marry a *khawaja* so that she would never have to work again. Had she been joking? Zahara was horribly afraid that she had not, and that an elderly Sudanese doctor (apparently single) might seem to Nura to be the next best target, in the absence of a *khawaja*.

'My parents don't live together but they are not divorced,'

she said, hoping she sounded more casual than she was feeling. 'My mother works as a nurse in England.' (No point saying Wales or Britain or even the UK to Nura, who probably thought all *khawajas* came from England, even Americans and Australians.) 'But she was here four months ago,' she added. 'For my brother's wedding.'

She watched Nura pass the iron languidly backwards and forwards over the sheet, her saucy eyes demurely lowered. She didn't believe for one moment that Nura was as untouched by this piece of information as she appeared. Perhaps Abu had already told her that Mummy had declined to stay in this house but had squeezed into their cramped flat with them for the whole two weeks of her visit. Nura turned the sheet and the pink tip of her tongue arched daintily against her upper lip. She was like an actress performing for an audience. Would Abu be up to resisting a strategic assault? Probably he would not even see it coming. He was so unworldly these days, so deep in his own thoughts.

I will talk to him about it tomorrow, she thought.

But tomorrow she did not. Nor the next day. She gave Nura another chance, and then another. She didn't want Abu to think her prejudiced. But she went to the house each day after school to check that Nura was doing the things she'd asked her to do, and each time Nura looked at her with those laughing, upward-tilting eyes. Almond eyes, I suppose that's what almond-shaped eyes are, Zahara thought (rather crossly, because she could see as soon as she came in that Nura had merely swept around the furniture, and not even that carefully – from the doorway she could see the tidemark left by the passage of the broom).

Nura inclined her head when Zahara pointed out the bits of floor her broom had missed and considered the evidence.

56

'I am too tired,' she announced. 'I will do it tomorrow.' She didn't sound the slightest bit abashed.

Bukra – tomorrow. It was turning out to be Nura's favourite word.

'Abu, that girl must go,' she said to her father later. 'I will have to try again.'

'You will do no such thing,' Hassan said, quietly but so firmly that she looked at him in surprise. 'She is young and inexperienced but she will learn. We will give her time.'

'But Abu, she is "resting" more than she is working! She won't accumulate much experience like that, except for inventing excuses. She's always too tired, or she's got a headache. Actually, she's stopped even bothering to make an excuse, she just says '*Bukra!*' and leaves it at that! And she isn't embarrassed to sit there watching me do her work.'

But Hassan was firm, as he said she too should be. 'She is young,' he said. 'Besides, she sings like a bird while she is ironing, it is a pleasure to have her in the house. And she looks like Nefertiti, which is amusing.'

She did look like Nefertiti, it was true, with her long slender neck and high cheek-bones and the upward sweep of her hair. And she did sing beautifully. But her ironing was dreadful, and at this rate she would be resting too often to do it anyway. Zahara went home and allowed herself a small weep on Ibrahim's shoulder. She knew he understood that her real problem was the feeling that she had somehow been displaced.

❧

'You are old enough now, Sandra, for me to talk about this,' says her mother. And begins to tell another story, not the familiar one of the handsome young doctor and the pretty young nurse: that is the framework, but this story is like decaying flesh filled in on old, familiar bones. The young nurse who got pregnant by mistake. 'He was a doctor, he was so much older than me, I trusted him, Sandra,' says Doris. And the fourteen-year-old Zahara nods but she is thinking, Yes, but you were a nurse! Surely you knew how babies are made?

(At nineteen, Zahara thought, Yes but she was a nurse, she was twenty-one, she must have known all about abortions and where you had to go to secretly murder your own baby. But she was glad to be alive and thinking this thought.)

'He was so much older than me,' says her mother to her fourteen-year-old daughter. 'He was so handsome, we were so much in love. But his father had arranged a marriage, back in Omdurman. He was putting pressure on your father to go home and marry this woman – not someone he knew, just some tribal connection his father and uncles considered important. You know how they do.'

(At twenty-eight, Zahara thought, Was it blackmail, then? Her mother trying to hold on to her exotic foreigner by the oldest trick in the book?)

'I thought he would marry me,' says her mother. 'Even though I had no money, no important family. But he was insistent that he must go back to the Sudan. He put his father first!'

('Not my father,' says Abu later, sitting in the *racuba* beside the Nile. He strokes her hair as she lies with her head in his lap. 'Not my father, Zahara. My people. My country. I had to come back and work here, it was my duty. One day you will understand. Your mother has never been able to.')

Her mother tells instead this other story, of tears and recrimination before Zahara was born, of shouting and anger in Grandma Pugh's claustrophobic little house. Of Grandma

Pugh throwing her out. ('I'll have no blacks in this house, you filthy girl! And I will not be shamed by you bringing a black bastard into this house!') So that Doris was homeless as well as disgraced. The landlady where she found herself a room to rent near the hospital looking at her suspiciously as if she were something dragged in off the street by the cat. 'A mean room in a horrible house with broken lino,' she says, 'and the stairway reeking of over-cooked brussel sprouts, or worse, and only an outside toilet with a cracked and dirty pan, and me with terrible morning sickness and a painful back.' A room she did not feel she could bring Hassan back to, even if the landlady had permitted it. The landlady was a dragon to out-compete even her mother.

'I will never forgive Grandma Pugh, never,' she says. 'I was her daughter, I was only twenty-one. She should have been more loving, she should have looked after me. She left all that to Aunty Audrey. Aunty Audrey was "a brick".'

And Zahara looks at her, wondering what comes next in this story, because the history that she remembers is so different: her parents calm and quiet, and, when she was smaller, anyway, affectionate. In the house Abu had built for them, with the pink bathroom, beside the Nile. The quiet river flowing calmly past, and red *kerkedeh* flowering in neat rows alongside the *simsim* and the maize and the groundnuts, in the fields beyond the lemon trees.

(Though she has always known a part of this other story: fourteen years after her own arrival in this world Grandma Pugh is still telling it for herself. 'Whoever thought any daughter of mine would marry a black! Not even a Christian black at that!' says Grandma Pugh, quite often. Saadiya and Nazmul just laugh and say she is old and can't help being silly, but Zahara hates it.)

Zahara wonders, as her mother tells this story, if her own reluctance to excuse Grandma Pugh is some pre-consciousness memory. In her mind's eye she sees a dark baby in a white shawl in the arms of the trembling young mother as she goes to the door of her mother's house in search of reconciliation. Grandma Pugh refusing to open the door.

But even as she is thinking it her mother says, 'She thought the world of *you* as soon as you were born. It was ridiculous really, but I suppose it was because you were her first grandchild – she let you win her over, even if she doesn't like to let it show. She likes to hide behind the old prejudices. They make her feel safer, Aunty Audrey says. Actually, Grandma would have thought the world of your father, too, if she'd relented enough to meet him. But she wouldn't, not for years, and by then it was all too late.'

'So what happened?' Zahara asks. 'How did you come to marry after all?'

'Your father does have some honour,' says her mother, as if surprised. 'And anyway, he was hoping for a son.'

The usual afternoon storm was threatening when he came in from the office – the heat building and bulking through the day, the clouds massing but in the end tramping off westwards to rain elsewhere. He cast an eye to the sky and then turned his back and tried to ignore it. He was so tired of wanting it to rain. But dusk fell earlier than usual and the wind was rising.

A mighty wind coming out of nowhere suddenly ripped through the house, banging all the doors. A sheet of rain as dense and horizontal as a squall of sea-spray hit the back wall of the verandah. For a moment he stood transfixed and disbelieving in the sitting room doorway. Then he was running along the verandah shutting windows and doors like a man running along the perilous deck of a ship to batten down hatches. He was still running when the lights went out.

He sat on the bed wrapped up in a sheet against the sudden chill, watching the continuous flicker of the lightning. The thunder massed into a single deafening roar. The electricity pole in the USAID compound over the road was struck and flared briefly with a fierce magnesium flame. He felt terribly and fiercely alone, like a minor animal, but exultant. So much fierce energy unleashed. The rain, at last. The longed-for rain.

Hours later the storm died away but it was only nine o'clock and he was restless. If only Bee and the kids were here, they would all be enjoying the novelty of the cold air but, alone, he couldn't get warm. He was as miserable as a wet dog by candlelight. The power was unlikely to come back before morning. The garden was four or five inches deep in water, the roads would be impassable. There was nothing else to do so he went to bed, huddling up in the sheet in all his clothes because he couldn't remember where Bee kept the cold-season blankets.

When at last he fell asleep he dreamed all night that he was pursuing Bee along the long windswept beach at Walberswick. In his dream she was running, keeping always just ahead of him, out of his reach, the wind in her hair and in her long blue skirts.

The rain had been widespread. The reservoirs and the *hafirs* were full. He went to the Post Office and telegrammed Bee to come. The man behind the counter looked up from the telegram form and grinned.

In the villages, a wave of frenetic activity had been unleashed, men and women rushing to plant at last. Two days after the storm, driving out of El Obeid to the south to look at the new vegetable nursery in Ban Gedeid, he was surprised how fast the green grass was shooting at the side of the road. Everything was in such a hurry as if held back, even the grass. In the village there was hardly anyone about, they were all out in the fields.

Saaid drove to the compound where the midwife lived and leaned on the horn. 'The strong woman' Saaid called her. A natural leader. Tall and fierce, with a nasal voice and powerful hands – it was hard to imagine a gentle delivery at her hands. Much easier to imagine circumcision. All those terrified young girls who must have known those hands all too intimately. The midwife came out of her impoverished hut ducking casually under the low doorway, and led them through the narrow lanes of the village to the garden. They walked between the irrigated beds. Women bent over their sowing, too busy to stop and talk.

Below the garden, on the edge of the village, the grove of mango trees on the far side of the dry river glowed orange in the sun as the afternoon faded. How peaceful it is, he thought. 'All the lands here,' – Faatma Mohammed's strident voice cut in – 'all the gardens and the mango orchards, are owned by wealthy merchants in El Obeid. We who live here are only labourers, we own nothing. And the landlords are withholding water from us so that we must pay. Unicef has not included Ban Gedeid in its water programme,' she said, looking at him sternly, 'because you think this is a wealthy place with ample water. There is no free water from hand pumps for us, we are going thirsty.'

What could he say? Nobody had talked of this before, he'd had no idea. He promised that he would see what he could do, thinking how lame his promise sounded.

It was sunset when at last they drove away, Charles and Saaid in the front of the pick-up and two local men who had asked for a lift to town in the seat behind them. On the edge of the village a solitary man was kneeling at his prayers outside the door of his hut. The fading landscape stretched endlessly in its unbroken roll, the single hut with the figure of the praying man tiny details in one corner of it.

How small we are, he thought. That man alone with his god. Me alone in this vast country with no family here, and no god at all. There is nobody watching over me. He thought of the merchants in El Obeid who wilfully deprived others of water and wondered if they too prayed at sunset.

Saaid stopped the car at the side of the road and jumped out hurriedly to pray. The two men got out and an argument broke out as to which direction they should be facing to pray towards Mecca. Charles went off to sit quietly under a thorn tree while he waited. A few minutes later he was amused to notice that of the three praying forms just visible in the dusk, one was pointing in a different direction from the other two. A huge affection bubbled deep in his heart: for Saaid, for the unknown men, for this whole enormous country in the gathering dark.

༄

She left Ibrahim sleeping and crept out of the house to load all the food into the boot of the Vauxhall. It was early enough for the sky to be pale, the air delicate and cool. Ibrahim would bring the girls later, at the usual time, in his brother's truck.

Leaving Khartoum on the Wad Medani road Zahara noticed that there must have been a brief shower of rain in the night: here at any rate the dust was damped down and the air smelled fresh. Between the road and the Nile each house stood in its own long rectangle of land, each with a mailbox on the road with an incongruous street number painted on the side.

She looked at all these details with a different eye this morning, wondering what Maggie would think. She very much wanted it to be good thoughts. After more than twenty-five years the house her father had so proudly built for his family was beginning to crumble. The sun was rotting the comfortable old seats on the terrace. The pink bathroom tended to smell of drains these days. But it was hard for her to see it with an objective eye.

Today, as she turned on to the bumpy track that led down to the house, she noticed how – even if the house was crumbling – everything around it was twenty-five years more grown. The lemon and orange trees had quite a girth on them now, and Jamil's neat rows of *simsim* and *kerkedeh*, groundnuts and sorghum, were prosperous-looking. More so than when they were children, when Abu had been dependent on an overseer to manage his farms. Now he had Jamil to look after them. She drove down the track that ran along one side of the ten-acre plot. At the last minute the ground dropped suddenly towards the river and there was the house, hidden from the road, fading gently in its magnificent setting perched above the Nile. The house was still magnificent too, she decided, even if – as she was painfully aware – the roof was leaking and the cess-pit could no longer be relied on. The irrigated kitchen garden was bright with leafy things in spite of the rains being so late. Bougainvillea tumbled riotously across the facade of the house, clashing vigorously with the red of the brick. She waved to Mustafa, the old man who came to weed and water.

Jamil won't mind if I take a big bunch of *jir-jir* from the garden, she thought as she parked the car under the trellis of bougainvillea and morning glory. She wasn't surprised to find she had got there before him. It was early yet, barely eight o'clock.

She was surprised, though, to find Nura sweeping the

64

verandah. Fridays were supposed to be her day off. Nura looked at her over one shoulder with that sardonic half-smile, clutching the drooping folds of her *thobe* to her buxom chest with her free hand while she swept with the other. Zahara stood, disconcerted, a box of groceries in her arms and her car-keys dangling. Nura finished sweeping, stood the broom in the corner of the verandah, placed her *thobe* carefully over her head at a particularly raffish angle, said 'Goodbye' in English, and left. It was only as Zahara stood watching Nura's hip-swinging gait – as the girl walked up the slope towards the road – that it occured to her how strange it was that Nura should have been sweeping in her *thobe*. *Thobes* were very expensive. Nura always carefully folded hers and put it in a safe place while she worked, for fear of getting it dirty or snagging the chiffon. Under the *thobe* she wore such tight, skimpy sleeveless dresses that it would be better really if she always kept it on.

Abu came out of the bathroom. 'You're early! Where's Nura?'

She thought she caught a fleeting look on his face, soft, almost lascivious when he thought for a moment that she was Nura, followed by a fleeting disappointment when he saw that she was not. A little bell in her head chimed a discordant echo. A hovering suspicion, suppressed until this moment, settled awkwardly into place. But she said casually, 'She left just as I came in. I've come to get ready. Will and Maggie Smith are coming for *fatur*, Abu. Remember? And somebody called Charles who also works for Unicef.' Her confidence faltered suddenly. For so many years she had been living between their two households, overseeing his as well as her own, but had she overstepped some unseen boundary, arranging this, even though Abu had seemed happy with the idea when she'd suggested it? Had he secretly minded and not said anything? She looked at his kind face and thought *No, it isn't like that.* Then she thought of Nura, beautiful and sly, and thought, *But she might think so!* 'I'll make you some coffee.'

'No need – Nura made me some earlier.' He turned back towards his study. 'I suppose I had better change.' At home he always wore a soft grey *jelabiya*, but it wasn't his public dress. 'Who is it we're expecting?'

'I told you on the phone, Abu – Will and Maggie Smith, who are going to bring those resource packs for me when they go on leave. And they're bringing a colleague of theirs from Unicef, Charles Walker. I'd been hoping that he'd be able to bring his wife and children because I want to thank her for bringing two boxes of school books for me, but Maggie said they don't actually get back from England until tomorrow. And there will be Maggie and Will's children, of course. They have two, a boy and a girl. But no Josie. Josie couldn't come.'

'Is it this the Will and Maggie whose children are at school with you?'

'Yes. The girls are excited they're coming. The children know each other from school, of course.'

He looked searchingly into her face. 'Good. It would be good for you, too, to have a friend.'

'I have friends, Abu.'

'You know what I mean. English friends. Contacts. You might need them one day.'

'Why, Abu? What are you meaning?'

'Nothing, nothing,' he said, and went to his study.

Leading the visitors into the lounge she turned to watch their faces. They were struggling to focus after the glare outside as everybody did coming here for the first time, so that they

66

didn't notice for a moment that the big open windows looked out over the river. But when they did, they exclaimed out loud and she was satisfied.

She had met Will only once before, and briefly. This was the first time she had met Charles. She looked at him with interest. A good-looking, arrogant sort of man with blond hair falling over one eye. She decided immediately that she was probably not going to like him, he looked much too sure of himself.

'I'm sorry you couldn't bring your wife and children,' she said when they were introduced. 'Maggie says they are not arriving till tomorrow?'

'Tonight. They'll be here tonight but very late.' He said it matter-of-factly. And when Maggie said, rather tartly, 'Freedom ending, is it Charles?' he smiled a stiff smile.

Zahara thought, These two don't like each other much! 'Shall I show you the house?' she asked. It was her way of saying she would show them where the bathroom was. As she opened the door to reveal the pink bathroom with its black toilet seat and its pink and black tiles she sniffed discreetly: not too bad a smell of drains today, she observed with relief. 'Very sixties,' she apologised. 'But it was my mother's pride and joy when the house was built.' Remembering too late that she hadn't explained about her mother. Maggie gave her an intense, interested look. I rather like this Maggie, she thought. Perhaps we could be friends...? Immediately, she tried to wipe the thought away. If only Ibrahim and the girls would hurry up – it would be so much easier if she wasn't doing all this on her own! And Jamil and Mastura were supposed to be here too.

Back in the lounge she brought a tray of iced *kerkedeh*, hoping they were not expecting alcohol. Abu came from his study and was introduced. They sat on the hot plastic sofas that her mother

67

had had shipped out at such expense many years ago, sipping at their glasses of sweet red juice, the two English children subdued with her because they were outside the familiar surroundings of school. She spoke to them encouragingly, thinking of all the things that were still waiting to be done in the kitchen before they could eat. If Ibrahim didn't come soon it would be a disaster! Then she heard a truck draw up outside and the girls' excited voices. They rushed in, Ibrahim following in their wake. He grinned at her apologetically. She was relieved to see that he hadn't forgotten the bread. She had asked him specially to buy some from the Greek baker in Omdurman, and she could smell that it was good. 'Tell the girls not to go out of the yard,' she said in Arabic as she took the bread from him at the kitchen door. He looked at her patiently, his eyes saying, *they know that!* 'It's different when there are other children around,' she said. 'They might forget!'

He patted her shoulder reassuringly. 'They won't forget. Do you want me to do anything?'

'No, just go and help Abu talk to them. I don't suppose there was any sign of Jamil and Mastura as you came in?'

He shook his head. 'You know what they're like! Better just to carry on as if we're not expecting them.'

She watched anxiously as they ate, wondering if they were familiar with Sudanese food. When would these people have had a chance to eat a Sudanese meal unless they'd been invited to a Sudanese household?

She jumped up and down from the table, bringing things from the kitchen, replenishing the bowls as they were emptied, fetching more bread. The children sat at their own little table in the corner and giggled and chattered and occasionally had to be shushed so that the adults could hear themselves speak.

'Zahara, you have excelled yourself,' Abu said, and she was embarrassed, not wanting them to think she had tried too hard. But it was true that she had gone to a lot of trouble. The best bread in town. Vegetables from Jamil's garden: fresh *jir-jir* and tomato salads, two different aubergine dishes. Spiced meatballs, kebabs grilled on charcoal, two small chickens made into a stew. All the dishes were laid out on the table with the basket of flat bread. Serving spoons in the dishes, and her mother's Sheffield cutlery carefully laid by each plate, because although she wanted to give them a Sudanese meal she could not quite brave the challenge of making them eat communally and with their hands the way the family usually did. She sat now, watching them eat, relieved to see how relaxed they all were, helping themselves, passing bowls to her father, talking all together just as if they were at home. It was easier now that Jamil and Mastura were here. And Jamil had come bearing beer. Everything seemed so bright and noisy, so full of movement as soon as he came into the room. His big presence filled up all the spaces that had felt self-conscious and hollow before. Their father relaxed and talked more freely. Ibrahim too looked as if he were enjoying himself. She sat watching them, exhausted. She looked at Mastura, sitting close to Jamil, saw the little secret smiles between them. She was almost sure that under the table they were leaning their knees against one another. She looked at Ibrahim (his face serious as he outlined the strengths and weaknesses of the year-old, democratically elected government) and remembered how sweet it had been to be newly married. How long ago all that seemed now! Their own heady days as students in Europe, out of the sight of probing Sudanese eyes when he used to come from London to stay with her in Pisa. How free and inviting the world had looked in those days! She half listened to Mastura talking in her hesitant English to Maggie, remembering how

69

life had seemed then and how very much in love she and Ibrahim had been. Still are, she thought, looking at her husband's delicate profile as he bent his head to listen to something Charles was saying.

'Mastura is training to be a doctor,' Jamil was telling Maggie, his voice very proud. 'In Wad Medani Hospital.'

All the faces at the table turned towards Mastura, who blushed. How strange, thought Zahara. Everybody looks at Mastura all the time because she is so beautiful, and she must be used to that, but now we all look at the same time and she blushes!

Mastura is getting even more beautiful every day – marriage suits her. She went to the kitchen for the fruit salad. *More beautiful than Nura. And certainly kinder.*

When she came back Mastura was telling Abu (in English, to be polite) about a family that had come into the hospital yesterday. She was telling Abu, but everybody was listening. The man had been working in his fields with his children, the youngest only a baby in the arms of a big sister. A mad dog had jumped over the irrigation ditch and bitten one of the children. And when the big sister went to beat the dog off, he bit her too, and then the baby. And he bit the other children, and the father as well, when he came running from the end of the field with his hoe and tried to beat the dog away. All of them bitten, every single one. And they were seven. They had walked to the hospital. It took them nearly two days, so of course it was much too late when they got there. The dog was rabid and they would all die. 'Slowly,' Mastura said, not looking up at her silent audience. Jamil put his hand over hers on the table.

Hassan smiled kindly at his daughter-in-law. 'It is hard and unfair, isn't it. But sadly, it is life.'

Jamil said hotly, 'It doesn't seem fair that even if you get to the hospital in time the medicine is segregated! Twenty-seven injections in the stomach if you're Sudanese and if you're lucky, but only three in the buttock if you happen to be a foreigner and can get hold of the new French vaccine!'

Zahara looked up quickly but the visitors did not seem offended.

'You don't have to be a foreigner,' Abu said quietly. 'I have a small stock of the French vaccine in the fridge here.'

'Have you?' Jamil sounded disconcerted.

'You should take some with you to the farm. It has to be kept refrigerated but you should keep some there. Nobody wants the twenty-seven injections if they can help it. You remember your mother!'

'As if we could forget!' Jamil said with feeling. And he told the visitors how their mother had been sitting reading on the verandah one day, in the house they used to live in, when without warning a mad dog had jumped over the fence from next door and bitten her on the arm. She had to go to the hospital every day for twenty-seven days for the painful injections in the stomach while they all waited in terror to see if the rabies would develop.

'But now,' Abu said, 'as you know, we have this new French vaccine, which is very expensive but we hope that one day it will be available to all. And that is progress. Everything must begin somewhere,' he said, giving Jamil a meaningful look.

Will said, 'You must have seen many changes in your time as a doctor, Doctor Hassan?' and the conversation moved on, to health care programmes and issues of international aid. Mastura, shy as she was and her English hesitant, was in the thick of the discussion, Jamil helping her when she didn't know the words. Ibrahim was planning to write a book of his own about the

71

economic impact of aid on developing countries, so he had lots to say too. Only Maggie and Zahara were silent. Once or twice Maggie tried to join in but nobody heard her speak. She looked at Zahara and raised one eyebrow, a gesture so slight but so expressive that Zahara laughed out loud.

'Would you like to come and see the river?' she asked. It was time they checked on the children anyway, though she could hear their voices and knew they hadn't gone wandering off.

'The trouble is,' Maggie said as she followed Zahara outside, 'if you get two or more development experts in the same room there's never any space left for a non-combatant. They don't mean to do it, but they think that you can't possibly have anything to contribute because you're not another expert, therefore you can't possibly have spoken. At least when we go on leave it's different. No experts for Will to talk to then, I mean.'

'When do you go?'

'Wednesday night. The kids are that excited!'

'I've noticed,' Zahara said drily. Sam had been quite disruptive in class, but she would not mention it. 'Do you work? I mean, do you have a job outside the house?' she asked as they went down the steps to the backyard. (She had already counted heads and she was no longer anxious.)

'I'm thinking of getting one,' Maggie said. 'There's a voluntary job going with the new handicraft project that Calvin Dare's wife is setting up. He's the new head of Unicef. They're opening a craft shop. Have you heard about it? I suppose if I do some work with them I'll become a minor expert myself. If you can't beat them you just have to join them.'

Sam and Aasha were crouching together by the fence; the sun gleamed darkly on her braids and whitely on his blond head. The others were pushing each other on the two old swings that dated from her own childhood.

'Oh just look at them!' Maggie said, pausing to look fondly at Sam and Aasha, huddled together as they giggled furtively in the corner. But when they got closer they saw that Sam had pulled two legs off one side of a large ant so that it ran in circles. 'Sam! You little devil!'

He looked up, startled, and Aasha jumped guiltily. But the ant went on circling, and Aasha couldn't quite suppress another giggle. Maggie glanced at Zahara apologetically. Zahara shrugged. 'We're going down to the river,' she called to the girls. 'Do you want to come?' They came running from the swings with Cathy between them holding on to their hands.

Zahara unbolted the gate and stood aside to let the children through. They went ahead, down the twisting path to the bank. 'Careful!' she called, afraid that in the excitement of showing Sam and Cathy the girls would forget to be cautious. The path had dried off after last night's brief rainstorm, the red clay cracking and splitting, but already the dead grasses which reached over from either side were beginning to spring green in the middle of the clumps. Below them the river ran blue and serene. You might almost think you were in England, she thought as she looked at a distant red sail on a little dinghy, almost out of sight downstream of the island. Maggie was breathing deeply, her eyes half-closed. 'It's almost *fresh* down here!' she said. 'With that breeze off the river. What a lovely place!'

'That's Crocodile Island,' Zahara pointed at the big trees just across the water. Why had Maggie said it was '*almost* fresh'? The wind was almost cool, but certainly refreshing. 'The river is narrower here because of the island.'

'Why is it called Crocodile Island, Mummy?' Faatma's head

73

had popped up at her elbow. She said, as she said fifty per cent of the times she was asked, 'I don't know.' (The other times, she would tell a story. Of crocodiles with magic powers. Of sailors marooned with hungry animated logs for neighbours, and their feats of daring to outwit the sharp teeth and live another day until a passing boat could rescue them.) 'There aren't any crocodiles. Not now.' And Faatma ducked away again, disappointed. Zahara stood beside Maggie on the bank and they looked at the trees dipping their branches down towards the water. Such a tranquil scene, the Nile so very blue today. 'Once, a German lady lived there, with her young daughter. She was quite mad, the lady. She didn't wear any clothes a lot of the time. Then her husband came and he took the daughter away. He said she was not a fit mother. After that she lived there quite a while on her own. I don't know what happened to her in the end. Perhaps they put her in a hospital.'

'How did she live there if she was mad? I mean, what did she eat?'

She shrugged. 'Local people brought her food sometimes. She drank water from the river. People used to come on Fridays to look at her, as if she was a tourist attraction. She raved a lot, and she had tangled yellow hair all down her back. That, and her not wearing any clothes – I suppose that is what they came to see. Actually, it was sad.'

'That's a strange reversal!' Maggie said. 'German tourists go to see the Whirling Dervishes in Omdurman, Sudanese tourists go to see the crazy naked German lady on Crocodile Island.'

They walked side by side along the steep embankment, watching the water flow steadily by. It ran deep here, and muddy when you saw it up close, now that at last the rains were beginning, upstream of here.

'What happened to your mother?' Maggie asked. 'I mean, she didn't die, did she, when the rabid dog bit her?'

'Oh no. She lives in England now. Well, in Wales, actually.' She felt Maggie look at her and carefully composed her face so as not to invite further questioning.

Instead Maggie said, 'That was a wonderful meal!'

So she relented. 'I was fifteen when she left. Jamil was only five. Would you like to see the kitchen garden?' They climbed the path again, to a terrace at the side of the house where the vegetable patch was lush in the afternoon sun. 'Of course it all has to be irrigated. But we have an electric pump; we can lift water from the river. It is Jamil's garden, really. He looks after it, when he comes back from the farm at the weekends. Though it is harder for him now that he and Mastura are married. We have a cotton farm in the East,' she explained. 'My father bought it many years ago and now Jamil has taken over the running of it.'

'So the newly weds don't see much of each other during the week?'

'No. She is in Wad Medani during the week anyway. They only have Friday and Saturday together, and only if she is not working.'

'She's such a beautiful girl! Such amazing skin. And all that hair! I love the beads.'

Zahara smiled, accepting the compliment on Mastura's behalf.

Maggie stood looking round her. 'You don't know how nice it is to be out in the country and in a real vegetable garden!'

But she did, and she didn't think Maggie's house in one of the smart suburbs could be nearly as cramped as their flat in Souk Two, especially now there were six of them living in it. 'Do you not have a garden at your house?'

75

'There is a garden at the back but it's not all that big. And you know what it's like – if you fail to water just once everything dies. Our *gafir* is very old, and between him being forgetful and me not being much better, we've managed to kill a lot of things. So we just stick to bougainvillea now. It's a shame – in Kampala we could grow everything, even snapdragons.'

Zahara wasn't sure that she could remember what snapdragons looked like. She began to walk round the vegetable rows, telling Maggie the Arabic names of the plants.

Maggie said suddenly, 'If your mother left when you were fifteen, had she already taught you how to cook?'

Zahara looked at her carefully and could see that it was a kind of compliment. 'Our housekeeper taught me – old Faatma. She was like a grandmother to us. We had a Welsh grandma but not a real Sudanese one – my father's mother died soon after I was born. Old Faatma used to look after the house, and then when my mother went back to Wales she looked after us as well. Shall I show you Jamil's cow?' There was no sign of the others, just the sound of their voices drifting through the open French windows. The children had already run on ahead. 'Come, I will show you the cow. It is not like an English cow, though I have met Welsh cows a bit like it!'

Maggie laughed and followed her up the path. Lemon and orange trees made dark shadows against the pale blue sky as they climbed the slope towards them. On a patch of rough grass between the trees a black cow with a rope tied round sharp-looking horns pawed the dust fiercely and snorted. The children had already squealed and retreated well out of reach. As Maggie and Zahara approached, the skinny little cow charged again, its head snapping back with a jerk when it got to the end of its rope. 'It's all right,' Zahara said reassuringly, 'the rope is strong.' But they kept a cautious distance. 'Let's go and look at the *simsim* and the *kerkadeh*. What do you call *kerkadeh* in English?'

'Hibiscus.'

'I used to know,' Zahara said, 'but now I forget.' There was laughter behind them: the other adults had finished putting the world to rights and seemed to be coming out to see the cow. 'Who's volunteering to do the milking?' they heard Jamil ask. He shouted up to them, 'Maggie, Will says you want to milk the cow. Shall I bring the bucket?'

Maggie laughed and shouted back, 'Not today, thank you – I'm in my glad rags.'

Zahara looked up in surprise. Glad rags? She hadn't heard that phrase before. She looked back at the others. Both white men were the same wiry build as Ibrahim, smaller and slighter than Jamil, but unlike Ibrahim they looked scrawny. And in their pale, loose-fitting clothes they looked rather crumpled. Ibrahim and Jamil looked so neat and bright in their pressed jeans and coloured shirts, she thought proudly. She looked at Charles's chiselled features, thrown into relief now by the late afternoon sunshine. He had a way of pushing his heavy fringe up off his forehead, almost a nervous tic. Beside him Ibrahim looked younger, though they might be much the same age. Maybe it was because Ibrahim was less sharp and angular, as if he were more at home in his skin. Watching him as they came up the path towards them, she thought that actually Ibrahim was the more attractive. It was a long time since she had looked at him with such objective eyes. He looked up at her as they came close and his eyes twinkled. A little shiver of pleasure went through her. Poor Ibrahim, between the exhausting politics of work and the daily scurrying around after work that was needed just to keep things afloat at home, he rarely had a chance to have fun and simply enjoy himself.

How lively and happy he looked now after so much talking! How handsome and wholesome beside the pale Europeans. She sneaked a look at Charles and decided he was not that good-looking after all. There was something about him that made her feel wary. *Cocksure*, she thought. What an odd word that was, it sounded terribly rude. Had she just made it up? She turned to walk up the path behind Jamil and Mastura just in time to see them secretly clasp hands when they thought that no one would see.

'I'm going to make some tea,' she said, feeling suddenly drained and exhausted. It had been a lovely afternoon, and perhaps they would repeat it one day, perhaps another time Charles would bring his wife and children. But at this moment all she really wanted was for the visitors to go so that she could sit in the kitchen over a cup of tea with just Jamil and Mastura.

Chapter 5

The official on the gate into the new Arrivals Terminal waved his hand apologetically when Charles showed his diplomatic pass: new terminal, new rules. Strictly no entry now except for official personnel.

Excluded by the glass partition, he watched them come into the baggage reclaim hall, familiar, white-skinned points of reference among the dark-skinned crowd of arrivals. Bee was pushing one of the shiny new luggage trolleys. Adam was trying to climb up on it and was being reprimanded, Danny was looking vague. Kit was chattering as usual, and as usual his shirt was hanging out at the back and tucked deep into his underpants at the front. Charles laughed. That was so like Kit. And how Catrin had grown! His little girl. She was wearing pink dungarees and had the tatty bit of pillow-case she called her clothie clutched in one hand. The children saw him and started waving excitedly. All of them cheerfully, he noted with relief, though they must be tired after their long journey, and it was way past the children's bedtime.

How sensuous Bee looked in her well-filled skin. She was wearing the dress he liked best, the flowing blue dress which emphasised the colour of her eyes, and blue canvas shoes he hadn't seen before. She looked at him. Even from this distance he could feel the intensity of her gaze. He grinned back. Her hair was trimmed boyishly short. It suited her. He longed for them to be through the doors so that he could take them all in his arms. He leaned on the glass, trying to be patient, as they stood distantly by the new luggage belt.

It was a long wait. He shifted his position. Began a discussion about politics with an elderly Sudanese gentleman who was waiting for his daughter and son-in-law. Laughed at his children's distant antics. Catrin was dusting the motionless conveyor belt with a feather. Adam – unusually, but he was tired and had just fallen off the luggage trolley – was sobbing loudly. Charles could see by the way she was standing looking down at him with her arms folded that Bee was saying, 'Told you so.' Danny was squatting against the wall reading a book, quaintly studious-looking in his new glasses. Kit was still talking. Charles studied them one by one, drinking in the forgotten details.

At last the conveyor belt creaked into action. He watched as Bee lifted the heavy cases off the belt with difficulty. Nobody offered to help and she was looking hot and harassed now. Adam was obstinately trying to climb on the trolley again in spite of her visibly sharp reprimands. Half an hour later and they were still waiting. Bee gestured to Charles from where she stood by the nearly empty belt, a pile of boxes and suitcases beside her: it seemed that one of their cases had failed to materialise. Most of the other passengers had already left. It was after eleven and Catrin was hanging onto one of Bee's legs. Adam, bawling because he had fallen off the trolley again, hung on the other. Charles paced up and down on his side of the glass in helpless frustration. He collared a passing man in uniform and said in Arabic that his wife was having problems retrieving her luggage. The official promised to see what he could do.

The belt revolved slowly, quite empty now except for one disreputable cardboard box and an equally suspicious-looking suitcase, which kept reappearing on each slow circuit. An airport official came up and asked her to follow him. He went out through a door beside the conveyor belt and she followed with some difficulty as she had a child clinging limpet-like to each leg. Outside the night air was warm and sweet after the air-conditioning of the arrivals hall and there on the tarmac, beside the moving belt, sat the missing suitcase. She retrieved it in relief.

The man looked at her kindly. '*Itneen awlad?*'

'*La, arbaha,*' she replied. Four boys, not two. She was too tired to start explaining that Catrin, in spite of her pink dungarees, was actually a girl.

'*Arbaha!*' said the man, impressed. And then he said, in heavily accented English, that he hoped that God might now send her a daughter, for her pleasure. She thanked him.

'Are you my pleasure?' she said to Catrin as she wheeled the laden trolley up the baggage hall at last, towards customs.

Catrin looked up at her sleepily and smiled through her thumb. 'Nes.'

'No-o-o!' wailed Adam, predictably, given his over-tired state. '*I'm* your treasure!'

'No one's disputing that, pet. You are both of you my treasures,' she said. She smiled down into his anxious upturned face.

'Yes,' he said firmly. 'I'm your treasure. *Not* Catrin!'

But Catrin had caught sight of Charles, still the far side of the Customs Desk but close enough now to suddenly seem real. She was too busy shouting, 'There's Dadoo, there's Dadoo!' and she didn't hear Adam.

Customs was tedious, as usual, the search always meticulous, but (perhaps because she was a woman) oddly diffident. At last they were through and the children were throwing themselves into Charles's arms. He hugged them all. Then he hugged her, and kissed her warmly – after so long a wait decorum went out of the window. She saw that he too had tears in his eyes. They looked at one another and laughed.

The children were still sleeping when Charles left for the office next morning. It was too dark to read in the shuttered room so she sat quietly in the hard armchair, making the most of the stillness.

When the children woke at last she took them across the road to the main building of the hotel for breakfast. Climbing the two flights of stairs her legs felt as heavy as lead, as if she had walked ten miles. It was quite late. The dining room was washed in the sunlight that flooded down through the windows high in the roof and it was hot. Most of the guests had already breakfasted and gone. The waiters greeted Bee and the children affectionately and laid them places at the table nearest the stairs, asking how they had enjoyed their holidays.

The children sat quietly enough, Adam far away in a world of his own as if he had gone deaf. Danny was secretly reading his book under the table but Bee chose to ignore the fact. Catrin was tired and cross. She had forgotten all the critical details: the stale flavour of the cornflakes, the peculiar taste of the milk, of the orange juice, of the bread. Nothing pleased her, except for the little jars of jam. Only Kit was still bouncing. He looked at Bee with glowing eyes and said suddenly, 'It's good isn't it! All these seven and a quarter years I've had!' Her heart swelled with sudden emotion.

But a moment later, when he started hitting Adam over the head with the cornflakes packet, her feelings shrivelled up again. 'Stop that, Kit.' The habitual three words.

She talked to them quietly – mollifying Adam, calming Kit, coaxing Catrin, urging Danny – pushing and pulling them gently through breakfast and into the rest of the morning. But she could feel the familiar mounting of tension, like hairs pricking awake and erect in every follicle of the darker reaches of her consciousness. She had not felt like this all the time they had been away on leave. She'd forgotten it, just as they had forgotten the taste of the cornflakes. It was closing in on her again like a thorny corral, the forgotten taste of boredom and constraint. And it was only nine o'clock on their first morning back.

The short walk to the Sudan Club was never an easy one with a pushchair and small children because of the high, uneven kerbs and the haphazard holes in the pavements, and the traffic thundering past. The shops were tawdry and the streets were, as always, full of rubbish. Also of languid young men hanging about on corners, casting disapproving looks at her, a white woman out alone. She grasped Adam firmly by one hand and clamped it to the pushchair handle under her own. 'Danny, hold Kit's hand please, we need to cross the road.'

'I don't want to hold Danny's hand! I'm too old to hold hands!'

'Don't be silly, Kit. You always have to, to cross this road. The cars go so fast. I don't want you getting squashed, not here.'

'Why?' asked Kit, distracted into acquiescence and taking hold of Danny's hand. 'Wouldn't you mind me being squashed somewhere else?'

She ignored him, concentrating on looking for a big enough space in the traffic to get them all across the road in one piece. A lull came, and calling to Danny she moved briskly out, but

83

Danny was still staring dreamily at the black kites circling in the sky above. She shouted back at him to follow quickly.

They got to the other side safely, Kit looking self-righteous. 'See, I'd have been much more safer on my own!'

'Daniel!' she said as severely as she could, given that he looked sorry and was probably as tired as she was. 'You're nearly eleven years old! You really must start paying attention when we're crossing roads. It's all very well saying sorry afterwards but one day you'll have an accident and it will be too late then for 'sorry'.'

Catrin twisted round in the pushchair and peered at Danny. 'Danny bad!'

'No, not bad. Just hopeless,' Bee said, turning down the side street to the Sudan Club.

'I'm not hopeless,' said Kit. 'I've got lots of hopes. I hope that on my birthday I'll get a new bicycle, and I hope that my Lego is still in our house in El Obeid and the ants aren't in it. *And* I hope that today there's cream horns.'

At the mention of cream horns Adam came suddenly to life. He had been holding her hand but hanging back so that she was taking all his weight with one arm while she forced the pushchair through the soft sand of the unpaved street with the other. 'Cream horns?' he said, and began to hurry, as if that would make them come faster. There had only ever been cream horns once but the children had lived in hope of them ever since.

Out of the corner of one eye she saw a rat picking about in the rubbish at the side of the street. She ignored it. The scraggy cat which was sitting nearby, busily cleaning its grimy fur, ignored it too.

'Oh! Puss Puss!' cried Catrin, leaning forwards suddenly out of the pushchair and gesturing hopefully with her fingers.

'Don't touch!' Kit commanded sternly. 'We don't touch cats in the Sudan.'

'Oh bovver me!' Catrin said crossly and scowled up at him, 'I very fended wiv you now.' But she sat on her hands in the pushchair, as if to keep them safe.

They turned into the faded entrance of the Club and out of the hammering sun.

There was little about the Sudan Club that was Sudanese, Bee reflected, apart from the waiters and the cleaners. It was firmly British Colonial, an oasis in time and place, with its whitewashed buildings, indeterminately Turkish/Afro/European in style, and – under the big *neem* trees – a swimming pool glittering blue in the sun.

In the mornings, when they come to Khartoum for programme meetings, they usually have the place to themselves if it is term-time. Most mornings here they sit at one of the tables beside the pool and the children dawdle over their English school books in the shade of the big trees while the *gafir* clears fallen leaves off the surface of the water and she cajoles each of them through their sums and their writing (or in Catrin's case, being only three, her pretend-school pictures) with promises of a swim. This is their Sudanese life, when they are in Khartoum, these are their good times. But even here, in their haven, life is lived on a knife-edge: the shallow end of the pool is too deep for Kit to stand in, let alone Adam or Catrin. She must herd them all the time with *don't do this* and *don't do that*, until she is sick of the sound of her own voice.

As she was already, and today was not even a schoolwork day. Today they were simply recovering from coming back to the Sudan: no school books, and in and out of the pool all morning. And at lunch, though there were no cream horns,

85

there was fried chicken so the children were happy. And afterwards there was treacle pudding, with custard.

Bee bypassed the pudding and sat with her chin cupped in her hand while the children tucked in, considering her options. Catrin badly needed a sleep, though Kit trying to take her doll all the time wasn't helping. The walk back to the hotel in the fierce midday sun would be very trying: it would be so much easier to stay here, in the pleasant shade of the trees, enjoying the comfortable, familiar pattern of the Club filling up with people as they come in from work when the offices closed at two, to swim and sunbathe, to play squash, to order tea served in dented old silver tea-pots and sit gossiping round the pool or talking business. And now that the schoolday was over there might be other kids for the children to play with. But it was obvious that Catrin needed nothing less than a proper bed. Even Adam might sleep today (though he never usually slept in the daytime, in spite of being the second youngest), and Kit and Danny surely would because they always did. The long journey and the sudden switch in climate had taken it out of all four of them. They all might sleep, if she was lucky.

Maggie and Will lived near the Unicef office in a pretty little house rented from Chevron and furnished from Habitat. The house was full of rugs Maggie and Will had bought in Iran, baskets from Zimbabwe, and beautiful pots collected from their travels all over Africa. And they had lots of books, and music which they played on an expensive audio system, so Bee enjoyed coming here. But today was not a good time because Maggie was in the middle of packing.

'When will you be back?' Bee asked, reclining on the double bed while Maggie sat on the floor in a sea of packing cases.

'End of October. Twenty-sixth. Yeah, yeah – it's a stupid time to be going back to the UK with school just about to start again, but my brother's getting married on the twenty-fourth. The kids will just have to catch up when we get back. Thanks for getting those books, by the way. Zahara is almost painfully grateful. You haven't ever met her, have you? She'd been hoping to see you last Sunday when we went to her dad's place with Charles for *fatur* because she wanted to thank you herself. She was so disappointed when I told her you weren't arriving until the evening.'

'Another time, perhaps. She did thank Charles.' Bee watched Maggie stowing an electric kettle at the bottom of a box. 'Are you taking that back with you?' she asked, surprised.

'No. This is stuff I don't want to leave out in case the house gets burgled while we're away. Things like the video player. They'll be double locked in the store.'

'Not taking any chances then,' Bee observed wryly. 'I thought the *gafir* would be here?'

'Yes, but he's old, and there are so many desperate people in Khartoum these days, what with all the Eritrean refugees, and now the Dinka as well. I suppose it is a bit mean leaving an old man in charge. If we were robbed he might get hurt.'

Bee sat up and leaned back against the headboard. They always sat in here because it was the coolest room in the house. From the children's room came the sound of laughter and intermittent squabbling. 'Are you sure I can't give you a hand? I feel very superfluous just watching.'

'No, really – I've nearly finished. Just a few clothes to throw in a suitcase after this. Don't feel superfluous! You don't know how grateful I am to have somebody to talk to.' Maggie closed up the last box and taped the top down. 'Don't know why I'm bothering with this tape, the dust always stops it sticking properly. I'll have to do them all again with string. By the way, I'm really sorry about the house, Bee. I mean, that Bill's going to be using it while we're away. Otherwise you could have stayed here when you come up to Khartoum for the next programme meeting. I didn't know there was a problem over the *per diem* until Charles said the other day.'

'Don't feel bad about it. It may be all talk, anyway. But if they do cut it we won't be coming up to Khartoum with Charles any more. We won't be able to afford to stay in the Acropole on the *per diem* if they halve it, so we'll have to stay behind in El Obeid while he comes up on his own once a month.'

'Oh Bee! Sitting down there on your own while he has a good time here?'

Bee shrugged.

Maggie said, 'I hear they're talking about making El Obeid a Hardship Post.'

'That's all a nonsense. It wouldn't be so bad if they only gave us a bit more support. You know, half the time they even forget to send down our post? So much for the "Unicef Family"!' She sat up brusquely and ran her fingers through her hair. 'Sorry, sorry! I shouldn't be jaundiced, not when I've just had a good long leave at Unicef's expense.' She closed her mouth. But the indignation wriggled up all the same. 'It's just – they make all the right noises about looking after us but all the same I keep being left with the feeling that we've been shipped out here merely to service the Unicef employee. We're supposed to lie quiet when not in use.'

'Well, we *are* only animated baggage, you know,' Maggie said and Bee had to laugh.

The noise from the children's room reached a crescendo. Maggie got up, smoothing down her crumpled skirt. 'Come on, let's have some tea, and give those kids a drink and a biscuit before we find we've got a riot on our hands.'

In the kitchen the heat soaked back into their clothes like water into a sponge. There was no air conditioning in here; the kitchen was expected to be the province only of servants. The afternoon light glared at the windows in fierce streaks along the bottom edges of the lowered blinds. Maggie opened the enormous fridge. It was unusually empty but even so the contents were exotic compared with the modest fridge in their house in El Obeid, which never had wine or bacon in it and rarely butter but was mostly full of drinking water.

'Khartoum is like a foreign country compared to El Obeid,' Bee said. 'My El Obeid life is completely dominated by the boiling and filtering of drinking water, but here you can drink it straight from the tap.'

'Hmm, I'm not really sure that we should.'

But they did, and the tyranny of thirst was diminished by the simple fact that they did. And in this sealed house – protected by its air-conditioning from dust as well as from heat – the tyranny of sweeping was less, too. *But I wouldn't like the air-conditioning*, Bee thought, opening the packet of biscuits Maggie had handed her and putting them on a plate. *I wouldn't like being so shut in all the time.*

Danny appeared, looking flushed. 'It's getting a bit wild in there,' he said, helping himself to one of the biscuits on the plate.

'What are they up to?'

He picked up a second biscuit and took a bite out of both. 'Sam and Adam and Kit are hiding under the beds and Catrin and Cathy are pretending to be monsters and looking for them. Can I have another one?'

'Danny – even you can't eat more than two at the same time!'

'Want a bet?'

89

'It's all right,' Maggie said indulgently. 'They need eating up. Just leave some for the others, that's all. And don't tell them you've had a head start.'

'And don't let it spoil your dinner tonight,' Bee added. 'We're going to Calvin and Shirley's, don't forget.'

'We were over there the other night,' Maggie said, pouring out five glasses of lime cordial, from the duty free shop (that source of all precious rarities, purchased at huge expense). 'You'll never guess what Shirley said. I know she doesn't like it that so many Unicef wives spend their time slagging off the Sudan, but she said – and I quote – "Why do people make so much fuss about *haboobs* when they're so beautiful?"'

Danny said through a mouthful of biscuit, 'Why does Shirley want you to like her boobs?'

'Because she lives sealed up in air-conditioned splendour and doesn't do her own dusting,' Bee said.

'But what's that got to do with having big boobs?'

They stared at him for a moment, and burst out laughing.

'HABOOBS, Danny. Dust storms, not bosoms,' Bee said.

'Really, Danny!' Maggie exclaimed. 'Whoever told you beautiful boobs means *big* boobs anyway?'

Bee ruffled his hair and he ducked, but he looked pleased to have made a joke, even by mistake. Maggie handed him the tray and told him to take it in to the children.

'Without dropping it,' Bee added.

'Mum! How old do you think I am?'

'Eleven years and one month.' But Danny was already out of earshot.

'And another thing,' Maggie said, as she poured boiling water from the saucepan into the teapot, 'Cal's current catchphrase – so American, this — is 'Thumbs up for the poor!' He kept on saying it to Cathy and Sam the other night.

It seemed to be all he did have to say to them, really. He's not at ease around kids – have you noticed?'

'Nor women either. Not if they're wives, anyway.'

'You can guess what Cathy and Sam were saying to each other in the back of the car all the way to school next morning, can't you? "Thumbs down for the poor…"'

Bee snorted with laughter. 'Could you imagine an English person saying that? Or even a Frenchman? We Europeans must seem awfully cynical and unimpressed to them.'

'Speak for yourself,' Maggie said as she led the way back into the cool of the bedroom with the tray of tea things. '*I've* made it my personal motto. I say, 'Thumbs up for the poor' to everyone I pass in the street. It certainly makes an impression.'

'Did I tell you how Toby from CARE described Calvin?' Bee asked, making herself comfortable on the big bed next to Maggie. They sat leaning against the headboard with the tea tray on the mattress between them in their familiar gossiping mode. 'He described Calvin as the one with the wandering facial hair. And the very next time I saw Cal he'd lost the moustache and gained a beard. He was talking to me really seriously and I was struggling not to laugh!'

'Never trust a man with wandering facial hair,' Maggie said. 'The goatee's gone again, by the way. It's clean chin and droopy moustache now – a touch of the walrus. It was better really when you could see his lips moving.' She poured out the tea. 'We shouldn't bitch, though,' she said, suddenly serious. 'He does seem to be making a good impact, to be fair. New broom and all that. Will is impressed. And Shirley is going great guns with the handicrafts shop. She wanted me to get involved with it. I said I probably will. Why don't you, Bee? It would make life in El Obeid a whole lot more interesting for you. Especially with you being an artist.'

91

'Some artist. I never seem to have the energy to do more than keep the family just ticking over, bugger the art. Anyway it's almost impossible to get out of the house without the children in tow.'

'Doesn't Charles *ever* have them so that you can get out on your own?'

'He's very good at meaning to, but somehow something always crops up and he gets distracted. But having offered does make him feel nice and honourable for quite a while afterwards. And we don't have a vehicle of our own and I'm not allowed to drive the Unicef one. I could hardly ask the office to provide a driver for me.'

'Well you could for this, seeing that Unicef is putting up the funding for the initiative. It's part of their Women's Income Generation Scheme. I'm sure Charles *could* legitimately arrange a vehicle.'

Bee was unconvinced. She changed the subject.

The very thought of extra activity made her instincts jump up and say, Lie low and lie still because that way it will all be over so much the sooner. It wasn't even as if she didn't have plenty to do, and yet, looking back, there was so little to show for all the days she had already spent in El Obeid, so few paintings begun, and fewer still finished. So little achieved. So many days still left to fill. The empty days were stacked up in front of her and the old stagnation was already clawing at her throat before she was even back in town.

Bee wheeled the pushchair down the quiet street which led towards the dun-coloured cemetery, and beyond that the Unicef office. The boys ran on ahead. She wished Maggie wasn't going away just now. She saw so little of her anyway. How could friendship grow without a little more space than this?

She called to the boys to stay close in case a car came round the corner ahead of them. And then she called to Kit to stop shouting. He looked round at her in surprise. It was Adam who was doing the shouting, unusually.

Perhaps what most separated her from Maggie, she thought, was the habit of expatriate life, rather than the lack of space. Maggie and Will had been working in the Aid world all of their adult lives and they were accomplished at moving easily from posting to posting, philosophical about the more difficult ones like Khartoum and biding their time while they waited for something better. Friendships in such an existence must be loosely held and casually left. There would always be others to take their place.

They turned the corner into the long road that ran alongside the cemetery. Kit began to run. Adam followed after him on his short legs, earnestly straining. Then Danny sprinted past the two of them with the long-legged ease of near-adolescence and Kit shouted out in disgust.

'Don't go too far ahead, boys! Watch out for cars!' In the pushchair, Catrin was quietly singing.

The temporariness was what made living here bearable: they only had to last one more year and then they could go back to their normal life at home. But it made them different. They were surrounded by Europeans who were also transitory, who would say to one another when they were old 'And was that Kampala or was it Delhi, or was it Khartoum?', but she wouldn't. She would always know, without question. And oh the enormity of two and a half years when it was stretched out thinly like this and sandwiched in a sliver between the two halves of an interrupted life! She knew it wouldn't last forever, that it was therefore precious. Yet here she was, crawling through the experience like an unwilling snail, and to her secret shame she was impatient for it all to be over. She thought that, afterwards, she would never be free of this sin. People would ask her about her wonderful experience and she would have to lie, or admit that she had hated it.

Nearly every single minute of it, she thought, as the pushchair snagged suddenly in a hole in the pavement and made her stumble. She manoeuvred the wheel out. Catrin had gone quiet. She had fallen asleep and didn't wake when the pushchair jolted, sitting with her head tucked up uncomfortably against the plastic of the buggy and sweat running down the side of her cheek in a dirty streak.

Would she have settled to this life better if she hadn't thought of it as temporary? The very things which kept her sane (the scent of home, the expectation of return, above all the precious dollars they were saving and the freedom in the future which that money represented) were also the needles of her despair. Would she regret this afterwards, shocked at the waste of thirty months of her precious, frighteningly finite life?

It seemed to make her ponderous, this waste. There was Maggie – pretty, lively, clever Maggie, so tart and quick in her observations, not seeming to be weighed down by her own existence at all. Next to her, Bee saw herself as a large, lumbering woman, heavy with restraint. Not physically unprepossessing, she thought, but nobody would ever have described her as pretty, even when she was younger. And now her inner light felt subdued. She wondered what Maggie could see in her, apart from her ability to make Maggie laugh.

How it saps you, this life, she was thinking wearily as they reached the office. All her networks left behind. All her ordinary self-confidences lost, as if they had fallen out of the plane on the way back here.

Chapter 6

El Obeid, and they are home again. If this can count as home.

Back in this jaded blue room, which they can't afford to paint. To the heat, bleeding her children limp so that they lie about on the *angarebs*, endlessly pushing the open window backwards and forwards with one listless foot, robbed of their energy, transforming under her eyes to different children. Where have they gone, the bouncing, busy children of a week ago?

Back to lonely weekdays, and child-dominated Sundays when the children are at home (the Comboni being a Catholic school) and Charles is supposed to be, but – being a workaholic – he is not. And black Fridays, when all the offices are officially shut. For all the difference that makes.

And yes, it *is* home. Familiarity, it turns out, does count for something, after all. The children, welcoming themselves back into it when they got back, were like sentimental old-age pensioners revisiting somewhere they had lived during their youth, Catrin (astonished because she had forgotten she was connected to all this) singing all the way from the airport into town, 'Ello, Beid. Ello, Beid.' Which is perhaps what she thinks the name is.

So it is home, in its way. But it isn't homely. The caustic sun, the intensity of shadow: the daytimes are vicious here.

And how the heat encloses them. She walks out into the garden and it reaches into the folds of her loose dress and weighs her down. Her bracelet strikes hot against her arm, like a manacle, her pendant earrings burn as they touch her neck. So she retreats. She encloses herself with a barrier of walls and a roof of shadow.

On Friday she forces herself to take Adam to the *souk*, because Charles is at home for once. But there is nothing to buy there because nothing is open. No *jir-jir* for salad, no spring onions. No little satchels for Adam, ready for school. Dust and pepper make them sneeze. His earnest little hand is hot in hers, and the sand scuffing into their sandals burns their toes. A sad little expedition, but Adam clings desperately to the special pleasure of being alone with her and the high-point of excitement, for him, is the sight of their own footprints undisturbed in the sand as they return home. They seemed light years old, those footprints. The timelessness of half an hour in an empty *souk* when it is carved out in the earth...

Time is a strange thing. As soon as they come back it grinds almost to a halt. Every day lasts twenty times longer than at home. Where at home she would give anything to make time stand still, now it drags at a punishing crawl. Days full of nothings. So many visitors, but all to talk to Charles, not to her, Fridays giving no respite: they come on business, just the same, unintentionally exclusive. All the talk of places she will never see, of people she doesn't know and will never meet. Endless discussions of the alien intricacies of things called Supply Call Forwards, and the internal workings of the water pump called a Donkey, and who might have siphoned off the consignment of cement before it reached El Obeid. She watches them, people on the other side of a glass barrier from her, all of them sharing something she will never share, and

Charles is there with them. He is not here with her. He has travelled, and grown. She has travelled thousands of miles to stand still and shrink.

She looks at the puddles, green with algae and thinks of stagnation. She smells the incense-smell of fallen leaves being burned in a neighbouring garden and smells the falling note of autumn, permanently suspended in the air. This perennial perfume of burning leaves, fragrant and sad from one season to another. She watches a plant pushing its way out of the anxious soil with an air of struggling growth in a world of perpetual ebb. And she feels like that plant, struggling against odds.

But there are unexpected beauties half-hidden among the remorseless details. A crumb of food falls and ants cluster like black jewels rising out of dirty floors. The limpid rise and fall of voices as the army runs and sings in the early morning, in their vests and faded trousers. There is no uniformity at all in their uniforms, or in their height. Small, a lot of them, as if malnourished. But you can believe them fierce, in spite of the sweetness of their singing. And at nightfall, as a backdrop to the noisy karate club across the road in the small, drab park where nothing grows except the weeds in the cracked tennis courts, the universal moon swings in the electric blue of the cloudless half of the sky, pendant under a black curtain of approaching storm.

These are the things she sees and that she could write about in letters, but somehow she can't. She is inhibited by the things she cannot tell. She writes to her parents, to her friends. To Charles's mother. And all her letters are their usual predictable selves. Then she begins a letter to Kay, along the usual acceptable lines.

But suddenly she thinks, *Oh to hell with this!* Takes another sheet of paper. Begins again, not 'Dear Kay' but 'Dearest Kay'. And writes the things she cannot say.

Dearest Kay, I am so sorry. I should have said something sooner, not left it till it was nearly too late. My Misplaced Stoicism, you called it once, my Post-Sudan Abstraction. But it wasn't what you seemed to think. Dear Kay, it wasn't me finding you lacking. It was me feeling how lacking I must seem to you.

And she writes about the confusion of her feelings, coming home, when she had to brace herself all the time for the coming back. How that had made her terribly homesick, even in the middle of being home. She knows that Kay, coming to El Obeid last Christmas, had thought their lives exciting, as she herself had thought for the first few months. It wasn't the weeks nor even the months that were the problem, it was the reality of the years. *I've never had your energy or drive,* she wrote. *I suppose I'm more like Dad in that respect, even if you're the one who looks like him – I have the same tendency to retreat.*

This is safe, she has said this before.

She adds, *And if it was you living this life instead of me you'd probably be making a much better job of it.* (That is safe too, because it is flattering to Kay.) But then, boldly, she writes, *I'd been so looking forward to your coming last Christmas but when it came to it, it made me feel more lonely than if you hadn't come at all. That really hurt because I'd looked forward to your coming for so long. And then you said one night, in the kitchen here that perhaps I would find it all more bearable if I could stop sitting so much on the outside looking in.*

I thought that you saw me as failing to pull my finger out. And I thought you were probably right.

Perhaps my real problem is I've lost my sense of humour, as Charles says I have. In which case I could start looking for it in the children's bedroom – there's enough mess in there to lose anything. Fatouma looks at the chaos and sighs crossly and I quake and try to tidy it up before she gets in there to sweep. Not me being

98

overly housewifely – I've found her sweeping Lego out of the house with the dust before now. Toys? Waste of time! One of life's natural ascetics, Fatouma. Not very thorough but very energetic. There's dust on all the surfaces since she doesn't believe in dusting but the Lego is efficiently swept right out into the garden.

She writes the letter, but then she crumples it up and puts it in the bin. Only the last paragraph will do. She is not a woman who voices inner things, this is not her kind of letter, but it is enough just to have written it. She calls Adam and Catrin and they go out to meet Kit off the noisy school bus.

The air in the ice-cream parlour was only slightly cooler than outside in the street. The girls sat at one plastic table with Miriam's two naughty boys, while Zahara and Miriam sat at another. The fans whizzed round over their heads and the air-conditioning laboured noisily but the ice creams melted almost as fast as they could eat them.

'I wonder how near a cow this ice cream ever went,' Zahara said, peering suspiciously at the bright pink slurp in her bowl.

'It'll be powdered milk,' Miriam said authoritatively, and licked her spoon.

Zahara thought it unlikely that it was even that but she didn't say so. She watched Miriam enjoying her ice. Miriam had always liked sweet things but she used to be thin. Now she *looked* as if she enjoyed them: the hand holding the spoon was dimpled, the fingers bulged slightly round the gold rings. Bright, brash gold – Saudi gold. Miriam had lived in Saudi Arabia since before her boys were born because her husband worked for an import-export firm, but they came back to Khartoum every year for their holidays.

It wasn't just that Miriam had got plump – she never used to wear a *thobe* either, but now she does. Elegant fabric

99

threaded with gold. 'Do you always wear one these days?' Zahara asked, leaning across the table and fingering the fine cloth. 'Is it silk?'

'Genuine polyester,' Miriam said proudly, and added wistfully, 'I could manage another one of those…' Zahara was only picking at her ice, and at the next table the children were still eating theirs. 'Believe me, Zahara, *thobes* are freedom! You should see what some women have to wear in Saudi. Wearing one has become a habit now, and Osman does prefer it. Boy!' she called, leaning over the back of the shocking pink plastic seat and snapping her fingers. But it wasn't necessary: the man at the counter was watching them with a hopeful grin, poised to bring them more. They were probably his only customers of the day.

Zahara pushed her bowl away and half-turned in her slippery bucket seat so that she could see down to the entrance, filled now with the glare of afternoon sun. How often as teenagers they had climbed that long stairway, past the framed photographs of Alpine lakes and snow-capped mountains, to the indoor terrace where they were now sitting. Everything was still in the same sixties colours – pink walls, plastic seats in purple and lime-green, yellow tables. How swanky it had seemed to them then – it was quite like the National Milk Bar in Cardiff, so even to her and Saadiya it had been glamorous. They used to come here after school, hanging out in a giggling crowd in their neat school uniforms and consuming quantities of ice cream as garish as the plastic seats. She rarely came any more, and when she did the place was always more or less empty, there were no giggling schoolgirls these days.

'Yasmina!' she exclaimed, shocked. Yasmina had just leaned over the table and hit Tahir on the shoulder.

'He pinched me under the table Mummy!' Yasmina said hotly in English. 'He leaned under the table so you wouldn't see and pinched my leg hard!' She looked as if she might burst into tears.

'But still, you must not hit,' Zahara said in Arabic. She looked at Miriam. Miriam appeared not to have noticed. Her English had always been minimal, but her boys were spoiled: probably she would not have reacted, even if she had understood what Yasmina was saying. Tahir was pulling faces at Yasmina now. 'Go and get yourselves some Pepsi,' Zahara said to distract them, though she didn't have much money left in her purse. She turned back to the table. 'It's a good life, then?' she asked, thinking – expensive *thobe*, rings, gold earrings – Miriam certainly didn't look deprived.

Miriam saw her looking at her jewellery and laughed. 'Oh we are very small fish. You should see how the Saudis live! But yes it is a good life. We have a nice flat, and a four-wheel drive, and the electricity always works. We are a long way down in the pond but still we have several servants.'

'Big fleas have little fleas,' Zahara murmured in English.

'What?'

'Just something my mother used to say.' She translated. Miriam frowned. At the next table Tahir had turned his attention to Jamila and was flicking ice cream at her. Could she – should she? – ask Miriam to tell him to stop?

But Miriam had seen him. She laughed and said indulgently, 'Don't be naughty, Tahir.' Tahir just grinned.

Ahmed flicked some ice cream off his spoon, too, and it landed in Jamila's hair. Before Zahara could say anything Faatma said, 'Give you an arm wrestling match, Tahir.'

Zahara turned back to Miriam thinking she would stay out of this.

'Such a dull place Khartoum has become these days!' Miriam was saying. 'And so dirty! I don't know why you go on living here. Why do you?' She gazed earnestly into Zahara's eyes, her own eyes seeming smaller than they used to be in her new, plump face.

Zahara laughed. 'I wouldn't want to live in Saudi! Even if I was willing to give up driving the car and going about bare-headed – I wouldn't want that kind of life, however nice the flat.'

'I never drove so I don't mind not being allowed to. But I didn't mean Saudi. You've got an English mother – you could go to England, couldn't you?'

'England?' (Miriam had never got her head round Wales.) 'We could, but it always rains so why would we want to?'

Miriam laughed.

At the next table Faatma had forced Tahir's arm down to the table and was grinning victoriously while her sisters cheered. It wasn't fair really, she was older and taller, but judging by the expression on Tahir's flushed face it had probably done some good.

It was past ten o'clock but Catrin was still up. Or more accurately, she had slept for an hour before climbing out of her bed and padding barefoot into the sitting room to complain to Bee that she could not 'sleep a blink'. Now she lay sprawled on her back across Bee's lap, clothie clutched and thumb in mouth. Bee stroked her head with one distracted hand while in the other she held her book at an awkward angle so that she could carry on reading.

'Lead me a storwy,' Catrin lisped through her thumb.

'Read me,' Bee corrected automatically without looking up from the page.

Catrin sat up suddenly and twisted round to look at her in amazement. 'But I can't lead!'

'*Read*, not lead.' She looked up from her book reluctantly. 'I was correcting you, poppet, not promoting you. No, I will not read you a story. You had your story two hours ago. Now you're supposed to be asleep.'

'I not sleepy.'

'Well sit quiet then until you are. Or you can go back to bed and practise if you like.'

Catrin flopped down again quickly and Bee stroked her tousled head and went back to her book. Charles came in and Catrin sat up hopefully as he bent to kiss Bee's neck over the back of the chair. 'What are you doing up, you little minx!'

'She's not really here, she just appears to be.'

'I want a storwy,' Catrin suggested hopefully.

'And I said no more stories tonight.' Bee looked up. 'How are the Japanese visitors?'

'Better now they've got the electric back. You know what they're like, these Japanese – they travel with every kind of gadget. Samurai they ain't. One of them plugged something in and fused the whole Rest House but I managed to find Ugandan John and he's sorted it out for now. We'll have to have another look at it tomorrow. Fingers crossed it keeps going till the Japanese leave for Kadugli at six.' He tickled Catrin's bare foot. 'Come on you, shall I put you back to bed? Shall we let Mummy read her book?' He tipped the book up so that he could read the title. 'Oh that. Calvin didn't think much of that.' Bee looked up in surprise. 'He started reading it when he was here. He said, "You won't want to bother reading this, it's no good."'

'Oh,' she said, unimpressed. 'The eleventh commandment. And did he, from his mountain top, say why…? No, I thought not. In fact it would be the twelfth commandment – the eleventh was delivered a while ago: Thou shalt get a donkey.'

'Yes, he did remember your reaction to that suggestion.'

'Did he? I can't even remember now what I said. Was I less than enthusiastic?'

'You were. He seemed rather bemused by your response.'

She looked at him fondly, crouching on the floor beside her chair. 'Oh dear, did I risk compromising your career prospects?' She rumpled his hair. 'Thank God he's only going to be your boss for another sixteen months. I'd hate to have to try to butter him up.'

'He was talking about that, too,' he said, picking Catrin up and heaving her over one shoulder like a small plump giggling sack.

'Don't get her all excited – she's supposed to be settling down.'

'He talked about extending my contract. He suggested five years. He's looking for a five-year commitment, he said.'

'So was he disappointed?'

'Disappointed?'

'When you disabused him.'

'I didn't say anything. Best to keep him expectant, I thought. By the way, he does think they're going to make this a Hardship Post. Which will mean no families to be posted here in future.'

She snorted. He knew what she thought about that.

Kit came off the school bus cheerful but missing a good number of his shirt buttons. He was as red-faced and sweaty as if he had just emerged from a particularly vigorous football match. 'What have you been doing?' she asked, but he just said, 'Playing'.

After they came into the house he disappeared. She went

looking for him after a while, a little worried that he was so unusually quiet. She found him fast asleep on his bed. Across the room, on her own little bed, Catrin was asleep too, equally tousle-headed and innocent. She tiptoed out. Adam had his lunch by himself at the table on the back verandah. He ate his bread and Syrian cheese and she sat at the table with him, sewing new buttons on Kit's shirt while he chattered about the usual things – the sparrows that lived in the holes in the high wall just beyond the verandah netting, and Mustafa. They had never seen Mustafa. They knew him only by his voice, because they could hear him playing on the other side of the wall, a small bright voice among the low, melodious voices of women. They heard the women call him by name so they knew he was called Mustafa, but they had never seen him. It had become a family pastime to spot possible Mustafas, in the street or in the *souk*. He sounded as if he was about three years old.

She often wondered what their neighbours must make of the pantomime that went on on their own side of the wall. From their side, what they heard mostly was Mustafa's voice as he played by himself or chattered to an adult, but the most frequent sound was the solitary clatter of somebody washing up in a basin. Whereas from their side there were shouts and laughter, jokes and tantrums and fights, and the graphic, detailed sound-effects of the children's games. And over it all, Charles's voice and hers, often angry or chastising (usually of the children but occasionally of each other), teasing, laughing, arguing. Their two voices equal, and robust. And they must be audible, every word, from next door.

But today they were as peaceful as Mustafa. Adam cocked his head, listening to Mustafa's chirruping voice on the far side of the wall. 'He's my friend,' he said suddenly. 'He's same age as me and when he comes we do jigsaws.'

'Do you?' she said, surprised. He didn't like jigsaws but his small fantasies were never much concerned with real life.

'Yes, he does jigsaws and I watch. And afterwards we play with my cars.'

'Can we have the last chapter?' he asked suddenly. His favourite book, third time round. She nodded and he ran to get it. He sat with his teddy in his arms, listening intently as she read, his eyes on the sparrows on the back wall. 'Oh,' he said when she read the last page and closed the book, 'It *is* a sad story. But in the end it happies.'

'Yes, sweetheart,' she said, smiling. *The Little Wooden Horse* had always been her least favourite book, it did go on so.

'Danny's come!' he exclaimed as Danny banged in through the netted door, overheated after the long walk home from secondary school in the midday sun. He rumpled Adam's hair in passing with the vague affection of an eleven year old for a mere four year old and came to tell her in minute detail how well he had done in his maths test.

At last Kit emerged, rubbing his eyes and cross, and soon afterwards Catrin, her clothie clutched tight against her sweaty little chest and all her hair standing on end.

From the kitchen, as Bee cut up more tomatoes, she listened to their languid talk at the table. They were watching a big lizard on the compound wall. Who would have imagined the diversion afforded by a ten-foot wall just outside your verandah? The mud bricks, worn and hollowed like a sandstone cliff, were populated by homely house sparrows and ugly big lizards. The sparrows looked as if they had just stepped off the Clapham omnibus. The lizards looked prehistoric.

She sat down with them to eat. There was no knowing when Charles would come in from the office. At last they heard him come through the metal gate into the compound. Catrin clambered down from her chair and ran to greet him.

'Hi kids!' He stood looking down at them, raking his fingers through his hair. He had been out since before six and now it was after three and he probably hadn't eaten in all that time. Not surprising he's getting thin, she thought. Not just thin, either. Verging on the gaunt.

'There's a plate of tomato salad and cheese for you in the fridge and some bread wrapped up in the tea towel on the counter,' she said. As he passed behind her chair he paused to kiss the back of her neck.

'Salty!' He licked her skin suddenly and quickly, his strong tongue making her think of lizards.

'Get off!' she said, laughing. 'If I need a bath I'll use water, thank you very much!'

'Can't stop – I need the salt! Stop me getting these terrible cramps in my shins.'

Adam was looking up at him wide-eyed and slightly worried as if he wasn't sure that this was friendly. She shrugged Charles off and passed him the salt pot. 'Here, make do with this instead. I suppose you've got to go back to the office?'

'Nope! I am yours till tomorrow,' he said, dropping to his knees and burying his face in her lap. 'Do what you will with me, lurv lurv.'

'Get up, you great fool ! And don't call me lurv lurv. Are you capable of getting your own lunch out of the fridge or do you want me to fetch it?'

The little ones drifted off to play and Danny came back in to recount another detail of the maths test he'd forgotten in the first two tellings. She went to the kitchen and made a pot of tea. When she came back to the table Charles was reading an old *Guardian Weekly* and Danny was reading Tintin.

As she poured the tea she noticed a pair of sparrows copulating on a ledge high up the wall. The male had a little routine: he jumped on, jumped off, took one hop sideways and wiped his beak on the brick; one hop back, hop on the female again. She nudged Charles and nodded towards the wall. They began to count in silent unison while Danny sat behind them innocently reading his book. Four, five they counted, no sign of fatigue yet. Six, seven, and eight. Nine, and the cock seemed to be getting a little dizzy: he hopped off to the left instead of the right and found himself facing backwards. He turned round, a little shakily, she thought. Charles sniggered. Twelve, thirteen... Behind the two birds a particularly large and ugly lizard, with a yellow crest like a dragon, emerged from the nest hole with an egg in its jaws.

'Win some lose some!' said Danny's clear voice behind them.

She burst out laughing. Charles grinned. Up on his ledge, the cock-sparrow was still at it.

Suddenly the little hen lunged at him and grabbed him by the tail. For a moment he swung, ignominiously, upside down. Then she released him and he fluttered off dizzily.

'Story of my life, counting sparrow fucks,' Bee murmured, but nobody heard.

After lunch they retired to bed, carefully shutting the children out. In the shuttered sanctum of their inner room they could listen to soothing Schubert from the adjacent sitting room. Or they would have been able to, if Kit hadn't been riding Catrin's truck round and round the house.

They lay entwined on the pink sheet, naked under the slowly revolving fan. At every point where their bodies touched, the sweat pooled and ran. Their damp skin squeaked and sucked as they moved against one another. It made them laugh, but trying not to make any noise was also erotic. Not that they would have been heard anyway, drowned out by Kit on the truck as he passed on his circuit, banging noisily up the step to the sitting room just outside their door, and down again as he came out at the other end of the sitting room, onto the back verandah on the far side of their bedroom.

'I could think of a more peaceful design of house,' Charles said, probing her ear with his tongue.

'At least it keeps him quiet.' She turned her head back and kissed him under his chin. 'Relatively speaking.'

Schubert stopped abruptly in mid Rondo. There was a brief silence, and then an unseen hand put on... *The Three Little Pigs*.

'Oh well,' she whispered, turning over to face him. 'You did always say you could make love to anything. Remember? When I had that passion for Leonard Cohen?'

The bump and whirr of the passing truck resumed another circuit. It paused just outside their room. A small hand came through the dusty louvres of the door and wiggled about. They heard Kit giggle.

'Kit!' Charles said severely. 'You're supposed to be asleep!'

'Been to sleep,' Kit said.

'Liar.'

'I'm afraid – for once – he *is* telling the truth,' she said.

The truck clattered up the step. A moment later they heard him in the sitting room rebuking Catrin. Her voice rose suddenly in shrill protest. Probably he had hit her. He usually did when provoked.

'Somehow everything seems to be against us,' she said wearily. 'And I'd have given anything for a sleep this afternoon, too.' She got up and pulled on her dress. The thin cotton felt unbearably hot and heavy. He was watching her from the bed but the lust had gone out of his eyes. She had no doubt he would sleep now, while she kept the children quiet. A tiny sword of resentment raised itself in her heart and twisted. She knew he worked hard, but it was hard for her too: he was always either absent, or he was asleep. There seemed to be nothing in-between.

Chapter 7

Daz came into El Obeid riding on a camel. He had a red and purple Mohican under his check head-cloth and an earring. He'd been on the road from Khartoum for nearly a month and the wooden saddle had given him swollen balls.

The first tragedy of his trip: he was ripped off about the camel. He wanted to groove among the people and a camel had seemed a good way of going about it. (Anyway he liked animals. His dad worked on a farm.) The trader in Omdurman had sworn it was a young one but he was soon told otherwise, when he was two days out on the road south and it was too late to go back. He had also apparently paid way over the odds, even for a much younger camel. He could have lived with all of that, were it not for the second tragedy: the beast (which he called Sammy) was – even for a camel – particularly intractable. He'd found this out before he'd even left Khartoum.

So Sammy was evil-tempered, but maybe that's what camels are about. He could learn to live with that, too, but it was harder to be responsible for him biting and kicking other people. Or even other camels. And since Daz had never been much good with knots, Sammy didn't have to be much of a Houdini to escape from his attempts at hobbling.

All in all he had suffered a good few humiliations on the three-hundred-kilometre journey from Khartoum and he was very nearly at the end of his own tether when he rode into El Obeid one fine, windy morning, not least because the third tragedy was the dreadful things the sun was doing to his face in spite of the head-cloth. His nose was peeling so badly that he could see it glowing red from the corner of his eye and it was getting on his nerves.

He found his way to the leather quarter in the *souk* where the camels were hobbled, rows of them sitting with their knees neatly akimbo, sedately erect in the stoical way camels have and chewing thoughtfully while they looked about them with arrogant eyes. They were parked within a whisker of the leather workers who were busy immortalising deceased camels into red bolsters and saddle cushions, but although Daz looked into their eyes for signs of rebellion the camels appeared unmoved.

At last he succeeded in getting Sammy to crouch down at the end of the back row and said a silent prayer while he hobbled the camel's legs with a length of rope. Then he hobbled off himself to look round the *souk* while he considered his next move.

An English woman was standing at a stall that sold cloth. A small boy at her side was bossily telling her which fabric to buy. Daz had hardly seen a single white face since leaving Khartoum and he could feel himself gawping with stupid enthusiasm at this one. She was in her mid-thirties, he guessed, a tall, striking woman with strong bones. Not conventionally pretty and he thought, looking at the way she moved, that she was self-possessed but probably had no idea that she might be considered handsome.

The little boy had noticed him and was staring. He was the first child not to have burst into tears at the sight of Daz's face since he'd left the capital. He grinned down at the kid, who promptly crossed his eyes and pushed up his nose with one

112

dirty finger. Daz crossed his eyes and stuck out his tongue. At that moment (but of course) the woman turned and saw him.

Bee saw a young man in a dirty *jelabiya,* with a red and purple Mohican, grown out enough to show ginger roots, and an earring in one ear. Apart from the fact that he appeared to be pulling awful faces at Kit, he had the most horribly sunburned nose, which was peeling badly. Oh God, she thought, not a beggar! I couldn't cope with a washed-up European begging.

'I'm terribly sorry to bother you,' Daz said, 'but I'm looking for an English man who lives somewhere near here. *Are* you English?' he interrupted himself suddenly, because her bemused expression apparently suggested incomprehension.

'Yes. Who are you looking for?' she asked cautiously, hoping it wasn't going to turn out to be Charles.

'A guy called Toby? Toby Sutcliff?'

'Oh,' she said, relieved. 'Yes, I know Toby. I can tell you where he lives.' Not adding, but I think he's just gone off on a field-trip, because she didn't want to find herself burdened with a dopehead.

'How do I get to his house? Is it far?'

She tried to tell him but it was too complicated, the *souk* was a labyrinth of alleyways and she could never remember how it all fitted together until she came out at one end or the other and could re-orient herself. Besides, she only knew the way to Toby's house from her own. Eventually she offered to show him, if he would wait until she'd finished her few purchases.

'I'll have to get my camel.'

Kit pricked up his ears. 'Have you really got a camel?'

'Yep.'

'A nice friendly one?'

'Nope. A particularly nasty one.'

'Oh,' said Kit, disappointed.

'I'll just go and fetch him. I'm Daz, by the way.'

'Oh,' she said, and wasn't going to say anything more but Kit said, 'I'm Kit and this is my mum.'

Daz chuckled, and then swore: a camel was coming towards them, trailing a rope from one large flat foot. He walked cautiously towards it and lunged at the dangling head-rope but the camel swerved past him with surprising nimbleness. Bee leaped out of the way, clutching Kit to her as the camel trotted past and loped off down the alleyway. Daz disappeared after him, shouting and waving his arms like a madman. His skinny, gingery legs pumped up and down as he ran with his *jelabiya* hitched up in one hand. He was wearing pink socks.

She thought this might be the moment to slip discreetly away, but when they got to the corner where the alleyway joined one of the main thoroughfares through the *souk* they found Daz limping dejectedly towards them. He'd gone up a dead end, he said, and found no Sammy at the end of it. Sammy had escaped. He sounded almost on the verge of tears and she looked at him more closely. He was younger than she had first thought. She was beginning to feel sorry for him.

'Come on,' she said, in the tone of voice she used with Kit when he needed special encouragement, 'I don't suppose he'll get very far.'

'Pity,' Daz said. 'Just at this moment I'd happily lose him all together.' But he turned and walked with her towards the middle of the *souk*.

They could guess at Sammy's passage round the market by the shouts and laughter and the crashing of stalls as he was pursued by a horde of boys. Once they caught a glimpse of him crossing from one side-alley to another with an intrepid

114

boy hanging on his tail, the running camel as ungainly as an old woman with overlong legs. 'I hope to goodness that kid doesn't get kicked,' Daz said with feeling. In his agitation his voice had acquired a rural burr she hadn't noticed at first.

'Where do you come from?' she asked, suddenly curious.

'England.'

'I guessed that bit.'

'Suffolk?' he offered.

She looked at him sharply. 'Where in Suffolk?'

'Blythburgh.'

'Blythburgh?' she said suspiciously. 'I know Blythburgh.' She would have asked more but a group of boys had appeared leading Sammy demurely down the alleyway towards them. The boys were laughing and joking excitedly, pleased with themselves for capturing the crazy *khawaja's* camel. What else could you expect of *khawajas*? *Khawajas* should stick to Land Cruisers.

Daz thanked them in clumsy Arabic and the boys stood, draping themselves over one another's shoulders, nudging each other and laughing hopefully.

'I think they're expecting you to give them some money.'

'I know they are,' he said, and she saw he had gone very red. 'But it's dead embarrassing because I haven't got any left, not a bean. Not until I've changed some more travellers' cheques. I was hoping to borrow some off Toby to tide me over till tomorrow.'

Well *that* was predictable. Silly boy! How old was he? Nineteen? Twenty? She took some notes out of her purse, watched by the gimlet eyes of the disreputable-looking brown boys, and handed them to the disreputable gingery one. 'Do you think that would cover it?'

'Jesus, I don't know. What's the going rate, d'you s'pose, for recovering runaway camels?'

'Try it and see, I should.'

He handed the money over. The tallest boy took the money courteously, then looked down at the notes in his hand and grinned with obvious delight. The other boys thanked him and they ran off hastily before he changed his mind.

'I think we must have given over the odds for escaped camels,' she said, watching them go.

'Yeah, I think that was obvious. I'll pay you back, Kit's mum, as soon as I've got the money. Honest.'

He had a nice face, in spite of its ugliness, in spite of the intimidating plume of hair. There was something unexpectedly innocent about him. 'I'm Bee,' she said, relenting. 'And my husband is Charles. Charles and Bee Walker. Come home with Kit and me and have a cold drink. You can park your camel in our compound. You look as if you could do with something to eat and drink.'

He said, regretfully, 'I don't think you'll want us in your nice garden – I'm afraid Sammy's rather partial to flowers.'

'It's not a nice garden. It's a prison compound with some bushes in it. There isn't really that much he can damage,' she said. 'We'd better go. I said I'd only be out for three-quarters of an hour.'

She left Daz in the compound making another attempt at hobbling Sammy in the middle of the sandy courtyard, well out of reach of the bushes. 'Come into the house when you've done that,' she said as she left him, and he looked up with an apologetic grin.

She went in search of Charles. He was in the sitting room, stuffing papers into his briefcase. He looked up irritably and glanced at his watch.

'I know, I know – I'm sorry,' she said. But she did wish he

wouldn't do that. 'I met an English boy in a spot of trouble in the *souk*. He's in the back garden now with his—'

'Sorry darling, I really haven't got time! I was supposed to be in a meeting ten minutes ago.' He kissed her hastily. 'Tell me about it later,' he called over his shoulder as he hurried out through the front door.

She stood in the middle of the room listening to his footsteps sharp on the front path. She had over-run her allowance and he was annoyed. It made her feel caged, as if she had just rattled the bars.

She heard Daz's gruff voice approaching along the verandah. The children seemed to have appropriated him already. Kit was trying his best to assert finders-keepers' rights but it was Danny who was doing most of the talking, his voice doing its sudden squeaks and plunges today. He would be hating that. 'And this is our sitting room,' he said grandly, ushering Daz through the door.

'Wow. This is like a palace,' Daz said, looking admiringly around the shabby blue room. 'It's cool!'

'Have a seat,' she said, though he did look very grubby. 'Don't crowd him, you lot!' She thought, Any minute now he'll say to them 'You're doin' my 'ead in.' But he didn't. He even looked as if he might be quite enjoying himself. She went to the kitchen to make a drink.

Standing in the kitchen on the edge of the shaft of sunlight that cut across the floor, she was heavy on her bare feet and knew that her legs had, as usual, swollen with the heat. But she couldn't shut the sun out of the kitchen without also shutting out the passage of air. It was always a compromise, and the breeze usually won. She cut the hard, wizened little lemons into halves and laboriously squeezed out the juice to make up a jug of *limoon*. A house designed by men, this. Every consideration given to the proper maintenance of the women's seclusion (a high inner wall separating the compound from the front garden, a large public reception room at the front of the house and the women's quarters tucked demurely away at the back) and then they stuck the kitchen on the hottest, sunniest corner of all. It was the most uncomfortable room in the house. But it wasn't such a bad place to be this particular morning, given that there was a fine bright breeze blowing in and not one of her children was hanging hotly around her skirts.

She could hear distant squeals of delight from the sitting room. She could see the camel through the kitchen window, grazing on the bougainvillea. Do that no harm to be cut back, she thought. She fished the ants out of the sugar and poured a generous quantity into the jug of bitter juice and stirred vigorously. She took a bottle of cold water from the fridge, and the last of the ice cubes, reminding herself that she must fill the water filters this morning. They never seemed to have enough drinking water, it was an endless struggle keeping sufficient water boiled and filtered to keep up with the stream of visitors on top of their own heavy demand. There is nothing quite as dispiriting as half-cooled water when you are thirsty, either.

She found a packet of biscuits in the cupboard – a bit stale, but she doubted if he would be fussed, and the children certainly wouldn't, they were only allowed biscuits as a special treat. She took the tray to the sitting room. Daz had said it was cool but he couldn't be feeling cool, not at the moment. He was sitting in the armchair with Catrin perched on one knee and Adam on the other. Kit was hanging on the arm of his chair and Danny was sitting admiringly on the floor at his feet. Catrin was ready for her morning sleep. She had her thumb in her mouth and was clutching her clothie. She reached up to pat Daz's Mohican and said, wonderingly, without taking her thumb out, 'Wed!'

Kit corrected her authoritatively, 'Not red, Catrin. That's purple. Isn't it, Daz?' He seized Daz by the chin and turned his face towards his own.

'Kit—' she started, but Daz cut her off ''S all right. I like kids. Anyway, makes a nice change to be with kids that 'int scared of me.'

'Yes,' she said, looking at his nose and wondering how much it hurt.

Catrin was studying his nose too. 'Wed,' she said again, in an awed voice, and this time Kit didn't contradict her.

'You need something for that sunburn,' Bee said as she poured out the juice. 'Does it feel as bad as it looks?'

He laughed ruefully. 'Don't know how bad it looks. But yeah, it is getting me down. Specially when kids start crying at the sight of me.'

Not really surprising that they do, she thought. All in all. She said, 'Fancy you coming from Blythburgh.'

'Why?'

'My family has a holiday house in Walberswick. We've had it for three generations. One of those wooden shacks down by the harbour.'

'Blimey!' he said. 'Small world.' He sounded disconcerted. It was a bloody long way to come only to find yourself bumping into somebody from the next village. 'Which one is it?'

'The green one on the end, next to the creek. End Point, it's called.'

'Blimey,' he said again.

'Whereabouts in Blythburgh do you live?'

'One of the cottages in the row next to the church. Or my dad does.'

'Is that where you grew up?'

'Yeah. I don't live with him any more, but I suppose it's more home than anywhere else is—'

Kit interrupted, 'Have you had lots of ventures on your camel? Can we have a ride on him?'

Daz looked at him quizzically. 'Do you really want to?'

'No,' said Kit, capitulating instantly. He raised his shoulders nervously and gave a shudder. 'He is a bit big,' he said, very seriously.

'Too right he is,' said Daz.

She sat, half listening as he recounted mild little tales of his journey from Khartoum on the back of a bad-tempered, self-opinionated camel. The children hung on his every word. Her own thoughts drifted back to Blythburgh, wandering past the familiar little row of cottages beside the church that this over-grown boy thought of as home. Then she was outside the wooden house down by the creek, where the River Blye runs into the sea, the house that she dreams of nightly, with its Elsan, and its draughty floors. The wind whistling under the house among the stilts, and up through the floorboards, lifting the rug in the hallway. Her mind runs over the building, touching its details like a secret mantra. The weathered old boarding, smelling of salt. The way the light falls into the rooms. The ugly modern windows that her grandfather installed (his one small rebellion) after her grandmother's death, that look out over the dunes towards the sea in one direction, up river towards Blythburgh in the other, and out over the grassy flats towards the village in the third. And the one upstairs window that winks over the studio roof towards the river. She can hear the summer wind sifting round the bright, open windows in July, and see the bruised red sunsets over snow in December. In her ears, her grandmother's voice drifts back, scolding her and her cousins from the doorway where she stands crossly, a small woman in an apron, long dead now. Scolding them because, using her studio as a dormitory during the long summer holidays, they are talking and giggling when they should be sleeping. Her grandmother, whose obsession with painting she alone has inherited, who must have been so put out by their coming every summer, because she couldn't paint again until they had all gone home again at the end of August.

She wonders at that now. And if she alone among them has inherited the painting gene, they have all of them inherited the house, and even though it is the house she loves most in all the world it must be shared, in perpetuity, between the two sisters of her mother's generation and the six cousins of hers. But when they go home on leave it is where they stay, the weeks that it is free, their own house in Norwich being rented out.

So many questions she wants to ask Daz now, to hear the familiar names from the mouth of a stranger. The Bell, and the Ship, and the Harbour Inn. The trendy vicar and the woman who runs the village shop. The Old Pottery. The path that leads over the sandy common, under the Heronry, along the tidal river, from Walberswick on the coast to Blythburgh, four miles inland. All these small remembrances so suddenly and oddly transposed into this blue room in the middle of the Sudan, drinking *limoon* while the bulbuls flit about in the bushes at the windows and a camel browses ungraciously in the back garden. She thought them, and she said nothing. But once Daz looked up and caught her eye. 'I've been missing my pint of Fish,' he said. So he was thinking about it too.

'Fisherman's Ale, and draught sherry in the Harbour,' she said, and he grinned. He was testing her, and she had probably passed. But the children claimed him back, anyway.

121

The morning slipped gently away. Catrin took herself off to bed, reducing the pressure a little, but Daz seemed to be holding his own. Even possibly to be enjoying himself. She left him to it and went to the kitchen to boil water and fill the water filters. She made some more *limoon* and carried it back to the sitting room. Danny had fetched his model aeroplanes to show Daz. Adam was still sitting on his knee and Kit was standing beside his chair, one arm leaning nonchalantly on Daz's shoulder while they solemnly discussed Dihedrals and Uplift. Man's talk, she thought. It was the nicest Sunday ever. Sundays were usually such a trial, with all four of them at home and bored and Charles absent at work

'You've got yourself a fan club,' she said to Daz. 'You can come and entertain them any time you want.'

'Yes! Yes!' shouted Kit, jumping up and down, clapping his hands. Adam looked at Kit and dutifully echoed him. Daz grinned, and blushed.

The metal gate to the compound banged open and shut and she jumped up guiltily. That would be Charles coming in for lunch and nothing was ready yet.

She found Charles standing just inside the verandah door looking tired and cross. 'There seems to be a camel outside and it's eating the flowers and shitting everywhere.'

'It's Daz's camel. I'm sorry – I haven't got lunch ready yet, I got distracted.'

'Daz? Oh you mean that English kid from the *souk* you were talking about this morning? He's still here?'

'He's entertaining the children in the sitting room. He needs your advice. He wants to do voluntary work but he doesn't seem to have much idea how to go about finding any.'

Charles went into the sitting room and his heart sank. He recognised the type at once: yet another romantic, wanting To

122

Do Good. There'd been a lot of it since BandAid. He'd had more than his share of trying to fit awkward volunteers into the system. Most of them were more trouble than they were worth. He asked a few questions, feeling gruff and unfriendly.

Daz saw a handsome, fair-haired man who reminded him of David Bowie, so a potential hero. But this brusque older man made him self-conscious. He knew he wasn't expressing himself very well, and although Charles promised to think about where he might try offering his services, Daz didn't really believe he would. He excused himself not long after and took Sammy off to go in search of Toby's house, leaving behind some raggedly pruned shrubs and a large pile of camel dung.

'Good,' said Bee as she saw him out. 'Fertiliser. The bushes will be grateful. And so am I – you've kept the children out of my hair all morning. You can come again, any time, with or without the camel.'

'I think he's going to be a bit of a liability in town. I don't know whether I'll stick around El Obeid for long,' he said. 'Anyway, I'll go wherever I can find some voluntary work. I want to do something useful.'

How quaint. How very young, she thought. I hope he doesn't hurt himself in the process. He was, perhaps, only eight or nine years older than Danny: it didn't seem so very much. And he was plucky. She had glimpsed it now, through his armour of hair and bravura. She had seen his fear and his uncertainty and they made him seem more human, and much more courageous. She watched him leading his camel off along the street, an odd clumsy figure not the slightest bit disguised by his *jelabiya*. She smiled, and went back inside to have lunch.

His first serious field trip since Bee and the kids had come back. Saaid came to the house early, just as it got light; at the veterinary department Dr Ali was ready and waiting. They bowled out along the dirt road towards Dilling. How the grass had grown since his last trip! The whole world looked different, like seeing a man with long hair who you used to know with a crew cut.

After half an hour or so they turned off the main road and bumped along sandy tracks through scrub trees and seeding grasses, chatting good-humouredly. They were all glad to be out of town.

Hours later they were sitting outside the fourth cheese station of the day, waiting so they could observe the nomad women come with their milk. They had sat in the shade for one hour, then another. Giant dragonflies skimmed the slick, muddy waters of a large pond nearby. Beyond the pond, a colony of green ridge tents was pitched among the trees: a government veterinary team was vaccinating nomad cattle against anthrax and rinderpest. The cheese technician had brought out chairs for them to sit on. They sat with him, in a row in the hot narrow shadow along one wall of the building. They talked of the passing season and the dwindling supply of milk, of the proposed cheese-making project and what might be gained from it. Of the government, and the SPLA rebels and their leader, the charismatic (and Ali thought wicked) John Garang. Then they sat in easy communal silence, patiently waiting. None of them had eaten since before six that morning and it was now after three.

Charles sat sideways on his metal chair, trying to emulate their stoical stillness. His drowsy head buzzed with thoughts. What a lot they had seen today. The cheese stations hulking barn-like in tree-studded grassland, the oil drums over smoking fires where large flies drowned slowly in greasy whey and paint flaked off the walls of the drums into the cheese.

Curds drying, white and pristine, on rough wooden tables in the sun. He marvelled at the smiling energy of the young technician who managed this place, who had learned his quaint English on a dairying course in Aberystwyth. How could Mahmoud have moved so cheerfully from the spotless stainless steel of rainy British cheese-making to an oil drum over a wood-fire in the open bush and a wooden table in the sun? A bright, intelligent young man, living here in the middle of nowhere for months at a time. The cheese itself, so casually made, was whisked off to Khartoum by lorry to be sold at a hefty premium to the urban rich. A little anomalous, Charles thought, shifting uneasily on his chair and surreptitiously easing first one stiff buttock and then the other, but it brought money to the people who owned the cattle so it probably was a good thing.

It could not be more peaceful. In the nearby encampment the government vets were resting under the canvas awnings of their tents. The sound of their voices drifted gently. Dr Ali came back from one of the little stalls set out under the trees with six paper screws of freshly roasted peanuts and Charles accepted one gratefully, aware that his stomach was beginning to gurgle audibly. Ali's voice, as he commented on the scene in front of them, was half wistful, half calmly proprietary. Charles inclined his head, listening to the sound of Ali's certainty about his own roots, the nearly universal attachment of urban people here to their recent rural past. He thought about his own uncertainties, never able to say where he belonged, never truly certain where he would return. Being born in Kenya, going to boarding school in Sussex, to university in Durham, living since then in London and in Norwich – none of those places was really home, not even Norwich where they owned a house, paid rates, elected politicians. He didn't have Bee's anchoring certainty, nor did he share her yearning to be firmly placed. Suffolk to her was home and was where she was aiming for. Not just the county but the small, precise location which she knew so well that she could travel round it in her mind when she was far away, mentally visiting detail after detail. He felt that he only paid lip-service to the idea of home, as if in his secret heart he had none. For him this moment – what was in front of him, in this particular place, for one fleeting afternoon – this was all he needed... The unforeseen which flowed into his experience, flowed round him and away again.

He became aware of a mouth-watering smell of meat being cooked somewhere. He didn't like to broach the question of food because really this was Ali's trip. A small boy brought them more ground nuts. He shifted on his seat again, this time to disguise the rumbling of his stomach. Some women were walking along the sandy track towards them with enamel buckets balanced on their heads. At last! This was what they'd been waiting for.

The women queued in a long line, laughing and calling to one another, chattering. Almost certainly he was the subject of some of it, but he couldn't follow the unfamiliar dialect. Thin, wiry women, they were either young or they were old, as if life were too sudden and precipitated them from the one condition into the other with nothing in-between. They were shy in his presence, hiding behind their *thobes* and averting their faces when they came close, addressing him through Ali or the technician, never directly. But even so they were direct in their curiosity. He could tell by the questions. Was he married? (Laughter at a comment from further back down the queue, and from Ali's grin he could guess what sort of comment it had been.) Had he children? He was foreign to them, a *khawaja,* a white man, therefore without race or space, straying across the surface of their complex, absorbing lives and then away again, brief and irrelevant.

The sweet white smell of new milk filled the air. Some women had brought as much as a gallon or two but many had only a few pints. He wondered how far they had walked for the small amounts of money or sugar that their milk was worth They sold protein for sugar, he observed with interest. That was an anomaly in under-nourished lives! How much milk did they consume themselves or was there too much pressure to sell it all? He sat, unconscious now of his discomfort, his mind busily processing what he was seeing. He listened to the rise and fall of their voices and the splashing of milk into the measuring pail. Their *thobes* – there was another anomaly. So expensive to buy, so little suited to thorns and burrs and corrosive sun (and they were all faded and snagged), but these women who had probably never seen a telephone or a dollar bill or a transistor radio were wearing cloths with these alien images printed all over them for decoration.

The last of the women measured out her milk. Ali commanded three of them to stand forward and answer Charles's numerous questions. Afterwards they strode away cheerfully, back along the path to their encampments in the bush.

Outside the building, when he emerged stiffly with Dr Ali and Saaid, a table had been set up under a tree. The veterinary technicians called them over to join them in a meal of millet pancakes and mutton stew.

It was well after five when they began the long drive back, with the cheeses they had all three bought from the technician stowed like precious booty in the back. The green of the trees against the bright, cloud-scattered blue of the sky, the winding sandy tracks through the scrub: you could imagine meeting the Suffolk seaside round the next bend, or the next. Saaid drove fast between trees and thorn bushes, passing an occasional man on foot carrying a stave, or riding gravely on a donkey. The only other vehicles were horses and carts, turning into the side of the track to let them pass.

As they drove the homeward stretch on the newly graded main road, the light was rapidly falling away and birds were gathering on the warm surface of the road in their nightly droves. He would store the memory of this day like a seed pearl, deep inside. He could never share it, although he would try to: he lacked the language to hand it on to someone else, even to Bee. It was his alone, a part of his harvest.

Zahara sat in the window seat, musing. Aasha lay sprawled beside her, asleep with her head in Zahara's lap, Mastura sat nearby on the sofa studying a book of anatomy. The silence between them was easy and familiar. They had spent many such hours together since Mastura had joined their family. Jamil and Abu were outside somewhere, surveying the sorghum, Ibrahim was reading in Abu's study, and the girls' voices drifted up from the courtyard below the house: another Friday, happily routine. The river swung past in its safe, familiar way, spinning its blue trail of splintered light against the sun, which reflected off the choppy surface of the water, restive in the hot, buffeting breeze. Round the bend of the river two white sails bore briskly upstream against the wind and passed out of sight to their right. After a while the sailing dinghies came back, heading downstream towards Khartoum. She smiled at the sight of them, thinking of the boat they had once had, in which Abu had taught her to sail, until (like other little pleasures) the boat had fallen into disrepair and rotted away. She wasn't sure what had happened to it in the end. Jamil kept talking about getting a dinghy but he was too busy, always off down at the farm, or – now that he was married – much too preoccupied with his new wife in his new flat, whenever both he and Mastura managed to be in Khartoum together. And when he was here, seeing to his crops and his cow.

'How she is sleeping!' Mastura said suddenly.

Zahara looked down at Aasha's face and passed her hand protectively over Aasha's hot, damp hair. 'She's still exhausted by school,' she said. But she guessed suddenly what Mastura was thinking about. So many times in her life that women have asked her about this. Frankly curious questions about herself, because of her 'English' mother, which border on the voyeuristic. The questions about her daughters more veiled.

'Can I ask you a question?' Mastura was leaning forward on the sofa, her books tumbled about her. Not a tidy girl, Mastura, except in her own neat, slender self, poured into her slinky dresses as delicately as if they were a second skin. 'Jamil tells me you are not circumcised.'

Zahara stroked Aasha's hair with one unconscious hand and shrugged: 'My father was a doctor,' she said, as if that alone were sufficient explanation. But Mastura's father was also a doctor, and Zahara had always wondered. That same semi-voyeuristic curiosity: women in two camps, each wondering what it could possibly be like for those in the other, so remote from their own. But she had never liked to ask.

Mastura said, 'So was my father a doctor. And he forbade my mother to have us girls circumcised. She agreed, of course. But one summer when we were staying in the village with my grandmother – my mother's mother – my mother had to go back to Khartoum for some reason and while she was away my grandmother called in the midwife and told her to

129

circumcise us. By the time my mother came back it was too late. My grandmother always said that what she did was for the best, that nobody would marry us if we were not circumcised, that we would be unclean, and we would smell bad, and other people would have to leave the room if we were in it. You know all the things that are said!'

Yes, of course she knew. She had lived with them all her life. The sly looks in the street from men who thought that she was European. The things they sometimes called out from the safety of the shadows as she walked past. The odd comments that were sometimes made by women, which might or might not be allusions to the fact that she was different from them. And worst of all, the frank bullying at school, for one painful year of her life when she was thirteen. Even as an adult this insinuation of uncleanness could still make her feel degraded when she felt the attention of other women upon her.

'And the girls?' Mastura asked.

The inevitable question. Zahara said, hastily simplifying her own feelings, 'Of course not! I would not inflict on them what Saadiya and I were spared.' She looked at Mastura's sweet, open face, gazing down at Aasha now with such a worried look, and was suddenly curious. 'Would *you*, if you had a daughter?'

'No, I would not. In the hospital I see some terrible cases. We were lucky, my sisters and I, the midwife in my grandmother's village was skilful. So many are not. Girls are sewn up badly, or they bleed all the time until they become anaemic. You know how much suffering there is because of it. But I have a friend who was not circumcised as a child and she is wanting now to be circumcised as a woman because she is afraid that this is why nobody has offered her marriage. I hope I have only sons and then I will never have to make such a big decision! But that is not the reason I was asking. You know, families come to us in the hospital and ask for us to circumcise their daughters. Do you think it is better to do it properly, with good hygiene, so that we protect the daughters from dirty knives and rough women? Or should it *never* be done?'

'Abu spent his whole professional life worrying over the very same question,' Zahara said. 'You should have this conversation with him.'

But they didn't talk about it any more. Aasha had begun to wake up.

Later, Zahara went to the kitchen to make tea. She could hear Abu and Jamil's voices coming from down by the swings where the girls were playing. As she passed the study she looked through the open door. Ibrahim had fallen asleep at the table, his head resting on his arms on top of the book he had been reading.

In the kitchen, she put the pan of water to boil on the gas stove. So Mastura *was* circumcised! She and Saadiya – when Saadiya was here for the wedding six months ago – had sat up late one night having a sisterly gossip just like old times and they'd wondered then whether she might be, but they'd decided that she probably wasn't, given who her father was. Very hard on the husband, Zahara had always thought circumcision. There was so much pressure to perform quickly in this culture but then all the geography was taken away!

She lifted down the tea caddy. In her father's house she made a hybrid tea: the tea leaves stored in an old tin caddy of her mother's with a view of a horse-drawn coach and ladies in long dresses painted on it. The tea made strong, and heavy with sugar, Sudanese style, but served in the Crown Derby teapot and the delicate Crown Derby tea cups, which her mother had left here to remind them of her, heirlooms from Doris's own grandmother that had travelled with her such a long way south.

The dark blue and gold was faded and worn, the tea set more precious to Zahara now than it had been when she was younger and angrier. She lifted down the cups and saucers from their shelf but the teapot was not with them, though she knew she had put it back in its place the week before.

Nura! she thought immediately, ungenerously.

Once, this had been her mother's kitchen, which old Faatma, as servant, had shared during working hours and they had inhabited, as children do, with unthinking certainty that things would always stay the same. In this kitchen, Zahara was near her mother, even now. When she made tea in that teapot she was bringing her mother silently to the table. But today there was no teapot. She began to look in all the cupboards.

Hassan looked up as Zahara came in.

'Abu, I found this hidden in the cupboard, behind the flour bin.' She looked at him carefully, thinking it was possible he had broken it but unlikely – if he had – that he would have hidden it. 'Did you know it was broken?'

She saw, quite clearly, his mind working fast. There was just that moment of stillness while he decided what it was best for him to say.

'I'm so sorry, Zahara. I know how fond you are of that old teapot. I'm afraid I broke it yesterday. I was going to try and mend it before you came next Friday.'

She knew he was lying. If he had broken it he would already know it was beyond repair. A piece was missing – she had already looked to see if it might be glued. He looked her steadily in the eye. Nura had not just invaded the kitchen, she had invaded the space between Zahara and her father. She looked at him and did not know who he was any more.

132

Chapter 8

On Wednesday mornings, between six and seven, the familiar hum of engines overhead would announce the arrival of the Unicef Twin Otter and if she went out into the compound she could usually see the white and blue gleam of the small plane as it circled towards the airport. Soon there might be a bundle of letters (if the Khartoum Office had not forgotten to put their post in the bag), and often visitors too – aid people, or journalists speeding through as they sniffed out tales of drought and disaster – who might come back to the house with Charles for breakfast. Men who had been in London yesterday morning, or in Geneva last week, bringing with them the taste and smell of an outside world, so distant but suddenly come up very close. Nearly every one of them was white, and quite a few of them were being knocked sideways as the reality of the Sudan swallowed them up. Charles ran around picking up pieces. Bee put the kettle on and made them English tea, or coffee they would recognise, she kept water that they could trust in her fridge. She put fruit and bread and local cheese on the table, occasionally even butter, knowing their visitors would have no idea how precious these things were: the cheese an expensive luxury available only from the Syrian shop; the butter like gold dust because the only place where you could buy it was the duty free shop in Khartoum (and only if you were lucky enough to be in possession of a duty free card). Even the water was precious, because so much labour went into preparing it. She would put these things in front of them for their casual consumption, and then she sat down beside them to wait for morsels of news from Europe.

Charles saw the visitors as a duty and an unwanted distraction. The government in Khartoum was getting increasingly nervous because of the war in the south and new travel restrictions had been brought in because of the influx of foreign personnel moving about the country. Nobody in the Unicef Office in Khartoum seemed to take the new regulations seriously, however, and he was spending more and more of his precious time in the police station trying to sort out travel papers for people who had been sent down without them. He could feel the rising tension in the officials he was dealing with and he had some sympathy. It looked like arrogance to him, too: We are *right* because we are bringing help to your peoples, therefore anything you do to make our movements more difficult must be *wrong*. It was surprising really that tempers didn't get more frayed than they did. Usually it was the expatriate experts who got loud and angry. The Sudanese officials remained courteous, discreet, patient.

Their social pattern had re-asserted itself but so many familiar faces had gone – their fragile social network, carefully built up, had been fragmented by departures. Even dogged old Toby was due to leave before long, to a new posting in Mozambique. And Sandy was going to Mali. In their wake would come others, filling the vacuum. The long process of friendship would have to be embarked on all over again, but most faces came and went and were never seen again. Daz too, Bee couldn't help but notice. They hadn't seen him or his camel since the first visit and Toby was vague about where he'd gone. The children waited eagerly for his return. They talked of him hopefully at first. Then wistfully.

Unicef in Khartoum was full of unfamiliar faces too. The old wave (jaded and disillusioned and baulking at Calvin's vigorous new regime) had gone and in their place came fresh faces. Instead of being the newcomers needing guidance, Charles and Bee found themselves looked to for advice and information. Carlo the languid Italian asked Bee anxiously if she felt that the Sudan was a suitable environment for a wife and children. She was amused when she found later quite how new the wife was: eighteen, to Carlo's thirty-two, and the children entirely hypothetical. If she had said no, it isn't suitable, would he have postponed Greta's arrival and cancelled the children all together?

Among the new faces in Unicef in Khartoum was a big Canadian doctor called Jonathon Knappf. He had close-cropped greying hair and a beard, a thin nasal accent and a habit of saying 'Hmmm,' while stroking his chin. She had first met him in May, sitting in the dusk by the pool in the Sudan Club. The children had been in their usual state of fractiousness at the end of a long day and Jonathon had sat back in his chair watching them with an expression of incredulity, occasionally murmuring 'Hmm.'

'And what do *you* get to do, besides mothering these?' he had asked her. 'Not a lot,' she'd replied.

Now he was in El Obeid for two weeks, to monitor the progress of the vaccination programme. He was staying in the government Rest House but he spent his evenings with them. He was attentive. It boosted her flagging self-esteem, this reminder that she and the children might be of some interest in their own right. It was impersonal, she felt. He was of an age to be wondering if he too should get round to having a family: she and the children merely represented examples of something his mind was busy with. But she quite liked that because it made him less threatening. And she enjoyed the acerbic edge to his observations. He woke her up intellectually and made her pay attention.

For those two weeks, instead of eating with irritable children at dusk as they usually did, they had adult suppers, just the three of them, drinking Charles's home-brew of *kerkadeh* wine and laughed so much that Kit got out of his bed to come and complain that they were keeping him awake.

One night Charles invited the three new VSO girls for supper with an eye to introducing Jonathon to some eligible single women. They're so young! Bee thought, watching them. Twenty-six or twenty-seven – barely six years younger than she was, but they seemed a lifetime away, separated from her by far more than age and circumstance. She envied them their courage, their ability to find their way into new jobs, in a foreign language and in a difficult environment. They were careful of local sensibilities in what they wore and how they behaved in public. And then they flouted those same sensibilities by living in a mixed household – the house Toby and Sandy also shared – even though they were none of them married. Where they also held lively parties. She couldn't really make them out, and she knew that she was just as remote to them, a woman living at home and doing nothing beyond looking after her husband and bringing up her own children.

So they came for supper, these three eligible women in their loose-fitting dresses and their dangly earrings. Jonathon cast a rapid eye over them, told them some funny stories, and then abandoned them to Charles, instead keeping Bee company in the kitchen where she was making waffles. And while the young women talked serious stuff to Charles in the sitting room,

136

Jonathon entertained her with a stream of rude jokes in the kitchen and made her laugh so much she kept burning the waffles.

The VSO girls left at midnight. Jonathon didn't offer to walk them home.

He was a lover of words and games. The next night they played Scrabble, Charles growing increasingly silent. Fatigue, he said, yawning. But he looked bored.

'You can't have "can't", it's got an apostrophe,' Jonathon said primly when Bee put her letters down on the board.

'Oh my sainted aunt, I can't have can't, but I *can* have cant!' she chanted gleefully. 'Even if Americans can't speak properly, we English still carn.'

'*North* American,' he corrected, crossly.

'Sorry. I have to confess I keep forgetting you're actually Canadian.'

'Ouch,' he said.

She was sitting wearily on the back verandah in the Sunday version of her domestic isolation (Charles at work, children all at home) trying to get English schoolwork out of three of her four children so that they shouldn't pay too dearly for their years away when they got back to the UK school system.

Jonathon came in to get a drink of water between field trips.

He paused on his way past the table to glance over the children's work. Danny was dragging his heels over his maths so much that he was boring himself and Kit was doing no better with his sums, dropping his pencil every few minutes with monotonous regularity. And Adam was completely stuck on his word cards, unable to remember them for two minutes together. Looking at them might help, she thought, unmoved. Catrin alone was enthusiastic, nagging relentlessly for more drawings of bricks to count.

'Does Charles always work Sundays?' Jonathon asked. In Khartoum the office was closed on Sundays. Here, Charles usually went in to work. 'I guess everybody in this place does work Sundays so he has to,' he said, answering himself.

'Come on, Adam,' she urged, resting her arm on the back of his chair. (She could feel the glow of Jonathon's attention even though she wasn't looking.) 'I just told you. You can't have forgotten already.'

Adam stared meditatively at the sparrows on the back wall as if they might have the answer. Jonathon caught her eye and raised his own eyes to heaven. He went into the kitchen. She heard him take water from the fridge and pour himself a glass. He came back to the doorway and stood watching them as he drank. She bent over Adam self-consciously.

'Hey – would it be okay if I took a bottle of this water with me?'

'Yes, of course,' she said, looking up. The sunlight streaming in through the kitchen window made him a dark silhouette surrounded by an aureole of gold. She could see all the hairs on his arms profiled against the light. 'I meant to tell you: feel free to take as much as you need.'

'If I take this one that only leaves you two bottles. Is that enough?'

'Yes – I've just filled the filters.'

He disappeared into the kitchen again. She could hear him lifting the lid of one of the big filters that stood beside the sink. His voice boomed, echoing inside the tall plastic container as he peered inside: 'Jesus, that's liquid mud on those filter candles!' The lid clattered as he put it back on.

He came out onto the verandah. 'How long do they take to get like that?'

She laughed ruefully. 'Not long. I scrub them and boil them

up once a week. Smells like a pond inside those containers, doesn't it.'

'Yeah. And they make that room damned hot, too. It must take a good while for them to cool down. Hmm. You do boil the water for ten minutes?'

She looked away, uncomfortable. 'No, I don't, I just boil it. And that takes long enough. I'd spend my life doing nothing else otherwise,' she said, irritated with herself for being defensive.

He must have heard it because he came over and patted her on the shoulder. 'You're doing great, Bee. Hey you guys, be nice to your mom! Okay?'

Then he was gone. She smiled to herself, feeling the pressure of his hand on her shoulder, nicely balanced somewhere between paternal and friendly.

At night, with Jonathon safely disposed of to the government Rest House, he had Bee back to himself. As they got into bed he realised quite how rattled her distraction, her near-absence, had been making him feel. And when, lying quietly side by side under the tent of the mosquito net, she moved against him voluptuously, arching her soft, hot body first against him, then away, he was momentarily shocked, well aware that it was the excitement of Jonathon's company which was the spur to any sexual high spirits. But he wasn't one to brood, especially not in bed, and Jonathon would be gone tomorrow, back to Khartoum on the Unicef plane. He pulled her towards him.

And she, turning into his arms with sudden pleasure, didn't even think about Jonathon, who was an irrelevance. It was the fragile flame of her self-esteem, which Jonathon had reignited, that was the source of her small burst of energy.

Peter, the Dutch water engineer, strode into the office shouting 'I go from a fokking mess here to a fokking mess in Port Sudan and another fokking mess in Khartoum and now I'm back to *this* fokking mess again!'

A difficult man, Peter. He criticised Charles for things way beyond his control, he was rude to the Sudanese who worked for him putting in hand-pumps, and he couldn't stand his opposite number in the local office of the Government Water Corporation. And – Charles thought gloomily – Peter was going to be working in the El Obeid office for the next six months. He could only hope most of that time would be spent out on the road. He looked at Halima, whose eyes were averted as she busied herself filing papers, then at Aziz, who widened his eyes very slightly in response.

Peter caught the look and erupted: 'And you! The least *you* can do, Charles, is give me your support!'

He made conciliatory noises but inwardly he felt hostile. What was this assumption that he owed Peter loyalty simply because he was a fellow *khawaja?* He would never identify himself with Peter at Aziz's expense – irritating as Aziz might be at times, Charles had to work with him day in and day out. He depended on his goodwill far more than on Peter's. And anyway he liked Aziz more than he did Peter. He hid his reaction in the depths of the Unicef pouch that Peter had brought with him from Khartoum.

Bloody hell, he thought. Now they're sending me a film crew. That I could do without!

There was also a memo in the pouch confirming that the *per diem* in Khartoum had been halved. So he would have to go to Khartoum for the next programme meeting alone. How would Bee feel, he wondered, sitting alone with fretful children while he went off on the plane?

Charles came into the house looking shifty. He had no one with him today: the only visitors on the plane were going on to Nyala.

She raised one eyebrow, knowing that look, waiting for the confession.

'Sorry, darling – looks like you can't come to Khartoum.'

She said nothing. She turned away from him, looking through the kitchen window at the bright morning beyond the rustling papery pinkness of the bougainvillea. It was worse than if she had shouted at him. He couldn't think what to say. After a while, when she stayed with her back to him, he went over and put his hands on her shoulders. She stood perfectly still, too still: he realised that she wasn't breathing because she was holding back tears. His heart contracted. 'I'm sorry...' he said again, adding lamely: 'it's not my fault.'

She moved away and put a pan of water on the stove, thinking, Of course it isn't your fault, I didn't say it was. Does that change anything?

There was another thought lurking here, deep and terrible. Unlooked at, but she knew it was there. He had brought them all here. He had brought them, *knowing*. All that he had hoped for – that the strong dollar would enable them to save money so that they could buy their cottage in Suffolk, his assurances that they would be able to live here comfortably on his local currency salary and save the dollars, that they would be able to find a girl to look after the children leaving her free to paint – all of this had fallen by the wayside. It wasn't within his sphere of influence, he could not be blamed for it. The pound had risen against the dollar for the last twelve months, steadily reducing the value of the international component of his salary, while inflation here had eroded his local currency pay so fast that these days they could hardly afford to buy the most

141

modest day-to-day items, sometimes not even food, without changing precious dollars. The promised girl had not materialised, as the Irish nun had told her would be the case, waiting for the plane to El Obeid that very first time – an apparently obvious fact to which Charles, in his enthusiasm, had managed to be blind. All the difficulties of living here – the sapping fierceness of the climate, the discomfort of the gritty environment, the toll of even the shortest trip out of doors, that trapped them as surely as the heat did in the house, the fact that there was nowhere to go, nothing to do – *all this* he had known. He'd been coming here for years. He could have seen all this, had he looked with an objective eye. The thought lurked like a sea monster, and she turned her back on it, refusing to acknowledge it, but she knew it was there waiting for her. She averted her eyes, but still it filled her with inarticulate turmoil. She presented him her calmest face and waited for him to go back to the office.

She could see it all in advance: the casual departure of the chosen on the Unicef plane while she and the children sat alone and abandoned, somehow state-less without the official stamp of his presence. Everything about their lives circled round him: he managed their movements, arranged their connections, translated for them, shopped for meat and bread and cheese in places she couldn't reach on foot with a three-year-old in tow: in this place she was suddenly rendered 'dependent wife'. Then the organisation, which liked to call itself the Unicef *Family*, took him away and she was left with the children, all of them lonely, their world irretrievably smaller without him. It was almost beyond bearing, and her inability to deal with it – the rank taste of failure that it left her with – that was the most unbearable of all.

'Go back to the office,' she said at last, when he was still hovering. She gave him the briefest of smiles so that she might be left in peace and could lock herself into their bedroom, out of the way of Fatouma's stern observing eye.

He was relieved, but he was hurt too. Being shut out.

In the evening they sat in the living room after the children were all safely in bed. They might have talked, but they didn't. She watched Charles sitting over his paperwork in the easy chair. Sinewy, dust-stained, his thin summer clothes crumpled in the heat, but recognisably the same Charles who had walked into Mr Plummer's bookshop that first time, that December day several lifetimes ago. He was the same man, but was she still the same woman? A day in late December with a blank rain falling and Christmas decorations everywhere and the last-minute shoppers hurrying. There is a time, turn turn turn. Before the time for loving, the time for marrying, the time for having children, the time for coming to the Sudan, there had been a lifetime where it was just her and him. His grin infectious, like a cat that had got the cream, coming back again and again to the bookshop. A book for a present for his mother that first time, two days before Christmas. (Swanky photographs, he'd said, not much text – coffee table fodder.) For an uncle, the following day. (Anything – just show me what you've got... so that she couldn't help but think it might be a chat-up line, that the uncle was mythical, as indeed he turned out to have been.) Then the third time, for a friend (and this time she knew it was an excuse, but by then she was glad). After that he'd given up on camouflage and asked her out. What had he seen in her? She'd never understood that one. Next to his bright, charismatic self she had always felt like a shadow. But he had seen something, and he kept on coming.

What does he see now? she wondered, watching him turn

a page and frown, turn the page back again. A cantankerous, unreasonable woman? But the truth was, he didn't see anything much now, not of her. Not of what made up his home. Home was merely where he came back to, where he went out from: most of his life happened outside it. But she was in the house, dependable, comfortable, making the household function, producing children and nurturing them, facilitating his life, and nothing much of her own life happened out of the house. Not these days. Not even the shopping – Charles did most of that, having the vehicle, not to mention no children slowing him down. She didn't need to be looked at any more, she was simply *there*. After all, she didn't know who he had become and she was looking, so how could he possibly still know her?

It's being here, she thought. He can't help it. I can't help it. It'll be different when we go home. But a little worm in her brain was turning: habits change, people change. When they go home they will never be the same again.

Chapter 9

Eleanor's new baby glowed with the translucence of skin perfectly poised between Sudan-dark and English-pale. Her black eyes squinted up at the ceiling fan as she lay in Bee's arms. Catrin, half resentful, half fascinated, hung over the arm of the chair and thrust her finger into the baby's tiny grip.

'This could make me dangerously broody!' Bee looked up to where Eleanor was restlessly pacing the room, picking things up, putting them down.

'Eleanor's baby likes me! Eleanor's baby likes me!' squealed Catrin as Tamara smiled up at the ceiling. 'What's boody?'

'Never you mind,' Bee said. 'Careful – don't lean on her like that, you'll squash her. She's only little.'

'I hope she'll be all right, going back on the bus.' Eleanor picked up two pieces of Lego, pushed them together, pulled them apart. 'She's nearly sixty, my mum. I hope the bus doesn't break down.'

'I'm sure Charles would have got her on the plane if he possibly could,' Bee said. His exact words last night had been I don't operate a bloody taxi service, for God's sake!

Eleanor was a tough cookie but her gruff movements suggested she was close to tears. Ex-VSO, living in a single room in Dilling and married to Karim (who, according to expatriate rumour, was probably a junkie – Eleanor's defensiveness of him suggested there might be some truth in

145

it) she had never seemed vulnerable before. Bee watched her, intrigued to see there were cracks in the armour and that Eleanor was human after all. 'Did Karim get that job?'

'No,' Eleanor said gloomily. 'Everything seems to slip out of his hands, somehow. He *does* try, you know. I know that's not how it looks, but he really does try. He hasn't got much confidence in himself, that's the trouble.' Her voice trailed away. She came to a halt beside Bee's chair and stared at the photographs stuck on the wall. (Once, she had criticised Bee for only being interested in images from home instead of taking inspiration from the world around her.) 'It isn't very responsible, is it – bringing a baby into all of this.'

Bee looked at Eleanor's troubled face. She wasn't yet thirty but she was thin and pregnancy had left her looking gaunt. There was no point not being kind, even though she knew that when Eleanor was feeling more robust their relationship would return to its critical distances. She said gently, 'You're feeling low because you've just had a baby, not to mention saying good-bye to your mum. It'll all look better in a week or two.'

Eleanor shrugged.

'She seemed to be taking it all very much in her stride,' Bee said, casting about for something reassuring to say. 'Dilling must have come as something of a shock after Chiswick—'

'Dilling's not so bad!' Eleanor interrupted, defensively. 'Dilling's all right.' Then she conceded, 'Well, I suppose it must have been quite hard. Those toilets – long-drop latrines, and nosey kids looking in the windows all the time, and no running water. But she's pretty tough, my mum.'

Bee heard the note of pride and retreated. She felt an unexpected twinge of envy, for what, she wasn't sure. For the relationship? For the tough genes, handed down from mother to daughter? Not that she envied Eleanor her life, nor could she see that Eleanor had much future here. But Eleanor possessed something she lacked. She was depressed now – not surprisingly – but she was by nature strong and decisive, a natural survivor. She was famous for having once fallen into a long-drop when the floor of the latrine had collapsed. She had got over it, with no ill effect, just as she had survived pregnancy, and marriage to a complicated, unemployed man. Bee was slightly in awe of her. She suspected that Eleanor despised her for her luxurious expatriate life, her lack of gainful employment. Eleanor had already arranged her own return to work with Oxfam: as soon as Tamara was a month old she would be back in her job. With Karim out of work she didn't really have a choice. Privately, Bee put the chances of those two staying married as very low indeed.

'Why won't you come, Bee? It's a heaven-sent opportunity! We don't know when we'll have another chance like this! I don't understand why you won't…'

She didn't answer. She stood chopping onions, leaning against the cupboard with one bare foot resting on the other, in her soft green stripey dress. He watched her hands. Chop chop chop. So quick and efficient. What was she chopping onions for anyway? They'd only just had lunch.

'Come on, sweetheart,' he coaxed. 'Leslie might not ever want to kidnap Danny and Kit again. We might not have another afternoon with only two kids in tow for months.'

'We might not have the whole of this one, if she gets tired of them squabbling after an hour and wants to send them home.'

'They won't squabble. They'll be too much on their best behaviour.'

Kit and Danny had gone home with one of the VSO girls to make kites: Leslie had called in on her way home from work and asked if she could borrow them. It was Sunday and they were bored, so the boys' faces had lit up at the prospect of being taken off to a household of single men and women in their twenties who would spoil them rotten and treat them as sort of grown up. It didn't seem to Charles that Bee was taking the opportunity in the right spirit. She seemed determined only to see pitfalls.

A piece of onion fell on the floor by her foot. He looked at it. The sight of her bare feet, so vulnerable looking, so ordinary, reminded him of the shock of coming back to the UK from Kenya when he was a child. A family friend had brought him back alone, leaving his mother to pack up after his dad suddenly died. He'd been only seven when he had suddenly landed in his Presbyterian grandmother's household. He could hear her voice still, shrill in its Scottish cadences: Charles! Put on your shoes! (She never ended her sentences with a preposition.) It's not hygienic, Charles. Put on your shoes in the kitchen! And when he'd argued she'd gone sideways: One careless moment and a dropped knife and your toes could be sliced off! He smiled at the memory. Poor old bag, she just couldn't grasp how impolite and uncouth it had seemed to him to wear your shoes indoors, after a world where everybody took off their shoes at the front door.

Bee scraped the onions into a bowl of chopped meat. 'This meat's as tough as old boots,' she said, peering into the bowl. 'I was going to marinate it with the onions and yoghurt and garlic to try and tenderise it. Perhaps I will come, after that.'

His spirits leaped. 'After you've done that or when the meat's tender?'

'How long have you got? A week? This meat feels as if it

walked a very long way to the *souk*.' She went to get the yoghurt from the fridge. 'You'd better fill the big water container then, if we're coming with you.'

Bumping out along the Ban Gedeid road, the hot wind scorching their throats, the light so bright and white, she watched the landscape with a heavy heart. No, it did *not* make her feel better, coming out. The landscape was like something blitzed. The thin shimmer of the grass sprouting through the sand was like hair after radiation. You couldn't walk through that sparse sward without scratching your legs and filling your clothes with burrs, and all the bushes had thorns. Even the *limoon* tree in their garden had thorns. And only one *limoon*. There was nothing at ease about this place, not even a lemon tree.

The nomad huts were different from the villages: the rounded tents of matting pegged over hooped staves and shining like great grey ticks sitting out in the sun were scattered singly through the bush. There were gourds and baskets hung in the branches of the surrounding trees, and beds sitting idle in the shade under them. They sped by, looking for the Health Project Land Rover and Suleman Ali, who was showing films in the hope of encouraging the Baggara women to bring their children for vaccination.

They found him setting up his screen and projector apparently in the middle of nowhere. A circle of folding chairs had been set out in the sand. Already a few old men were settled on some of the chairs, clutching staves and spears the way old women at home clutch handbags, nodding and cackling toothlessly and calling out witticisms to Suleman Ali who answered good-naturedly. Charles and Saaid got out of the Land Cruiser and went over to talk to him. Bee, with

Catrin on her knee and Adam beside her, waited in the vehicle. After a little while Charles and Saaid came back and got into the front seats and they drove off.

'Is that it then?' she asked.

'What?'

'What we came to see?'

'Well yes. But only a bit of it. I thought we might go and talk to some of the nomad women – see if they'd be interested in producing anything to sell through the Handicrafts Project.'

She was silent, scenting a trick. He wanted her to take an interest in this Handicrafts Project.

Charles and Saaid talked to one another in Arabic as they drove off through the acacia trees. After a few miles they stopped near some nomad tents and the men got out and began an animated discussion with the sinewy men and women who emerged one by one from among the trees. There was a lot of laughter. She sat watching from the back of the Land Cruiser. Would it be easier if she had mastered enough Arabic to follow a conversation? Probably. She was always, inevitably, on the outside, waiting to be included as a generosity, not as a right. On a level with the children. She didn't even know if they were asking the way to somewhere or if these were the people they'd come looking for. Catrin was bouncing up and down boisterously on her lap, looking at her reflection in the driver's mirror. Adam was having a long conversation with his teddy. She had tried to learn Arabic but languages had never come easily to her and the words seeped out of her head as fast as she tried to stuff them in.

'Ouch, Catrin. Please don't dig into me like that.'

Charles came over. 'They want to show you inside their tent.'

She climbed out of the Land Cruiser obediently and turned to lift the children down. Outside in the fierce sunshine there was a lot of shrill commentary over Adam's blond hair and much chucking of Catrin under the chubby chin, which Catrin was suddenly too shy to resist. One of the women signalled to Bee to follow and ducked under the low doorway into the tent. It wasn't really a tent, it was a portable hut. Inside it was very dark and surprisingly cool. The wind blew through and under the matting walls. The interior was mostly taken up with a bed – a frame of lashed poles like a small four-poster, and on the frame a stout mat made of palm ribs woven with leather, which could be rolled up for travelling. The woman rolled and unrolled this mat, explaining something that Bee couldn't follow. Everything was arranged neatly, hung from the frame of the bed or stowed underneath it, or slung from the arching ribs of the hut. As her eyes got used to the gloom she realised she was looking at a well-polished rifle, hanging in the shadows. Catrin and Adam ran in and out excitedly: it seemed like a toy house to them, an outdoor house in the middle of nowhere.

There were so many flies. How did they ever get used to them?

The woman pulled a nearly completed leather-and-basketwork container from under the bed and handed it to her. Bee turned it in her hands, admiring its construction, and she was suddenly deeply impressed, struck by the austere grandeur of a life so finely honed to its essentials.

They went back out into the sunshine. Charles asked questions about their lives and translated for Bee as the nomads described their slow annual progression northwards, following the rain, and southwards as the rains receded again, encumbered by few possessions but those they had much prized. The ones they made themselves were beyond commercial value, they said, because they made them only for their own use, slowly and intricately, out of the things they had about them: the fibre from the palm trees, horn from slaughtered animals, and leather from the skins. They were objects with a condensed aesthetic of purpose because they had to be loaded on the bulls or the camels and carried to the next resting place. The woman showed her the basket she used to carry the tea glasses in. The texture of the palm fibre and the leather was worn with the sweat of frequent handling to a dark, supple gloss. Bee looked inside and marvelled at the unexpected sophistication of the interior. She handed it back, noticing as she did so that the woman – who at first she had seen only as gaunt – was made beautiful by her vivid smile.

The sun began to drop and they were still sitting with the nomad family beside their little fire, talking, and listening to the lowing of the cattle that were being driven in for the night. The dust rose until the air was thick like fog. Dark wiry figures of small boys, laughing and calling, flitted about among the cattle. An hour ago this space had been empty and now it was full. The goats were brought in and marshalled into a corral fenced with dead thorn and the sheep were corralled in another. A herd of camels came past, roaring ponderously. The huts where they were sitting were enclosed by a thorn stockade, making an island of stillness in the middle of the heaving, bellowing animal crowd. As the sun went down the dust-congested air turned orange. A lanky boy, nearly seven foot tall and dressed in a green *jelabiya* and turban, came up to greet them. On his upper arm he wore a finely wrought silver dagger in a leather sheath. The woman who had shown Bee round the hut sent him off with an aluminium pot and a few minutes later Bee could see him going round the cows, milking off a little here, a little there. He brought the pot back and set it to heat on the fire. As the milk came to the boil the woman threw a handful of tea leaves onto the rising milk and stirred briskly before whisking the pot off the fire and adding a large measure of sugar. It was the most delicious tea Bee had ever tasted, and she sat on her low stool with Catrin on her lap thinking how very far away El Obeid seemed, and how Other her life in it. If it could be like this all the time, she thought wistfully. But she knew that the reality was flies and vicious thorns and dirty drinking water. The deliciousness would prove ephemeral.

All the same, it was pleasurable to be sitting there in the dusk, the camels just beyond the thorn fence looking like a race of tall, crazy kings in the shadows. The woman who had made the tea so full of laughter, especially when her little daughter, a similar age to Catrin, complained querulously that her glass of tea was not filled up the right amount. Two boys sat side by side on some sacks of sugar, two more were perched on an upturned drum which had been hollowed out of an enormous piece of wood. The woman saw Bee looking at it and said to Charles that this was the drum that the women used to call the men back from the bush when it was time to eat. But only if the women felt like sharing the meal, she added slyly, and the boys laughed. The dusk had deepened and only their grins were visible in the firelight.

On the way home, as they passed close to the health project Land Rover, they could see the film Suleman Ali had brought flickering in the dark. The shifting colours glinted on the white turbans and silvery spears of the circle of men watching. The vast spaces of the bush reduced to a cinema, Bee thought, amused, and apparently one showing spaghetti Westerns, not the dry health-promotion film she had imagined. 'Bait,' Charles said, seeing her surprise. 'To lure the women in so they bring their children to be vaccinated.' But if there were any women, they were invisible in the shadows.

It felt very late when they got to Toby's house. She was sure they'd been away much too long but Kit wasn't pleased to see them. 'We're not ready yet. Go away,' he said, waving an imperious hand.

'We made ice cream but it's not frozen yet. Do you want to leave them a bit longer?' Leslie, dark and thin, was hardly any taller than Danny as she stood there between him and Kit, Kit looking anxious in case they said no.

'I'll come back for them then,' said Charles. 'In half an hour?'

Bee carried Catrin screaming to the car – she wanted ice cream too, so did Adam. But Bee wanted them suppered, bathed and in bed. She was as exhausted as they were.

Zahara had not forgotten that the protest march was scheduled but she didn't have any choice: they had run out of cooking gas and she had to take the car to go and get some more. When she got to the depot, however, there was still no gas (though a delivery had been expected now for weeks), so she had to go to the *souk* to buy a sack of charcoal instead. And on her way home she ran into the traffic jam caused by the marchers.

She sat in the stifling car, waiting for the march to pass. She was relieved that the girls weren't with her. The memory from her childhood was still powerful. She could hear these men, too, long before the column came in sight. A harsh, angry sound of rhythmic chanting. And when they came, marching past the cars which had pulled into the side of the road to let them pass, they looked angry, saluting with raised fists and scowling grimly into the hot sun. She thought about the old memory, trying to remember what the occasion of those riots had been. It was Southerners, she did remember that.

154

❧

It is 1964. The city is full of refugees. The camps on the edge of Khartoum spill over. People come into the city looking for work, but there is no work, and no money unless it is stolen, and hardly any food, and the people are getting angry. Not the people who have come, but the people who were already living here. It is a common enough story: it happens every few years. There are demonstrations, strikes. Sometimes there is fighting.

They are in the car, the five children, and their mother is driving. Abu is at work in the hospital, and they are going swimming. It is the school holidays and they were to have gone to England but there has been a problem and their journey is postponed for two weeks. Zahara is thirteen, old enough to feel the bubbling of resentment in the air of the streets, beyond the parochial bubbling of their own household. She knows that they have been arguing, Abu and Mummy. But that is a private simmering. It can be ignored. This other bubbling is something different, this is all around them on the outside. It has been there for weeks, though most of the time, tucked away in their house on the bank of the Nile outside the city, they are immune, and they only notice it when they are going to and from school. Today they have come into Khartoum to go swimming with family friends in their private pool.

As they drive up the road near the airport a crowd is walking along the street towards them. The men are wielding banners and their faces are dark and scowling. The car in front of them on the road has a Greek family in it, people they know by sight. The car hesitates as the press of people comes forward, and then it stops. Mummy slows down too, peering ahead. Then they have to stop because there are too many people. There are women among the men, that means they must be

155

Southerners. The women look as furious as the men do. They are shouting at the people in the car in front; they mill around the vehicle, hammering down on the roof with their fists. A man comes up with a can of petrol and pours it all over the Greek car, even though there are foreigners inside it, and somebody else comes up with a box of matches. But they are Chinese matches: match after match, they do not strike and the man throws them angrily aside. Mummy still has the engine running. She is looking behind her but the crush of people is so close, filling the space between their car and the one in front and blocking the road behind them. The crowd has wrenched open the doors of the other car. Fierce hands are reaching in and pulling the *khawajas* out onto the road. 'Hold on,' shouts her mother, slamming the gears – she turns back to look over her shoulder and puts her foot down hard. They shoot backwards. Zahara turns to look back too, cowering in the front seat beside her mother. People are jumping out of the way and shouting. Fists hammer down on the roof of the car but her mother keeps going. There is a smell of burning rubber now as well as dust. They back fifty yards or more along the road. 'You can turn now! You can turn now, Mummy!' shouts Zahara, understanding suddenly what it is she is trying to do. The car shudders as her mother brakes violently and changes gear and then they are away, down the side road, driving fast, back towards Souk Two. The roads are empty, the air is still full of the roaring of voices but more distant now.

They have gone about a mile when another crowd of demonstrators comes in sight ahead of them. Her mother turns suddenly down a side-road to the left, but round the corner the road peters out in some wasteland. 'Don't cry, don't cry,' Mummy keeps saying to Saadiya as they turn back along the way they have come. Jamil has gone very pale when Zahara

looks back at him. He is tucked up against Saadiya like a little
bird. 'Don't fret, children, it'll be all right,' her mother keeps
saying, and turns so suddenly down another side-street that they
are all thrown about inside the car. 'Sorry, sorry,' Mummy keeps
saying. This street too is empty. Everybody is hiding indoors,
there is not even a house-girl or a beggar in sight. This street,
too, peters out in wasteland – they can see it ahead of them.
'Quick,' says Mummy, stopping the car suddenly. 'Get out,
quickly! – Follow me.' And they race up the driveway of a big
new bungalow, all its shutters shut down firmly like blind eyes,
and Mummy hammers on the front door. But nobody comes.

Behind them the street is eerily still. The birds are singing
but they can hear the marchers over the top of the birdsong
and the noise seems to be coming closer. Mummy straightens
up and looks at the houses on either side. 'Don't say I've
chosen the only one which really is empty, she says. Come on!'
They run down the path again and up the path of the
bungalow next door. Every house has a little patch of ground
in front of it. All of the houses are new, all of the small gardens
are bare with just the beginnings of grass poking up like green
spears, and new bougainvillea shrubs planted in round
irrigation holes. The ones in this house's garden are wet as if
they have only just been watered but nobody comes to the
door in answer to her mother's frantic knocking. The voices
of the mob are closer now. Perhaps only a few streets away.
Mummy bends down and shouts through the letterbox, 'I am
an English woman, I am with my children, please help me,
please!' There is just a whisper of a noise on the other side of
the door, a flicker of movement. Her mother closes her eyes
as if she is going to faint. An eye appears at the other side of
the letterbox. A dark Sudanese eye. A voice whispers, 'Are you
alone?'

'Thank Christ,' Mummy says as she bends in relief to show her face to the eye at the other side of the letter box. 'I am with my children but we are alone, my husband, Dr Hassan Moussa Mohammed, is working in the hospital today.'

And then there is the sound of bolts being pulled rapidly back and the door swings open and they tumble inside.

It is a whole week before it is safe for them to leave. By that time the elderly Sudanese professor and his wife have become friends. 'The kindness of strangers,' Mummy says. And a kind of justice in it – the couple's own family dispersed, all living abroad now, in America and in New Zealand. 'And I turned up with all of you, and suddenly they had a substitute family for a week!' her mother says, when they talk about it again years later. 'How they spoiled us, too. I wonder,' she says – looking out at the so-different street where she is living now, in Cardiff, at the cheap modern houses opposite – 'I wonder if it would have been different if Abu's mother had lived longer. Perhaps I would have found it easier if I'd had more family in the Sudan.'

But Zahara, brushing little Faatma's hair out ready to re-braid it (the child struggling but only half-unwilling), thinks her mother is being overly sentimental. Zahara is not yet thirty when they have this conversation, she is not yet at the fading stage and she is still critical. Easy enough to descend out of the blue, she thinks, on one sophisticated elderly Sudanese couple who, it turns out, have spent a significant part of their working lives living abroad. And then to go away again and only visit them now and then when you feel like it. It wouldn't have been so easy with the real thing. They had never, after all, seen much of Abu's father, or of his three surviving wives who had been like surrogate mothers to Abu when he was growing up, his own mother so often ill and more or less an invalid. 'Oh them,' says her mother disparagingly. 'We had so little in common with them, Zahara. They were village women, really. And they didn't like me. They'd wanted him to marry that cousin woman – I was all together a disappointment -- no tribal connection, no dowry! It was always easier for him to go and see them on his own. And I think they hoped he would divorce me and marry again, so they didn't want to get too friendly with me. It suited me not to get involved. You know how it is.'

⁓

And now she too was thirty-six, the same age her mother was when she left the Sudan and went back to Wales. Sitting at the side of the road, waiting for the angry men to march past, she was struck more by her mother's courage than by her shortcomings. Would I be as brave? she wondered, and she didn't know the answer. She thought again of the last time they had talked about this memory, that day in Cardiff in her mother's house. She could see herself as she was then – a younger, brighter, more confident version of herself as she is now – braiding Faatma's fluffy toddler hair while the ice-cream van whined outside in the street. She could hear in her inner ear the intonation of her mother's voice telling the story. Have I been too hard on her? she wondered. Would she have the courage her mother had had? Would she be found wanting, if the moment came?

What had it *really* been like for her mother, those fourteen and a half years she had spent in the Sudan, a country she was only connected to by marriage? Zahara had known her mother's story her whole life but had she ever really considered it before? She did so now, sitting in the car watching the men march past. The fear, that was what remained of that particular day: that being white had made their mother a target, at risk of being killed. And for what? For the sake of living in a place for which she had felt no more connection than Zahara felt for Wales. Less, even. A place her mother was connected to but in which she had no sense of belonging; history but not blood. 'Kith but not kin,' Josie said once when they talked about it. Would I have stayed even as long, had I been her? Zahara wondered now, surprising herself, as the tail end of the march passed, a few stragglers running to catch up with the back of the procession, their grim faces wet with sweat. The traffic began to move again.

Should I have stayed as long as I have? she thought, as she turned into the familiar road they called home. It had become such a struggle. Working so hard, but the money they earned barely enough any more to buy the things that they needed (even when there was anything in the shops to buy). The school so fragile, caught between economics and unhelpful bureaucracy. Ibrahim's job little better, and she knew how much he worried: at any moment the fragile new democracy might fall, and if that happened the right-wing Islamic fundamentalists could make life very difficult indeed, especially in the universities. It was beginning to feel as if they were living on borrowed time.

Sudan could become a wealthy country yet, if the petroleum companies did find oil after all. Nothing was the same forever: they could go and they could come back again. Ibrahim had been talking about it again last night. If it were not for Abu she would consider it now, even though she didn't like Britain much – such a dull, insular place, and the people coarse and unfriendly! She would prefer America. But America was not on offer, and the UK – with her precious British passport – was.

160

The girls would be better off in the English school system now, she was thinking as she parked in the street outside their flat. They could no longer afford to put them into a good secondary school here. She went round to the boot and pulled the sack of charcoal out of the car. She began to drag it up the outside staircase to their flat. How much of their old, comfortable life had slowly eroded away, little by little. Even if Abu helped with the school fees it wouldn't change any of that. Maybe her mother's advice (repeated in every phonecall, in every letter) was right: the time might have come to consider going to live in the UK for a while, until things improved again here. Zahara had always resisted before. Leaving the Sudan was too much like betrayal. It would be like leaving her father for her mother, as Nazmul and Saadiya and Ali had before her. Ali and Saadiya were sitting on the fence, the one in New Zealand, the other in New York, but Nazmul had crossed the fence, all the way to Newport, just up the road from Cardiff. They claimed all the old allegiances – to their father, to their country – but all the small betrayals hid in their shadows. 'It's so dirty!' Saadiya kept complaining when they came back for Jamil's wedding. 'The Kiwis have such a can-do culture,' Ali said, looking askance at Khartoum. Nazmul had said nothing, but his silence had said everything.

Jamil would never leave. He had never forgiven their mother, even if the others had and she had too, in her own way. Abu would never want to live anywhere else. They could not go away and leave him with only Jamil and Mastura to be his family.

It would be such a betrayal if she too crossed to the other side.

161

Chapter 10

The days had a physical force to them when Charles was away. It felt as if, looking up, Bee would see them lined up, wide and empty like boxes cut off at top and bottom by the darkness. She saw herself marooned with her children inside each of these successive boxes, like frames of a film slowed down to nearly static.

He had gone down to Muglad on the Unicef plane. Muglad was difficult. Refugees and angry inhabitants. Quarrels erupting and turning into fights. And the sneaking, underhand tentacles of war, creeping ever northwards, infiltrating refugee camps, laying mines on the edges of roads. He was tense and anxious going, she was tense and anxious waiting for him to return.

Her own days, by comparison, were so safe, so killingly dull. They got up very early, before the heat. Danny set off to walk to his *madrassa* soon after six-thirty and Kit went on the primary school bus an hour later. Soon Adam would be joining him. In their wake, five dragging hours of tidying, cleaning, preparing, maintaining, and entertaining the endlessly needy Catrin. As if I had never had a creative life at all, she thought. I did more painting when I used to work all day in the bookshop.

I need to structure myself! She thought it nearly every day, embarking in the fresh of the morning. But the hours reared up and sucked her down. And anyway, would it not be a greater guilt to sit idly painting like some Victorian lady of leisure?

Selwa Mohammed – she of the mighty bosom and the broken-down plastic shoes – turned up, as she often did, between buses, in search of a bed for the night, a meal or two. They had known her for years. As a student of Charles's in Norwich she had worn jeans and woolly jumpers and played a mean game of rounders, whacking the ball into the bushes on the university lawns, tripping in her trainers from post to post, laughing too much to run properly.

Probably she can't run, Bee thought now, looking at Selwa as she sat sipping tea with her little finger crooked politely above the glass. Or perhaps she had been able to once but had changed. Back here in the Sudan she was a different Selwa. She would never admit to trousers, not now. Shrouded in her *thobe*, tripping languidly around the dusty offices of the public health department in her plastic shoes, her energy seemed all used up in the effort of being single in a world where it was unusual for a woman to be twenty-five and unmarried, let alone thirty – heaven forbid Selwa's thirty-five. She had been looking for a husband back then, in Norwich. Eyeing up Charles, Bee remembered. Selwa was still waiting for that elusive proposal of marriage, though as her chances grew more slender her aspirations seemed to grow ever more demanding. She did not want an old husband, she said to Bee, stirring three spoons of sugar into her tea. Nor one who was younger. And she wanted a husband who would accept her having a career, who would not mind if she earned as much as or more than him. And now that she owned a house (it was rented out – she still lived with her parents in Khartoum) she was not at all sure that she wanted to hand that over, as hand it over she must if she married.

163

Bee sat across the table and listened to the litany of Selwa's fears. The list had grown longer since the last visit. She had seen the look in Selwa's eye when she flirted with Charles last time she was in El Obeid. It was clear she was even more tempted to consider a second-hand *khawaja* husband now than she had been five years ago in Norwich. She wondered idly if Selwa could offer anything that she could not. On the whole she thought not. Selwa was a formidably handsome woman but she did have very annoying habits. And besides, Charles was a father of four. He had a fair amount of baggage himself.

Goodness, she thought – when Selwa was making sheep's eyes at him in Norwich five years ago he was only a father of two. Two and a bump. How time flies. Or it used to. Here, it loiters under dusty bushes and dawdles endlessly in hot corners.

Selwa finished her tea and a piece of the cake that Bee had made that morning – a rare domesticity, in this life of endless domestic obligation. A rather dry cake, made with tired eggs, and dates she'd had to soak for three days before they were soft enough to chop. But the cake had just disappeared down Selwa nearly as fast as it had down Catrin, who sat next to her at the table dressed only in her knickers and a necklace of Bee's.

Catrin, cake all over her face, watched admiringly as Selwa unwrapped her piece of chewing gum from the corner of her *thobe* where she had carefully folded it before embarking on the cake. 'What's that?' Catrin asked as Selwa popped the gum into her mouth. 'Can I have some?'

Bee's heart sank. But Selwa said, 'Not now, darling. It's my last piece. Your mummy can buy you some in the *souk*.'

Catrin looked at Bee expectantly but she was saved from replying by Adam appearing at her elbow. 'Yum, yum,' he said, eyeing the single piece of cake left marooned on the plate.

'No, Adam. I told you – that piece is for Daddy.'

He studied the plate gravely. Then he looked up at her. She could almost see the little cogs and gear-wheels of his thoughts in motion. 'Daddy wouldn't know,' he suggested hopefully.

She raised her eyebrows. 'Wouldn't know?'

He grinned sheepishly. 'I wouldn't tell him.'

'But Catrin would.'

'I'd let her share it.'

'Adam!' She was quite shocked. He always seemed so demure, so law-abiding, so very un-Kit-ish. 'That would be rather mean to Daddy, don't you think?'

He laughed, as if he had only been teasing. His face went serious again as another thought struck him. 'But when will Daddy eat it?'

'I'm going to put it in the fridge. He can have it tomorrow when he gets back.'

He gazed mournfully at the plate. It was true, the piece of cake did look rather pathetic. And it would be even drier tomorrow than it was now. 'Oh, what the hell,' she said, and cut it into four pieces. 'Take the plate to the bedroom and share it with the others. Try not to make any crumbs for the ants.' Catrin hurried after him. 'Sorry – I should have offered you some too.'

Selwa shook her head. 'I have a lift coming. I'm going out for tea. I have to get ready.'

A little later, in the sitting room, Catrin stood planted in front of Selwa, transfixed, one knicker leg riding up over a small white buttock. Oh the mysteries of lipstick, and kohl to a child whose mother didn't even use mascara! The magic of little mirrors. Selwa bared her teeth at the mirror, then smiled graciously at Catrin over the top of it.

'I take it you'll be wanting a bed tonight?' Bee said. 'If your bus is tomorrow?'

165

'Of course. I will come back later. Don't wait up –The *gafir* will let me in.'

All afternoon, while Selwa had slept on the *angareb* in the sitting room (after carefully closing all the doors to keep the children out), Bee had been hushing children and sorting quarrels before they got out of hand. She had made the cake, and sat over grumpy schoolwork, cleaned the kitchen and mended Kit's kindergarten tunic because Adam would be needing it soon when he started school. How sweet and angelic he looked in it, as Kit had done before him. Like a small Italian sailor-boy. Soon Adam too will be climbing on and off that crowded cattle-truck of a school bus, like a little sailor climbing aboard a dirty ship. Dirty little coaster with a salt-caked smoke-stack, she thought as she sewed. But so very far from the sea. And like a mother worrying over her little cabin-boy gone to sea, she will be worrying then. How can he possibly find his way through the short school day in Arabic? Kit will not be there – he is in the primary school now. How will Adam manage the dreadful latrines? Will he remember not to drink from the big water jars in the schoolyard but only to drink the boiled, filtered water he has taken from home? Will he make any friends? Kit has had to do all these things before him. He has settled, unexpectedly, and made friendships, though he still (after more than a year) seems not to speak a word of Arabic, except for *la*! – no. She sewed the sleeve of the polyester tunic back onto the body with small, neat stitches. Kit had progressed now to khaki shorts and a white shirt: after kindergarten the tunic was replaced with more masculine wear. He was already teasing Adam about the navy tunic with its square, white collar, calling it a dress, as if it had not been his for a year first. Adam was in danger of losing his nerve about this school business before he'd even begun.

166

At the far end of the house, the doors to the sitting room clattered open and Selwa re-emerged. She looked well-slept. Stately Spanish galleon, thought Bee, as Selwa ambled towards her down the length of the side verandah on her mis-shapen bare feet.

'You're just in time to have some tea and cake with us,' she had said.

Now the long afternoon was cooling, the light was going dull, and Selwa was preparing her face in the sitting room while Bee sat in the armchair opposite with her book. Across the road, the Karate Club did their usual noisy exercises. In the distance the Khartoum train whistled. At last Selwa pushed her feet into her shoes and stood up. She wound her *thobe* carefully about her and tucked the end under one arm, picked up her large plastic handbag and tucked it under the same arm. 'Bye bye,' she said roguishly, waving her free hand over her shoulder as she went to the front door. Bee wanted to say, *Be good*, but it didn't seem appropriate.

The long evening routine began, pushed – like yet another little British coaster – out of port: all their strange British habits and needs and formalities, like a small vessel on a foreign sea. Supper-time, bath-time, bed-time. Don't think, don't think! she told herself, as she did every night. There should be more to life than this! her angry voice said, and her philosophical one replied, And there will be again, one day. But the slow, deadly present seemed to be swallowing up the future and tonight the angry voice was winning hands down.

And then, the children in bed at last, she began the long solitary routine of picking up toys and books, a discarded sock, Charles's shoes which have done a mysterious walk-about, no doubt on Catrin's feet. Toys into baskets, books piled outside the children's room to be put back on their shelves in the morning, discarded clothes into the washing basket.

From the sitting room came the low murmur of a man's voice.

A man! Malik never let a man into the house without first checking the whereabouts of Charles so how could there possibly be a man in her sitting room? She hurried along the verandah.

In the middle of the floor, on cushions, very close together, sat Selwa and Mustafa Abaker. Another former student of Charles's, with a pretty little wife of his own, so what was he doing on the floor of her sitting room, murmuring with Selwa? They looked up calmly as she came into the room. Mustafa smiled and nodded in greeting, but they went on talking in Arabic in low voices so that although she sat down politely in the easy chair it was obvious that she was surplus to requirements. After a while she went to the kitchen to wash the supper things. She felt like a Victorian matron, blushing at the antics of a wayward protégée. Which was ridiculous.

But it was a relief, some time later, to find the room empty, her visitors gone. And when Selwa came back soon after ten they neither of them said a word about it.

In the night, Bee tossed and turned under her hot sheet, strangely disturbed. Everybody seemed to be canoodling, one way or another, except for her and Charles. Even the feral cat was canoodling – she could hear it scratting about now in the bushes next to the verandah. A moment later it began to yowl. She got up and, pulling on her dressing gown, went to fill a bucket of water from the bathroom tap. She padded back to the verandah on her bare feet. The cat was still yowling. She could see it just the other side of the insect netting, tight in the grip of an ugly ginger tomcat under the shrubs, too

168

engrossed the pair of them to notice her. She threw the water through the netting. The cats ran away.

From the sitting room, there was a muttered groan as Selwa turned in her sleep.

She froze: was Selwa not alone? But it was a crazy thought – Selwa had been settling down for sleep on the *angareb* while she was still sitting in the armchair reading.

She climbed back onto the pink-sheeted expanse of her own high *angareb*, under the majestic tent of the mosquito net, in the pink-walled shadows of her bedroom. Where was Charles sleeping tonight? Was he lonely too? Was he afraid? Outside the night was utterly quiet, now that the cats had gone. The wind whispered, the town slept. A single dog barked and fell silent. It felt like an umbilical separation when he wasn't here. He was their lifeline, they were attached to him.

An amplified voice sang out in the darkness. The muezzin. She lay listening to the mournfully falling cadence. A call to prayers, yet when she heard it she always felt as if she were the only soul left in the world.

'Are you sure it's a good idea?' Ibrahim asked.

She stopped setting out chairs and looked at him. 'Why not?'

'It's only suspicions, isn't it? There's nothing you actually know…'

It was true. It was *thobes* and teapots and insolent glances, nothing substantial, but Jamil was her brother, he deserved to know the little that she did know. She pushed her hair back off her face and looked round the classroom, feeling unusually irritated with Ibrahim. She wanted to talk to Jamil about Abu and that girl – brother-and-sister talking, not husband-and-wife talking.

169

'Is this all right here?' Ibrahim was asking.

'Push it more into the middle. But why do you think I shouldn't talk to him?'

'Because,' Ibrahim said patiently as he shunted the table across the floor, 'you might be wrong. It *is* possible. Will this do?'

'Well if he thinks I'm wrong he can say so, the same as you. But he *should* know! If you had seen her, Ibrahim – the way she looked at me! As if she knew something I didn't. I don't like the thought of her sharing secrets with Abu.'

'But looks and thoughts, Zahara – those aren't facts. Even if they hurt,' he added, coming over to her and touching her gently on the shoulder.

'But the teapot was a fact, Ibrahim! However trivial. And I don't like the way she behaves. Yes these are little things, but they do add up. Jamil will understand what I mean.'

'And so do I, sweetheart. I *do* understand! But I don't want you to get hurt and it is easy to be hurt if you accuse people of things they have not done.'

'It's not about accusing, it is only about telling. I want to talk to Jamil. I want to share it with him.'

He stroked her face. 'She's disturbed you, hasn't she, this Nura.'

She shrugged. She couldn't say to him, she makes me feel pushed out, I'm not certain of belonging any more in my father's house, because if she said it he would know she was no longer sure about a lot of things.

'You look tired,' he said tenderly. 'Do you not think, though, that talking about some things can make them more dangerous?' He was gazing at her as if there was more he might say.

'What? Say it.'

170

'Would it really be so bad if he *were* doing what you are afraid of? It is so long since your mother left him, after all. Even when she comes back she stays with us, not him. She doesn't come back as his wife.'

She drew in her breath sharply. She did not like any hint of criticism of her mother from anybody else, not even from Ibrahim. She turned away and looked out of the window at the blue sky.

She is fifteen and they are at the airport. Her mother is hugging Jamil to her and saying his English name over and over: 'Colin, my little Colin,' she says, 'never forget that Mummy loves you.' When she looks up, Zahara sees that she is crying. 'You will all come and see me soon,' her mother says and Zahara thinks it sounds like a command. 'You'll all come and spend the summers with me, just as soon as I've found us somewhere to live.'

Zahara wants to be generous, she knows this must be difficult for her mother too. But how can she bear to leave them? And even if she, Zahara, a gawky fifteen year old, is leavable, what about Jamil who is only five? He is standing there now, looking so lost and little, so confused and uncertain. He is pouting in the way that he does when he is angry, or when he is going to cry. She goes to him and takes his hand. She looks up at Abu and he is looking very stern. How can Abu let her mother go? He could forbid it, she knows he could. He has had to write a letter giving her permission to travel abroad alone, otherwise she wouldn't be allowed to get on the plane. Zahara cannot understand what possessed him to write it.

Then her mother kisses them each in turn (except for Abu, because they are in a public place and it would not be seemly).

171

She picks up her bags and goes through the door to the plane, and suddenly everything looks empty, the terminal building echoing as though there is nobody left in it, though it is as crowded as it ever was. Zahara looks up at Abu and his face is so sad. She goes to him, pulling Jamil with her, and puts her free hand in his.

When Zahara is nearly grown up her mother tells her the other story. 'I applied for a job in a hospital in Cardiff,' she says, 'I didn't really expect to get it, but when I did, he refused point blank even to consider coming with me.'

He refused, she says, to discuss the possibility of sending the five of them to Wales for their education. Though it would have saved him so much money, if they had been resident in Britain before they applied to university. 'Stubborn,' she says to Zahara, years afterwards, bitter now where once she might have given Abu credit for allowing her to leave herself. 'He made me choose,' she says. 'He said that I was free to stay or to leave, but he insisted that you children stayed with him. So unreasonable of him,' she says. 'No mother should be forced to make such a choice. It was the worst time in my whole life,' she says, and Zahara nods sympathetically, but she thinks it was a battle of choices, one of them forced to lose and the other to win, in a competition that her mother alone had created. Like Abu, she too was shocked by the desertion then, and secretly – when her mother tells her this at twenty-one – she still is.

Ibrahim put his hand on her shoulder again and said gently, 'He has been so long without a wife. Well, hasn't he? A man needs female company, it's not necessarily about sex at all. And anyway, it's not as if you're worrying that *he* is taking advantage of *her*, is it? What's the worst that could happen? He would never marry her. That would just not happen, even if your parents got divorced.'

'Jamil should still know,' she said stubbornly, going back to setting out the chairs around the tables ready for school tomorrow. Though she would not dream of telling Saadiya (New York was too far away, Saadiya would no longer understand the nuances of life here and it would all sound much too minor to her), nor Ali (New Zealand was even further). And Nazmul, in Newport, was too close to their mother these days mentally as well as physically. Only Jamil would understand the delicate complexity of it, and why it was making her so miserable. After all, even Ibrahim seemed unable to understand.

And then she thought, Maybe Jamil won't understand either. Maybe he will think like Ibrahim. Is it a male/female thing?

'You've got it so nice in here now,' Ibrahim said, standing in the middle of the classroom and looking round at the fresh white walls and all the things the girls had helped her stick up on them this morning.

She and Josie had been painting into the small hours last night but it was worth it. She looked round her, wishing that she felt more pleased, but this sly feeling of unease that had been growing for weeks was getting in the way. She knew it was more complicated than she had been making it sound: she wasn't sure herself how much her being disturbed about Nura was actually a cover for her being disturbed about herself and Jamil. He was her little brother, she wanted to claim him, and to protect him, but he had Mastura now, and she was not sure any more quite how they all fitted together.

They moved the last cupboards back against the wall. 'You look so tired,' Ibrahim said. 'Come on, let's go and find those girls and take them home. I will make the supper.' He paused by the door. 'I wish we had the money to employ people to do the heavy work,' he said suddenly. 'You and Josie should not have had to do the painting. And we should have a girl in the flat to help with the cooking and the housework...'

'We would have more money if I worked for someone else,' she said. 'I would make more money if I had an ordinary job and didn't have to put so much money back into the business all the time.'

'Hush,' he said, drawing her to him quickly and leaning his forehead against hers. 'Don't even think it. It is best as it is.'

The film crew arrived, as threatened, early in October: six of them, and all enjoying themselves with such gusto that it wasn't possible to stay resentful. Charles sorted out vehicles and arranged trips, Bee fed them in the evenings. The third evening – their last – they all went out for a picnic, to a dry river-bed outside the town, and ran races on the clean river sand and cooked beef sausages on a charcoal stove.

As the sun went down she sat in the last glow of the evening, deliciously child-free. The sun was poised on the point of dropping below the horizon and the sky was the usual evening riot of golds, mauves and reds. A single tree stood in sharp silhouette against the molten light where the road bridge crossed over the *wadi*. A woman passing under the tree on a donkey was momentarily transfixed against the sun.

'What a wonderful country!' the cameraman, Simon, said softly. She looked up in surprise. He was sitting a little distance away, leaning back on his hands and turning his tanned face to the last ruddy warmth of the sun. Behind him, the others were running races again. She watched them for a moment, wondering where they got the energy, then looked around her at the fleeting richness of the western sky, the delicacy of the thorn tree silhouetted against it, the grey of the dark cloud bank on the eastern horizon, the earthy reds of the distant *jebel* exaggerated by the sunset. For a moment she saw it with his eyes. Why did it not move her more? It was easier when it was new. It had been easier at the beginning. Now it was as if she were jaded inside. Afraid of it all, perhaps. Her inner eye shut, waiting to go home. *Homesickness is a terrible thing*, she thought, looking at Simon's calm, contented face. *It bleeds the life out of experience.* But he had made her look. For a moment she had paused and really looked.

She felt an abrupt, unexpected rush of happiness. For a moment she wanted to be nowhere else – a moment she would hold on to, except that already, with the last echo of sun fading out of the landscape, it was growing dusk and Adam was getting jumpy, standing nervously at her shoulder as she sat relaxed on the rapidly cooling sand. He was afraid of the dark, even out here where it felt so safe, so empty.

'Anyway, Mummy,' he said, as if continuing a conversation they had just been having. 'You do have to be careful. Cos there *is* cockerdials. In rivers. In Africa.'

She laughed and hugged him to her. 'Not where there isn't any water, my pet. It's quite safe here.'

There was a burst of laughter behind them. Charles had picked Catrin up and was running with her to the stick that marked the finishing line of their improvised race track. He plonked her down in the sand and held up her arms in a victory gesture. Kit roared his indignation. 'You wouldn't have won anyway,' Daniel said disparagingly. Bee looked at Charles's face, flushed and laughing. He is a good father, she thought. When he's present. The trouble was, he hardly ever was present. Simon probably thought they did this sort of thing all the time but the truth was they hardly ever did. If Charles wasn't out of the house he was usually deep in paperwork, or he was asleep. Present, but somewhere else inside himself.

It isn't enough, she thought. For all the crumbs that fall from the master's plate, it isn't enough. Kit's roaring had given way to giggling because Charles was tickling him. For the children, it probably is. But not for me. She got up and started to collect the plates. And of course, Charles was always at his best when he had a wider audience. Simon jumped up to help her. His attentiveness surprised her, reminding her she did exist in her own right. She asked him about his two daughters, who were a little older than Danny. The mosquitoes were beginning to bite.

'Will you be coming to Khartoum with us tomorrow?' he asked. She shook her head, afraid that if she spoke her resentment would be audible. Charles was going. It would feel very empty in the house when the film crew left on the plane in the morning and Charles went with them.

In the morning the plane arrived promptly. She heard it from the kitchen soon after six as she made breakfast for the little ones. Danny was getting ready for school. They wouldn't see Charles again for five days.

The front door banged. She heard him running down the verandah and went to meet him, afraid that something was wrong, but he was grinning. He shouted breathlessly, 'You can come!' and threw his arms round her so vehemently that she staggered against him.

'How? How can we come?'

'A message just came with François, from Jonathon. He's persuaded old Bill to move in with him for the next five days so we can have Will and Maggie's house after all! And there's

176

room on the plane, but we have to be quick – François is champing at the bit. I wouldn't trust the old fox not to go without us. Hurry! Throw some things into a case. Let's go!'

She couldn't think straight. Clothes. A few toys. She bundled things unceremoniously into a suitcase, calling out instructions to each of the children, urging them to hurry. Danny, so nearly on his way to school, was gleeful but Catrin was disturbed. Passports, identity cards, duty free card. Sun hats, spare sandals in case they lost the ones they were wearing, Catrin's favourite doll – the familiar rituals but speeded up. Make sure the gas is turned off at the cylinder. Quick, get the computer into the cupboard, tape deck too, and turn the key. Lock the inner doors, lock the outer ones. At the last minute Catrin remembered her clothie, still tucked inside her bed. Charles ran back for it, unlocking and re-locking doors in a frantic hurry. Then they were speeding out along the airport road in the old pick-up, towards the purple *jebel* which was still only just showing the sun its face. The two Mig jets stood dark and hawkish on the tarmac, scowling, and unmoved. The red zinnias made their usual gaudy show in the rectangular beds of the airport garden, where the usual corpses slept, heads covered against the rising day.

'Are they really dead?' Kit asked anxiously.

'No, darling,' she murmured, kissing the top of his head. 'Daddy was just being facetious.'

'What's fecious?' asked Adam.

Catrin was chanting, 'Bye-bye 'Beid, Bye-Bye 'Beid.'

They hurried round the end of the airport building to where François was strutting impatiently, looking at his watch. 'Aha, you 'ave come,' he said grimly. 'Into ze plane, if you please. We 'ave a schedule to keep to.'

They climbed up the steps and into the last seats on the

plane, to cheers from the grinning film crew who were already strapped into theirs. François surveyed his full cargo of passengers and tutted fretfully. There was no seat for Catrin and she had to sit on Bee's lap. François looked at her and frowned as if he might say he couldn't take them after all. Charles said suddenly, 'Christ! I never even thought about travel permits for you and the kids. Fingers crossed this isn't the day the police do a check!'

So even animated baggage needs a permit to travel, she thought. She sat in anxious stillness, waiting for the cabin door to be shut, for them to taxi safely away.

There was a long pause. François was fussing around outside somewhere. It was hot inside the plane. 'Need a poo,' Catrin observed benignly. Bee ignored her. Closing her eyes she counted to twenty, waiting for the demand to be repeated. She'd got to eleven when she was interrupted by the sound of the engines coughing into life. At last François came round and shut the cabin door from the outside. He walked back to the front of the plane and climbed up into the cockpit.

The door from the cockpit was abruptly slid back and François's hawk-nosed face glared round at them. 'Okay? Zen we go!'

She relaxed.

Taxiing down the runway towards the town, the airport buildings already looking unreal, the Migs like toy planes. The slow deliberate turn as they swung round on the tarmac. The rising stationary throb as the engines roared to full power and then the innocuous lurch as they began to roll down the long black line of the runway, bumping over the pot-holes, gathering speed towards the little *jebel* which was pink now as the sun rose higher. That heart-murmur pause at the moment of lift-off, and the sudden weightless swinging as the plane lifted, clumsy as a mechanical moth, buffeted by the thermals that were already rising off the warming ground. François's precious schedule: the relentless timetable of heat and sun that made flying a thing of the early hours, sandwiched precariously between daylight and heat.

They rose swiftly, rocking this way and that. The red earth dropped away, the *jebel* was already like a toy beneath them, its spine like dragon's teeth, blocky in sun and shadow. They passed over the town, the station visible as a square matchbox beneath them, their own house briefly identifiable by virtue of its position on the corner opposite the park. On the edge of the town the road to Khartoum fanned out over the red plain in a splay of wheel ruts, shadowed sharply by the rising sun. In this light the dry stream beds were clearly visible, giving the village locations a logic they lacked on the ground. Had water ever run in those courses? It was hard to believe it. But here and there a shiny Unicef hand-pump could be seen on the dry stream bed, complete with its crowd of tiny figures collecting water. Then, for miles and miles, little to see except for the occasional village, merging with the brown of the earth, and the occasional *jebel,* until the first glint of the Nile appeared in the distance.

Adam said dreamily, staring over his egg sandwich at the leaves above them, 'Who looks after God? Does God's wife?'

She couldn't help laughing. What was the answer to that? Kit popped up in her line of vision like a relentless jack-in-the-box. 'Can I go swimming now?' he demanded, impatient because today it was Adam's birthday and Adam was getting all the attention: he had opened his one present and his two homemade cards before Charles left for work. Now they had a whole day in the Sudan Club, to be eked out between swims and swings.

But in the evening Charles came, bringing Jonathon Knappf and Bill Stephens with him to supper. Then the film crew turned up unexpectedly, for their last evening before flying home, and the meal turned into a party, seated at a long table hastily set out for them in the dining room with Adam in the place of honour at the centre. The room was noisy, the conversation careering about between water and poverty issues and funny stories, and crazy toasts drunk in Pepsi. Simon went out of the room and came back with a pink birthday cake, which they'd had made in their hotel. He placed it ceremoniously in front of Adam and everybody cheered. Adam's face went all pink to match. He slipped from his chair suddenly and ran to bury his face in Bee's lap. She took him by the hand and led him gently back to his place. They all sang 'Happy Birthday' and she helped him cut the cake.

'And how old are you?' someone asked.

'Five,' he answered proudly, safer now that he was on Bee's knee.

'And starting school next week, aren't you Adam,' called Charles from the far end of the table.

'Mummy, I don't want to go to school!' he said suddenly, turning anxiously and cupping her face in his hot sticky hands.

'Yes you do, you've just forgotten. That's why we bought you that nice green satchel in the *souk*, remember?'

He looked unconvinced.

A sudden crash made them jump. In all the excitement the rumbling of the approaching storm had gone unnoticed. Catrin gave a terrified squeal and ran to Bee. Through the open windows the night sky lit up haphazardly, followed almost immediately by another crash of thunder.

Was it Jonathon who suggested it? A birthday swim in a thunderstorm? But suddenly they were all in the water, even the children, who were scared of storms, cavorting in a kaleidoscope of lightning flashes. Rain began to fall in big splashy drops.

'Are you more likely to get struck in a pool, do you think?' asked Bill.

She whisked Adam briskly past him through the water so that he wouldn't hear.

'Who cares anyway!' shouted Jonathon over the roaring thunder. 'Let's go out in style!'

The elation of doing something utterly unexpected, probably forbidden, (possibly foolish), in the face of the raw elements! The rain began in earnest, cascading down. The lightning was like a crazy discotheque. Charles grabbed her in passing and kissed her hard. 'I'm so glad you've come, darling!' he yelled, but she had to guess what he'd said, the thunder drowned his voice. Adam was clinging to her, trembling with scared excitement.

'And is *this* my birthday too?'

'Yes, darling,' she said, hugging him close as Catrin whirled past, propelled through the water by Jonathon, Kit chasing after them like a small shark, head down and skinny bottom jutting up out of the water. 'This has all been laid on especially for you.'

Chapter 11

This house is full of bloody wildlife, she thought crossly one lunchtime. A large black rat had just jumped out of the oven. What do you do when you've had a rat in your oven, anyway?

No rains now for weeks. Perhaps they had ended. The natural world seemed to know. Ants progressed in columns in the garden as if they listened to the ground and heard secret messages. The kitchen gecko was back. He had grown so big on last season's cockroaches that he hit his head as he ran under the fridge whenever she went into the kitchen at night. She was glad to see him back – there were baby cockroaches everywhere, mere red and white shadows of the treacly brown monsters they would soon become. He would have his work cut out this winter.

Toads in the bathroom, hedgehogs in the garden – what a strange life it was, so full and empty both at once.

And their own wildlife too: secret shifts and changes below the surfaces of things. Adam the schoolboy, unexpectedly self-possessed; Kit, now his protector, suddenly wise. But in their wake, Catrin – alone at home all morning – is bored and bad-tempered, kicking Bee's leg when she sits down to a rare morning treat of Beethoven. 'Dis not Thomas a Tank Engine! Dis not Thomas a Tank Engine!'

They go out on a Friday to visit a *hafir* that Charles has been enthusing about – all blue calm water, and a flock of pelicans too, just as he'd promised. The sun strikes hot through the bare thorn trees and Kit shouts, 'It's just like England!' He jumps up and down in his excitement. The track follows the town water pipe. At every leak, a group of birds clusters. She looks at them. The Sudan has birds instead of flowers, she realises. Birds of passage, going somewhere else.

It isn't only the wildlife that is moving. Without the cover of the rainy season the war is shrinking back again as the SPLA withdraws into the humid forests a long way south. The pattern of Charles's work shifts: from the acute and the crisis-driven, back to projects and development. He is away less often. The tension in his face eases. All those things he's seen, she thinks, looking at him. Poor love.

'Sam!' Zahara said, more sharply than she intended. He looked up, his pale face almost sullen. Poor child, he was just over-tired. Maggie said they had only arrived back from England the day before yesterday. She said more gently, 'Go back to your place and I will come in a minute. And while you're waiting, work out how many eggs I would have if I had eight chickens and they each laid one egg a day for four days.'

'Easy peasey Jakanesey,' said Sam as he went back to his chair.

'Easy peasey Sudanesey!' Jamila corrected him, and giggled as she bent over her workbook. She said it again. A chorus of other voices began to join in.

Zahara hushed them gently: 'This is Quiet Time, remember? Aasha! Don't hold the book so close!'

'What if one of the chickens dies?' Sam asked, looking up at her. His eyes had woken up.

'None of them die.' She watched him for a moment as she

waited for Betsy to read to the end of the sentence. He frowned as he wrote out the sum, sticking his tongue out in concentration. In the next room Josie's class was going through its tables. Winter was coming: it was not quite so hot and the mornings were beginning to be pleasurable again. The day outside was bright, and the sky was very blue.

It was clear from Toby's voice that the children were definitely not included in this invitation. It was his and Sandy's farewell party and Charles would have liked to go, but he could just imagine Bee's reaction if he were to suggest it. She had hardly been out of the house since their return from Khartoum nearly six weeks ago. It would do her good to get out. The more he thought about it, the more he thought so. The more he said so, the more non-committal she became.

It wasn't all that far to Toby's house but she wasn't used to being out alone at any time of the day, the more so after dark. She let herself out of the compound by the side gate so as not to have to run the gauntlet of Malik's disapproval and hurried down the road, the only solitary female figure in a street full of men.

The party had barely begun when she got there, although it was after nine o'clock and they'd been told to come at eight. A group of giggling Sudanese girls hung around in an awkward group, their *thobes* carefully folded and stacked on a table by the wall. They were wearing tight, frilly dresses made of shiny material, very skimpy. Some of the girls had braided hair hanging almost to their waists, so hidden under their *thobes* in public that she hadn't seen hair like it before. Most of them were pretty and a few were extremely beautiful; they were all exotic, like tropical birds. She wondered where Toby had rustled them up from. Or, indeed, how they had persuaded their families to let them come. Among them she felt like a plump, middle-aged sparrow. The girls crowded in a gaggle at the far end of the room while Leslie and the other two VSO girls who shared the house with Toby and Sandy mixed easily and unselfconsciously with the assorted men in the middle of the room. John the Ugandan electrician was there, and an Eritrean friend of his. The rest of the men were white. The music was loud and conversation was difficult.

Sandy came in carrying a crate of Pepsi, and behind him, carrying another, came Daz. She was surprised to see him. She had forgotten Daz. He no longer sported his pink and purple Mohican. Instead his gingery hair was shaved close to his head. He was wearing a *jelabiya* but no head-cloth. He noticed Bee and grinned at her from across the room.

Later, as she sat talking to Leslie, perched side by side on a table that had been pushed up against the wall to make room for dancing, Daz materialised out of the shadows at her side. The room was lit only by candles, which made jumpy shadows on the walls. The low lighting softened his awkward features.

'Hi,' she said.

'Hi. Did Toby get that money to you?'

She was confused, then she remembered: the reward for the runaway camel in the *souk*. 'Yes he did. Thank you.'

'How's the kids?'

'Well. More or less. Though they don't look it – they're all getting over impetigo. How's the camel?'

'Don't ask,' he said darkly.

She chuckled. 'Been running away again, has he? Haven't you got the hang of that knot yet?'

'Worse than that. He dropped dead under me,' Daz said mournfully. 'Don't laugh, it was tragic. One minute we was ambling along minding our own business, the next he was flat out and I was in a thorn bush in the middle of nowhere and that was that – he was stone-cold dead. Relatively speaking.'

'Oh, Daz,' she said, trying to be serious. 'Did you lose an awful lot of money on him?'

He shrugged. 'Put it down to experience. It was my fault for being too hasty. I shouldn't have bought him on me own.'

'Will you get another one?'

'Naa. Don't think so. Too much of a liability. I did have some good times, though. Saw things I wouldn't have seen without him.'

'What sort of things?' she asked, intrigued. One might, from the silent height of a passing camel, see things better not seen. (She'd commented once on how eyes-front the camel drivers were as they glided past the house, only their heads visible above the compound wall, rocking gently to the strange motion of their unseen camels, and Charles had said it was self-protection: they could be killed for looking into a compound.)

But Daz said, 'Sunsets.'

She peered at him in the semi-darkness. Something indefinable was different about him. As if he were older, wiser. An audible change, like a resonance in his voice. He didn't look any older, just better tanned, less acute; his nose was no longer raw with sunburn. The tan suited him, making him look, in this light at least, auburn rather than gingery. He lingered beside her, chatting about this and that.

Toby changed the tape on the cassette player and he and Claire began to dance in the middle of the empty room. The Sudanese girls watched, eyes glittering, as if they were waiting for something.

'Going to dance?' Daz asked.

She shook her head. 'But don't let me stop you.'

He hesitated a moment, then muttered 'Oh, what the hell…' and went over to join in. His *jelabiya* immediately wrapped itself awkwardly round his legs. The Sudanese girls tittered happily, discreetly, into their hands.

The music was good — some mix of Toby's — eclectic, jumping from old favourites to recent stuff Bee hardly knew but all of it good for dancing. You couldn't help but want to get up and move to it. She sat, foot tapping, too awkward to join in. The Sudanese girls were suddenly in the middle of the floor, dancing shyly in a group. Gracefully. Laughing a lot. She watched them, amused.

Daz tangled his legs in his *jelabiya* again and nearly fell. 'Oh shit!' he exclaimed, and suddenly he pulled the garment up over his head and flung it into the corner. The gaggle of girls gasped and clasped slim brown hands over their mouths, their shocked laughing eyes flicking from side to side in the candle-light. Underneath his *jelabiya* he was wearing long blue and white stripey drawers from the *souk*, tied with a draw-string at the waist.

She smiled, and sipped her Pepsi.

Relieved of his *jelabiya* he began to dance with abandon. He capered about, twisting and gyrating. A leather amulet round his neck bounced wildly against his taut skin. He had a surprising body: thin, yes, but muscularly slender, not skinny. Shapely. His drawers kept slipping down around his narrow hips. She heard the Sudanese girls' sharp intake of breath as for one moment they thought – as she did too – that he was about to lose them all together. He stopped to re-tie the drawstring, and winked at her.

The gaggle of girls was dancing wildly now, and Daz was leaping in and out among them, making them laugh. She

187

ached to join in but she felt overweight and self-conscious so she stayed where she was, sitting on the table against the wall.

He came over and threw himself onto the table beside her to rest for a while with his back against the cool wall. Sweat was running in rivulets down the hollow over his breastbone and he was breathing hard with exertion. 'Wow,' he said, 'this is some party!'

The leather amulet on its cord hung between his tense pink nipples. She carefully averted her gaze.

'Aren't you going to dance?'

She shook her head.

'Why not? Don't you like dancing?'

She shrugged, saying nothing. She felt isolated. Everybody except her seemed to be high on something, though if there was any dope around she hadn't smelt it, and there certainly wasn't any alcohol. She felt his gaze resting on her.

Why was he focussing on her? Or was it displacement therapy, to avoid engaging with any of the lovely girls, perhaps? Not just the intimidating Sudanese gaggle, but Claire, who was very pretty, or Leslie, who was lively and amusing. Was it because she was so much older than him and married, so he felt safer with her? She looked at his earring, trying to remember which way the significance of left ear/right ear went. Left ear. Did that mean he was gay? He stood up.

Suddenly he'd grabbed her by the hand and was pulling her off the table and into the middle of the room. She laughed uncertainly. She was disconcerted, having forgotten he was tall, to find herself on a level with his left nipple as she stood there beside him. She looked away. Next to him she felt short and squat. She began, out of sheer self-consciousness, to move gently to the music, if only to blend in.

Gradually her tension slipped away, dissolving into the safe darkness where the music enclosed her, blocking out thought. And no one, anyway, was watching.

Daz was very struck by Bee's dancing. She moved with unexpected grace. He felt exposed, dancing beside her, his antics laid bare beside the economic fluidity, almost languid, of her movements. She reminded him of the way an animal is transformed as it enters the water, changing its nature as it changes elements. She looked transported, her eyes half closed. It was almost disturbing, like watching someone who was having sex. It also made him want to grab her attention. He cavorted the more, twisting around her, jumping about. She opened her eyes, laughed, and closed them again. At every leap there was a titter from the Sudanese girls, who, as he well knew, were watching his every move.

'What?'

He bent forward to repeat it closer to her ear: 'They remind me of my dad's turkeys.'

Her eyes shot open and she looked round at the girls. 'That's a bit mean, isn't it? They're so much nicer than turkeys!'

'I didn't mean it like that,' he said hastily. She didn't catch what he said. He had to lean very close to her to repeat it, smelling her smell, sweet with soap and shampoo, sharp with sweat, all jumbled up in one heady mix. An elemental womanly smell, it seemed to him. He leaned in again, close to her ear, and added, 'I just meant… my dad's turkeys, every time you do something in the shed, they react. Just like that.'

Bee smiled and nodded, and moved back slightly. Nose to nipple she felt a bit uncomfortable. She looked up to see him staring down at her anxiously. Funny boy! Perhaps he thought

189

she was backing off. She smiled up at him reassuringly and closed her eyes, swaying to the beat.

Was she being provocative? Her mind brushed over the thought, half concerned, as she rocked her hips, drew her hands through the air, inclined her body first this way, then that, dreamily, as if through water. Perhaps she was. Who cared, anyway. There was no one really to see. She ceased to feel bothered, setting the thought to one side and drifting away through the spaces of her mind. The music, the movement, was all.

It was two a.m. when the party ended with the sudden departure of the Sudanese girls. Who they were she never found out. CARE girls, probably. Their wild dancing abruptly gave way to a departure en masse, demurely wrapped in their *thobes*, as immaculate after more than four hours of frenetic dancing as they had been when they arrived.

She wasn't. She was sweaty and dishevelled. But not the slightest bit tired. She smiled to herself, thinking that this was one way to lose weight, if only by sweating it off. She hadn't done anything so energetic since coming back to the Sudan three months ago. Was it really only three months?

Realising how late it was, suddenly ill at ease at the prospect of walking home alone, she hesitated by the door. Daz detached himself from the group of people who were staying in the house and came over. 'I'll walk you back. You shouldn't walk on your own.'

She smiled up at him gratefully. He went to get his *jelabiya* from the corner where he had flung it and pulled it back on, an ignominious figure as his blue and white drawers and skinny legs wriggled their way up inside it.

The night outside was cool and empty. The fizzing in her

ears after the loud music fused with the fizzing of the brisk wind. An over-sized low-voltage moon was hanging over the end of the road. The street was completely empty but full of the movement of the wind – the bustling turbulence of jasmine hanging over a compound wall, the tumbling surge of dust and rubbish blown along the surface of the road like snow in the dull moonlight. An empty tin can rolled and knocked fitfully. She breathed deeply, smelling the dust, but beyond that the faint, wild smell of open spaces beyond the town. Above them the stars arched in their silent millions.

She felt him looking down at her looking up at the stars. He was silent, and she was grateful. There was an awkwardness between them now, like self-consciousness. She had enjoyed his attention; she didn't want to make a fool of herself by mistaking it for interest. The sand scuffing into her sandals was cold.

He walked with her to her front gate and stood in the road watching until she was safely in the house. Malik, on his *angareb* on the front verandah, cleared his throat with a grunt and raised his head to greet her. '*Salaam Alleicum, ya sitt.*' The greeting came grimly from the shadows. He could hardly be expected to approve. She returned the greeting in a whisper, '*Alleicum Salaam,*' as she kicked off her shoes at the front door.

The sitting room, scattered with books and toys, looked familiar and homely. She padded silently to the kitchen, looking in at the sleeping children as she passed. She drank two large glasses of water, then a third, not feeling the slightest bit sleepy. At the window the bougainvillea moved restlessly in the wind, scratching against the mosquito netting. She stood for a long time leaning against the window frame, watching the descending moon, aware of the sweat drying on her skin.

The image of Daz floated about in her quiet mind. Strange boy, so young, so old, all at once. Had he really been interested in her? Or was it only an illusion of her self-referencing imagination? Their awkward silence walking home had lasted all the way to the front gate. She realised guiltily that she hadn't even been interested in him enough to ask him what he was going to do now, without his camel.

Chapter 12

In the long blue shady room the sunshine scutters across the tiled floor, buffeted by a hot breeze. Beyond the netted windows the eternal bulbuls flutter and fidget in the desiccated shrubs. Today is a Friday, but every afternoon here is like an endless Sunday at home – the smell of bonfires, the empty garden, the quiet street beyond.

Out of the reach of the hot fringe of sunlight that marches across the tiled floor she sits drawing, in her blue dress. Probably she looks serene, her outside self. But inside she is not serene at all.

How is it, she thinks, that all the things I most hate from home have followed me here? The bulbuls irritate, chack-chacking like blackbirds constantly alarming in uneventful suburban bushes. A truck passes on the road and takes the corner with a crashing of gears. Children's voices rise in an angry crescendo from the verandah where she has left them with the plasticine. The plasticine has gone hard, she doesn't expect it will keep them quiet for long. She can hear Danny's exasperated voice trying to keep the peace. She can hear Kit's predictable resistance. Charles, of course, is somewhere else. It is supposed to be his day off but a man called more than an hour ago and they went off together. For ten minutes, he said. He'd missed lunch.

Above her on the wall is a watercolour she did once, it feels like a lifetime ago. In the foreground a rickety old black shed with a roof of rusted orange rears up shakily against the sky. In the middle distance the stumpy silhouette of a sail-less windmill, an old water pump long disused, stands stiff and desolate. The flat, passive reach of the marshes stretches back from the foreground to a wooded rise beneath a turbulent expanse of stormy clouds. It is her favourite among her own paintings. It hangs there, collecting disfiguring dust, a brave reminder to keep her stoical, to remind her of the value of endurance.

She is having trouble with her drawing. It is difficult to remember the absurdity of a camel when there are none in sight, too easy to inadvertently tidy it up. She intended this for a Christmas card but the exercise is dispiriting, and anyway anything she writes now will not arrive until well into January. It's difficult to feel any incentive. How can you write Christmas cards from the remoteness of your own summery isolation, to people so busily wrapped up in communal winter and approaching festivities that they have even more difficulty than usual guessing at your strange, incommunicable reality? She feels dislocated, and so homesick that it is like a physical pain. The consciousness that April, when they expect to go on leave, is the far side of a winter that is still in its early stages at home makes the prospect seem endless. She has no measure for winter here, only the intellectual exercise: this is December, it will be getting cold and grey at home. Whereas here, today, it is well up in the 90s, the temperature of blood, even if at night it is cold enough to need a blanket.

In her private self she feels as if she has been abandoned, not just by Charles, who is still half here, but by those she has left behind. Though the movement was all hers. It isn't anyone else's fault if she has become remote, so far on the outside of all their lives at home that she is only a memory, and a foreign

194

stamp on a Christmas card received in January. And yet she does feel abandoned, as if no one can reach her. Nor does she believe that anyone is trying to.

'Do you celebrate Christmas?'

Zahara thought for a moment before answering. The question was not unexpected in the house of Maggie-Who-Always-Asks-Questions but it was not Maggie who had asked, it was the young Italian woman. Greta was gazing earnestly into her face, her big eyes glinting in the darkness. She repeated the question, thinking, perhaps, that Zahara hadn't heard over the loudness of the music: 'Ow do you celebrate Christmas?'

Oh, she thought, that question. Not the other one. 'We usually go to the American Club.'

Greta laughed. A light-hearted sound. How old was she? She looked no more than twenty. 'We too, we go to the American Club. Carlo take me to the Sudan Club once but I did not like it. All that architecture, it is very nice, but very stuffy, I think. Sorry, sorry!' She put her hand on Zahara's arm. 'Maggie tell me your mother is English?'

Zahara smiled, considered for a moment whether to correct her, and as usual didn't. 'Yes, but I don't like the Sudan Club much either. We used to be members, a long time ago, when I was a child. But I like the American Club better. As you say, it is not so stuffy.'

'Isn't it a nice party!' Greta exclaimed, looking round at the coloured fairy lights festooned on the garden fence. At the milling crowd of people, all nationalities jumbled together, having a noisy good time. The lights from the house spilled out over the grass. Maggie was flitting about, organising the food. Zahara could see Ibrahim, talking to Will by the table

195

of drinks. She noticed Greta shiver slightly. The night was cool and she was wearing so little. She looked as if she might bounce right out of what she did have on. So much firm, youthful flesh bulged exuberantly over the strapless top that Zahara had difficulty knowing quite where to look.

'I saw you dancing,' Greta said. 'And Carlo tell me you 'ave four children!'

Zahara looked at her bright, guileless face. Clearly Greta thought she was very old.

Had nobody told her she was in a Muslim country? Did Greta not mind that she was the only one there with so much bare skin? It reminded her suddenly of being a student in Italy: how shocked the old women had been at the young people's skimpy clothes, and she had been one of those young people then. She remembered the strict notices on the church doors ordering women to cover their hair. Fifteen years ago. How very long ago it seemed. Greta was talking of this and that. Their two dogs mostly. Zahara guessed she was lonely, and probably homesick. She should talk to her about Italy, she was thinking, just as Greta smiled, touched her briefly on the arm, and moved away to talk to someone else. Zahara had not revealed that she could speak Italian, that she had lived in Italy for three years when she was at university – longer than she'd lived in the UK. I'm such a coward, she thought, as she went to the kitchen to see if Maggie needed help.

The kitchen was nearly empty. It was cavernous and hot. The only person in there was a man in a paper hat who looked drunk. He was rummaging in the fridge. 'Ice cubes. There must be some ruddy ice cubes somewhere,' he muttered. Then he saw Zahara. 'No ruddy good having gee and tee without ice,' he said defensively as if she had asked a question. His face was flushed and the paper hat had slipped sideways. She went back out into the garden and wandered around the crowded lawn, wondering if there was anyone here that she knew.

Christmas had always been an anxious time when they were young. Her mother's fraught preparations, her father's bemusement. The jolly Christmas dinners at the Sudan Club, all lined up at long tables on the lawn, wearing silly hats and pulling crackers, eating roast turkey flown in by plane, and awful Christmas puddings that she had never liked. And her mother usually getting a bit tipsy, and once embarrassing them dreadfully by crying in public in the middle of the festivities. It's easier now, as an adult. She could stitch together her past and her present, taking just the best bits and making modest, private ceremonies of their own, her and Ibrahim. They buy the girls little presents and wrap them in some of the paper she has got the children to make in school with poster paints. They go to the American Club and eat tasteless turkey and play team games afterwards in the pool, though usually it is too cold to enjoy going in the water. And in the evening they always go over to her father's house with Jamil, and now with Mastura too, for supper. Afterwards they play cards and word games. It is one of the three nights in the year that they unfailingly spend with him. The others are New Year's Eve and the Eid at the end of Ramadan. The points of their family compass. Their family's agnostic version of the two religious traditions, and the universal pivot of the New Year.

She found Maggie sitting alone in the shadows. She must be tired, thought Zahara, who never had parties and could not imagine all that effort and preparation. She sat down on another chair nearby.

'Have you found enough people to talk to?' Maggie asked. 'I saw you talking to Greta earlier.'

'She seems a nice girl.'

'Pity about the clothes,' Maggie said. 'I wonder if someone should say something to her. Larger than life, our Greta.'

Larger than life? Zahara savoured the phrase and stored it away. It was a nice phrase. It suited Greta well. 'I think she will learn. Men will say things in the street and she will learn.'

'I'm not sure Carlo and Greta are really the learning type. Did you hear about the Porsche? And the Irish Setters?'

She frowned. 'What is an Irish Setter?'

'A very expensive, pernickety breed of dog, with long silky hair. Like the very expensive wife with the long silky hair, but red hair in the case of the dogs, not black like our Greta's. And I don't think our Greta is particularly pernickety. Just naïve. Oh and the Porsche is red too.'

'Where can he drive his Porsche in Khartoum?'

'I think he's limited to a mile and a half of road. There aren't too many pot-holes on that new bit near the museum, apparently.'

Funny people, these aid people, thought Zahara. Importing dogs for fun, and cars they couldn't drive anywhere, while she had so much trouble importing educational books for school. She suddenly noticed a familiar, unexpected figure on the edge of the lawn, her glasses glinting as she stood watching the crowd of dancers with a glass in one hand. 'There's Josie!'

'Oh good,' Maggie said. 'She did say she would come if she could.'

Yes, but Maggie could not know how unlikely that was! Zahara stood up and made her way across the grass.

'This takes me back!' Josie said, leaning forward to kiss her, her words almost drowned out by 'Twist And Shout'. There were lots of people dancing on the grass now, singing along with the music. Zahara leaned towards her and shouted over the din, 'I didn't expect you to be here!'

198

Josie looked at her. 'Things are changing, girl.' Her eyes were impenetrable behind the glasses. Normally they did not talk about Josie's private life – she had just disclosed more than she had in years. Zahara stared back at her, wondering. Josie looked away and sipped her drink. There was a slice of *limoon* floating in her glass. Was that water, or was it gin?

She hooked her arm through Josie's and turned to watch the dancing.

Years ago, Josie had lived a public life as well as a private one. Zahara knows this from her mother, and from what she remembers of the days of her childhood when Josie was her mother's only real friend. She had come to Khartoum as a young teacher on a two-year contract. 'She was lively in those days,' Doris says, now. 'Noisy, if anything.' Until she began a secret love affair with a married man, an American diplomat whose wife had chosen not to accompany him on this particular posting. 'Well he pretended to be a diplomat,' Doris says. 'But we all thought he was a CIA spy. Anyway, Josie fell in love with him and she sort of forgot to go home. Her passport went out of date and she didn't do anything about it. She wasn't a legal resident – I don't suppose she is still. He stayed on, and so did she. He was a lot older than her and he should have been due for retirement, but there he still was, going native in his house in Omdurman and dropping out of European circles. And there she still was, living in his house with him. But she never talked about him. The story was that he was a drinker. With other secret vices, if you were to believe all the stories. And she started living two lives – the one we all knew about, at the American Club, at the school where she worked, and the other one she never talked about, at home. It was hard on our friendship,' Doris says, telling Zahara this story, years afterwards, as they walk round Marks and Spencers in Cardiff. 'This woman I'd known really well, becoming so mysterious.' And Zahara nods, only half listening as she picks up children's clothes and puts them in her basket, worrying about the prices but knowing her mother will probably pay. She knows Josie differently and the silences do not bother her.

Standing beside her now, her arm through Josie's, she felt the warmth of that familiar, bulky body and out of the corner of her eye saw Josie's face, calm behind the reflecting lenses as she sipped her drink. What did it mean, things are changing? A little flutter of fear made her shiver, and Josie turned her head to look at her. 'Wind's quite sharp,' Zahara said.

'You should be dancing. That would keep you warm.'

But Zahara did not like to dance unless it was with Ibrahim, and Ibrahim, on the far side of the lawn, looked as if he was much too engrossed in conversation to want to dance again. She tightened her arm against Josie's slightly. What if Josie should decide to go home, back to the States? She had never really countenanced the possibility before, it had always seemed too remote, but now for some reason it suddenly didn't seem remote after all. How I would miss you! she thought, squeezing Josie's arm again. In the darkness, Josie calmly squeezed back.

The Christmas tree was made of two palm fronds Charles had found discarded in the *souk* and a small branch off the dead mango tree in the garden. She sat for hours with the children making decorations to hang in the tree and round the room. It was a cool, happy time, like the best of summer days at home.

On the day itself, instead of stockings, the children had little baskets from the *souk* filled with the few odds and ends she had been able to find in Khartoum and a few that she'd secretly brought back with them in August. There weren't many presents but nobody minded. There were two visitors. One was from work, although it was supposed to be a public holiday (Jesus being one of the prophets). The other was a hopeful beggar. Christmas dinner was a frozen chicken from the American Duty Free in Khartoum, which had been sent down on the Unicef plane, and a proper Christmas pudding Bee had made, all washed down with Charles's *kerkedeh* wine. Afterwards, hot and uncomfortably stuffed, they played an endless game of Monopoly, which Kit very noisily won, and then had a tantrum anyway because it wasn't a proper Christmas, not like they had at home.

She knew what he meant. It was their second Christmas in the Sudan but it still seemed as if they were only pretending, hot and sweaty in their summer clothes as they were. It was quite a relief to give up pretending after just the one day and go back to normality. That's Christmas out of the way, she thought, hanging up the new calendar (Christmas present from her parents, views of National Trust gardens) under the old one (last year's Christmas present from Charles's mum, views of kittens) that still had six days of the old year left outstanding. She had already marked the date on the new one of them going on leave in April – it was the only event she could think of to pencil in. Nothing else scheduled between now and the fourth of April. Six days of the old year, ninety-five days of the new: only a hundred and one days between now and going on leave, but each one of those days a lifetime long. A hundred and one lifetimes – and then two months at home which will vanish in the blink of an eye.

Wishing my life away, she thought, but all the same she went off to the kitchen with a lighter step. Numbers were manageable. And after that blink of an eye there would be only six and a half months left until they went home for good. Six and a half months: another one hundred and ninety-eight days: a finite number.

But first she must get through the last six days of 1987.

On New Year's Eve they went to the *souk* at dusk to buy one of the big circular mats, intricately patterned, which were used to cover the trays of food dishes to keep the flies off. *Tabaqs* were very expensive but they had decided they would buy one as a belated Christmas present to one another, because they hadn't had anything to give on Christmas Day.

It was that lovely colourless time when the sky hovers on the dark side of daylight but there is still a faint glow from the departed sun. The long negotiations over the *tabaq* were interrupted at six by evening prayers: the trader excused himself and, picking up his rolled prayer mat, went off to join the rows of praying men in the broad central alleyway. They stood by the car waiting for him to come back. The praying figures, all in white turbans and *jelabiyas*, chanted quietly, moving through the ritual sequences, bowing their foreheads to the ground in one mass of up-ended bottoms. Kit, watching them through the car window, suddenly said, 'That's rude!' Bee chuckled, turning to look. What must it look like to an uncomprehending child? What did they any of them look like to him? What would he remember, looking back when he was twelve? When he was twenty?

A figure in a *jelabiya* came skirting round the praying men towards them. Her eye rested on him with detached curiosity, her mind elsewhere. It was only when he came closer that she realised it was Daz.

Afterwards this fact intrigued her: when she had first met him he'd stuck out a mile, for all that he was dressed in the

202

same white *jelabiya* that most Sudanese men wore. Now he seemed to have taken on some quality that made him merge in. What was it?

He greeted them enthusiastically, ruffling the children's heads, shaking hands with Charles. (Who instantly became reserved and distant, but Daz seemed not to notice.) He nodded at Bee and grinned. She was surprised how pleased she felt to see him.

He lingered while they completed their purchase, entertaining the children who had been beginning to grow fractious with boredom. When Charles and Bee came out from the stall with the big *tabaq* (acquired at vast expense), Daz was still standing by the car telling the children jokes. She invited him to come back with them for the evening, not really expecting him to say yes because he would surely have some New Year celebration arranged with the others in the VSO household, but Daz had come back from travelling to find they'd all gone off on a camel trip and he seemed glad of the invitation.

Back in the house, Charles said to her in the kitchen, 'What did you invite him back for? I've got a lot of work to do this evening!'

'But it's New Year's Eve!'

'We didn't do anything last year. I assumed we wouldn't this year either.'

She stood in the middle of the kitchen, a *limoon* in one hand, a knife in the other, looking at him. Why weren't they going to celebrate? And if they weren't, if he was too busy, couldn't she have a sociable time even if he chose not to? Suddenly she felt rebellious. She went out with a tray of *limoon* and joined in the high-spirited game that was going on in the sitting room with Daz.

Charles, left behind in the kitchen, didn't wonder why he felt so upset. Instead his mind jumped to considering what he should do about the Water Corporation and the inappropriate new hand-pumps that had been proposed for the Governor's home village. He went into their bedroom and sat down at the computer. Usually he helped with the supper but tonight he was damned if he would. Let her do it.

When she came back into the sitting room to tell Daz the children were in bed and waiting for the promised bedtime story, he was inspecting the picture on the wall above her work table.

'Is this one of yours?'

She was surprised that he had guessed. She'd never told him that she painted. 'Yes. Recognise it?'

'Yep. It's the marshes between Walberswick and Dunwich, in't it?'

She nodded.

'It's good.' He said it with confidence. She looked at him, her eyes narrowing.

'You paint a lot?' he asked.

'I did. But not here. Here – hardly at all.'

'Why not?'

He was watching her so closely that she felt suddenly quite uncomfortable. She began to pick toys up off the floor and put them into the baskets where they belonged. 'I don't know. Not really.'

There was a silence. She felt he was still watching her, though when she looked up he was going round the room looking at the other sketches and half-studies that she'd put up on the walls, more in an attempt to spur herself on than anything.

'I want to paint – painting has *always* been my passion. Obsession, even. I've always painted. Right through having the children, right up until we came here. I was selling stuff too. I was just beginning to think I might even earn a modest living from it. I had a bit of illustration work coming in. I thought being here would be a chance to really get some work done.'

'But?'

'But – it didn't work out. Charles had thought we'd be able to find a girl to look after the children so I could concentrate on my work but it just didn't happen. And anyway, people back home forget you if you're a long way away. They find other people closer to hand.' He wasn't looking at her. He was examining a small charcoal study of horizontals (cattle with their wide, sweeping horns) and verticals (shadowy camels), a slight sketch she had made after they had visited the nomad encampment back in September. One of the only things she had done since coming back from leave. She said, 'It didn't help that everything dried up.'

'The ideas?'

'The paints.'

He propped the drawing back against the wall and stood back, scrutinising it.

'But the ideas have all dried up too. Nothing really inspires me.'

He shot her a disconcerting grin. 'Which is odd, innit? Given that half the time here it looks much like where we come from, only without the sea.'

Where we come from, she thought, pleased that he had included her in the place where she most wanted to belong, so that the rest of what he'd said didn't sink in for a moment. As soon as it did it seemed extraordinary that she hadn't had the same thought herself because it was true. Had she been subconsciously trying to keep the two landscapes separate? There were surprising echoes. The thought was disturbing. She shook her head, trying to disentangle her reactions.

'You don't think so? No, I suppose it is a bit ridiculous, but it's what's always struck me. Around this bit of Northern Kordofan, anyway. I wouldn't say it about some of the other places I've been in.'

She looked at him, wondering. He talked a lot, but somehow she never knew what the pattern of his life was, or where he had been before he'd turned up on his ill-fated camel. Or even since. Reappearing as he did erratically, as if out of nowhere. Vague and evasive when she asked direct questions.

Kit appeared at the door to the sitting room, as angelic in his little white *jelabiya* as a fallen angel. 'We've been waiting *so* long,' he said, aggrieved.

She laughed. 'How long?' she asked wickedly, knowing Kit's idiosyncratic sense of time.

'About seven-and-a-half minutes!'

Without a word, Daz whisked him up by his legs and carried him upside down by his ankles, along the verandah to his room. Kit giggled, struggling to pull his *jelabiya* up to cover himself.

Later, Daz came into the kitchen and helped her cut up onions and aubergines as if he'd done it so often before that nothing needed to be said. He seemed perfectly at ease. He had taken ages putting the children to bed, telling them story after story. If he had noticed Charles's cold manner and rude withdrawal he ignored it. He was as cheerfully talkative with her as he was with the children and as full of absurd jokes. It was refreshing, after the customary evenings of serious debate that made up most of their socialising.

Outside the kitchen window she could hear the distant echoing soundtrack of an Egyptian film at the open-air cinema. The night smelled fresh after the day's dusty heat, and she listened half-consciously for the whispering scratch of the bougainvillea on the netting of the window. Sometimes, for moments together, she *could* feel happy here.

It was the last night of the old year. She wondered where they would all be at the end of the next. Her mind slipped away to Suffolk, to the image lurking always at the back of her consciousness. The red-tiled, flint-walled cottage, unspecific but vivid, for which she hungered as if it were a missing limb. A cottage with the wide sweep of the marshes beyond it, within a curlew's cry of the sea.

'Let's go to the races!' Jamil said. 'It's years since we last did.'

So they all climbed into his battered pick-up, she and Mastura in the cab with Jamil, Ibrahim in the back with the four girls, and off they went, through the quiet, Friday streets, to the outskirts of the city where the races were held. It was New Year's Day so there would be camel races as well as the horses.

The air was very clear, the colours lively against the orange earth and the blue distances. The racecourse was so big that the far end of it was almost out of sight. There were already many riders milling about at the town-end of the rough track, camels in one group, horses in another. The horses were frisky, fidgeting impatiently while their riders made a show of control, pulling their mounts' heads up, turning them about. A little distance away, the camels stood tall and serious, their haughty profiles turning from side to side, considering the world and finding it dull. The camel men sat quietly, perched high up on the wood and leather saddles decorated with long ropes of cowry shells. One of them had a black waistcoat over his white shirt and a bright red fez on his head. He looked down at Zahara and Faatma and Yasmina through his little round sunglasses and grinned.

'I'll go for that one,' she said to Ibrahim over her shoulder.

Ibrahim studied the sunglasses for a moment. 'I think you would be wasting your money,' he said. 'Anyway, you are supposed to be betting on potential, not on the rider's looks.'

She laughed. Suddenly the day felt very good. The clear air was still fresh, the shadows quite cool. All around them, the rise and fall of voices and the grumbling of camels. A pony neighed, men were laughing. Everywhere people in their Friday clothes, come to enjoy the races, place a modest bet or two on the quiet (not publicly, of course – that would not be legal), enjoy a picnic. Behind the long untidy line of cars and trucks drawn up on one side of the course, bright gaggles of gossiping women laid out plates of food on coloured mats. Their men-folk huddled round the riders, considering form. Children were running about and getting over-excited. She could see Aasha perched on Jamil's shoulders and Mastura holding Jamila by the hand. Faatma and Yasmina, arm in arm, heads together, had drifted over to look at the horses.

'Don't get too close, girls,' she called. 'Don't forget horses can kick.' Thinking how sad it was that they had never learned to ride, had never really been around horses. Their lives were so much smaller and more confined than hers had been.

She is fourteen and Saadiya is twelve. They are no longer quite so good and tractable as they once were, when they were little. In fact they are feeling downright rebellious. A feeling that has been growing for months now as their parents bicker, and the

208

confines of the house beside the Nile seem too narrow, and the pink bathroom is no longer a novelty, and they want to be grown up, and preferably not to be girls any more – boys have so much more fun than girls do.

It is the holidays, but only for them, not for their parents: they are in the railway carriage for a month, parked in a siding in the middle of a vast landscape which has little in it apart from some scattered thorn trees and a distant *jebel*. A landscape in which, as the day progresses, the horizon becomes vagrant and shimmers in the heat so that nothing is fixed. Boundless space, which is half inside your head as well as out, under the pressure of the light. Every day people walk out of nowhere to queue patiently for their father the doctor to see them. For their mother the nurse to give them the medicines as he instructs, to hold down a patient while Abu breaks and resets a fracture, or pulls a thorn long gone septic, or cleans and bandages a dagger wound. A man comes in with his forearm pinned to his upper arm by the spear his enemy tried to kill him with. Another has a gunshot wound in his foot, but his wound is self-inflicted – he shot himself by mistake. Abu speaks to these men sternly. Mummy murmurs sympathetic nothings in English, which the patients cannot understand. And together they vaccinate babies and children, examine expectant mothers and talk to them about child-care, and advise old men to give up smoking if they want their bad coughs to go away. Though the old men prefer to believe it is the winter that is affecting their chests.

Zahara is supposed to be watching Jamil, who is four and very mischievous, and Ali, who is eight and bored. But actually she and Saadiya are racing the local boys on their nimble little ponies: they have grown tired of watching the boys ride all afternoon. They can ride too, they have had hours of practice

209

on their cousins' fat little ponies in England. It isn't fair that just because they are girls and they are not in England they must only sit and watch. So they demand their turn. The local boys are shocked into silence, Nazmul and Ali both look worried. But Zahara and Saadiya, too anxious to prove themselves to be inhibited by their cotton frocks, clamber quickly astride the bare backs of two of the skinny little horses, pick up the rough leather reins, and take off like devils. The village boys scramble back onto their ponies and whoop excitedly as they speed after them. The girls keep ahead, they round the big rock and race back towards the small distant dot which is Nazmul, with Jamil and Ali smaller dots on either side of him, and the village boys are gaining on them, totally lacking in style or refinement – their reins flying, daylight visible from thigh to ankle – but, as usual, their lack of style does not slow them down. The girls do not win (the local boys always win) but something has shifted. They have become honorary boys. They are no longer excluded.

But later one of the boys tells his father that the doctor's daughters were riding like men. The man reports them to Abu. They are all severely admonished: two of them on the grounds of modesty, all of them on the grounds of safety. 'If you splintered a bone here it could cost you an arm or even worse a leg,' Abu says. His face is dark with anger. 'Never let me catch you doing anything so stupid again,' he says. They have never seen him so fierce.

And their mother looks at them crossly and says, 'I told you to look after Colin and James, not to risk breaking your own necks. That was very irresponsible of you, Sandra. You too, Susan. You should all have known better. None of you should be riding on those ponies. It isn't anything to do with modesty; it's just a question of common sense.'

The races began. They climbed up into the back of the pick-up to get a better view. Mastura was sitting on the roof of the cab with Yasmina and Aasha on either side of her, telling them stories about when she was a little girl and used to stay in her grandmother's village. Jamil was looking through binoculars as the camels lined up. They had placed their small bets with the man at the back of the big Land Cruiser who was pretending not to be a bookie, under the eye of the policeman who was pretending not to see, and Zahara had instructed Ibrahim to place hers on the man in the sunglasses. Not that she expected him to win. It was all just for fun.

What a pity we did not ask Abu if he would like to come, she thought as she looked up at Mastura giggling with the girls. He would have loved this, once. But now she was no longer sure. These days he seemed tired, always. A little distracted and distant. Last night, when they had all gone there for supper to see out the old year, he had said to her again that he thought they ought to go to England. She wished he would not do this! She knew he was only trying to do what was best for them but every time he said it, it felt like a rejection. As if he was saying that he did not need them after all. That he would not miss her if she went. So this morning, when Jamil suddenly said, 'Lets go to the races,' she said nothing about Abu, and neither did anyone else. But he would have liked to be here, she thought sadly, feeling she had been remiss. He would have sat up there beside Mastura and the girls and told tales of his own childhood. If he hadn't been too tired to come.

The gun went off with a distant crack. The group of camels shambled off, untidy as camels always are. Their lower lips drooped and wobbled and began to shed gobbets of white foam as they stretched out their necks and ran. A man in a green turban was out in front. The men in the watching crowd roared encouragement, Jamil and Ibrahim too.

At the end of the first straight the rider in the green turban carried straight on instead of swinging into the turn. They could see him pulling and beating at his camel, trying to turn it, but it kept on running, out into the desert. The sound of his angry screaming drifted back, his camel bellowing in protest as he tried to pull it round. The spectators were roaring with laughter. The rest of the camels circled the end of the course demurely and raced down the long straight on the far side. The knot of animals had spread into a long line, with a tight little group neck and neck at the front. The riders bounced on the high saddles, whooping as they whipped the end of the camel ropes, in the air over their heads or against the animals' flanks. The camels roared and blustered. Even a racing camel still looks as if it's only loping along, she thought. The man in the red fez – her rider – was, surprisingly, among the front runners. Jamil was peering through his binoculars. 'Who's winning? Who is winning?' she asked him excitedly, but he couldn't really see, the riders were coming towards them now round the last bend and he couldn't make out which was in front. A cheer went up. The camels thundered over the finishing line.

'Did yours win, Mummy? Did yours win?'

'We don't know. Abu is just going to find out.'

A few minutes later Ibrahim came back with Jamil. They were laughing. Ibrahim, unusually, looked sheepish.

'Well?'

'He's got a confession to make,' Jamil said, slapping Ibrahim on the shoulder. 'The man in the red hat won.'

'The red fez? The one in the sunglasses?'

'Yes, that one. But – 'and Jamil looked at Ibrahim and spluttered with laughter. 'But he was jealous so he didn't put your bet on that one, he put it on the man in the green turban. Same as he was betting on.'

'The one in the green turban? Oh, Ibrahim!'

Chapter 13

In January Charles went down to Kadugli for six days. Long days they were, in his absence. Nothing much to stir the monotony, except for the arrival of the blue-naped mousebirds in the bushes outside the window, displacing the bulbuls for a while.

They were sitting at the table, the children picking at their supper. I really must go to the souk tomorrow, Bee thought unwillingly. It's a bit hard on them, expecting them to eat aubergines.

'Daz!' yelled Kit suddenly, jumping up from the table.

They herded him in like a trophy. He sat opposite Bee with Catrin on his knee. 'Aren't you eating this?' he asked, shocked. A moment later he was finishing off all the leftovers.

Later she bathed Catrin in the big bowl on the verandah floor filled with warm water from the kitchen, while Daz read *Ivor the Engine* to Kit and Adam, with noisy sound effects. Danny was hovering, listening too. Catrin commanded Bee to make less noise splashing the water because she couldn't hear the story. 'I not want you read me!' she said, when Bee had finished drying her and told her to go and fetch a book. 'I want Daz.'

She bathed Adam, organised Kit through his own washing. Daz had moved on to *The Cat in the Hat*. She moved on to the washing-up in the kitchen. And finally, when she had finished clearing away and Daz was still in full flow (if he went on at this rate he would get through their entire repertoire of books at one sitting), she moved on to the sitting room and read her own book in stolen peace, to the lovely Englishness of Elgar, until she was called to deliver goodnight kisses.

When the little ones were safely in bed Danny brought the playing cards for Daz to teach him card tricks and they sat together on the floor, absorbed and self-contained, while she moved about them putting away the toys. Then she sat down with her sewing. She watched them covertly as she pinned together the tedious pleats and tucks of a new dress for Catrin. Daz towered over Danny but in some ways he seemed barely any older. The same earnest concentration suffused his face, the same youthful enthusiasm made him loud. And at times even squeaky, though his voice was so much deeper than Danny's still unbroken one. She went to make a pale omelette for their supper with the last of the eggs. They ate in the sitting room (Danny joining in an illicit second supper), with their plates on their laps, and when they had finished they left the plates on the floor beside their chairs and plunged into a riotous game of Cheat. Little black ants swarmed over the greasy plates unregarded. The game was a long one. Bee won.

When Danny went – unwillingly – to bed, Daz stayed on. They talked idly of this and that. Of things he had seen here, of shared things from home. That common link of home loosely uniting them in a mantle of friendship. It was easy to find things to talk about; it was easy to be silent too. He was curious about her and his curiosity was like oil, easing her out of her solitude. When she said to him that she found life here difficult it didn't feel like a confession, and in his presence she did not feel like a failure. Perhaps it was the way she had met him, at his most undignified, or perhaps it was simply that dignity was not an issue with him.

She was letting him out onto the street at the back gate, away from Malik's inquisitive eyes, when he mentioned casually that he was going down to Babanusa next week to join a charity-run feeding programme. He'd got to know one of the nurses working on it and she'd persuaded the expatriate in charge to take him on as a volunteer.

She stood looking up at him in the wind-blown shadows, the street light tossed about by the jasmine overhanging the high wall. In that moment, as he looked down at her, the atmosphere between them shifted. She saw him smiling down at her, no longer as young as Danny but somehow as old as her. There was a calmness in his look, an unlikely gentleness in his voice as he said softly, 'I'll come and see you when I'm back in El Obeid. Don't know when that will be, though.'

'Have a good time,' she said primly, the older woman to the very young man, firmly establishing distance. But she knew he had seen her eyes, and that her eyes had betrayed her. She watched him disappearing down the street, a jaunty figure in his grubby *jelabiya*.

They sat in the tiny box room they laughingly called their staff room, Josie at the desk, Zahara on a low stool, leaning against the wall. All the children had gone home, even her own: Ibrahim had come at two to fetch them. The university was closed today. Demonstrations. Ibrahim was depressed.

'I sure don't like Khartoum when it gets like this,' Josie said. 'Too much bitter feeling. I've seen it too often before.'

Zahara was silent, thinking of all the times within her own memory that trouble had flared and died down again. It was like water rising in a blow-hole until the pressure makes it erupt, and then it all dies down again, feigning silence.

'I was driving past some of the refugee camps on Friday,'

Josie said. 'There are so many displaced people in Khartoum now! Ethiopians, Dinka – you would wonder how the government keeps them all fed!'

'Ibrahim's afraid there's going to be a coup.'

'Well we've seen that before too.'

Josie looked tired, she thought. Once – hazy within her memory – Josie had been tall and athletically built. Abu used to call her the American Amazon. Now, in middle age, she had grown big and misshapen, untidy. Her long greying hair was stringy and looked unwashed. Her clothes were only just the respectable side of scruffy. Zahara worried about her. She wondered whether everything was all right at home but she could never ask. Josie looked down at her suddenly and grinned.

'You remember your mother's story? About the time you were all in the bathroom with those rebels?'

'It was always Abu who told me that story. I don't remember Mummy telling it.'

❧

She is small. So small that Nazmul is only a baby. They are living in the old house, in the leafy part of Khartoum not far from the Nile where all the houses have big gardens and the roads are quiet. But whenever there is trouble an army tank takes up a position at the crossroads near their house because that is the highest point of the flat sprawling suburbs, with the longest views down each of the four straight roads. And the tank is there today, and they are hiding in the bathroom.

Abu, when she asks him now, doesn't remember why there was trouble at that particular time. There were so many times: rebellions against the government, starving refugees driven into Khartoum by drought or by civil war in the south. But, for some reason that he cannot remember either, each time the troops are out and there are fugitives running through the city, he takes his family into the bathroom to hide. Oh yes, he says – it was because we could lock an extra door.

It is a big old-fashioned bathroom, all white and shining, with a cast-iron bath and cracked white tiles. They are crouching in the corner by the washbasin, Mummy against the wall with the three of them in her arms, Abu in front of them, between them and the door. Old Faatma squats on the floor opposite, crouching down between the end of the bath and the wall.

Suddenly they hear footsteps running through the house. Someone tries the handle of the door. There are men's voices just the other side of it, whispering in the passageway. A moment later there is a crash and the door bursts open, the lock broken, and three men come tumbling in. It is easy to see that they are rebels. They look wild, their hair sticks up all over their heads in dry little dreadlocks. Their *jelabiyas* are dirty and torn. They are wielding sharp-looking knives and they threaten Abu in low voices, and Abu talks back to them, quietly but sternly. There is a distant roar as the tank on the crossroads fires its big gun and almost immediately afterwards shots are fired just outside in the garden and somebody starts pounding on the front door of the house. Two of the rebels duck down and hide beside Faatma. She looks at them with distaste and leans away. The third climbs quickly into the empty bath and lies down flat. 'How did you get in?' Abu whispers urgently, because the front door is now being chopped down. 'Through the kitchen window, Sah,' says one of the rebels politely just as the front door caves in with a splintering sound and all the outside noises come indoors, men's voices shouting, feet in heavy boots pounding in the passageway. Boots, so it must be soldiers. And then the broken bathroom door is thrown open.

'Out! All of you, out!' shouts the soldier, gesturing angrily with his gun. They are pushed out into the garden, all of them together, and the soldiers in their uniforms look at them as if they are all the enemy, but Abu is talking to them. The little soldier with the glasses, the one who seems to be in charge, tells Abu to stand to one side with his wife and the children. 'And Faatma!' Abu says urgently. 'She is with us, she is not with them!' The soldier hesitates, then he nods at old Faatma to go to them. The three rebels are standing now in the middle of the lawn, and the soldiers have lined up, pointing their black guns at the men, and Mummy is screaming: 'Not in front of the children!' She keeps shouting, 'Please, not in front of the children!' But the soldiers ignore her as if she has not said a word. The rebels start throwing their arms up in the air. 'We are going to Allah,' they shout, and one of them begins to do a little dance. 'Quiet!' says the soldier with the glasses, but the black guns are not steady any more. 'Allah is good,' shouts one of the rebels, 'I am coming, Allah, I am coming!' He looks like a whirling dervish, and the others start dancing too. The soldier in the glasses hesitates and the barrels of the guns begin to shake. Then, with a little gesture of his hand to his men, the soldier in the glasses tells them to lower their guns and he says to the rebels, 'Okay, okay, you can go. Go quietly. We didn't see you.' In a moment the three men have slipped away into the bushes towards the next garden.

They looked rather disappointed, says Abu. And they ask, as they always do at this point in the story, But why didn't the soldiers shoot the rebels, Abu? And he says, Because if the rebels thought they were going to heaven, then where would the soldiers be going, if they were the ones to send them there?

219

'Tell it me again,' said Josie now, in the staff room of the little school that takes so much effort out of them both that they wonder sometimes quite why they are doing it. 'I forget the details.'

So she told it again, her own version, but hearing Abu's voice in her ears, his familiar phrases.

'You have so many stories!' Josie said. 'We never had stories in my family. I suppose some families tell them, some don't.'

Zahara said sadly, 'I only have stories from the past. My present doesn't make stories.'

Catrin was trying to persuade Bee that she really had seen a 'snowmam'. Just now. She sat on the arm of the chair, clothie clutched in the hand whose thumb she was sucking, taking her thumb out to expand further on the subject. Bee was sitting in the chair trying to write letters.

'And my daddy said "Tax!" And a tax did come. And we did go to where the snowmams were. And we did fly in a Concorde. And my daddy was four and I was three.'

'Yes,' she said, not listening.

'I tell you a joke?' asked Catrin, leaning over to peer into her face so that she couldn't see what she was writing. 'There's a fly in my soup. We dead it wiv hot water.'

Bee chuckled. Children are so absurd. You can lose yourself when you live too much in their world. She worried sometimes that, sucked down into their midst, she was too weighed down to see them properly and enjoy their fleeting little selves.

Pleased with the success of her joke Catrin pushed her advantage. 'You want make coffee? I want a biscuit!'

'You,' said Bee, pulling her off the arm of the chair and tickling her chubby tummy, 'are just one big stomach.'

'No I not!' Catrin said. 'I got two legs!'

Fatouma came in to sweep the floor and Bee took her letters to write on the back verandah where the morning sun reflected rosily off the wall outside and the sparrows chattered. Catrin got her biscuit. Then another. Biscuits used to be only for treats, Bee thought weakly. So many old boundaries gone. As she put the packet back in the high cupboard, away from the ants, she wondered, Was I a better woman then, or is all this improving me? It was too exhausting to think of an answer. She went back to her letters.

She was in the sitting room re-arranging the chairs (a wordless disagreement she and Fatouma had every morning – Fatouma favoured the doctor's waiting room look, with all the chairs pushed back firmly round the walls) when the front gate clanged and sandalled feet strode swiftly up the front path. She looked up in surprise just as Charles opened the front door. 'You're early! I didn't expect you till tonight – perhaps not even then!'

He slipped his sandals off in the doorway and kicked them out of the way. He was very grimy from the journey, his white trousers stained and his face masked with dust, but he was grinning. A moment later he was hugging her tight. 'We'd got the work done – there was no reason not to come home. God I've missed you!'

She leaned against his firm, familiar body. He looked tired. There were dark circles ringing his eyes from over-late nights sitting up talking and over-early starts, but there was a vigour about him, an energy. It lit a small flame in her, as it always had. She kissed him again, and wondered if they might sneak off to bed, if only for a cuddle. But with Fatouma in the house there was little chance of even an out-of-bed cuddle. Charles didn't seem to mind. He was talking animatedly about Kadugli, how he wanted her to come and see it for herself. I do love you, she thought. 'Do you want some coffee?'

221

'I will have to go to the office in a minute,' he said.

She felt like the donkey whose carrot has just been whisked away. She stiffened and drew back a little. He said gently, 'Sorry.' But she knew too well what would happen. He would be sucked into the office – she wouldn't see him again until nightfall. The day had unexpectedly woken up, and now it had just closed down again.

He watched her face shut down, shutting him out. He felt guilty. Then he felt resentful. She seemed always to want something from him that he somehow did not have and could never quite identify. What he had to give was never adequate. He went off to shower and change his clothes.

Chapter 14

February: forty-two days marked off on the new calendar, fifty-three still to go, and a major event interrupts the slow ticking off of days. But not one that has been pencilled in, because until a radio message comes via the office the night before Bee has no idea that Maggie is coming. She arrives on the Unicef plane on her first-ever trip to El Obeid, bearing money from the Handicrafts Project and instructions to buy baskets from the villages.

Bearing gossip, too. Carlo's red Porsche was having a hard time. The Irish setters weren't doing much better, their long silky coats not designed for hot climates, but he already had a waiting list for any puppies among the expatriate community. If they ever managed to produce pups he stood to make a big profit.

'He could try selling the wife, too,' Maggie said. 'You should see the clothes she wears! Even the European men go goggle-eyed!'

It became a running theme between them – the bride, the dogs, the car – reducing them to giggles, confusing Charles when he came in from work late that evening. He looked helplessly from one to the other, unable to extricate the truth from the growing fiction, not sure that they weren't making fun of him. But Bee looked happy for the first time in ages and he was glad Maggie had come. He had arranged a field trip for Maggie the next day to one of the basket-making villages. It was a Friday and his day off so he would stay home with the kids and Bee could go too.

The wind was cool, almost shockingly so, as if the heat had been leached out of it and swallowed up by the bare sand.

Riding in the back of the Land Cruiser, she turned her face to the bright keen air and felt the familiar desiccation as the moisture was sucked out of her skin, cracking her lips, drying the underside of her eyelids. Saaid was driving, preserving an amused, distant silence while Maggie and Amna talked busily about the Handicrafts Project in Northern Kordofan. Bee watched Amna's pretty face, amused to see that under her *thobe* she was wearing curlers.

It felt as if something heavy had lifted off her back. She realised with a shock that she hadn't been out beyond the garden gate for six days. Leaving the graded dirt road with its busy traffic of trucks and lorries, they bounced across the wide open plain towards a small *jebel*, raising a fine cloud of sand behind them. They passed boys herding goats and elegant turbaned men perched on the haunches of white donkeys, riding towards the town with short, tripping steps. A lorry swept towards them out of its private cloud of dust and passed by to their left. The plain was covered with tyre tracks, spread out expansively through the thin, brittle grass that was as yellow as straw.

In the village a tall woman came out to greet them and took them to the wood-lot. They sat in the shade of a thatched *racuba* while they waited for the women to come with their baskets. The wooden posts of the *racuba* were rough and crooked and the thatch was old. Big ants filed endlessly in and out of a large hole in the sand at the bottom of one of the posts. They sat on low stools and talked idly. It was a pretty place. When she looked up at the roof over her head the sun pierced the thatch in magnesium dots, needling her eyes. She looked down again, seeing black dots like shadows.

At last the women began arriving in ones and twos. She had not expected that there would be so many. They crowded forwards, jostling one another with their baskets as they tried to claim attention.

She sat very still on her low stool, watching the women's faces, the children, the bare-bottomed babies. They were all so absorbed, so excited. Laughing, argumentative, pushing forwards until the space under the *racuba* became claustrophobic. Her right ear throbbed with the powerful voice of the tall woman, the village midwife, who was sitting beside her. The smells of stale synthetic cloth, the sweat of hard work, the incense smell of musky perfume overlaid with garlic, made it difficult to breathe. A wave of such utter misery ebbed through her that it felt as if the bottom of her stomach had fallen away. For a moment she even thought she might faint, the falling sensation was so strong. A strange, demanding grief clutched at her throat. In this garden, in the thick of an event so stimulating that everybody else's eyes were shining – the village women's eyes, Amna's eyes, Maggie's eyes – she alone sat silent, excluded by her own sudden misery like a leper.

She is nothing. She is beyond contempt. Unable to enjoy anything. Unlovable. She, least of all, likes the person that she is.

What's wrong with me? she wondered. Am I ill?

Maybe there is something secret and fatal, eating her out from the inside, unseen.

Suddenly Amna – her almond eyes fierce and angry – picked up some of the baskets that were being pushed at them from all sides and flung them to the back of the crowd. The women scattered, laughing and grumbling, to retrieve their precious work. Amna commanded them sternly to form a queue. They did as they were told, making a long snaking line in the sun, each with her baskets carefully set on the sand beside her. The pressure eased and the noise level dropped. The dark oppression of Bee's mood lifted as suddenly as it had descended.

She sat very still, deeply shaken. Cautiously feeling her way back into some kind of normality like a swimmer regaining the surface, she concentrated on what Maggie was saying as if it were a lifeline by which she might haul herself back up. Maggie was explaining what the shop would buy, and what it would pay. Her voice was hoarse from trying to make herself heard over all the shouting. Amna was translating.

'We should do this more often,' Jamil said, brandishing a wooden spatula over the charcoal stove. The stove was made out of an old cheese tin. He had ledged it safely on the slope, wedged between some rocks. Below them the water lapped gently on the shore of the Aulia Dam. Black and white kingfishers stood around on rocks and now and then a large fish plopped in the water, leaving a pattern of fading ripples. Brother fish to the one that Jamil was cooking. Zahara smiled, remembering the fish and chips in Shendi on the way back from their trip to the pyramids when they were children. Jamil would not remember; he had only been a baby.

Mastura brought the other cold-box from the pick-up and Ibrahim carried over a crate half-full of Pepsi. 'He's not lost his knack at cooking then?' he said as he put the crate down beside Zahara. 'After a whole year of married life?'

Jamil snorted with laughter and looked sideways at Mastura.

'He says he's going to start doing the cooking at home,' she said. 'He thinks my cooking is dull.'

'Not dull,' Jamil objected, 'but fried meat and salad for *every* meal does leave some room for competition, don't you think?' He deftly turned the fish and poured more sauce over it from the jar at his side, sending up a sizzling haze of aromatic smoke.

'He always liked cooking,' Zahara said, a hint of pride in her voice. 'And he always thought he was better at it than anybody else – apart from old Faatma, of course. It isn't just you, Mastura.'

'But I have to admit you do make the best mutton stew, big sister.'

Big sister! She had been smaller than him for years. The sun was going down just behind his shoulder, from where Zahara was sitting on her mat. Beyond those hills, she knew (but could not see), the tyre tracks splayed out over the sand like the fingers of a hand, pointing outwards across the desert towards El Obeid and Darfur and far, far away the dead volcano of Jebel Mara, and to the south the besieged city of Juba, swimming in its sea of jungle and of war. All these places that she knew of but had never seen. So many places. The trucks and lorries which they could hear roaring distantly along the main road would be crossing the bare desert just the other side of those hills, each in its own cloud of dust, the bleached bones of cattle and camels laid out like markers along the side of the route pointing the way. My lovely country, she thought, I wish I knew it better. The air was warm and gentle and the calls of the kingfishers sounded mournfully from over the water, beyond the rise and fall of the girls' voices. She watched the girls as they moved along the water's edge. How vulnerable they looked, stepping along the shingle like elegant, long-legged stilts. She felt the familiar quiver of anxiety as she watched them. Children grow up so fast! The air was still and she could hear their sisterly conversation quite clearly. They were discussing Nile perch.

'This is a treat!' she said. She had put the bread and salads out on the big tray, covered with the *tabaq,* and now there was nothing to do except sit side by side with Mastura on the mat and wait while Jamil juggled his fish over the hot charcoal.

'Would you teach me how to cook this mutton stew?' Mastura asked her. 'Or is it difficult?'

'Not difficult, so long as you get the right spices together at the beginning and don't try to rush it. Of course I will show you how to make it! Next time you're free and Jamil isn't making you work too hard in the flat –'

'She never works hard in the flat. When she isn't frying meat and cutting up tomatoes she lies around on the sofa all day and watches Egyptian soaps.'

'I do not!' Mastura exclaimed, but she was laughing. 'It's Jamil who watches the soaps. I'm too busy washing his clothes.'

'Why wouldn't Abu come?' Zahara asked suddenly.

Jamil said, 'He had a headache. And he said he likes to be in bed early and we won't be back till long after his bedtime.'

It sounded a bit feeble to her. Down at the water's edge the girls were skimming stones across the glassy surface. She hoped they were being careful – there might be scorpions hiding under those stones. The water was rosy, the same colour as the sky, and the hills on the other side of the dam were smoky shadows.

Jamil stared out over the lake as he waited for the fish to cook. 'They're having terrible problems with water hyacinth in the dam. It's gone rampant, clogging everything up. They're going to have to use herbicides to kill it off.'

'Oh!' said Zahara, 'I do hope they don't! That's our drinking water!'

'It will be perfectly safe,' Jamil said soothingly. 'These modern herbicides have been thoroughly tested. Come and get it!' he yelled suddenly, lifting the fish off the stove.

Later, they sat on the mats on the stony ground as the sunset went dark and then faded into night. Big bats were flitting. Ibrahim fed dry twigs onto the dying charcoal to keep a small flame burning. How bright everybody's eyes shone in the firelight! Zahara sat with Aasha between her legs leaning drowsily against her. She could feel Aasha's limbs loosening as she drifted towards sleep. Jamil started humming a haunting melody, gazing up into Mastura's face as he lay on the mat beside her.

'What is that?' Mastura asked. He sang it again, with the words this time, and they both burst out laughing. Mastura slapped his shoulder.

'Why did you hit Uncle, Aunty?' Aasha asked, suddenly awake.

'I thought he was singing me a love song but it was a song to his she-camel.'

'It *is* a love song. Just a love song to a camel. Nothing wrong with that.'

'I know one! I know one!' shouted Yasmina. She knelt on the mat as they turned towards her and began to sing loudly, 'Chitty Chitty Bang Bang, Chitty Chitty Bang Bang, Chitty Chitty Bang Bang I love you!'

One field trip was enough. Besides, Catrin was petulant, resentful that she'd been left behind the previous day, and although it was Saturday the school was closed for a one-day holiday. Anyway it was obvious that Charles wanted to go on

229

this trip himself: he'd done the setting up in these villages, not Amna, and he had other business to see to in the same district. He went through the motions of asking if she wanted to go but she could feel he was anxious that she might say yes.

Early in the morning, soon after five-thirty, she heard Maggie and Charles in the quiet camaraderie of early breakfasting without waking anyone else: the scraping of a chair, the muffled clatter of plates, the low murmur of their voices. She heard their feet in tandem as they walked out through the compound, and the clang of the metal gate behind them. Then she fell asleep again. By the time she woke it was nearly eight o'clock and the sun was already hot, and high enough to reach across the floor of the verandah and strike the wall of her bedroom. It was like waking in a prison.

Maggie sat in the front seat next to Saaid, Charles sat in the back. As soon as they left the town he felt his spirits lift. Getting out of El Obeid had become addictive and that was disturbing. He struggled for a few minutes to work out why he should feel it but then he thought he would rather not know.

There had been a shift in the usual tension between him and Maggie these last few days. She was more forgiving. At some point the barbed comments had mysteriously ceased. For his part, he no longer felt the peculiar need to provoke her that he always felt at social gatherings in Khartoum. Perhaps it was just that he was too absorbed in his everyday life to take much notice, rushing around as he was in his usual state of over-drive.

He sat behind her, listening to her talking to Saaid in hesitant, incorrect Arabic. He was impressed: not many expatriate wives learned Arabic. He remembered then that she had a degree in languages. Her face was just visible in the wing-mirror, partially obscured by a large pair of sunglasses. He

230

watched the movements of her mouth as she talked, and the back of her neck, slender under the curling wisps of dark hair that was pinned up on the back of her head. He wondered what she saw in Will, who was so earnest and so dull. Then his mind wandered away, to the rehabilitation of *hafirs*, the reservoirs on which so many communities in Northern Kordofan depended.

In Um Gelgi they looked round the wood-lot while they waited for the women to gather with the baskets. Maggie was curious about everything and her questions were stimulating, jumping all over the place so that he had to rack his brain sometimes for answers. What varieties are the trees? Where are all the men? Do camels eat thorn trees? When are the crops harvested? When the women came she made him translate her questions, direct and probing. How many children do you have? Do they go to school? When do you have time to make baskets? Where are your husbands? Are widows and divorced women free to marry again? The women replied, sometimes with enthusiasm, sometimes embarrassed, but always appreciative. In one hour he learned more about the village than he had during his numerous previous visits. It wasn't just the fresh energy of her curiosity, it was the fact that she was a woman, and she was curious about things he had never thought to ask about. The women responded to her differently from the way they did to him.

He watched her secretly, with new respect. Of which she seemed quite oblivious.

In Hamdan the women brought out some big shallow baskets with an edging of purple and blue. Maggie pounced on them. 'Now *these* – these are wonderful! Look at them! Simple, but really striking.' She looked up at Charles, who was watching her with amusement as she squatted on the sand

231

beside the baskets. 'Tell them we can take almost any number of these.'

He laughed: that might prove rash. He translated. The circle of women nodded solemnly. He was willing to bet that on his next visit he would be inundated with plain baskets with blue and purple rims.

After the meeting, the *gafir* of the wood-lot came up to him and complained that the women were too busy making baskets to work in the wood-lot any more, they wanted to pay him to do the work instead. Charles was amused: it wasn't what had been intended when Unicef had set up the two projects side by side. Human inventiveness sometimes had a way of re-writing projects from the bottom up.

They stopped in Bara for a late *fatur* of beans and bread. In the shady street, sitting with Saaid at the metal table, Maggie took off her sunglasses and looked around her at the quiet scene spread out along the broad sandy road under the *neem* trees. Saaid was leaning over towards the men on the next table, discussing family connections to see if they had relatives in common.

'You are lucky, living out of Khartoum,' she said, looking Charles very straight in the eye.

'I know.' Then he added gloomily 'But I'm not sure Bee feels the same way.'

She looked at him seriously, with a directness that was quite disturbing. 'She isn't happy, is she.'

He said nothing.

She went on, 'She looks strong. Outwardly she's so calm and serene. But there's something about her that feels vulnerable. It's as if there's an awful lot going on underneath but you can't see what it is.'

'I've always felt that and I've been married to her for nearly thirteen years. I never know what she's thinking.' He picked at his bread moodily. 'I feel I'm letting her down all the time. It was a big mistake, really, bringing them all out here.'

Maggie looked at him sharply. 'That bad? I know she's not happy but I didn't think it was as bad as that!'

'Perhaps it isn't. I'm not sure I can handle it any more, that's all.' He'd said more than he'd meant to. More than he'd even consciously thought. He was aware that Saaid had turned back to the table but was excluded because they were talking in English. Abruptly he changed the subject. 'Really, while we're here, I ought to visit the drilling rigs north of Bara. Would you mind? It'll make us pretty late back.'

'Course not – I'd love to!'

He smiled, and translated for Saaid.

The rig, when they reached it, was in the middle of drilling a bore-hole. Sand spewed upwards into the afternoon sunshine and the team of men were shouting to one another over the high-pitched whine of the drill, their voices hoarse and expectant.

They stayed for a long time, waiting and watching. The spewed sand became damp. Then wet. Suddenly, water shot upwards in a spume, full of stones. A cheer went up and the men patted one another on the back. They grinned at Maggie, white teeth shining in dirty, sweat-drenched faces.

'Wow!' she said as they walked back to the vehicle. 'That was worth waiting for!'

The foreman wanted a lift back into El Obeid to fetch a spare part. Two of his crew asked for lifts as well. They piled cheerfully into the Land Cruiser, the foreman and one of the workers in the front, the other in the back with Charles and Maggie.

233

The conversation was fast and furious in Arabic, all the way back to El Obeid. Saaid joined in, so did Charles for a while, until the effort got too much: they were all talking at once and too fast for him to follow.

He felt Maggie's warmth beside him, the pressure of her arm and thigh against his as they were thrown about by the jolting of the vehicle. It was uncomfortable but rather nice. She began to talk again about Bee, and in their squashed seclusion he found himself talking about things he had told no one, not even admitted to himself. How remote she was, how lonely that could make him feel. How she seemed unreachable, and his efforts to reach her anyway so poor and clumsy that often they seemed to push her further away. He said things that alarmed him, drawn out unexpectedly by the situation they were in, bumping along a sandy track at the end of a long day, side by side, without eye contact, in the company of strangers and under the cover of their noisy, incomprehensible conversation.

She listened. She asked him questions he couldn't duck. She said wise things that made him feel heard, and others that made him look at things differently. She was Bee's friend. It made it feel safe to talk to her, and very comforting.

Everything Bee did was wrong. First she put the wrong jam on Adam's bread at breakfast. Then she hadn't washed his teddy, as promised, after the bear's encounter with a bottle of ink yesterday. They were all punishing her for going out on the field trip without them but Adam was the crossest.

'Anyway,' he said, coming back to hound her in the kitchen as she washed up the breakfast things, 'Anyway, Fred can't go in the washing machine cos he'll get dizzy.'

'No he won't,' Bee said, near the end of her patience, 'Teddies are made to go in washing machines.'

'No they isn't!' he screamed. 'Anyway, teddies isn't made. They're borned!'

There was a momentary lull. She went on washing up. Suddenly a small boy flung himself on her from behind, kicking fiercely at her legs as he shouted through his tears, 'Anyway you're cruel! You mustn't put teddies in the washing machine! You mustn't!'

'Adam! Adam – stop that! You're hurting me, Adam!' She turned, half crouching and tried to pull him to her to comfort him and stop him hurting her, but he was like a crazed little animal. So quiet compared with Kit, yet when he got into a rage (usually unexpectedly and always shockingly) he was almost frightening. He fought his way out of her grasp and ran crying to the bedroom, where he slammed both doors.

Alone at the sink, she realised she was trembling.

Later, when Adam had re-emerged, distant and stoical, and the offending bear was soaking safely in a bucket of water, she realised that the nausea she was feeling was physical, not emotional. Then she had a bout of diarrhoea. This probably explained Adam's behaviour, not to mention her own strange little crisis yesterday in Ban Gedeid. The thought – and a second bout of diarrhoea – made her feel a little better but she watched Adam cautiously, waiting for the worst. They were often ill like this, one or another of them, going down like skittles, and then after an uneasy interlude they just as suddenly bounced upright again. (Except for the time Catrin turned out to have amoebic dysentery, and the two occasions when she'd had malaria.) This time, Adam was very pale but nothing happened. There was no sudden throwing up, or desperate and ineffectual rushing for the toilet.

Her own legs felt weak. It was not un-pleasurable, this rag-doll emptiness, so long as you didn't have to actually get anything done.

235

It was dusk when Charles and Maggie came in, cheerful and thoughtless, full of their own day. Neither of them asked very much about hers before going off, one after the other, to shower in the cold, draughty bathroom. She bathed the little ones on the verandah in the big red washing bowl with a pan of hot water, wondering quite what the point was since the water came out of the tap dirtier than they were. She read them their stories. Then she began to chop up the usual onions, courgettes and aubergines to make yet another variation on the same supper. Charles came into the kitchen and offered to give her a hand but by then she had nearly finished. Maggie seemed to be reading the children another story when they'd already had one from her.

Next morning they sat on the floor packing up baskets for Maggie to take back to Khartoum on the Unicef plane tomorrow. Bee felt better this morning, and more forgiving. Maggie made her laugh with stories of the village women yesterday.

They drifted into their familiar pattern of talk. 'He puts so much of himself into his job,' Bee said, 'There's nothing much left over for me and the children.'

But Maggie replied, 'Poor old Charles! He is doing his best, isn't he?' She was looking down, tying a label onto a stack of baskets, she didn't see Bee staring at her coldly.

She didn't say a word. She clamped shut like a flower curling in on itself. This was not the way the conversation was supposed to run. Besides, did Maggie think she *did not* know how hard it was for Charles? Did she not understand that this knowledge was part of the trap?

'Of course I know how difficult it is for you,' Maggie said hurriedly when she saw the look on Bee's face. 'All I meant was, isn't it worse if you blame him when you might be friends together? You know, in adversity?'

Bee got up and went out of the room.

Maggie came to find her in the kitchen. 'I'm sorry, Bee. Did I upset you? I didn't mean to...'

'You didn't. I'm making coffee.' She kept her voice carefully neutral. 'You carry on with the labelling. I'll bring the coffee in a minute.'

When she came back Maggie was on her knees among the baskets. They sat for a while, Bee on a chair, Maggie on the floor, drinking their coffee in their separate silences. Then Maggie said, 'But isn't it true, what I said? Isn't it true for both of us? We can't afford not to be on the same side as them. Or as each other, come to that.'

She ducked the issue by simply staying silent. A little while later she made an excuse and left the room. This time, Maggie did not follow.

In the kitchen, Bee washed up the coffee cups, relieved, aggrieved and furious all at the same time. How dare Maggie patronise her like that! Coming down here like the Queen of Khartoum and telling her how to live her life!

'Here you are, pet,' she said to Catrin, handing her the plastic beaker of water. Catrin seized the cup with both hands and drank thirstily. 'Steady on poppet!' She said the words and laughed the laugh but her mind was somewhere else entirely, black thoughts bubbling up like tar.

It was nearly six when he got in from work and the light was fading. The atmosphere was strangely charged: he wondered if they'd had an argument. But they got through the evening rituals of feeding and bedding the children without any revelations. Maggie suddenly said she was going out for a walk, even though it was dark. 'Why don't you come, Bee? We haven't been out of the house all day! '

Bee looked up from her book. 'No, I don't want to come for a walk.'

Maggie said, an edge of pleading in her voice, 'Wouldn't it do you good to get out and have a breath of fresh air, same as me?'

Bee went back to her book. 'No it wouldn't. And I am *not* the same as you.'

Betrayal, she was thinking. I speak in my code – our code – and you've been replying in his. I'm not supposed to have to explain myself to you, another woman, supposedly my friend! We're supposed to speak the same language. You know how it feels – how worthless I feel, how unconsidered, a kind of possession, to be exported and then overlooked. I shouldn't have to explain this, or defend my position. Not to you. You of all people should understand that I know I'm being unreasonable but what else can I be in the space that is left for me?

And what is it that is going on between you, between you and him? That you speak for him and do not listen for me? That you take his side, against me? The excitement between you – which I chose to overlook before – the way he looks at you, and the way you look back? That feeling of special attention between you, as if your senses are on alert whenever you're both in the same room. Excluding me. Overlooking me.

I've known it all the time. I chose not to see it before.

And if he is not there for me, why am I here at all?

Charles, in the kitchen helping Bee make a late supper, looked at her warily. She kept her face averted. She was angry, that much was clear, but he still had no idea who she was angry with or why. What had he done now? Or was it something

238

which had gone on today between her and Maggie? Was that why Maggie had left so hurriedly to go out for a walk? But then he had heard her asking Bee to go with her and Bee had refused. He couldn't spot any clues but something told him it would not be wise to ask her what was the matter.

He sighed. Felt her look at him as she stood, closed off into herself, chopping onions by the sink. He sighed again, unconsciously.

She had always been complicated to live with – he was used to getting by on a trial and error basis. But it was getting to be really difficult to keep up with her chameleon moods. One minute she'd be normal, blithe and even-tempered, the next she'd withdraw into herself. And most often he had no idea why. But it was made so much harder by the fact that he felt so damnably guilty, for putting her through this at all. And it was difficult to know what to do about it, short of taking her back to England, and he couldn't do that. He didn't even think she would want him to if he could. It would feel like failure to her, not to have stuck it out to the end. She had said so, more than once.

They sat uneasily at the table on the back verandah, eating their supper in near silence under the bare light bulb and the fluctuating voltage. A cold wind was blowing briskly through the mosquito netting. Maggie had come in from her walk looking subdued but reasonably cheerful. Chares looked at her now and then as they ate, still watching her and Bee for some clue to the continuing undercurrent of tension. After a while, since Bee outwardly behaved as if nothing was wrong, he began to feel impatient. If she was going to make no effort to be sociable then he damned well wasn't going to let her moodiness dominate. He began to talk about the Handicrafts

Project and Maggie responded. The tension eased a little. Bee remained largely silent, monosyllabic in her replies, and after a while the other two gave up trying to draw her into the conversation. In any case their own enthusiasm got the better of them. The discussion became animated.

Maggie insisted on doing the washing up and he stayed in the kitchen to carry on the conversation. Bee moved around them, clearing up, her silence oblique and significant. Maggie looked at her, smiling, asking her some question. She affected not to have heard and made no reply. She left the room and didn't come back.

'Is she all right?' Maggie asked Charles anxiously, under cover of the clattering of plates.

Taking the plate from her to dry it, he said, 'I was going to ask you the same thing.' It felt conspiratorial, side by side at the sink, carefully not touching, hyper-sensitive to the spaces between and around them, one of which was filled by the black cloud of Bee's mood.

'Oh dear,' Maggie said. 'I think it's probably my fault then, but I don't know what I said that was bad enough to make her quite so angry with me.'

Charles said gloomily 'I hardly ever know.'

And Bee sits in the sitting room, a book on her lap, but in her head she is walking from the steps of End Point, along the restless river. Past the wooden shacks, past the old ferry hut, inland along the river dyke towards the bridge. Hold on, hold on – only another fifty days to go, she tells herself. Away from the river across the common, back to the village. Down the street, counting off the houses one by one. The long calming ritual of her childhood and her youth. Past the shop, the solicitor's run-down cottage with its faded plaque, the garage which hires out bicycles, the public toilets. *Fifty days.* Past the Old Pottery, past the village green. *Fifty lifetimes.* Past the Bell Inn, over the sea wall and back to End Point, where the tide in the creek is running out and the sea smell is rising salt and wild.

Chapter 15

'Hello!' Mastura's clear, light voice rose up the outside staircase. 'Hello!'

Faatma ran to the door to let her in. Zahara, washing up at the sink, could hear Mastura saying to Faatma, her voice slightly breathless from the stairs, 'Today we speak in English, yes?' and Faatma's laughing reply, 'Of course, Aunty.'

'Come in, Mastura! We're in the kitchen,' Zahara called in English.

Mastura appeared in the doorway, a plastic bowl covered with a cloth under one arm, a big bag of vegetables in her other hand. She took off her *thobe* and folded it carefully.

'Oh Aunty, I like your hair!' Jamila said, holding onto Mastura's arm and gazing up admiringly at the long narrow plaits, which had been freshly braided. The beads in the braids clinked and chinked musically with every movement of her head.

Mastura put her bags down on the table. 'Today we speak in English, no?'

Zahara nodded. 'Have you got everything off the list? I got the *jir-jir* and the mint this morning.'

'Oh, slowly, slowly!' Mastura exclaimed, holding up her hands. '*Jir-jir* is English word?' she asked, surprised.

'No, but I don't know what it is in English'

'Rocket, Mummy. Sam's mum said it's called rocket in

English,' Faatma said as she peeked under the cloth that covered Mastura's bowl. 'That's an awful lot of meat!'

'Your uncle very hungry man.'

Aasha suddenly squeezed between them and plucked at the front of Mastura's dress. 'See, Aunty? See my new...' She hesitated – looked at her mother for help. 'What is they called in English?' she whispered.

'Glasses.'

Aasha turned back to Mastura and said, suddenly shy, 'I got new glasses!'

'Yes, I see them. You have new glasses. Very beautiful glasses,' Mastura added as Aasha gazed up at her anxiously through the blue steel frames of her unfamiliar spectacles.

Aasha grinned. She had not been sure, in the calm of this morning, whether she was so pleased with these new glasses after all. 'She only got them yesterday,' Zahara said. 'Now we know that the reason she couldn't read was because she could not see the words. But now you can see them, can't you Aasha? Now you will be able to learn to read properly.'

'I see everything now!'

'She could see the spider behind the bathroom sink this morning, too,' Faatma said. 'She wasn't so pleased about that.

'I not like spiders,' Aasha said. She peered into Mastura's shopping bag. 'What this?' She pulled out a paper bag of spices.

'Careful!' Mastura said quickly in Arabic. 'You're getting chilli on your hands. No! Don't touch your face!' She led Aasha to the sink and lifted her to wash her hands under the tap.

'Are we speaking Arabic now?' Aasha asked as Mastura bent to dry her fingers carefully, one by one.

'No, no. Now you learn me English and learn me cook too.'

'Teach you,' Zahara corrected, putting knives and chopping

boards out on the table. 'Now we will teach you English, and I will teach you how to cook the mutton stew that Jamil particularly loves.'

'Particularly?' said Mastura. She tried the word out again, experimentally: 'Particularly.'

'Do you want to play snakes and ladders with me?' Jamila asked Aasha.

'Sneks? N'leders?' Aasha said uncertainly, wrinkling up her nose. Faatma translated for her. 'Yes yes! We play that!'

Zahara said 'Not in here – you can't play in here while we are cooking, we need the table. No, not there either, Jamila, we will fall over you if you play on the floor in the kitchen. Take it to the living room. Or your bedroom.'

'Do we have to play in English?' Jamila asked anxiously, pausing in the doorway. 'No, only the kitchen is an English zone today,' Zahara said. Some days they spoke English for practice in every room all day long. 'First, we shall cut up the meat.'

She looked at Mastura sitting at her table – her gleaming skin, her shining eyes – cutting up meat. Blood stained her slender hands, and Zahara looked at them, thinking that she cut the meat like a surgeon, precise and regular. And like a surgeon, complained that the knife was not sharp enough. And as they gossiped and worked, and laughed at Faatma's very bad jokes, and explained things to Yasmina who in her eight years had done even less cooking than Mastura had in her twenty-two, Zahara realised that what she was feeling was happiness. Life shifted and let Mastura in, and they were truly a family again.

Yasmina was standing by Mastura's shoulder as she sat at the kitchen table, gazing at Mastura's long braids. She put out her hand and touched the clinking beads gently.

Mastura looked up. 'Will I braid yours, Yasmina?'

'And me, Aunty!' Aasha squealed, arrested on her way to the tap for a drink of water. 'And me! I want beads.'

Mastura pulled her onto her knee and smoothed down her fluffy head. 'It is short for braids but we will do little ones.' She looked up at Zahara and her eyes were like water in a rock pool, full of light. 'I will ask my grandfather to invite you and Ibrahim and the girls to his house in the Gezira. You will like it. It has a place for a fire. You know, made of brick. A fireplace, my grandfather calls it?'

'A *fireplace*?'

'Yes. A real one.' She giggled suddenly. 'It was an Englishman's house once. But if you can have a fire – I do not know. It is just to look, I think. You come to my grandfather's house and we will braid all your hairs and henna all your feets.'

Two weeks after Maggie's visit, getting ready to go up to Khartoum for the first programme meeting for several months, Bee thought cautiously about Maggie, testing her feelings. The bad thoughts had largely abated. She remembered, chiefly, resentment. That she should be disregarded even by those she loved.

Jealousy was more dangerous. She pushed the word away.

There were no flats or houses available in Khartoum this time; they must dip into their precious savings again and book a room at the Acropole. How strange it was that she – who cared little for material things – should find herself behaving so much like a miser. She was not so much miserly about money as about the future. The future had no shape or colour. It had a vague form – a house near the Suffolk sea – but it made her vulnerable. The present stretched so interminably that it threatened to swallow up the future. What if she should die here? Every time they flew she thought this thought. She

245

saw her existence framed by this ugly landscape and she felt diminished. If she were to die, this would be all that was left of her identity, she would become Bee Who Died In The Sudan. She would be swallowed whole.

Khartoum is grim, a heavy *haboob* grips the city and wraps its hot, gritty blanket around the streets in a vicious embrace. The brown fog exaggerates the acrid stink of rubbish and the traffic fumes. The glare of the hidden sun strikes downwards through the thick air and glances painfully off the windscreens and the roofs of the cars.

At the Sudan Club the pump has broken down and the swimming pool is full of dirty brown water, though there are still people swimming in it. 'No, you can't swim!' she says, and the children are too awed by the colour of the pool to protest much.

Everywhere in Khartoum the drinking water tastes foul. It has a strange chemical smell to it. But they are so thirsty that they drink it all the same.

They go for supper with Maggie and Will but it isn't like it used to be. The easy friendship has gone. Charles and Maggie hardly speak to each other at all. It seems to Bee that they barely look at one another.

Until the moment of leaving. That is the moment when she catches a look between them, full of unspoken meaning. Instantly jealousy returns, cascading down on her head. She says goodnight stiffly, kisses Maggie distantly. Harbouring her suspicions like a winter store, settling them in ice.

It is a relief to go back to El Obeid.

Thirty-nine days left.

Malik was still watering the front garden when they went to bed but they'd had to be up at four that morning to get on the

246

Unicef plane and they were all exhausted. Lying in bed, Charles at her back already snoring softly, she didn't go to sleep at once. She could feel the long line of his spine resting against hers. A tremendous sadness seeped through her, like blood leaking from a wound. Once, if they went to bed early, it would have been to make love. She lay wondering when they *had* last made love. Not in their hotel room in Khartoum, shared with the children, nor the week before that. A month ago? She couldn't actually remember. They seemed to sleep like strangers in the same bed, back to back.

She shifted away, trying to get cool. The air was heavy, full of stillness in spite of the slow revolutions of the fan. No wind whispered tonight and the thermometer had hardly dropped at all after dark. The mosquito net, hanging festive and bridal over them, seemed to enclose and exaggerate the heat. It smelled of dust. She lay for a while feeling the faint stirrings of desire like a half-forgotten language she was losing for lack of practice. I'll be thirty-four next birthday, she thought, and life is slipping away. I'll be old and it will all be too late. A hot tear spilled from the corner of one eye and slid down her cheek-bone to pool in her hair. Too late. My life drained out of me here, in this dusty expanse of landscape where I have no colour and no energy. A pale shadow without much meaning. A fat, pale shadow, she thinks, remorselessly. Who would want me now? Charles, the children – they want my presence for the comfort of it, but do they really want me? Do they even see me?

Thirty-three, thirty-four in November. My best time passed already. Invisibly. Like water down a drain. Suddenly life is half over before I was properly ready.

Is this all there is?

247

There was a loud banging on the metal gate of the compound. It roused them only slowly from the depths of sleep, disoriented, unsure what had woken them. The banging came again, urgent, insistent. Charles took his Thai sarong and wrapped it hastily round his waist as he hurried, bare-chested, out to the gate.

She drifted back into sleep, then woke suddenly with a start. It was very still, very quiet. Not a whisper, not a rustle. Charles had disappeared. She lay listening, her heart suddenly pounding rapidly. She could hear nothing else at all.

She got up and walked, naked, along the verandah to the kitchen. In the bushes, a hasty rustle betrayed the presence of the feral cat and her single kitten. They stared up at her through the netting, suspicious-eyed and wary. She padded on towards the kitchen. A gecko ran across the verandah floor and up the wall, a colourless secretive shadow against the brash green brick. In the kitchen, disturbed by the light, the cockroaches made for the cracks. There was the usual clunk as the kitchen gecko ran under the fridge. She got herself a glass of water and went back to bed.

It was never fully dark in the house unless there was a power cut, and there had been fewer of those since the Dutch had arrived to up-grade the power station. The street light made eerie shadows across the verandah. There was no breeze. She listened.

Not a sound.

Back in bed she waited but Charles didn't come back. The stillness and the silence began to feel ominous, like the lull before disaster. She wondered where he could have gone. Where could he have gone dressed only in a sarong? The oddness of him going out of the house without dressing began to weigh on her. Something must surely be wrong. She lay very

248

still and listened intently. The blood pounded in her ears. She swallowed nervously and it sounded loud. It was as if the whole world had disappeared, leaving her solitary and unguarded. She must go and make sure that the children were still there, sleeping safely in their beds.

They lay, innocent in the grip of sleep. She stood looking down on them, one by precious one. Even Danny, whose room she rarely ventured into, respecting his privacy now. She looked at him sleeping quietly beneath his mosquito net. How much a child he looked, growing up fast as he was. Reassured, she went back to her own bed. But the fear still lurked.

If something had happened, if there was some kind of silent uprising and Charles had been spirited away, how would she know? It would sound like this – a conspiracy of silence. It would feel like this – the slow realisation that the stillness had no innocence, that disaster had struck sideways and without tremor, like suffocation with a pillow in the secrecy of sleep. And what would she do? If they came for her now, what would she do? If, out of the night's opaque stillness, the attack came?

Mentally she mapped it out. How she would run, gathering the children. She would pull them under their double bed (it was big enough to hide them all) clapping her hands over the little ones' mouths, imploring silence from Kit who was never silent, from Danny who always argued, whatever he was told to do. She would—

The gate clanged open and shut.

Charles came in, cheerful and ordinary. 'That was Louise and Ed. You know, from Dilling. Their vehicle broke down on the way back from Khartoum – they've been on the road for more than eighteen hours! They wanted me to take them to the Rest House for the night.'

'What time is it, for God's sake?' The abruptness of relief

made her sound irritable. She could feel the fizz of the blood subsiding in her veins.

'Nearly twelve.'

She fell back on the pillows, disoriented. Of course! They had gone to bed so very early, it had made it seem much later than that. Four o'clock and her fears seemed not unreal. Less than midnight and they looked foolish. But her heart was still pounding as if she had been running. He clambered back into bed.

Embarrassed now by her private fears she avoided his eye, and when, lying beside her, he put his hand on her breast she kept her face averted, pretending she was already asleep.

Chapter 16

He set out for Kadugli before dawn, on his own. He had tried to persuade her to come with the children but she wouldn't. So he went alone on the Unicef plane, looking down on the landscape he knew so well now from the ground. Even here in the Nuba Mountains everything was as brown and burned off as it was further north in El Obeid. But still he wished that she had come. Something felt askew between them and the trip to Khartoum, instead of giving them the positive break he'd hoped for, had only exaggerated the feeling of distance. She couldn't – or wouldn't – find enthusiasm for anything any more.

The children, thankfully, seemed okay, though as going on leave loomed closer they were getting a bit unmanageable. On the whole though this was the only life they really knew, except for Danny perhaps, and he was naturally stoical and didn't seem to mind that he was missing so much that other boys had at home. Charles watched him with some pride, seeing himself at the same age, self-contained and strong. Kit was more awkward, but then that was Kit – always on the go, always on edge, never still. Adam and Catrin simply accepted things as they found them. If only Bee weren't so unsettled they would be surviving quite nicely. They might even be considering seriously whether they might stay on.

Watching the hills circling beneath him as the plane swung

251

round to line up with the dirt strip that served as Kadugli's runway, the thought that had been lurking darkly in his head, just under the surface, suddenly reared up and stared him in the face. How was he ever going to adjust to life back in the university? To living in safe, ordinary Norwich, or safe, ordinary Suffolk? He had managed to bury himself in the present and put all that to one side, a future he didn't need to face head on for a while yet. But time was passing and the end of his contract, at Christmas, was already being talked of by his superiors. Calvin at his back whenever he was in Khartoum murmuring, 'Thought about that extension yet, Charles?' Staring at him with those piercing blue eyes, the mouth unreadable under the moustache. Calvin, who always seemed to know clearly what was right and what was wrong, with his Shirley at his back, as sure as he was, like two Crusaders mounted on one war-horse. 'Port Sudan is yours, if you want it,' Calvin had said last time they met, pausing as he rushed between meetings with the minister, with the Prime Minister (Calvin was moving in high circles now). And Charles was flattered but he gave no clear answer. 'Why not make your career in Unicef?' Calvin had shot back over his shoulder as he left the room.

He had told Bee nothing of this. It wasn't that he hadn't tried to, but in her remote and touchy state she was liable to misunderstand him and go off at tangents. It was as if he was talking in a foreign language: he thought he was saying one thing but she seemed to hear another. Why don't you come to Khartoum, he'd said before the last programme meeting, we'll fork out the money and stay in the Acropole. I'll miss you, and I'm worried about leaving you behind, he said. But she had somehow heard, I need you to come so that I can feel better. How could he embark on so formidable a discussion as the extension of his contract?

He seemed to have lost the art of making her happy. Perhaps he'd never had it but it hadn't been exposed before. Were they growing apart, or was it just the pressures here that made them so distant from one another?

He thought of Maggie as the plane rolled to a stop and François came round to open the door and let them out. Her enthusiasm and vitality were deeply attractive. He had been thinking a lot about the day they had spent out in the field together. Trying not to think, If only Bee could be more like that!

He wondered idly, as he climbed down from the plane and stretched in the sun, had they been in different circumstances, might they have had a thing going, Maggie and him? But it was a meaningless thought, too hedged around with the realities of her life with Will, and his with Bee and the kids. She was like a ray of light, though, flashing across his life and lighting things up. He'd have liked to get to know her as a friend but he knew he never would. Too dangerous, for one thing. And for another, she and Will were likely to be leaving soon, if Will managed to land the job in Accra that he'd applied for. It was just as well, really, since Bee seemed to be watching them now like a hawk. If jealousy was the reason she was so angry with him it was sadly ridiculous – the only private conversations he'd ever had with Maggie had mostly been about Bee. But she was right to be suspicious. He was suspicious of himself.

He had arranged on the radio that he would stay with Dave as usual. Dave from Derby, by nature impatient but particularly so with him. Dave seemed to see him as a jumped-up academic with little experience of the real world, while he saw Dave as bullish and liable to make significant mistakes. It would have been better if Bee and the children had been here: they would have taken the edge off things. But it wasn't only that. When he got to Dave's pretty little house and found it full of people and very lively he knew she would have enjoyed it. Louise and Ed who worked for Action Aid in Dilling were here, and two French doctors from *Médicins Sans Frontières*. And a couple of pretty English girls who Dave seemed to have picked up somewhere, who were doing some kind of study for the health department but were having trouble getting travel permits so they had been stuck in Kadugli for several weeks. They were on the verge of giving up and going back to Khartoum. Dave told Charles this wistfully, as if he had tried unsuccessfully to persuade them to stay longer.

The days in the office were hectic but the evenings were sociable and fun. They sat out in the garden under the oleander trees, hardly troubled by mosquitoes, under a wealth of stars and a young moon. His regret that Bee hadn't come faded as he began to enjoy himself. And since she had chosen not to come he didn't feel guilty for being happy in her absence.

He was aware of the eyes of one of the girls, lingering on him admiringly. She was… well, she was quite beautiful. He felt himself responding like a cat, stretching, purring. It was obvious that Dave fancied Liz himself. He glowered at Charles in her presence by night. By day he found fault with each and every suggestion that Charles made. Even down to his suggestion that they might take a look at the new latrines before they went out of town to look at the hand-pump programme.

She had always liked the thock… thock… sound the rackets made as they hit the balls. A lazy summer sound that made her think of grass, and daisies, though tennis was a winter game here, played on dusty brick-red courts. They never seemed to have time to play much these days but this afternoon, after work, Ibrahim had announced that it was high

254

time Faatma sorted out her serve before it got too hot to want to play at all.

They were in the middle of a gentle game of doubles, Ibrahim and Faatma against her and Yasmina. In the corner of the court Jamila and Aasha seemed to have reverted to a private game of French cricket.

'Like this,' Ibrahim said, demonstrating the arm movement to Faatma. How she was growing! She was nearly as tall as him now. Her long lanky body was beginning to develop shapes – hips, little chest buds. Zahara noticed this with surprise. If you don't watch your children all the time they change while your back is turned! Faatma's white shorts were getting too small, they really ought to get her some new ones. It made Zahara feel sad, looking at her growing up so fast. Anxious, in the way the sheer speed of a fairground ride makes you feel nervous. They were all growing up too fast, her little chicks! Faatma beginning to be knowing and womanly. What sort of a future will they have? It was a bit outrageous to ask for four doses of luck as great as her own had been, finding Ibrahim. Would they all find husbands as good and as generous as he was, or would they find husbands like Miriam's Osman who would make them wear *thobes* and take away their small freedoms?

Yasmina stubbed the ground with the end of her racket. 'Don't do that,' Zahara chided automatically, but the racket was really too big for Yasmina and she was probably finding it heavy.

'I'm bored, Mummy. Can't we just *play*?'

'Abu wants Faatma to learn to play properly.'

'But proper playing isn't so much fun!'

She smiled. 'No – it isn't, is it? It's always so much more fun being improper.'

'Improper?' Yasmina pounced on the new English word but Ibrahim was calling out that they were ready to play again.

255

A few volleys later there was another pause, another discussion of technique.

'I'd rather go and play with Jam and Aash,' Yasmina said.

'But Faatma needs us. Just a little longer, Yasmina,' she pleaded. The ball came sailing nicely over the net and she ran to her right to knock it back. It really was getting too hot for this. Yasmina ran for the next ball and sent it back to Faatma neatly. No Jamil and Mastura at Abu's house last week, but they were all invited this Friday, to Mastura's grandfather's house in the Gezira, and Abu had agreed to come too. It would be the first Friday they had all gone out together for a very long time. It would be fun, but it would be proper. Certainly nobody would be in shorts. If they were female, they wouldn't even be in trousers.

There was a knock on the front door. She opened it to find Leslie standing there, her usually cheerful face anxious.

'Bee – I'm glad you're here! I thought you might have gone down to Kadugli with Charles.'

It struck her, not for the first time, how other people always seemed to know where Charles was and what he was doing, possibly better than she did. 'Why – what's the matter?'

'It's Daz. He's in our house. He's ill, I don't know what with. Could be dysentery, but he's really sick and I'm worried about him, with all of us out working in the daytime. And he hasn't seen a doctor. I think he should.'

Bee stood nonplussed. She looked behind her into the room where Catrin was sitting on the floor absorbed in a jigsaw puzzle. She looked back at Leslie's worried face. She wasn't sure what she could usefully do. She didn't even know where the doctor's surgery was – it had been Charles who took Catrin there last time she had malaria.

'I was wondering, you couldn't have him here, could you? I know it's a lot to ask but I don't like him being on his own all day long, if only because he's getting very depressed and that's not like him.'

'What if he's infectious?' Especially not now! she was thinking in her secret heart. Not now when there are only twenty-three days left to go.

'I knew you'd say that. He probably isn't particularly, not if it's dysentery and you're careful. But of course you're right to be worried, with the children.'

Resilient Leslie, small and wiry, who strode round the town at such a brisk pace that she was known by the locals as 'the woman who walks' – she wasn't looking at all resilient now. She looked tired and rather miserable. Bee took pity on her. It wouldn't do any harm at least to go and see him quickly. But she had to ask Leslie to stay with the children while she did.

It felt very odd, walking into someone else's house, but nobody answered when she knocked on the metal gate to the compound. She opened it, and crossed the hot, silent yard to the front door. She banged on the door for form's sake, then opened it and listened. The house was dark after the brilliant sunlight and very still. She called but nobody answered. She kicked off her canvas shoes and went in. In the middle of the shadowy room she stopped and listened intently. From one of the rooms opening off on the left her ear caught the slightest sound of a groan.

He was asleep, dressed only in the stripy drawers she recognised from the party, lying on his back with one hand resting across a bare chest which was no longer slender but painfully thin. She was shocked at the sight of him. His face was haggard, even in sleep. The bones of his rib-cage stood out. A sparse, gingery stubble discoloured his pale cheeks. He moaned again, shifting restlessly, and frowned in his sleep. As he turned his head towards her his eyes opened and he stared at the part of her blue dress that was level with his eyes.

'Daz,' she said softly.

Slowly his eyes travelled up her dress to rest on her face.

'Blimey,' he said faintly. 'Are you an angel?'

'What in God's name have you been doing to yourself?'

'Don't come too close – don't know what I've got. Could be something exciting like bubonic plague...'

'You look dreadful.'

He grinned weakly. 'Thanks!'

'You're terribly thin.'

'Well it ain't no picnic, not in Babanusa.' He closed his eyes as if the effort of talking was too much. He looked so young and vulnerable. She couldn't leave him like this. Her mind moved rapidly, thinking out strategies. A bed at home, at the end of the far verandah they didn't use much, beyond the bathroom: that could be shut off. That would be possible, if she told the children to keep away. Which they would find hard to accept, but not when they saw him, probably. And get him to a doctor. That was essential. But how to get him home?

'Are you fit to walk? You don't look it.'

He said, not opening his eyes, 'Don't know. Haven't tried to walk further than the bog for a few days. My head's busting. I'm aching all over like I'm about to fall apart.' There was a long pause. His eyes flicked open and looked up at her. 'Problem is, my guts aren't all that reliable. Tendency to get taken short. Embarrassing.' He added in a murmur, 'Specially in the circumstances.'

What did that mean? His eyes had flicked shut again. She stood looking down at him, feeling helpless. Perhaps if she went over to the office she'd find someone there who could fetch him in a Unicef vehicle. And ferry him to the doctor's. But she wasn't sure if she would be within her rights to ask it, not for a friend.

'Walk where, anyway?' came his voice, from far away, his eyes still closed.

'I'm taking you home to my house. You need looking after.'

He was smiling, his eyes still shut. 'That's the best thing I've heard for weeks.'

'But how do we get you there?'

If she were to go to the office first it would take her a long time, and in the meantime Leslie was stuck in the house with the children. Where were the others – Claire, Melanie? John? Would they be in soon from work?

''Spect I could make it as far as your house,' he said slowly. 'If we took it nice and gentle. Shall we give it a whirl?'

She looked around for his *jelabiya*. It was crumpled in a corner, on the floor. Daz was as untidy as Danny. He sat up slowly, clutching his stomach as if in pain. She helped him feed his thin arms into the awkward garment. He paused, exhausted by the effort, sitting hunched on the edge of the bed.

He groaned. 'Think I'd better take a precautionary turn to the shit-house first.' He got up stiffly and hobbled off to the outside latrine. She couldn't avoid hearing the ominous gurgling sounds, which came through the closed door across the small courtyard. When he came out he looked paler than ever.

'Sorry 'bout the sound effects. Still sure you want me?'

He was grinning bravely but he looked rather lost. Any residual doubts she might have had disappeared. If Danny were ever to find himself in such a fix, she would hope someone would take care of him.

259

'Ready?' she asked. 'These your sandals?'

'What about the rest of my things?'

'Leslie can bring them over later. Come on, I've left her with the children.'

After that they neither of them said much, putting all their effort into walking up the street. She made him put his arm round her shoulders and lean on her. They had to stop every hundred yards or so for him to rest. Passers-by looked at them curiously, and once or twice with antagonism. She feigned ignorance.

They had made it to the side-gate when Daz said hurriedly 'Oh shit!', and stopped dead with a look of panic on his face, staring at Bee. 'Oh shit!' There was a gurgling sound.

Kit was running towards them across the compound. 'Daz! It's Daz!' he shouted excitedly. 'Pooh, what's that smell?'

'Daz is very poorly, Kit. Go inside and tell the others, you must stay out of the way until he's feeling better. And in case it's catching,' she added darkly, glimpsing mutiny in his eyes. He went, hurriedly. She turned to Daz, taking his arm. 'Don't mind about it, come on.'

He didn't move. She looked up at him in concern, not realising he was crying until she saw the tears tracking down his cheeks. Her protective maternal instincts blazed then and took over. She squeezed his arm. 'Don't be upset – it doesn't matter. Come on, let's get you sorted out.'

'Some house-guest,' muttered Daz. 'Charles will be even more pleased to see me than usual!'

Saaid drove them to the doctor's surgery. Daz was doubled up in pain, and very anxious in case he embarrassed himself in public. The waiting room was full of women with pale faces and dark circles around their eyes: anaemia, very common here. She sat next to the hunched figure of Daz and tried to keep her mind off his digestive system by watching the women's anxious faces and wondering what it must be like to be circumcised. The few men in the surgery looked so much healthier than the women. It was difficult, really, not to begin to see all men as enemies.

The doctor came out of his consulting room. He noticed the two white people waiting and spoke hurriedly to the nurse. She summoned them to the front of the queue. Bee was too relieved to feel guilty, Daz was too far away in a world of his own to be aware. The doctor had a kind, intelligent face. He asked after Charles while preparing to take a blood sample from Daz's finger. They had brought a stool sample with them. To her surprise, although the doctor said Daz might well have amoebic dysentery or something similar, he was pretty certain that the primary problem was malaria, in which case the blood test would confirm it immediately. They would have to wait until the following day for the result of the stool test.

He prepared a slide with a drop of dark blood. It had taken several attempts to get any. 'None left,' Daz said weakly. 'That must be what's the matter with me.'

There was a lengthy pause while the doctor fiddled with the microscope and peered into it. Daz sat back in his chair with his eyes closed, clutching his arms across his stomach.

'As I thought,' said Dr Jamal. 'You have malaria, you'll be glad to know.'

'Will I?'

'It could be worse. Malaria usually responds well to treatment. I will give you a prescription for Chloroquin – you can get it from the pharmacy by the *souk*. Tomorrow you can call in and I will have the results of the stool test. I suspect there will prove to be dysentery as well. Good evening. My regards to Mr Charles.'

'Home,' she said to Saaid when they got outside. She wanted to get Daz safely back in bed before she negotiated the more difficult task of explaining the pharmacy bit to Saaid in her nearly non-existent Arabic and his equally minimal English. And anyway, poor Leslie was probably going crazy by now, she'd been stuck with the children on and off for most of the afternoon.

'Poor Leslie' was on her hands and knees in the middle of the sitting room floor and the children were leap-frogging over her back.

Bee didn't have to warn them to keep away from Daz – they gazed at him in awe and hung back. He did look pretty dreadful. She shooed him off to bed and Leslie came out with her to the pick-up to explain to Saaid about the prescription. She went off with him to the pharmacy leaving Leslie with the children again. When Saaid brought her back to the house he didn't want to leave two women alone in the house with a man, especially as the *gafir* had not yet come for the night. He was anxious to do the right thing by Charles. Leslie told him Daz was Bee's cousin. He looked surprised but he accepted it. She explained to him, on Bee's behalf, that Bee would need to go back to the doctor's, and probably to the pharmacy too, in the morning. He said he would call at the house at ten to pick her up.

She went to the far verandah where she had made up the bed for Daz and gave him his medicine.

It was late by the time she made supper. Leslie had long gone home. She sped through the storytelling regime, and did the routine kisses and tickles and hugs, and tucked in the mosquito nets. At last the children were all settled and quiet and she could go to Daz to see if he had changed his

262

mind about eating something, but he was asleep and she didn't wake him.

The subterranean friction between him and Dave was getting so bad it was making things awkward, but he didn't care. It was harmless, what was going on between him and Liz – merely a bit of fun which obviously wasn't going anywhere. He was, as Dave frequently and pointedly reminded him, a happily married man. (Unlike Dave, which was no doubt partly the source of the problem: Dave was probably looking for a wife himself, he *was* pushing forty.)

The more he watched Liz the more captivated he was. She had the clear-cut classical features, the creamy skin and dramatic, heavy blonde curls occasionally found in Italian women. Her eyes were wide, a very clear grey, dark-fringed with long lashes. And she had a classical figure to go with the face. He felt her eyes upon him in return, and experienced all the excitement of looking – or refusing to look – back. It was familiar to him, this game. All his life, since adolescence, he had turned heads with his chiselled looks. At parties certain women sought him out, others as significantly hung back, looking but not approaching. It was a game he enjoyed when he found the attracted attractive, but he had rarely pursued it, even before he'd met Bee. Finding more stimulus in the realms of tantalising possibility than in the mundane detail of reality. But this time it was somehow different. Liz's response to him was reassuring after the muddled negativity of his recent feelings. And what Bee didn't know needn't hurt her.

They cooked communal meals in the evenings, which they ate outside beneath the rustling oleander trees, the darkness lit only by a hurricane lamp. Power in Kadugli was fitful and occasional. They slept in a demure, communal row on *angarebs* under the trees in the garden. It was too hot to sleep inside the house.

There was something a little coy about it, the nonchalance they both pretended once she realised that he in his turn was attracted to her. Debbie, the friend, looked on with amused tolerance as if she saw right through them both. Dave bristled.

In the dead reaches of the night Daz woke, not knowing that he'd been asleep and dreaming. For a moment the eyes travelled with him, peopling the darkness. They pressed in on him – row upon row of eyes, following his every movement, watching jealously his every breath. Then they were gone, but the rancid stench of death remained. And as he turned, restless and frightened, the winding sheet tangled about his limbs, trapping him.

They'd got him. After all. Another fucking death, he thought. One more skinny corpse in the long row of winding sheets. He moaned, and realised then that he was sleeping but that he had moaned out loud. He opened his eyes. The darkness was total. He *was* dead.

On the fringes of his blank vision a golden light crept in, wavering unevenly. A blue figure, out of the shadows. A blue dressing gown drawn round a soft female body. Her. The Woman. Amazingly. Unexpectedly. A fantasy come true. As she bent forwards with her candle to look at him he saw, quite clearly, the heavy swing of her breasts under the thin cloth, the secret shadow between them. Hardly had he registered what he was looking at than she had turned away to put the candle down on a box beside the bed and was briskly pulling the sheet from under him. Not a winding sheet: a sheet. He wasn't a corpse.

Quite distinctly he heard her say 'Oh you poor boy. What a mess.' The sheet was whisked away. The stench of death faded.

264

He sighed, and smiled. And sank again into sleep, a golden sleep this time, infused by the light of a candle he could see through half-closed lids, feeling her hands gentle upon him, turning him this way and that. He slept, and dreamed of angels.

At this rate she was going to run out of sheets before the night was over. And it was difficult to see what she was doing by candlelight. The power had gone off at midnight and hadn't come back on.

She was a little frightened, seeing the blood-coloured liquid that had flowed out of him, but the doctor's calm voice from earlier in the evening sounded in her ears and she put her faith in his judgement. Poor kid, he had eaten so little in the last week – it was amazing he could pass anything at all. He was too ill to know what was happening, at least he was saved that indignity.

She fetched a bowl of lukewarm water and a fresh bar of soap and a flannel. She rolled him with some difficulty onto a large towel; he was surprisingly heavy, being so tall and so limp, for all that he was skinny. She began to wash him down with careful, caressing strokes. He looked fragile, lying there. Lanky and disorganised in the utter abandon of exhausted sleep.

What an awful night. This was the third time she'd been up to him. She hadn't heard the muezzin – perhaps it wasn't four a.m. yet. The nights were so long here, nearly eleven hours of darkness. Summer weather, winter nights – it still surprised her.

Her mind wandered gently, trying not to be frightened of what might be happening. She didn't want him to be so ill. It would be awful if he were to die. What would Charles say if he came home and found a young man – of whom he seemed to be oddly jealous – dead, or dying, in his house? And it would be really awful for the children; she would feel dreadful that she had exposed them to it. Not to the infection (if it was malaria that wasn't even a risk) but to the emotional trauma. Especially that it should be Daz... their Number One Favourite Person, as Adam had solemnly told her that evening as he went off with Catrin and Kit to draw Daz a get-well picture.

Why was she thinking about death? So far as she knew death was not an option for a grown man, well-nourished. As he had been, once. Unless it was cerebral malaria. She began to feel alarmed. What should she do? What *could* she do? Relax, relax, she told herself. It's just night panics. After all, he's sleeping easily now.

She looked at him, lying on his back on the damp towel. His bony, hairless chest was rising and falling with reassuring evenness and he wasn't feverish any more. He slept with his head turned towards her. Under the crack of his eyelids she could see the glint of his unseeing eyes. She sponged down the length of his body. The hands loosely resting on his chest were relaxed. She tipped him gently towards her to sponge down his neat little bottom. The tight creases under his thin buttocks made him seem like a child. She turned him back. It got everywhere, this stinking mess. He'd be sore tomorrow, probably. She grinned suddenly, wondering how he'd react if she offered him the zinc oxide cream they used to use on Catrin's nappy rash. She parted his legs gently and washed between them, under the wrinkled scrotum and the slack penis. Rarely had she been so close to someone else's private parts, other than Charles'. And never without their knowledge. She looked, in guilty fascination. His penis was long. How innocent and ridiculous it looked, lying there, jiggling about gently as she dried him. No doubt it wasn't innocent at all. You'd hardly expect it to be, not someone as lively and as enthusiastic as Daz. Not someone with a Mohican. She looked up at his safely sleeping face. After the first time she had met

266

him he had kept his hair closely shaved in a thick, even stubble but she still thought of him as the Boy With The Mohican. She began to wash his thighs. The way the skin of the scrotum moved continuously was like the perpetual lunar ebb of the tide over corrugated sand, the sparse reddish hairs standing proud like seaweed. She stopped to watch. How peaceful it was, sitting here beside a naked man in the solitary dark, musing about scrotums. Should the plural of scrotum be scroti, or scrota? He shifted in his sleep and hastily she went back to washing his legs. She patted him dry with a towel. Finally she rolled him carefully, forwards, backwards, onto a clean sheet. He hardly stirred. Before she went back to bed she bent and kissed him gently on the forehead. She left him the candle, at a safe distance, in case he woke again and didn't know where he was.

She didn't hear the alarm clock go off at six. It was after eight when she was woken by Fatouma rattling the door, trying to get in. The house was quiet with the stillness of late-sleeping children. The floor tiles burned her bare feet as she hurried to unlock the door. She went back through her bedroom to the far verandah. Daz was lying very still on the bed, his open eyes turned in a fixed stare towards the high garden wall just beyond the mosquito netting, mud-red against the perfect blue of the sky.

'Daz?' He blinked, and swivelled his eyes to look at her. Her heart had missed a beat – for a moment she had thought the very worst. 'How are you feeling?'

He considered for a moment. 'My guts still hurt,' he said hoarsely through cracked lips, 'but the rest of me feels…'

'A little better?' she volunteered hopefully.

'No, not better. Just – neutral.' He gave a long sigh. 'Wonderfully neutral…'

267

She bustled about him, straightening his sheets, plumping up the hard cotton pillow. As she turned she saw Catrin. 'You mustn't come in! Daz is too poorly for you to see him yet. Go and tell Adam and Kit, I'll come and make them some breakfast in a minute. They don't have to go to school today, tell them that. And they mustn't come and see Daz till I say they can.' Catrin wandered off, thumb in mouth and still sleepy but proud to be given so important an errand. From the further bedroom Bee could hear her loudly proclaiming: 'You no go school today. You no see Daz. Mummy tell *I* when you can see Daz.' Kit appeared, seeking confirmation. She shooed him away, promising she'd follow in a minute. She turned back to Daz, who was lying like a waxen shadow, strangely flat in the bed.

'Do you want anything to eat?'

He grimaced.

'But you should drink. I'm worried about you getting dehydrated. There's some ORS in that glass – Oral Rehydration Salts, standard Unicef issue.'

He lifted himself with an effort and picked up the glass but his hand shook so much that the water splashed on to the sheet. She went to the bed and took the glass from him. Sitting beside him she put an arm round his shoulders to support him and lifted the glass to his lips.

He drank cautiously. 'Yuck!'

'That's what Catrin said when we tried to make her drink it when she had malaria. But I do expect better from you!'

'Yes ma'am.'

'Drink some more.'

He did, partly to oblige her, partly for the excuse of resting his head a little longer against the firm mass of one full breast. He'd had such peculiar dreams all night, half of them dark and terrible, half of them decidedly pleasant.

He asked softly, 'Did you come in in the middle of the night, or was I dreaming?'

'I did. Not just the middle of the night. On and off all through the night.'

'Oh. Sorry!'

'It was hardly your fault. It's a relief to see you looking a bit better – you were really ill…'

'Thought I'd pop me clogs, did you?' he said in amusement, catching the worry in her voice. 'That'd have been awkward!'

'Mum, it's half past eight and I haven't gone to school!' Danny, forgetting the rules, had walked right in.

'Out!' she said, more sharply than she intended. She followed him into her bedroom. 'Sorry, love, I didn't mean to shout at you, it's just I'm worried – you mustn't get too close to Daz, not until he's getting better. Just in case. I overslept. I thought it would be all right if you missed school for once.'

His face lit up. She added, firmly 'So long as you do some English schoolwork instead.'

'Great!' he said. 'I'm going back to bed to read my book. That's work.'

'What are you reading?' she asked suspiciously.

'Tintin.'

She raised an eyebrow and cocked her head at him.

'Well, it *might* have been in French. And it's old – even older than you – so it is sort of history. Can I go on the computer after?'

'And when would you fit the schoolwork in?' she asked suspiciously. The computer was just an expensive toy as far as she could see. All Danny seemed to use it for was games.

'After I've done my schoolwork, can I go on it?'

'So long as you're nice to Kit and Adam you can.'

He sighed. They could never leave him alone for a minute

when he was allowed to (as Catrin called it) pootle on the pooter, but at least that would stop them bugging her so much about Daz.

They had just had time to finish breakfast and she had got some of the sheets into the washing machine when Saaid arrived. She made Kit, Adam and Catrin come with her, never liking to leave them alone in the house with Fatouma since they couldn't communicate with her. Besides she wouldn't have trusted them not to sneak in to see Daz as soon as her back was turned. 'No computer, mind,' she said to Danny as they left the house. 'I expect all your schoolwork to be done first!'

They had to wait for some time at the pharmacy. The stool test had shown up amoebae but fortunately nothing else. The drugs were expensive.

Daz pulled absurd faces at the medicine. She laughed at him mercilessly: Catrin was forced to down her chloroquin syrup every Sunday – he was making even more fuss than she did! He slept most of the day. She wondered what Fatouma made of his sudden appearance but since they had no common language she would probably never know the answer to that and there was little point worrying about it. Malik, when he came at dusk, had no reason to know at all. So efficient at fencing her in, she was amused that Malik was obliviously fencing a strange man in with her without even realising it.

By eight that night she was exhausted. She went to bed with her book, praying that tonight the power would stay on and let her read. But she found it hard to concentrate, her mind tugged away by the thought of the young man just the far side of the wall from where she lay. Perhaps it was the effect of fatigue but her mind buzzed with uncomfortable excitement. She was appalled at herself – thinking repeatedly of his body,

270

her own intensely aroused. This is sick! she thought. It felt predatory – more to do with his passive oblivion and her inadvertently having power, perhaps, than genuine desire. And how foolish she would look, if he were ever to guess that she had been thinking about him like this.

But with the children there, and Fatouma by day and Malik by night, nothing was going to happen anyway. It couldn't, even had he been an eligible figure instead of being a Daz. She let go of her thoughts, her book unread, and travelled slowly in her mind's eye down the long bony reaches of his body, till she fell asleep somewhere vaguely near his knees.

Jamil drove the pick-up quite fast along the causeway. Egrets and stilts picked their way elegantly in the water of the irrigation channel on their right. The flat, low-lying fields stretched in regulated blocks on either side of the road. The girls sat with Ibrahim in the back of the truck, squealing happily as Jamil took the corners just a little too fast on purpose to make them squeal. The Gezira is a grid of dykes with narrow roads running along the tops of some of the causeways: there are a lot of right-angled corners.

'I used to bring your mother here sometimes,' Hassan said. 'I thought she would like it, but it always made her homesick.'

Zahara, sitting behind him in the back seat with Mastura and Aasha, looked at the back of his neck. So familiar, that neck. The collar of his white safari suit was beginning to fray, she noticed. She wondered whether he would replace it when it got too old. He'd had it for years – the last of his work clothes – and he always wore it to go out of the house, though at home he usually wore a grey *jelabiya*. *Clothes are funny things*, she thought. They said such a lot. Neither Ibrahim nor Jamil ever wore a *jelabiya*, though in the heat it would be more comfortable.

271

Perhaps it was partly because they both liked to wear brightly patterned shirts, perhaps it was merely a statement about who they were: modern men in a world of flux.

She looked through the open window at the flat landscape with its endless ridges of cultivated earth, dark in the sun. Just like Cambridgeshire fenland, her mother used to say, only hot, and with egrets. Zahara had had a reverse experience: when she and Ibrahim were living in London, when Faatma was a baby, they had taken the train once to Cambridge and then a bus to Ely to visit a friend of Ibrahim's. And how it had made her homesick! Those flat, black fields with the long straight cuts of water between them, the regimented crops, the narrow roads on banks turning at right angles. But no hot sun, and no egrets. It had made her long so painfully to come home. She could remember the taste of it even now, that longing.

Jamil swung through another corner and behind them the girls dutifully squealed.

'Mummy, I wanted to go in the back. It's much more fun,' Aasha complained.

'But you get very dusty in the back,' Mastura said. 'And it is not very comfortable, especially with your uncle driving. Can you remember the way, Jamil?'

'No problem,' he said. 'I used to work here, remember. I know it like the back of my hand.'

Such a different world he lives in, Zahara thought. All those things he has done. He knows things I will never know. She looked at the back of his neck, so different from Abu's because his hair was black while Abu's hair was going grey. She looked at the shape of Jamil's skull under the closely cut hair and noticed how similar their two heads were, though Jamil was so much taller and broader. A great surge of protective love washed through her suddenly, for her three men, the two in

272

front and the one behind. For their shared, complicated past and their fragile-feeling present. Why does it feel fragile? she wondered, looking away to the clusters of trees on the dyke coming up on their left. Why does it never quite feel safe? But she knew the answer: because they are nine now, their truncated, partial family. They are exposed nine-fold. And their lives are suspended in uncertainty and she cannot feel their futures, she can only think them, and thinking is full of conflicting possibilities.

Friday: the weekend and a day out of the office. Dave suggested a picnic beside a lake an hour's drive from Kadugli. Perhaps he hoped Charles would be too busy catching up on paperwork to come with them. If so, he was disappointed. They set off in the two office vehicles around eleven, driving into the hills past herds of bellowing camels with their leggy calves.

The lake was the same colour as the brown hills that encircled it. They took the metal boat, which bobbed disconsolately at the end of an old jetty, and rowed cautiously round the lake for a while in the harsh sun. The water was rife with bilharzia and the hills trapped the heat like an oven. It was more pleasant off the water, sitting under the trees.

They made a barbecue and cooked strips of tough mutton to eat with bread and a salad of tomatoes and *jir-jir*. Afterwards they sat for a long time, idly skimming stones across the still water. The MSF doctors were talking about the new HIV disease, which the Sudanese authorities were dismissing as a purely western problem, a phenomenon of western decadence, but it seemed to be flaring up in Kenya so it was hard to believe there really were no cases in the Sudan. They moved on to politics – Thatcher at home, Sadiq al

273

Mahdi here – rambling talk in the turgid heat. Even Dave was relaxed for once, as if being off work made it easier for him to let go. Charles, sitting with his back against a tree, felt utterly contented. Out of the corner of his eye he could see the tip of Liz's dirty tennis shoes. He could feel her there, not talking much, behind his right shoulder, sitting on a rock. He smiled to himself and asked Dave how he rated the chances of the civilian government in Khartoum surviving into a second term.

Mastura's grandfather was standing at the gate. He had seen them coming when they were way back along the dyke, he said. His white *jelabiya* and turban were spotless. His big moustache was spotlessly white too. He had the upright bearing of a man who has spent his life as an army officer, but he was tiny now, and emotional. He welcomed them out of the pick-up, helping the girls down, shaking hands all round. He embraced Jamil. Mastura came last. He pulled her to him and it was clear that he loved her very much. Zahara remembered him weeping at the wedding. With joy, he had explained – joy that his son's daughter, his eldest grandchild, should be marrying. 'Come, come!' he said now and bustled them into the house.

It was a very English-looking house. It had two storeys and a pitched roof with red tiles, and windows looking out on every side. It stood in a garden full of flowering bushes with a low mud-brick wall round it. And all round the wall there were trees, so that the farmland was half-hidden except through the gaps in the leaves. The sun shone down from high overhead and the trees shut the heat in. The *gafir* stood by the path, his *jelabiya* very drab next to the general's shining white one, and nodded and grinned as General Bashir ushered them past and

274

up to the front door, which had faded red paint and a brass knocker. Faatma exclaimed at the knocker. Above it was a brass number '1'. She looked at her father questioningly. Behind her, General Bashir said in English, 'You see! You see! This was the foreman's house, so this was Number One. We are in Number One house!'

'So where is Number Two house?' Faatma asked, because they had not passed another house anywhere.

'Oh there was never a number two. Only a Number One house, and now we are living in it! Come, I will show you.'

In the dining room three elderly ladies, as tiny as the General, were sitting in upright chairs. Two of them, as widows, were swathed from head to foot in indigo silk so dark that it was almost black. The third was wearing bright red. They got up a little creakily and came forward to greet them. 'My wife,' said the General, 'Batul Omer Rahman. And my wife's sisters, Amna Omer Rahman and Rashida Omer Rahman. We have all met before, of course. At the wedding! But we forget, don't we – we old people.' He laughed mischievously as he laid a hand on Hassan's arm. (Hassan inclined his head graciously.) 'And now, of course, we are family.'

Mastura said 'We will speak in Arabic now, because my grandmother and my great-aunts do not speak English. Although you like to speak it, don't you Grandfather?'

'I like to, but I don't speak it so often now. Life gets small when you are old,' he said to Zahara, to whom he seemed to have taken rather a liking. But she was a little distracted by the fact that the whole of one wall of the dining room was a giant photograph of an Alpine scene, looming over the table, with pine trees in the foreground and white-capped mountains beyond.

275

'You like my picture?' the old man said, still in English. 'It is Switzerland. It makes me feel cool when I look at it. I was in Geneva, you know?'

She did know. She had talked to him about it before.

'And now I will show you the fireplace!'

They trooped out of the dining room into a long sitting room with shady windows looking out over the garden. In the middle of the wall that faced the windows there was a large brick fireplace. It had a strangely unused look, the bricks painted red and shiny inside the fireplace as well as on the chimney breast. The cast-iron grate was painted glossy black as if it had never been used.

'You cannot use it, it is only for looking,' the General said. 'There is no chimney. Please, sit.'

A servant brought in jugs of *limoon* and glasses, and also a bottle of gin.

'Would you prefer whisky?' the General asked Hassan.

Sitting in armchairs side by side, Abu looked tall and robust next to the General as he inclined his head courteously in assent to the whisky. Yet somehow he did not look quite well, she thought. Nothing she could put her finger on, just a general tightening in his features, almost as if he were in permanent pain. A paling and fading of skin and hair. And with her, a slight distance in his manner that had never been there before. She sat beside Mastura's grandmother, listening while the old lady chattered, and tried to remember when her father had last looked properly well. Ibrahim told her she was just a worrier, but wasn't that really a kind of excuse? One *should* be concerned about these things. She glanced sideways at the girls. They were sitting politely in a row on the sofa. Aasha's feet were dangling some way above the floor. In a little while Mastura's uncle, who is also in the army, will come, and

Mastura's cousins, and then the noise level will rise and everyone will loosen up, as they do in crowds, and the women will go off to the bedrooms where there will be beading of hair and hennaing of feet, and the men will talk seriously and walk in the garden while they smoke and drink their contraband whisky, and they will put the world to rights the way that men do, but by the end of the afternoon the women will have exchanged more information than the men can even begin to imagine.

Daz was feeling rather better, and therefore bored. He had become a restless patient, wanting to be up and about, but she was cautious, still unhappy about the possible risk to the children. She wanted to be sure that he really was on the mend.

It was no easy thing keeping them separate. The children kept gravitating towards his corner of the far verandah beyond the bathroom as if towards a magnet, apparently seeing her determination to keep them apart as a challenge. His willingness to subvert her didn't help. Eventually she got cross, her patience sapped by a second day of having them all under her feet and not at school, since today was a Friday.

'I'm trying to protect them, not you!' she snapped when he protested that he felt strong enough now to have them come and see him.

He looked at her like a naughty schoolboy who'd just been shouted at. 'Sorry,' he said sheepishly.

A bit later, when she came in with some soup, he caught her wrist before she could hurry away and apologised again. 'I never meant to be so much trouble,' he said, searching her face.

His anxious expression made her laugh suddenly. 'More a diversion than trouble, really.'

'Honest?'

'Honest.'

'I don't like you being cross with me,' he said. 'It's rather scary.'

'So I've often been told,' she said dryly. 'Anyway, I wasn't cross with you in particular so much as with the world in general.'

He peered up at her, unable as usual to fathom quite where she was coming from. She was kind, warm-hearted, distant, abrasive. It was disconcerting. She laughed at his jokes and then got all serious when he wasn't expecting it. He didn't know where he was with her, except that he was in her debt and that made him feel vulnerable. In reaction he became anarchic, undermining her authority by ganging up with the kids against her, and then he felt terrible that he should have made her unhappy.

But she, suddenly, seemed to let go. She told the kids they could come in and see him, and later, when he had them all drawing on the floor next to his bed to see who could draw the ugliest monster, she came in and sat on a stool in the corner as if she really had forgiven him. He pronounced Adam's monster the scariest, Catrin's the ugliest (no big decision, since it was hard to make out what it was she'd drawn at all, it was so full of hairy bits and bunches of fingers in odd places), Kit's the funniest, and Danny's the cleverest, and they trotted off, well satisfied, to have their lunch. Which was a relief – they were great kids but exhausting at such close quarters. He was as tired as if he had no blood left in his veins and no muscles on his limbs.

He slept for a long time, so deeply that he didn't even hear the rituals of bedtime taking place just along the verandah from where he lay.

Now that the children were allowed to go and see him they accepted his sleeping without a murmur, one or other of them carefully creeping along to look at him at diligent intervals, coming back to report importantly that he was still asleep. When he was still sleeping hours later and it was getting dark they grew bored. '*Why* is he?' they kept asking. But they didn't try to wake him. Clearly he would still be there in their house in the morning.

'Do we have to go to school tomorrow?' Kit asked hopefully.

'Of course you do. It's Saturday tomorrow.'

'But who will look after Daz?'

'I will.'

'But he needs us! He'll be lonely without us.'

'I expect he'll survive,' she said.

'Anyway,' Catrin said, sitting up abruptly in her little bed where Bee had supposed her already asleep. 'Anyway *I* look after Daz. I do drawings for him. I do monster drawings.'

'You can't look after Daz, you're too little,' Kit said dismissively.

'I can. I'll be four tomorrow!'

'No you won't. Your birthday's not till next year.'

'Oh bovver me,' said Catrin, and putting her thumb back into her mouth she subsided quietly onto the pillow.

'Go to sleep now,' Bee said, tucking Adam's mosquito net in under the mattress. 'Daz won't be going anywhere for a while yet. There's no hurry.'

'Did Jamil tell you the news?' Zahara asked as they got ready for bed.

Ibrahim folded his trousers and hung them over the back of a chair. 'What news?'

'Mastura is pregnant!' She looked at him curiously. 'What *did* you talk about, then?'

279

'The military, mostly. What the generals think about the government. What the chances are of a coup. Not that Abdul would say what he *really* thought about that, of course.'

'Well now you know – Mastura is pregnant. It was a mistake, obviously. They had meant for her to finish her training before they even thought about having children. But that is why they were both so happy today. Didn't you notice?' He hadn't, she could tell by his face. 'It's due in November.'

'That's probably why Jamil didn't say anything.' He saw her sceptical expression. 'November is a long way away,' he explained. 'It's early yet – anything might happen.'

'Not for a woman, it isn't early. She's been dying to tell for two weeks but she wanted to be sure. I thought there was something going on.'

He climbed into bed beside her and leaned over to kiss her goodnight. 'You always think something's going on!'

She lay in the dark, thinking about the day, about all those people, all connected: Mastura's aunts and uncles and great aunts, her brothers and sisters and cousins. Only her parents missing, because they were in Nairobi on a month's vacation, but much talked of in their absence.

Ibrahim had plenty of family and so had she – all those relatives of her father's, right there in Omdurman – so why did she feel solitary? My family feels broken, she thought. Ever since Mummy left, it has been broken. Ibrahim stirred and reached out a sleepy hand to touch her, as if he guessed she was having sad thoughts.

Daz was still asleep when she went to bed. Later, she was aware of his footsteps going to the bathroom. A truck-load of ululating girls had pulled up in the road outside, intent on celebrating somebody's marriage at the photographer's shop next door. She listened to them for a moment, thinking how this seemed to be their only chance to let rip, these girls – someone else's marriage.

She didn't hear him at first, padding on silent feet through the open door of her room. Dressed in his blue and white drawers, now washed and ironed, he stood looking through the net at her lying demurely naked under the sheet, like a princess caught out in her curtained bed reading Iris Murdoch.

'You're up,' she said, to hide her own confusion while she discreetly checked that the sheet was covering her properly.

He grinned. 'Feeling rather better. It's nice to be vertical without wobbling.' He scratched himself under one arm, relaxed and at ease.

She felt shy and slightly nonplussed. She didn't like him to see her lying there like a beached whale, but he lingered as if he wanted someone to talk to.

'Actually,' he said, 'I'm a bit hungry. Could I get myself something to eat?'

'I'll get you something...'

'I do feel bad, about all this trouble I'm putting you to. I'm really sorry.'

She waited but he didn't move away. 'If you go back to bed I'll bring you something.'

'Actually I'm rather enjoying being upright.'

'I can't get up until you go out of the room,' she said, exasperated.

'Sorry – not thinking.'

But she'd caught the gleam in his eye and she wasn't at all sure he wasn't being wicked. It was discomfiting, eroding as it did her protective mantle of maternal superiority. She wondered suddenly if he was being downright provocative.

He went out of the room and she got up cautiously and slipped on her blue silk dressing-gown. When she came out onto the verandah he was waiting for her, leaning against the wall. He looked her straight in the eye, a potent, unmistakeable look. For a fraction of a second she hesitated, swallowing nervously. She saw the rise and fall of his Adam's apple as he, too, swallowed hard. Then she hurried away to the kitchen, leaving him to follow.

In the familiar, practical safety of the kitchen she set about heating up the soup she'd made for him earlier, only he'd slept so long that she'd had to put it in the fridge. The night felt open, dangerously exciting. She shook her head as if trying to clear it. She could feel him behind her watching her. When she turned she avoided meeting his eye.

How could she flirt with him like this? Was she in danger of seducing him?

However, he was too weak to stand for long and he had to go and sit at the table on the back verandah. She brought the soup out to him, with some bread, and the last of the butter.

He ate hungrily. She sat across the table, watching him while he was safely preoccupied with eating. But he hadn't eaten very much before he could eat no more. He sat back, rubbing his stomach tentatively. 'Hope I don't see that again too soon. Does make you a bit wary, doesn't it?'

'I hope I never have to wash sheets like those again!'

He looked at her in horror. 'I didn't mess on them, did I?'

She hadn't meant to tell him, if he didn't already know. Perhaps it was no bad thing, though, that she had. It took the dangerous edge off the night.

He said, 'All a bit bloody intimate, wasn't it?'

She shrugged, but when she looked at him again she saw he was grinning. Under the table his bare foot crept over the top of hers. She looked down at the table, but she didn't move her foot away.

He sat opposite her looking at the top of her head, tanned through the parting in her short bouncy hair. He could see the rapid rise and fall of her breasts under the dressing gown. The delight of her not taking her foot away filled him with sudden courage. He hadn't really expected this, though he'd fantasised about it often enough. Gingerly, in case he frightened her off, he moved his other foot to rub it gently against the smooth calf, out of sight under the table. He could hear his own breath coming huskily. She didn't move. Her hands were on the table top between them. He leaned carefully forwards and put his hands over the top of them. He could feel the tension in her immobility, the heat of it.

'I really want you,' he whispered, his voice coming out all awkward with pent-up desire. If he stood up now it would be so obvious anyhow he might as well admit to it, whatever happened next.

She swallowed. He waited.

At last she said flatly, 'We shouldn't.'

But the saying of it immediately exposed the possibility that they might, and even possibly that they would. His hands tightened over hers. 'Why not?'

'It's obvious why not, isn't it? The children are asleep in the next room! I'm married, for God's sake. And you're not strong enough.'

He chuckled. 'Want a bet?'

She looked at him, very serious. 'And Charles?'

'You don't want to, then?'

He'd caught her out, possibly not intentionally but nevertheless effectively. She'd exposed herself now. It was

283

obvious both that she wanted to, and that she'd thought about the implications already.

He didn't argue with her, didn't try to persuade her. It was more disconcerting that he didn't than if he had. He simply sat holding her hands and gently stroking her leg with his foot, a friend not an enemy, apparently accepting her resistance without a murmur. She felt oddly disappointed. Eventually he took his hands away.

'I hate to admit it but I really do have to be horizontal again.'

They got up, their chairs scraping in unison on the tiled floor. It was strange, walking side by side back towards her bedroom, through which he must go to get to his bed on the far verandah. She felt oddly let down, but relieved too.

In her room he left her. Independent now, not needing her help to get back into his own bed. She stood in the middle of the room, immobile. Which was dangerous because, when he paused in the doorway and looked back, he saw her watching him. He padded back.

'Goodnight. And thanks for everything,' he said, his voice still husky. He bent forward and kissed her on the cheek, a dry innocent kiss. He kissed her on the other cheek and paused, his mouth close to her ear. She turned her head and closing her eyes began to kiss him, on his ear, on his stubbly cheek, his forehead, his nose, and lastly, hungrily, on his mouth.

A few minutes later he was horizontal indeed, and she was pinned underneath him across the bed, thrusting upwards against his long, slight weight with all the furious pleasure of total abandon, while under the oleander trees, under the stars, Charles slept the sleep of innocence and the sickle moon slid slowly backwards down through the sky, to be blotted out behind the darkness of the invisible hills.

Chapter 17

She woke in the morning, alone in the big bed, besieged with doubts and chilling fears. What a stupid thing to do, what a terrible thing. What if the children had woken? What if the *gafir* had heard them? What if Daz was infectious? What if he had a relapse because of too much exertion?

What if amoebae and malaria weren't his only health problems?

For God's sake, what if she'd got pregnant?

And what about Charles?

Later, the ordinariness of the morning embarked upon, she found it difficult to look Daz in the eye. It was almost as if he had become an enemy after all, something dangerous she'd held to her breast only for it to inflict damage. She could feel him watching her, perhaps anxiously, but she wouldn't let herself look to see if it was anxiety or appetite that kept his gaze fixed upon her.

Eventually he said, 'Are you angry with me?'

She looked up, surprised at the tone. He looked steadily back, not challenging and not needy. It was as if he'd stepped smartly up to her and gripped her firmly by the arm so that she couldn't duck.

'Angry? No. Do I seem to be angry?'

'Well you won't look at me and you're looking pretty grim, so yes, you do.'

'Not angry. Worried, I suppose. About the implications.'
She added, '*All* of the implications.'

'I don't sleep around, if that's what you mean.'

'No I didn't mean that. I meant Charles.' But she was relieved, all the same. He too was very serious this morning, and consequently unfamiliar. She felt very uncomfortable. Thank goodness the boys were off at school, and Catrin – for a little while at least – was out of the way having a nap.

They were sitting in the easy chairs in the sitting room. He felt strong enough today to be out of bed. He was looking almost normal again, but painfully thin and still very pale. Fatouma came in and began pulling back the furniture and rolling up the big camel-hair rug to wash the floor. She looked grim and disapproving. They went out of the room to keep out of her way.

Walking down the long verandah towards the back of the house Daz said, 'My legs feel shattered! Too much shagging, I suppose.'

He looked at her sideways with a mischievous grin. She said, looking away, 'I don't think it was a good idea all together.'

He said nothing. They sat down at the table like two people meeting in a café with nothing much to talk about and nobody coming to serve them. She picked moodily at a bit of spilled food on her dress. 'There he is, working so hard, the lives of so many people dependent on it, and here I am cuckolding him.'

'I think it's technically me that did the cuckolding.'

'I'm not talking bloody semantics,' she said crossly. 'Christ, can't I even own my own misdeeds now?'

'Whoa! Whoa!' he exclaimed, putting up his hands as if to protect himself. He grinned: 'Let's go Dutch, then, shall we? Fifty-fifty on the guilt?' She didn't smile. 'Even women are

286

allowed to own half of that one here – when it comes to guilt. Under Sharia law we'd both be stoned.'

'That really makes me feel better.'

He came and crouched down by her chair and took one of her limp hands in his. 'It wasn't even worth the guilt, was it,' he said, not looking at her face. 'I usually make a better showing than I managed last night.'

She shrugged and gently removed her hand. 'You have been pretty ill.'

'All the same, it can't have made you feel any better that I fell asleep on you quite the way I did. Sorry.'

Another interminable day crossed off on the calendar at last, nineteen left to go. She lay reading in her bed, he lay distantly and silently in his. But she was thinking, what difference does it really make – having done it once – if we do it again? I'm guilty already. Won't I have to hide just as much, hiding the once?

She pushed the thought away but it kept sidling back. She went to the bathroom. Coming out again she thought she'd better just look to make sure he was all right. After all, you never know – when someone has been as ill as he'd just been – that they won't have a relapse. She went along the verandah to the corner where his bed stood against the wall.

He was lying very still, staring into space. At the sound of her footsteps he turned his head to look at her. The faintest of smiles twitched at his mouth. He shifted over on the narrow bed and made space for her without a word.

Dave was suddenly shouting at him, 'Don't think I don't know why you're here! I don't know what your game is but I do know why you've come!'

287

The outburst was so sudden – one minute they were quietly discussing the drilling rigs, the next he was exploding. Charles stared at him blankly.

Dave lifted one finger aggressively. 'I'm not stupid, you know! What do you take me for? A complete fool?'

Charles was about to say that it was stupid to fall out over a girl. He might even have added, a girl who doesn't fancy you, Dave. But he thought better of it and closed his mouth again.

'They've sent you to spy on me, haven't they?'

'What?' The man must be completely losing his marbles...

'I know you've been offered promotion. I know your type. They want you to find reasons for closing the Kadugli office down, don't they? Well I'm telling you this – over my dead body! This is my patch, my programme. They can go to hell and so can you! The drilling rigs are staying here – whatever the SPLA get up to come the rainy season!'

Charles looked at him in amazement. He began to laugh. 'I'm sorry Dave, you've got completely the wrong end of the stick. I haven't been offered a promotion, and I certainly haven't come down here "on their behalf". I've no idea what you're talking about!'

'You tried to get those rigs off me last August!'

'That was short-term, for a specific purpose – you know it was. It was an emergency, for God's sake! And I was quite clear that the rigs should come back here as soon as the crisis was over, I told you that at the time. And they did, didn't they? At any rate two of them did. You know as well as I do that there isn't enough work here for three rigs any more, not with the SPLA so active. But you got two of them back, didn't you, just as we'd promised?'

'There!' Dave pounced triumphantly. 'You said "we" – "we promised". That says it all.'

Charles said, still patient but irritated now, 'You know my thoughts about Calvin. I'm just as sceptical as you are, if for different reasons. But in that particular instance I happened to think he was right.'

'Of course you did! It was your damned proposal in the first place. You got into bed with him on that one, didn't you, whatever you might say at other times. You're a damned two-faced chameleon!'

There didn't seem any point arguing. In this state Dave was unlikely to see reason, even if he were able to at any other time. But the depth of Dave's dislike came as a shock. Until now Charles had thought they worked reasonably well together. Between his intellectual skills and Dave's practical ones they seemed to have the makings of quite a good team. He still suspected this was sexual pride talking but it hardly seemed appropriate to mention it.

'I want you out of here, now!' Dave snarled. 'You've got the information you came down for. From now on I do not wish to work with you. I shall be informing Khartoum.'

'But Dave, if you make trouble in Khartoum that could backfire on you. If you don't give a good enough reason.'

Dave glared at him as if Charles had just proved his point for him.

'Also, the plane isn't coming down again until Tuesday.'

'No problem,' Dave said acidly. 'I can spare you a vehicle and a driver.'

Charles shrugged. He could hardly stay on now, after this. 'I want to go and talk to the SGNED women about handicrafts first thing. But I suppose I can make myself free to go by late morning.'

'Good. And don't be in too much hurry to come back to Kadugli. I've got a hot temper and it takes me a while to forgive.'

289

'You've got it all wrong, Dave.'

'Have I? Are you really so sure? Perhaps you're more naive than I took you to be.' He strutted out, leaving Charles, tense and disturbed, to go off to his meeting and then return to the house to pick up his things.

On Sunday Daz was stronger. He was still weak, but clearly on the mend now, and eating as if he was making up for lost time. If he went back to bed for most of the morning it was hardly surprising, considering how little sleep he'd had during the night. The children were peeved: here they were off school and Daz was out of commission! But he made up for it in the afternoon, helping Danny make a big kite cobbled together out of two old ones. Kite-flying out on the *jebel* was Danny's next favourite past-time after reading.

She sat with her sewing and watched them huddled in a circle around Daz at the table at the far end of the sitting room. Perched on chairs and stools they made a comic study in concentration, watching transfixed as Daz and Danny cut and glued and discussed the next steps. Once Catrin fell off her stool and cried, but mostly they were so spellbound that they hung in their various precarious positions, crowding in so that several times Daz had to stop proceedings, complaining that he was getting too hot to think. Obediently they moved back but within a few minutes they had drifted in again. He was so good with them, making sure they each got a turn holding this, gluing that. He didn't talk down to them. In return they worshipped him, this unlikely hero with his plain face and gawky mannerisms. Yet in his own way he *was* stylish, she thought, watching him covertly.

Once or twice he turned to look at her, smiling his direct smile, confusing her thoughts. It was easier with the children around. The unease of yesterday had evaporated – or had that been Fatouma's presence, making her feel self-conscious and guilty? Fatouma was a Christian and didn't work on Sundays.

She wondered how much longer he could stay before he was well enough to have to go to wherever it was he needed to go. He had been on his way from Babanusa to Khartoum to sort out his visa when he got ill. Presumably he still needed to do that. Presumably he would then go back down to Babanusa to the feeding camp. He hadn't talked about it very much but she sensed that he was finding the work there exacting, even harrowing. His very silence said a lot, though Daz – for one who was so talkative – said remarkably little, always, about himself. She realised with something of a shock how little she still knew about him. They had talked about Blythburgh, Walberswick, Southwold; about the social possibilities of Yarmouth and Lowestoft, and the drug scene in Ipswich. But about his family and his home she knew hardly anything. While he knew so much about her. She shivered, remembering some of the things she had revealed to him last night. Not just her fat, horrible body but her horrible, haunting fears: that she had come all this way only to get smaller inside. Her strange, secret conviction that she was going to die before she could get home. She told him, and didn't feel demeaned by the telling, like a child-woman talking to a man-boy. He listened and his attention made her feel substantial again. Somewhere in the depths of the night she had told him how lost she'd been feeling – that being in the Sudan had made it feel as if Charles had floated a long way off, almost out of earshot, and how lonely that had made her. And how the experience of being here had made her begin to doubt his judgement because he, knowing this country – even knowing this town – had seen fit to bring them all here, putting his career first and their happiness second.

291

It was like spewing up a monster, telling him this most aching of sick thoughts, but immediately she had told it she felt less burdened. She had shared this with no one, not even Kay. Perhaps it was a double guilt, betraying Charles twice over.

Now, as she sat in the calm reaches of the sitting room, she vowed one minute that tonight she would hold out and keep to her own bed, alone; the next, her heart was turning over at the promise of the night to come. When he looked at her like that, turning from the table to catch her eye and flash that mischievous, irreverent grin, she knew he was thinking about it too.

They were on the back verandah giving the children their supper and Daz was wearing the emptied eggshell out of Adam's egg cup on his nose when Charles walked in. In the uproar, laughing at Daz's antics, she wasn't aware he had come in for a moment, any more than the children were. Kit was trying to hang his own eggshell on Daz's ear, and Catrin was banging the table with her teaspoon.

'Well, well, well,' said Charles, and they turned and saw him standing in the doorway watching.

'Darling!' She jumped up guiltily and went to him. Out of the corner of her eye she saw Daz taking the eggshell off his nose and trying to look solemn. Charles kissed her. He shook hands with Daz, rumpled Kit's hair and bent to pick Catrin up.

'I thought you were coming back on Tuesday,' she said lamely.

'That's a long story. I had a run-in with Dave, I'll tell you about it later,' he said, drawing her back into their privacy. And without a backward glance she went. She barely remembered even to explain Daz's presence properly. It sounded rather lame anyhow – claiming acute sickness for someone who'd just been caught with an eggshell perched on the end of his nose. He did still look ill, though, and Charles was surprisingly friendly towards him, not spiky at all. But with her he was strangely reserved. She stepped back into the magic circle of their marriage and felt – not at once, but soon – that she was quite alone in it. She kept looking for him, behind his outward smile.

Chapter 18

It was a long and arduous road journey at the best of times, but by lorry and in the oppressive heat of March (not to mention in the aftermath of a severe bout of malaria combined with a dose of amoebic dysentery) it was a test of dogged endurance.

Daz sat in the bed of the open lorry, his knapsack cushioning his back from the metal side. It was a relief to be out of El Obeid, once it got too complicated to be comfortable. Besides, he was anxious that he had been away from Babanusa too long already. He wanted to get his visa and travel papers sorted out as quickly as possible in Khartoum and get back down to Babanusa again. But he hadn't realised how weak he was until he was on the lorry. Every rut in the hard sand, every dry stream bed that they crossed, shook his bones painfully. His brain felt as if it had shrivelled up into a little ball and was rattling around inside his skull. For the first hour he managed to chat to the elderly man sitting beside him, who spoke a little English, but after that he had to concentrate on sheer survival. The voices around him rose and fell against the thundering roar of the engine, a background to fevered thoughts and half-dreams. He thought he was back with Bee in the house. She was leading him from room to room, a strange and lecherous look on her face, until in the last room she suddenly deserted him and he found himself instead face to face with Charles.

He woke with the sun in his eyes, completely confused as to where he was. The old man beside him was looking down at him in concern. 'Just dreaming,' Daz said, shuffling back into a sitting position and grinning through lips already cracked in the desert wind. He took a long drink from his water bottle. The old man nodded vaguely. The day edged on slowly and precariously.

They were still several hours short of Khartoum, crossing a steep-sided *wadi*, when there was an ominous crack like a gun going off. The lorry juddered to a halt. The front axle had fractured, as became clear when the passengers climbed down. Most of them had loud advice to offer the driver but Daz was too dazed by this time to understand quite what was going on. The old man made him sit in the shade of the lorry, leaning against the back wheel. He was not aware of the other lorry being flagged down, he was only conscious enough to be acutely embarrassed when he alone of all of the passengers was shepherded into the cab. He looked back to see the old man who had befriended him earnestly wishing him a safe conclusion to his journey, and all the other passengers watching impassively as he was whisked away.

How he got across Khartoum to the Rest House in Souk Two he was never very sure, though he knew the lorry had dropped him miles away, across the river in Omdurman. All he remembered afterwards was the anxious face of Nora, the Irish nurse who had got him onto the feeding project in the first place, gazing at him with exasperated relief as he staggered in through the door.

Next day, waking in an unfamiliar room, he got up slowly, gingerly testing his aching limbs. He was very stiff but he felt reasonably normal. He wandered out of the room to find Nora sitting reading a magazine at the table in the kitchen. She looked up at him sternly.

'Well, Mr Zimmerman,' she said in her sing-song voice, 'What have you to say for yourself this morning?'

Daz scratched himself under one arm, frowning. 'Why? What did I do?'

She laughed. 'Oh not much. Just disappeared for more than a week and had us all worried, only to turn up out of the dark last night looking like the walking dead! What have you been doing with yourself? I expected you to have all your papers sorted out and be on your way back to Babanusa by the time I got here but instead I found you'd never turned up at all!'

He shrugged. 'I got ill on the way up – malaria and amoebic dysentery. I was stuck in El Obeid. I got a lorry yesterday but it broke down the other side of Umm Inderaba.'

She looked him up and down. 'Looks to me as if you should have stayed in El Obeid a while longer. Have you seen yourself in the mirror? No? Well don't look!'

But he was already halfway into the bathroom to find a mirror. He howled. 'Me looks! Me looks – they've gorn!'

She laughed. 'Stop messing about, you great fool. Do something useful instead, like eat some breakfast. You'll be needing to get a bit of condition back on you before they'll have you back in Babanusa.'

Later, sitting over a long and desultory lunch, which Nora made but Daz only picked at (his appetite still very unsure of itself), she said, 'Seriously – I don't think you should be going back for a bit, Daz.'

'But I have to get back! I've been away long enough as it is. I *must* get back.'

'There's not much point you going back in this state.'

'I'm fine,' he said defiantly. 'A bit weak, that's all. Nothing I won't get over in a day or two.'

'I'm not arguing with you. That's orders. Doctor's orders.'

'You're not a doctor, you're a nurse.'

'I've been temporarily promoted. You are to take Rest and Recuperation in Souk Two for the duration of Dr Nora McNally's stay in Khartoum. No arguing.'

He eyed her with some antagonism.

'Seriously, Daz,' she said, suddenly grave, 'there isn't any point you going back till you're strong enough. You'll only go down with something else and need looking after, which means you'll be a liability. It wouldn't be fair on the rest of your team.'

He was silent, thinking it through. He'd been driving himself with the thought of getting back to Babanusa and it was difficult to let go of the idea. The truth was, he was completely shattered and a few days' respite in the city wouldn't come amiss. It was a difficult confession to make, though.

'You'd be doing me a real big favour if you did stay,' she said. 'Nobody I know seems to be around – it's not much fun being here on me own. I only came up now because there was the chance of a lift with the MSF team and we're getting that low on medication – I agreed to take my Rest and Recuperation early and get new supplies at the same time.'

'That's just the point, isn't it?' he interrupted, 'My team's due for R and R in six weeks anyway. I can have a good rest then…'

'The *point* is,' she said acidly, 'If you rest for a bit now you might do a good month's work between now and then. If you don't, you won't be worth the cost of keeping you.' She looked at his glum face and added, wheedling, 'Come on, Daz. I couldn't ask you more obviously. Keep me company for a bit. It's no fun being here on me own. That's all I'm asking for, a bit of company. Nothing too serious.'

'Okay, then,' he said, but still unwillingly.

'Honestly, Daz, you really know how to make a girl feel wanted!' But she was laughing. 'It's just as well you're not my type.'

Hassan's sixty-eighth birthday was going to fall on a Friday. Why not? Zahara had thought, months ago. We can have parties too, not just other people. Even if many Sudanese people had no idea when they had been born, Abu did – they could celebrate it, just like they used to years ago when Mummy was at home.

She began making secret arrangements. She wrote to her brothers and sister abroad, just in case – she did not really suppose that they would come, but there was no harm in hoping.

Saadiya phoned from New York (the phone had been working better just recently, even for international calls, but it was always difficult and Zahara preferred letters). Was it a mistake to tell Saadiya about the baby? she wondered, listening to the strangeness of New York city traffic noise in the background, thinking of Saadiya in her office high up in the United Nations building. She couldn't imagine Saadiya's office. The baby was Jamil's news to tell, of course, but he was not very good at keeping in touch with the others. So she had told Saadiya, swearing her to secrecy and certainly not to tell Mummy. If Saadiya knew about the baby it might encourage her to make the effort to come. But maybe she won't come now, Zahara thought as Saadiya chattered on about this and that. Maybe now that she knows she will decide to wait and come for the baby's naming ceremony instead. But Saadiya, when the conversation got round to Abu's birthday, didn't even say that. 'It's only a year since we came for the wedding. Maybe we'll

298

wait and make a really special celebration for Abu's seventieth,' she said. 'The air fares are so expensive now. And also we're all so horribly busy. I know Nazmul and Ali feel the same.'

So am I so busy, so is Ibrahim. But somehow it seemed to leave a lot more gaps in their lives than Saadiya or Nazmul or Ali had. And Saadiya seemed to have more to show for it, with her duplex and her big car, and her visits to Europe every other year. She has the money for her fancy holidays, Zahara thought as she sat on their old sofa and picked fluff off her skirt and said 'Ahuh, ahuh,' at suitable intervals. It was only the Sudan that was too expensive to visit. Ali was the same. He was the furthest away of them all, in New Zealand, but that didn't stop him going to the UK every third year or so. She thought of them all getting together, her mother and three of her five children, without her and Jamil. It hurt to be so left out. Did her mother miss her? Did she miss Jamil, whom she hardly knew? (Though she had come to the wedding and behaved as if she knew him well.) It was Nazmul who Mummy saw most often because of Newport being only just up the road from Cardiff. 'Martin' as Mummy still insisted on calling him, though he was Nazmul to his Sudanese wife and to all his friends and colleagues in Wales.

Sitting in her hot, dusty flat in Khartoum, hearing the faint hooting of cars in distant New York streets, she listened to Saadiya's voice and was not surprised by her answer, though she thought it was provoking fate. Who knew where they would all be in two years time? 'Oh yes, of course we are all excited about the baby,' she said when Saadiya asked. 'Especially Abu,' she added. She didn't tell her that, actually, Abu was behaving very oddly. He had seemed pleased, yes, but strangely distracted, as though he didn't quite take it in. She told Saadiya instead how intensely protective Jamil had

299

become, watching over his wife like a lion. She knew that Saadiya still thought of Jamil as the chubby little boy he'd been years ago, not as a grown man with a wife, even though she had been there at the wedding.

Saadiya talked on. It was her phone call, she could talk as long as she liked so long as they weren't cut off and Zahara loved to hear her voice, even though she hated the phone, with its buzzes and and clicks and the uncertainty of how long they would have before the call ended itself. But Saadiya's domestic arrangements seemed very far away and remote. She herself had so little news to tell. She sat on the sofa, the phone to her ear, and let her mind wander. It was very hot. The muslin curtains hung limply. They were looking very dingy again, it was impossible to keep them clean however often she took them down and washed them. She wondered how Ibrahim was getting on. He had taken the girls to the club for a swim, leaving her a rare moment of solitude and silence.

'Ahuh, Ahuh,' she said, whenever Saadiya paused. It sounded like a litany of shopping. Her mind wandered to Nura, who seemed to be working every day now, even on Fridays which were supposed to be her day off. She was never *not* there. What hold has she got over Abu? Zahara wondered as she gazed unseeingly at her dusty floor. Sometimes she thought that any other girl would have been better than the almost sluttish, almost clever Nura. Almost any other girl would have been forgivable, but not Nura, with her proud pretty face and her tart slick answers. Something's going on, she thought. I wonder if Abu is giving her money?

Every Sunday she went to her father's house to pay Nura her wages. The money was generous for the work that was actually done but pitifully small in terms of what it would buy in the *souk*. This morning Abu had suggested that they should pay her more but she'd pointed out that Nura did very little, actually, beyond sweeping, and minimal ironing. 'She cooks for me now,' Abu said, and she had been surprised. And hurt. 'I would cook for you, Abu, you know that,' she'd said, and he had replied, 'You have your own life, Zahara. Go home and look after your family. Don't worry about me.'

And now Mastura was pregnant. Would Abu tell Jamil, too, to go home and look after his own family now?

It took him several days of patient waiting around in offices to get his visa extended, and another day to sort out his travel papers. While Nora purchased all the medical supplies and found herself and her cargo a place on the Unicef plane for the following week, Daz sat on uncomfortable chairs in hot offices while bored clerks pushed his papers around under creaking ceiling fans. In the afternoons, taking advantage of their temporary free membership as emergency relief workers, they went to the Sudan Club and swam in the pool. There were other young people there from aid programmes such as theirs and they quickly made a loose circle of temporary friends. On the Friday they were taken to the American Club by two American nurses, to eat hamburgers and chips and play endless games of pool. On Sunday, the day Daz insisted was to be his last day, he and Nora went out for supper at the Acropole. A last-ditch attempt to feed him up, Nora said.

They sat in the crowded dining room waiting to be served. It was only 7.30 but Daz was anxious to get back to the Rest House: he had to be up early next morning to get a place on a lorry to take him back down to El Obeid, en route to Babanusa. At the other tables the diners were mostly

301

Europeans. An English family with two small children were sitting at the corner table by the stairs. They were just finishing their meal. Daz watched the children, tired and cranky, having their faces wiped. They made him think of Catrin and Adam – they must be about the same age. He felt a sudden, unnerving wave of homesickness for El Obeid when he thought of them.

The rotund waiter with the handle-bar moustache who had served him and Nora with their soup returned with plates of spaghetti.

'It's a bit like school dinner, isn't it,' Daz said, looking down at the large helping of pasta and meat sauce on the plate in front of him.

'That depends what sort of school you went to. Looks pretty good to me. There was one girl at my school used to smuggle lumpy rice pudding out of the dining room in her knickers.'

'What kind of a school did you go to?'

'Convent. Private. The worst sort, I dare say, as far as food goes – the dinners were truly dreadful.'

Daz forked in a mouthful and chewed reflectively. 'Tastes better than it looks.' It seemed woefully untimely to be regaining his interest in food just as he was about to leave Khartoum. The diet in Babanusa was limited, to say the least, and the bread was always full of weevils.

Nora was still talking about her school. He allowed his mind to wander away a little. He'd been bloody unsure about the wisdom of coming to the Acropole, knowing that Bee and Charles often stayed here when they were in Khartoum and that they were due to be going on leave any time now – he couldn't remember when, and he'd lost all track of time anyway. He really didn't want to run into them by mistake, even if part of him wanted to see her again – however,

302

wherever, whenever. Thank God, there was no sign of them. He heaved his mind back to what Nora was saying. She was a good sort and he'd been quite happy, really, to spend a bit of time with her, but an undiluted six days of her company was quite enough. He was relieved, since he was pretty sure she did fancy him, that she hadn't made a real pass at him.

The waiter came back to clear away their plates and serve them with bowls of rice pudding topped with dollops of jam. They looked at one another and burst out laughing.

Afterwards, walking back through the quiet and almost deserted streets towards Souk Two, Nora leaned against him and put her arm through his. He tried not to tense away. They walked along in silence.

After a while she said, 'Am I embarrassing you?'

'No,' he said, but he sounded false even to himself.

'Is it that there's someone else?'

'No. But it's not really done here, is it. Physical contact between the sexes in public, I mean.'

She sniffed, but she didn't let go of his arm. 'We've been together a whole week, quite alone in that house, and both of us must be desperate for a good screw, but you haven't shown any sign of wanting one. At least, not with me you haven't.'

They walked in silence for a bit. Two men passed them, hand in hand, as men often walked with men here. The men looked at them askance.

'Don't mind my asking, Daz, but are you gay?'

He stopped in his tracks, looking down at her in astonishment. Then he threw back his head and laughed. He laughed till his eyes watered.

'Excuse me,' she said crossly, 'But it's not doing my ego much good if you're not gay but you're so not interested in me that you don't take what's virtually been offered on a plate!'

'Oh Nora! Dear old Nora!' He bent down and boisterously kissed the end of her nose. 'No, I'm not gay. And if I haven't been interested in sex it's not because you're not a great girl. I'm sorry if you were waiting to be serviced and I was too thick to notice.' He chuckled again, tucking her hand back under his arm and starting to walk along the empty street past the blank, shuttered faces of the shops. 'The truth is, I thought you were a devout little Catholic under that cool exterior and I wouldn't have dreamed of shocking you by making a pass at you.'

At his side her suspicious voice came out of the darkness, 'And is that all?'

He said nothing. Her voice came out of the darkness, probing: 'There's someone else, isn't there? Go on, Daz – you can tell me.'

'No there isn't "someone else", because she isn't available, she's married, she's got kids.'

'Daz!'

He said, irritated, 'You shouldn't have asked if you were going to be shocked.'

'I'm not shocked, you pillock, I'm outraged! What did you go for a married one for when there's all us single girls sitting around waiting? What a waste! What were you thinking of?'

'Well there we are then. But that's where my mind's been, this last week. I'm sorry I haven't been giving you the attention you deserve and sorry I haven't been screwing you at every opportunity.'

'Okay, you don't have to make a meal of it, Sir Galahad. I know you don't fancy me, and if I do *quite* fancy you I can cope with that. There are other fish in the sea.' She sniffed.

She wasn't silent for very long though. 'Are you going to tell me about it then?' The possibility of plucking that brief fragment out of his thoughts and making it substantial by

304

talking about it was seductive. But he mustn't. In this small world where everybody knew everybody else he had already said too much.

'Daz!' Nora suddenly stopped dead and stared at him with a horrified expression. 'You've not been having it off with some Sudanese woman have you? You know you could be killed for that – whether she was married or—'

'No, she's not Sudanese.'

'Phew.' She put her arm through his again. 'She's European then. British?'

He didn't reply.

Suddenly she whistled. 'No! Not *her!* Oh Daz – I thought you seemed suspiciously nostalgic over your near-death experience! *Nursing* you, was she?'

He turned on her in horror. 'Don't for God's sake breathe a word, Nora! If this gets out I would land on you like a ton of hot bricks!'

She giggled. 'Don't tempt me!' Her voice went serious again: 'I won't tell a soul, cross my heart. I'd have guessed in the end anyway – there's only one married British couple with children to choose from in El Obeid. So it's Mrs Goody Blue Shoes, is it? You crafty bugger!' She gave him a playful punch in the ribs. A moment later she giggled again. 'Wouldn't do *him* any harm to be brought down a notch or two, I must say. Too clever by half, our Mr Charles Walker.'

He reached El Obeid without incident and managed to find a second lorry to take him down to En Nahud that same afternoon. From there it would be half a day's journey to Babanusa. He was uneasy until he was on the road again and travelling out of El Obeid into the late afternoon sun. Half of him was drawn towards her house, half of him was terrified of the complications if he should run into either of them. He knew he was one of those who knock on emotional front doors only to run like hell when the door is opened. He found it easy to come up close, but then he didn't know what to do next. As the lorry bumped out of El Obeid, along the wide dirt road, he turned his face resolutely to the setting sun and distant Babanusa and the prospect of five weeks of dogged oblivion.

Chapter 19

If she said something he would talk about it. Like hell he would! But she said nothing, so neither did he.

Her guilt was so obvious, if it had it been any other situation he would have laughed at the pantomime of her attempts to cover it up. He'd known as soon as he came into the house what was going on. It wasn't just the fact of that idiot's presence with *his* children and *his* wife in *his* house. It was something about the space between the two of them, so assured and intimate. It was the look on both of their faces, as if they'd been caught in the act. It was, above all, the fact that she changed the sheets on their bed while he was reading to the kids. As if he wouldn't notice! He might as well have caught them in bed together, he thought angrily as he read *The Cat in the Hat*.

'You're not doing the noises!' Catrin said. 'Daz does noises.'

'I'll bet he does,' said Charles. All sorts of thoughts and feelings were rushing through his head. Outrage that the two of them should have been carrying on while their innocent children were under the same roof (asleep perhaps but nonetheless close by). Disgust that she should have stooped so low (that useless creep, of all people!). Fear (who knew where he'd been and what he was carrying). But most of all, what flooded him was a terrible, numbing anger. He'd never felt anything like it. There was no heat, no urge to vent his feelings or lash out. Instead he felt shrunken under the shrivelling force of an anger so cold it seemed to burn like dry ice, reducing the inside of his heart to dust.

So he let her make her lame excuses and he said nothing. He waited, and when she didn't come to him with a confession he was disinclined to broach the subject for her. It was her mess; it was up to her to sort it out. After a while she seemed to think he hadn't guessed and she relaxed. He watched her, despising her simplicity.

His restraint in Kadugli with Liz felt like acute self-sacrifice when he looked back on it now. What a fool he'd been to be so cautious when Bee was making use of his absence the way she had! He wondered if this was the first time. He suspected not. His mind heaved about, delving into half-remembered scenes. Jonathon – he'd always been suspicious of him! That would explain a lot: her distance from him, her moodiness.

Well she wasn't being distant now. She hovered on the periphery of his consciousness, all attentive and loving. The more she looked at him but said nothing the less he wanted to reach out to her. He threw himself into his work, rushing around like a madman for the last ten days before they went on leave, setting everything in order for while he was away.

Five days left but she isn't even counting. The house is in turmoil. It isn't just the packing cases of things to be stored out of the reach of the dust while they are away, or the suitcases they are taking with them, or even the rowdiness of the children who are beside themselves with excitement. It is the turmoil within, under, over everything, of adult feelings in crisis, in total disarray.

She packs cases with so little concentration that she can't remember afterwards what she's put where. Charles is working

308

all the hours there are, trying to leave everything in good order before he leaves his job behind for a whole month. When he comes in from the office he's so tired that he cannot (or will not) look her in the eye. They have odd, half-ordinary conversations about where they will go when once they are back in the UK. They even plan their first trip round Sainsbury's, making a shopping list. Bacon figures on it, and sausages. Cheese, chocolate, and a really good bottle of red wine. But still he won't look at her properly. It's as if they are pretending that they're not pretending.

She doesn't say anything, because she can't think what to say. It was a madness and she wishes it undone. She is filled with self-loathing. She despises herself on every front – for letting herself go, for taking advantage of a sick and foolish boy, for being reckless. For risking discovery by the children. For not hanging on when it was only a matter of a few weeks more and she would be back in England and no longer so needy. She sees herself with a clear and brutal eye: an overweight, overwrought, stupid woman who is so self-indulgent that she stoops to using passing youths to prop up her own deficient ego. She is not at all surprised that Charles seems to have retreated from her. She wishes she could retreat from herself.

They spent three days in Khartoum on their way out of the country. The usual pattern of Khartoum days, with Charles in the office and her and the children at the Club, and two nights in the Acropole, paid for, this time, by Unicef because they were officially *In Transit*. The children's pent-up excitement made the time pass slowly, but the pump in the Sudan Club was back in order and they could swim in the pool once more, and this time there were no *haboobs*, and the water was no longer undrinkable, and Khartoum was not unbearable. She waited for the last interminable three days to pass. She made no move to go and see Maggie.

But Charles did. Choosing a time when he knew Will was in the office, and the children would be at school. He knocked at the door, his heart pounding. Half willing her to be out.

Maria, the Eritrean housegirl, answered the door. She asked him in and left him standing in the sitting room while she went to fetch Maggie. He was too nervous to sit down.

Maggie came in. She was wearing white trousers and a white open-necked shirt of some fine material. Her black hair was pinned up but curly tendrils escaped all round her tanned face. He had forgotten how pretty she was. Her expression when she saw him was one of complete surprise. Instead of coming across to him with a light social kiss of greeting, she stood rooted to the spot just inside the door. He realised this was significant. If he meant less she would have greeted him differently. He realised he had nothing at all to say. He said, 'I wanted to talk to you.'

She looks at him closely. Her dark brown eyes bore into him, revealing his bones, his lungs, his pulsing heart. Knock knock. It sounds in his own ears.

'Is something wrong?' she asks.

But he doesn't want her sympathy. He wants her secrets, buried beneath that white shirt, buttoned so neatly between those breasts. He steps towards her. And pauses, because a warning has flickered across her eyes.

'I'm expecting Will any minute. He's giving me a lift over to the American Club to play tennis because he needs the car today. I think,' she added slowly 'he'd find it odd, you being here. In the day-time, without Bee.'

He held her eyes with his. 'When can I see you?' he asked

in a voice so low and croaky with desire that he thought she couldn't possibly hear what he said.

'I thought you were going on leave,' she said at last.

His heart lifted. Like a hawk, rising off the ground and across the sun. 'I'll be back in a month,' he said. 'I'll come then.'

She said nothing, holding his fierce gaze unflinchingly. Without another word he turned. He found his way out of the room and out of the house without a backward glance.

ॐ

'Josie,' she exclaimed in delight as she opened her front door. This was a rare treat. 'Come in! Come in!' She led the way into the living room, where Faatma and Yasmina were sitting at the table cutting out paper patterns. 'Sit down and talk to the girls while I go get us some drinks.'

Josie sat at the table and picked up a string of intricate figures of cut paper. She held them up, squinting against the light. 'My oh my, but aren't these fine!'

'But they break, Aunty Josie,' Faatma said warningly. 'Specially the long ones. You have to be really careful with them. We got the pattern from this book.'

Josie looked. She picked up another piece from the table. 'So who did this round one? Let me guess! Could it have been – Aasha?'

Yasmina giggled, nodding. It was very untidy but it was supposed to be what the book called a 'doily'. From their bedroom came the sound of Jamila loudly counting, and then ruefully lamenting, 'Weeeee,' on a long, descending note, and Aasha's gleeful laughter. Josie looked up quizzically. 'What in the name of Moses are they up to in there?'

Yasmina listened for a moment, head on one side. 'Snakes and ladders, Aunty. Sounds like Jamila is losing.'

Zahara came back with a tray of glasses and the girls hastily made space on the table. She poured the *kerkedeh* from the jug. 'Faatma, take these on the tray to your room. And tell Aasha and Jamila, you can have a picnic in your room with the cookies, but try not to get crumbs on the floor or the ants will come. Oh look, we can try out Aasha's doily.' She slid it onto one of the plates, under the peanut brittle biscuits.

'Oh,' said Yasmina in surprise. 'Is *that* is what a doily is?'

Zahara handed Josie a glass and pushed the other plate of peanut brittle towards her but Josie shook her head. 'You know me. As usual I am reducing. Or trying to.' She looked round the room.

Looking at it with an outsider's eyes for a moment, it seemed to Zahara that everything had got very shabby, not just the curtains.

Josie said, 'It's an age since I've been in your flat. I'd forgot that wedding photo of you and Ibrahim. How is Ibrahim?'

'*Nus nus*,' she said. 'He's still got his job, anyway. For the moment.'

'Yo'all should get away, you know.'

She looked up sharply. Josie had never said such a thing before. But she couldn't read the expression on her face because Josie had got up from her chair to look at the photograph.

'Nice cushions!' Josie picked up one of the new ones that lay on the old sofa. They were very smart, and not like anything you usually found in Khartoum. Hand-woven in thick hand-spun white cotton. 'Is this Eritrean stuff?'

She nodded. 'Mastura got them months ago, for my birthday. They came from that new handicrafts shop, the one Unicef helped set up, near the Dolly Hotel.'

'I heard about it but I haven't been yet,' Josie said. She moved restlessly round the room, picking things up and putting them down again. Zahara sat quietly, wondering what Josie could want to say that would not wait until they were next in school. But she was glad, whatever it was, that it had pushed her into coming. It must be nearly six months since she had last visited them at home.

'I heard from my parents,' Josie said suddenly.

Zahara's head shot up. She had not known for sure that Josie's parents were still living. 'Did you?'

'They're neither of them very good. Haven't been for some time, but now my Dad's gone and got cancer.'

'Oh! Oh, I am sorry.' She looked at Josie uncertainly, not sure how she would be feeling about this news, she had been estranged from them for so long.

Josie sat down heavily at the table. 'Thing is, it's made me feel very strange. I thought I didn't care any more but now I find I do. I'm all they've got left in the world since my brother died. And whatever they did in the past I have to feel sorry for them now they're old.'

What did they do in the past? She had never known but she had always wondered. She didn't feel she could ask now. Perhaps her mother knew, but if she did it wasn't a story she had ever chosen to tell.

'I realised last night I haven't really got any choice,' Josie went on. 'I've got to go back to the States and see what I can do to help them now. I've decided to go at the end of this coming term, Zahara. I'm afraid we're going to have to find someone else to take my place in the school for the next school year.'

'Oh Josie! Do you mean you wouldn't be coming back?' It came out sounding stricken. She knew from Josie's expression

313

that she probably looked as stricken as she'd sounded. She had never expected such a thing. Josie had seemed, in reality, as fixed as she was, marooned in Khartoum just as she was, if with fewer obvious connections. She looked down at her hands but she did not see them, until Josie's big, firm hand suddenly covered hers.

'Don't take it too hard, girl. We'll find somebody to replace me. Someone your own age, with more energy than I've got now. You won't miss me after a bit.'

'Oh but Josie, I will!' She looked up. The slate-grey eyes behind the thick lenses were gazing at her. She could see tears in them, for all Josie sounded so detached and calm. 'Josie, I will miss you terribly! Are you meaning to say you would go and never come back?'

Josie shrugged. 'I can't assume I will come back.' She patted Zahara's hand absent-mindedly, turning her head to gaze fixedly at the curtains swaying idly in the breeze from the open windows.

'But Josie, what about Paul?' She had never said his name to her before. For all Josie knew she had never known it. But she said it now.

Josie looked at her calmly as if they had spoken of him every day of their lives. 'Paul is too far gone these days to notice whether I'm here or not. I might as well be the servant, for all he knows. Or for that matter, cares. Alcoholism is a terrible thing, Zahara. Hope that you never have occasion to understand what I mean.'

'Oh, Josie,' she whispered. 'I didn't know.'

From the girls' room, a gust of giggles. In her heart, a sudden emptiness.

'Well there we are,' Josie said, making it sound very final. 'Zahara, you really should get out of here, you know. You have got so much to offer, the two of you, if yo'all but gave yourselves the chance. Tell that Ibrahim to pull his finger out and go back to that journal – the one that offered him the job in London – see if they wouldn't offer it to him again now.'

'I can't, Josie. How could we leave? What about Abu? What about Jamil and Mastura?'

Josie gestured impatiently with her hand. 'You gotta take care of your girls, Zahara. You can't take care of the rest of your family too. Your dad can take care of himself. Even Jamil is a big boy now.'

&

At two in the morning they are in the departures terminal, short on sleep and high on expectation. It seems hours before they are on the plane, and then there is another long wait before take-off. The elderly English gentleman with the military bearing, in the seat across the aisle, harasses the stewardess for a whisky until she says imploringly, 'Sir, it's illegal to serve alcohol while we're in Sudanese territory, even on the plane.' This seems as incomprehensible to the old man as it is to Bee. The plane is so palpably a part of Europe, its textures, its smells, the sallow London accent of the stewardesses, the very absence of dust in the thick upholstery.

They fly through the dawn, the world cut into two smouldering halves of night and day, and then through the long sliver that hovers between the clouded globe and the dark blue vault of the eternal sky. She watches the trembling metal wing and wonders at the presumption of flight. The daring challenge of exchanging one world for another. At Heathrow, when they land, it is a rainy April afternoon and the sun is just breaking bravely through the wet to make rainbows everywhere.

315

They went to Charles's mother's house in North London for the first night, which usefully ticked off one family obligation before they went on to Ipswich and ticked off the other. Also, their car was housed in Charles's mother's unused garage. Glenda was pleased to see them and to tell them her news – all about the Bridge Club, and how much money she'd made on her shares this year. She hovered anxiously over the children with a cloth to catch spills from their cups on her polished tables, and surreptitiously checked the surfaces for marks from their pencils, and in the morning, when their car started at the first try, it was only Catrin who minded that they could leave so soon.

Driving to Ipswich, at the wheel of a car for the first time in eight long months while Charles sat back in the passenger seat, Bee felt nervous and emasculated like a grub exposed by the sudden turning of a stone and writhing tentatively in the light. Travelling through the familiar/alien landscape, that seemed to have carried on without them without even noticing their absence.

Their body fluids are working again – eyelids no longer gritty, lips no longer cracked. Skin returns to suppleness, hair regains its shine. And sand emerges, in hard wax balls, from the secret depths of ears. It is like being given their bodies back, detail by detail. She hauls them in, her trawl of precious detail, watching her children become themselves again. She has got her own body back: her legs have gone back to their normal size, just like that.

In her parents' house in Ipswich, her mother frets and fusses, her father retires behind his newspaper, both of them preoccupied with the fate of the early potatoes after last night's unexpected frost. By day her parents disappear into the windy expanses of their lush suburban garden, which is busily reawakening to the spring. 'Very nice, dear,' her mother says when Kit shows her his drawing of the Boeing. 'Very nice, dear,' she says when Bee tells her something about El Obeid. They stay the required number of days (two), filling them with useful things like shopping, and then they flee northwards at last, through the little market towns of Suffolk, to Walberswick and the house at the end of the village where the wooden shacks stand apart in the grass, and the river slides into the quietly sounding sea.

It was cold. On the beach, a north-easterly wind raked off the sea and into their eyes. The winter tides had deposited a bank of yellow pebbles all across the sandy end of the beach where the children liked to play. Catrin cried because the wind made her ears hurt. They retreated to the draughty sitting room of End Point and the valiant radiance of the twin bars of the electric fire.

He looked at her, in jeans and a baggy green jumper, and she was unfamiliar. She had had her hair cut short again while they were in Ipswich and now it was vigorous and wind-tousled and her face, still tanned from the Sudanese sun, was radiant as it hadn't been for a long time. He had forgotten this person. He looked at her in surprise and his heart lurched.

That night they made love for the first time in a long time. The wind tugged and buffeted the house and moaned at the leaky windows. Somewhere below them, at the far end of the long studio roof, a loose piece of iron banged now and then when the wind got underneath it. It was so cold they hardly dared move for fear of letting the night in under the quilt.

The children ran out of the house in the morning like horses released into the field at the end of winter. Danny and Kit doing cartwheels, Adam trying to. Catrin rolling like a puppy in the grass. Bee did cartwheels too.

But if the cold invigorated her and made her alive and alert it didn't have the same effect on him. He was a child of Africa; he had never quite lost the inheritance of his first seven years in Kenya. The cold always made him fold into himself. His felt his shoulders droop like wings narrowing his chest, he sat with his arms folded across himself to keep in the warmth. He had always found staying at End Point difficult when the weather was bad. It made him irritable. He began to find excuses to go off to the pub, not just for a pint of Fisherman's Ale but to sit by the fire. Sometimes, at lunchtime, Bee and the children came with him. At night someone had to stay with the children. She said nothing, but he felt the unspoken comment. When he came back in there were drawings on the table. A few slight sketches – the furl of a sail, a feather. She had come back, the woman he had been missing. But the questions – hers (What had she been doing?), his (What did he want to do?) – lay between them now.

They went to Norwich to visit friends, to sort out minor problems with the agents who were letting their house. It was strange to drive past the end of their road. They carefully avoided passing the house itself. At weekends, friends came to stay with them at End Point and the little wooden house was crowded and cheerful. One Saturday morning there was an excited toot from outside and Kay unfolded herself carefully out of her battered old mini. Bee stood on the steps, her hair ragged in the wind, looking down at her sister. Charles watched them, intrigued. There was so little outward sign of the intensity between them. They pecked one another gently on the cheek. But within a few minutes, as always, he felt profoundly forgotten, and he wasn't sorry when Kay left again the following evening.

Just once, he went into his Department at the University.

318

In the stale air of centrally heated offices his colleagues sat behind their incipient paunches at littered desks and swivelled their chairs to ask him briefly about the Sudan before telling him in detail about the abysmal quality of the current batch of students, the deficit they faced this financial year, and who was not pulling their weight, who was intriguing with whom. All the busy preoccupations of an academic institution. So familiar, but how strange that he should be considered a part of all this.

In the office that had been his, a pale-faced man of about thirty with a thin blond beard paused in his marking of essays to greet him cautiously. This was his replacement, a temporary contract to last the duration of his absence in the Sudan. It was a strange feeling, like meeting his own ghost. Outside the double-glazed windows the students passed and re-passed on the paths in the thin sunshine of late April, under trees just breaking into full blossom.

How could he come back to this? How could he pick up the threads of an existence so remote that he had difficulty believing he had ever lived such a life?

He knows he should talk to Bee. There is so much that should be talked about. But the one bit gets in the way of the other so that it is all clogged up. He hasn't told her about the renewed offer to extend his contract. He had argued to himself that he was taking time to work out what he felt before he troubled her equilibrium. But he does know, really, what he feels: if he didn't want the extension it would be easy to tell her about it. It is the force of his own burgeoning desire that makes it so difficult to broach. Because of course she will not want to stay on. It will be a straight conflict of interests, hers against his. Not the children's: they are happy enough wherever they are, they accept life as it comes. It is only Bee who seems unable to put her energies into the experience, who seems to refuse to try and make a go of it. Others do, so why can't she? Why *won't* she, for him? All he is asking of her is a few years in exchange for the rest of his life lived out in quiet academia here. Is that really so much to ask?

In another year or two they would amass enough savings to make life so much easier when they did come back. She would understand that: she'd been visiting estate agents in Stowmarket and Lowestoft and the sitting room at End Point was littered with particulars for houses and cottages in villages and small towns, and some which were miles from anywhere. The prices had shocked them. The steady rise in rural property values in the last eight months that they had been away had changed the picture. The value of their town house in Norwich and the savings in their bank account didn't match very well with the prices of the cottages she was looking at. Perhaps she *would* accept the argument that if they committed themselves to a further two years away they would be in a much more favourable position. Also, it wouldn't be another two years in El Obeid but in Port Sudan, which was a very different kettle of fish, being on the Red Sea. Swimming and snorkelling readily available, and more facilities. The sea, for God's sake! There would be her beloved sea. And a different kind of community from the one she was isolated in at present in El Obeid – far more Europeans, lots of families with children. The more he thought about it, the more he convinced himself that he could probably persuade her, if he went about it the right way and chose his moment. Was it not, after all, a fair exchange for his turning a blind eye to the Daz business?

As the month of his leave wore on and she still said nothing at all about Daz he found himself inclined to say nothing too. In Port Sudan they would be well out of Daz's way. He thought he should be generous. Daz was probably an anomaly she now regretted. She'd been having a hard time, shut in all day, every day, with the kids and he should be understanding about it Besides, not mentioning it kept things simple. It was better to suspect, sometimes, than to know. It left more space.

He filled the space with thoughts of Maggie. Driving to Norwich, walking with Bee and the kids on the dunes, sitting in the pub, Maggie was there all the time in the back of his mind. He was counting off the days until his return, though he tried not to. And he knew that because there were things he wasn't telling Bee there was a space between them into which other things seemed to fall. He forgot to tell her other things. He compared her and found her wanting. Small irritations grew larger. She sniffed on and off for hours after walks in the sharp sea air and he longed to say, for God's sake blow your nose! She listened endlessly to the radio and was too abstracted to hear him when he spoke to her. She left the lid off the toothpaste, and yesterday's knickers under the bedroom chair. None of these things had bothered him once, but now they began to grate like grains of sand that had got under his skin.

And he was bored with England already. Idleness quickly palled. After the first week, the pleasure of drinking beer again, of sitting by log fires in the pub, of buying whatever they fancied in shops and going for brisk walks – all these pleasures waned. He felt under-occupied and slightly ill at ease. There had to be more to life than this! The thought of that little life in Norwich waiting to grab them by the throats once again made him want to weep. He looked at his children and saw them as different from the whining kids who seemed to fill the shops everywhere they went. He didn't want to watch his own kids turning into ordinary children. In Great Yarmouth he watched Bee buying prepared meals in Marks and Spencers, and hair colouring in Boots. She bought a cassette tape of some band he had never heard of, that he found alien and hated at once, partly because he thought it was probably some influence of Daz's. He couldn't excuse these things as part of the innocent exuberance of coming home. They threatened him with separateness, part of an alien world personified by Daz. Do I know who she is any more? he wondered sadly. It seemed to him that something had changed between them, something irrevocable.

But he was in no condition to do anything about it. As the time approached for him to return to Khartoum all he could think of clearly was Maggie. His contract, his marriage, his own self, seemed all to be suspended in limbo, and he said nothing at all.

The children sat obediently in their chairs, waiting for her to open the classroom door and welcome in the mother, father, aunt or grandmother – whoever was waiting outside in the corridor to pick each of them up. It was a happy time of day, children's voices bright and excited as they talked about their morning in school, eager to show their work, but the little ones always sleepy. She watched them come in now, the assortment of parents. Her rainbow school, all nationalities and every mix of races. Some children would be whisked off home; some would be taken swimming before lunch in the Club. Arrangements would be made between families to meet up later, or to go home to play with friends. Her own girls, too. Or, if not, she would take them swimming and then they would come back to the empty classroom to eat the sandwiches they always brought from home (a necessary frugality), before going off to play quietly in the playground while she and Josie did some of the hundred-and-one jobs that must be done before they too went home.

Maggie came in late to pick up Sam and Cathy. 'I'm sorry, I am so sorry!' she said, breathless as if she had been running. 'I was playing squash and the clock in the court had stopped – I mistook the time.'

How pretty she looked, her colour bright and her hair escaping in tendrils all round her face. Zahara never felt pretty but always too thin and certainly too tired. She said 'You haven't forgotten my father's party is in two weeks time?'

'No, no, we haven't forgotten. We're very much looking forward to it.'

'I wondered, would your friend Charles be able to come too, do you think, with his wife?' It so pleased her, the thought of returning Maggie's hospitality, of showing her a Sudanese party, complete with a ram cooked over charcoal on a spit, and traditional musicians coming too – a friend of Ibrahim's who played the violin, and another man, a singer – but she was worried in case Maggie and Will wouldn't have enough people they could talk to. She was not surprised though, remembering the tension she had sensed between Maggie and Charles, that Maggie hesitated slightly and then said No, she thought it likely that if even if Charles was back from leave by then he would probably be going straight down to El Obeid, and Bee would not be back for several weeks after that.

'Never mind,' Zahara said, secretly relieved because the numbers for this party were escalating and she had not really been sure about asking these others to come.

'Zahara, there's something I need to tell you. We've just heard – we're going to Ghana. It's very sudden. We have to be in Accra by the end of this month. At least, that is when Will is due to be there, and I would like us all to go at the same time if we possibly can.'

'You mean, you are going on a visit?' she said, confused.

323

'No, it will be for good.' Maggie sounded genuinely sad. 'Your dad's party will make a very nice farewell.'

These expats, they came and they went. It was always the same. You should never let yourself get close to them, it was like never giving a name to an animal you were going to eat. Why had she let herself go against her own instinct with this one? Zahara tamped down her feelings resolutely, though she did allow herself to say 'I shall be sorry to see you go. *The girls* will be sorry!' Reminding herself that if it hadn't been this year it would have been next.

'The children have been very happy in your school. We *are* sorry to be leaving. But you know how it is, never in any place long. And I have told everybody in Unicef what a good school this is. I hope you will soon fill the places.'

Zahara nodded, not really listening. She would, she suddenly realised, genuinely miss Sam, for all his small naughtinesses in class. He had been one of her more stimulating pupils. But she would forget him before long, and Cathy too. There would, as Maggie said, be others. Pupils, anyway. Friends were far harder to come by.

భ

In her parents' garden, Bee stood watching her mother sticking peas. In a far corner of the neat vegetable plot her father was planting out cabbages, pipe in mouth, content in his own space as he always was. Her mother was more accessible. Bee stood on the path in the windy sunshine watching the small woman who bustled around, refusing her offers of help, and thought how odd it was that they were related.

The broad sowing of pea seedlings snaked slightly unevenly across the bare grey earth. As her mother worked, pushing hazel twigs into the raked soil, the white flesh of her bare upper arms swung slightly in the cruel sunshine.

She realised with a shock that her mother was growing old.

She looked at the sun shining harshly on the pale grey twigs, casting stark shadows across the pale soil and was reminded suddenly of Kordofan. The unexpected association made her shiver and goose bumps erupted on her skin.

It always did feel odd when Charles left, but it was much worse this time. This time there was no clean edge to the pain of him going. As time had gone on and still he'd said nothing about Daz, she had had to acknowledge to herself that he probably hadn't guessed, after all, and it was her own guilt that had created all the disturbance between them. His train would be arriving at Heathrow round about now. She thought of him sadly, as something very far away.

Her mother said, apropos of nothing, 'I don't know what we're going to do about your brothers.'

'I don't think it's a question of *us* doing anything, is it? I mean, if they're getting divorced, they're getting divorced – there's not much we can do about it. It's just unfortunate it should happen to both of them at the same time.'

'And I keep telling Karen—'

'Kay,' Bee corrected automatically.

'I don't know why you can't both stick to the names you were born with!' her mother said crossly. 'Anyway, I told your sister, it's high time she found herself a nice young man. She'll be thirty next month! It's time she settled down and had children or she'll be too old.' I don't think she isn't trying to, Bee thought. 'Well dear, at least you've done all that. At least I don't have to worry about you.' Don't you? she wondered mildly. Her mother always made her feel that needing to be worried about was the ultimate selfishness. 'Beverly, dear, do you think you could tell the children to be careful. I'm sure they don't take any notice of me. They'll have that ball crashing down on the cold frames before we know where we are.'

Bee sighed. The children were bored but they couldn't leave before lunch, not without causing a fuss, though she too longed to get back to End Point where there were no cold frames, or young seedlings, or prized roses, in which to land a football by mistake. The weather was getting warmer, though it would be cool beside the sea. The beach might be possible tomorrow. Or they could go for a walk inland, where the sandy soil heated up quickly in the sun and it was easier to get out of the wind. She had been away from End Point for less than twenty-four hours and already she was getting the shakes for it, longing to be back. Their last precious four weeks before they must return to their other life, like prisoners on parole. But only one hundred and ninety-eight days left of their sentence when they got back to the Sudan. One hundred and ninety-eight lifetimes. But a finite number

And by Christmas we'll be home, she reminded herself sternly. They could start house-hunting then in earnest. She knew already where she wanted to start but she hardly dared look yet. It was like a love affair: wanting not to look, wanting to look. The leap in house prices had been a nasty shock. Anything might happen yet, between now and Christmas. A terrible disturbed feeling gnawed at her insides. She couldn't bear to be swallowed up again into suburban life in Norwich. She knew so powerfully, so simply, what she wanted for her family. What if they couldn't have it in the end? All that time sacrificed for nothing, all those dead hours.

'Danny, be careful with that ball!' she shouted dutifully as the football sailed high in the air. It landed in a clump of delphiniums. He looked guiltily in his grandmother's direction. Across the garden the blackbirds chack-chacked harshly in the suburban trees.

❧

In a week it would be Abu's birthday. She had filled their small freezer and then Jamil and Mastura's with savoury dishes and sweet pastries. All Abu's elderly sisters and cousins had been visited and invited to the feast, and begged to keep it a secret. There was a moment when she was seized with misgivings. Perhaps he might find a surprise party intrusive, he might not be pleased at all.

Jamil bought a young ram in the souk. He was going down to Ed Damazin for a few days, he would not be back until the day before the party, so he bought the ram a week early and the night before he left for the farm he brought it round to Zahara's and tethered it in the yard behind their flat where the *gafir* could look after it and keep it fed and watered. Yasmina had decided she wanted to be a vet when she grew up. She christened the ram 'Feasty Beasty' and took him titbits scavenged from the kitchen.

The day after Jamil brought the ram, Zahara was in the kitchen preparing the evening meal. The girls were doing their homework at the table in the living room and Ibrahim had not yet come home from the university. Unfamiliar footsteps climbed the outside stairs. Just as she registered this she heard a gentle knock at the door. 'I'll go,' she called out to the girls, because they were not expecting anybody and it was nearly dark.

A young man was standing outside. She didn't recognise him but he greeted her formally, making it clear that he knew her by name. There was something very odd about his manner.

She returned the greetings, wondering at the embarrassed, solicitous look on his face because she couldn't imagine why he should feel in any way connected to her.

'I am the brother of Hawa Yusuf Mahtoub, Mastura's friend.'

Ah, that explained him a little. She nodded politely.

'Um, can I come in? I am sorry to call when your husband is not home, but this is urgent.' He added, seeing her hesitate, 'It is too difficult to explain out here.'

He kicked off his shoes just inside the front door and followed her into the living room. She wished Ibrahim was back. She had never met this man before, though she did remember Hawa Yusuf Mahtoub: a small, laughing woman, a friend of Mastura's since childhood and working as a nurse in the same hospital in Wad Medani.

The man stood uncertainly in the middle of the room. He clasped and unclasped his hands, staring at the wall as if he might find something to help him there.

'Girls, go to your room with your homework,' she said, guessing that whatever it was he had come to say he was unwilling to say it in their presence. The girls picked up their books and pencils obediently, looking at the stranger with open curiosity now that they had been asked to leave the room.

As soon as they were gone the man said, all in a rush, 'There is no easy way of telling this. There has been an accident. On the Wad Medani Road. My sister—'

Immediately she heard the words 'Wad Medani' she froze, her eyes fixed on his face. Out of the corner of her eye, she saw Faatma hovering in the doorway but Zahara was too distracted to signal to her to go away. The man struggled for a moment to collect himself. Then he said in a low voice 'They were in a car on their way back to Khartoum. A lorry hit them.

They didn't stand a chance. I am so sorry…' He added in a whisper, 'All of them. My sister too.'

'What are you saying?' she said sharply. But even as she said it, his words were hitting the back of her head like bullets, crack crack crack. He was saying that Mastura was dead? But Mastura could not be dead! This must be some kind of horrible waking dream. She shook her head slightly to clear the thoughts but he was nodding and staring into her face. The expression in his eyes confirmed that which she would do anything not to know. She collected herself abruptly. 'Faatma, go to your room, please.'

'What's happened? Mummy, what's happened?'

'I will tell you in a little while. Just do as I say now.' She shot Faatma an imploring look. 'Faatma, please!' Unwillingly – almost sullenly – Faatma detached herself from the doorpost. A moment later Zahara heard the door of the bedroom ostentatiously closed, and Faatma's voice muffled on the other side of it.

Her mind was racing. How could Mastura be dead? She who is more alive than anybody else Zahara has ever met. She was here only yesterday evening, borrowing cooking oil. How could she be dead when Jamil was not here to know it? It must be some mistake. 'How do you know?' Even as she asked the question she was seized with hope: it might – it just might! – be a horrible mistake.

'Their friends were in another car, travelling behind. Mohammed al Mahdi, my sister's fiancé, was one of them. They saw it happen – *he* saw it. The lorry was overtaking, it was on their side of the road – it hit them head on. Their car was thrown off the road. It burst into flames. They didn't stand a chance.'

He said (as if the saying of it relieved him of the weight of the words, delivering them into her care where they would fester for ever, untellable, trapped inside her head) 'They could hear them screaming but the flames were too fierce. Nobody could get close enough to pull them out. They tried. The lorry driver tried. He burned his hands and face. He is in the hospital now himself. But it was impossible. They were burned to sticks, all five of them, trapped inside the car. Mohammed al Mahdi came to tell me himself. He said he will never be able to forget what he saw today.'

She sways as if she will fall. The man takes hold of her arm and keeps her upright. All she can think of is Jamil – Jamil! But he is not here, he is out of reach.

Ibrahim put her to bed and brought her sleeping pills, but she could not sleep. He brought her food, but she did not eat. She heard, as if in a dream, the girls creeping about and sobbing softly in other rooms. She knew she should go to them but in her frozen state the knowledge did not touch her.

In Jamil's absence, Ibrahim helped Mastura's father make the arrangements for the funeral. He fetched Hassan, who sat for a long while with Zahara in the shuttered bedroom, saying nothing. Abu did not know that Mastura had been coming back to help prepare for his birthday celebration, and she could not bear to tell him. Ibrahim tried endlessly to get in touch with Jamil but the phone to Ed Damazin was, as usual, not working. The funeral could not be delayed.

All of Mastura's family was at the funeral the afternoon of the following day, her grandfather with tears streaming down his dignified cheeks. And all her surviving friends. Hassan and Zahara and Ibrahim and the girls were there too. But Jamil – the person who loved her most, whom she had most loved – Jamil was not there.

330

They buried the slight corpse in its white shroud in the big cemetery in Souk Two. Two days later, Jamil returned from the farm to find his wife already buried. She had been thirteen weeks pregnant.

Chapter 20

They were sitting in the main room of the Rest House, too full of food after the naming ceremony that afternoon to want to think about supper. Loud music and lively voices from the next-door compound made it clear that they'd left long before the celebrations were over, though they'd been there since *fatur* this morning and now it was fully dark.

The trouble with being back in Khartoum again was eating too much. Protein Shock, Colette called it: after the poor food in Babanusa they were all of them knocked out by eating so well. It seemed to Daz that it made him want to sleep all the time. Perhaps it was just the effect of stopping, after five weeks of non-stop grind in the camp.

They made a quiet, relaxed scene now, in the Rest House. Colette was reading aloud from a copy of the *Independent* which she'd filched from the Sudan Club yesterday. Mick was asleep in the corner, sprawled on a floor cushion with his head flung back. Chris was creeping over towards him with a large dead fly. He was probably about to drop it into Mick's open mouth. Sue was sitting at the table playing Patience and Jimmy, like Daz, was sitting slumped in a chair watching Chris.

'Aw don't!' Jimmy said. 'That's disgusting!'

Mick opened one eye and clamped his mouth shut without shifting his position. He eyed Chris challengingly. From somewhere far away came the muffled roar of an explosion.

Colette paused in her reading and looked up. 'That sounded like a bomb,' she announced casually.

Jimmy, who was also from Belfast, said 'More likely something going wrong in the industrial area.'

Colette went back to her article. She had finished the *Independent* and was starting on the *Sun* when the door suddenly burst open and American Carrie from USAID rushed in, her face ash-white: 'There's been a bomb – at the Acropole. Lots of casualties. They need medics! Can you come, Colette? Micky? Bring torches, the power's out. And dressings, splints – bring anything you've got that might be useful.' And she disappeared into the darkness again, the sound of her frantic knocking coming from the CARE Rest House across the road.

There was a moment of stillness. A bomb? At the Acropole? If they hadn't heard the explosion themselves they would have thought it must be some mistake. Mick moved first, shooting across the room to where his doctor's bag stood against the wall. In a moment they were all scrambling among their things for their torches, running to the store for the big box of bandages that was waiting to go down to Babanusa, finding tweezers to pick out broken glass – anything they could think of that might be useful. Daz ran out to the street with the keys to the old jeep which was kept for their use in Khartoum and jumped into the driving seat. He backed rapidly up to the door and the others piled in. Only three of them were medics, but they were all well practised in first aid and besides not one of them could have stayed behind. Though as they rushed through the oddly normal-looking evening streets each of them was worrying about what they would find when they got there.

Daz, concentrating on driving the ancient jeep, has hardly any space in his head for any thoughts at all, but what space he has is taken up by one thing only: don't let her be there! Please, don't let it be them!

It is a calm, ordinary night in the Acropole. The brightly lit building is homely, and alive with activity as usual. Upstairs in the dining room there is a clattering of plates and a buzz of voices as the evening meal is served. It is not long after seven-thirty and the room is crowded.

Halfway up the stairs, in George's office, it is also busy. The Dutchman is on the phone, facing towards the staircase. He notices the young Arab in a *jelabiya* who comes up the stairs because there is something funny about the way he is carrying his bag and the man seems nervous, but the Dutchman's mind is on the disembodied voice in his ear and he watches through the glass only idly.

At the top of the stairs the young man suddenly throws the bag over the balustrade towards the dining room and races back down. The Dutchman thinks, looking back, that somebody said, 'That was a bomb!' And then the whole thing goes up.

The Dutchman is at the bottom of the stairs when he realises he is still alive. He is lying where he has fallen, in terrifying darkness. Where his leg should be, when he puts his hand down, there is only a hot anarchy of splintered bone and blood. On the floor beside him, when someone comes with a torch, a dead child is lying. It is the little English boy he saw in the restaurant earlier.

The street was in chaos. People crowded the crossroads outside the hotel obstructing the police vehicles, everybody panicky including the police. Daz stopped the jeep and the others got out and ran the last few hundred yards, carrying the boxes of

334

dressings awkwardly between them. He backed the jeep up the street a little way until he could find somewhere to park roughly at the side of the road. As he leaped out and ran his heart was pounding in his ears. There were police everywhere, frightened and jumpy, pointing their guns. Glass and rubble lay all over the street and everything was pitch dark. Ahead of him he could just make out Colette. She was pushing her way to the door of the hotel through a pressing crowd of people. The others were close on her heels. He heard her say 'We're medics, let us in!' He pushed forwards until he was just behind Jimmy. The two policemen at the door had their guns trained on them. One of them was saying nervously, 'Sir, Madam, you not to enter!'

'We're doctors!' Micky shouted. 'We have to go in.'

'You *all* doctors?' the older policeman demanded suspiciously.

'Yes,' said Micky, and the next minute they were in through the front door, into the hallway.

There were bodies everywhere, some lying, some propped against the wall. Some of them seemed to be immobilised more by shock than by their wounds. Colette and Micky moved through the shattered hallway with the others close behind them. The raking beams of their torches picked out faces white with dust and spattered with blood. Some of the wounded had already been moved over to the annexe but there were others too badly hurt to be moved, and at least one of them was already dead. Daz followed Colette closely, holding the torch for her while she staunched gaping wounds and picked out shards of glass with silent concentration. Police were swarming like shrill, nervous flies, pointing their guns this way and that, apparently afraid that any one of them might be a terrorist. The two policemen on the door were still

335

refusing to let anyone in, but they wouldn't let anyone leave the building either.

An argument broke out. An American voice, male, protesting that the police must let him go up the stairs. 'No, no!' the policemen kept saying, their cocked guns dangerous in the erratic torchlight. One of the policemen, very fierce-looking in the jumpy shadows, said harshly, 'No one is left up there.' The American voice pleaded, sounding close to tears, 'Please let me just go up and see – I know my friend is up there! Let me go to him, please.'

'Your friend will be in the other building,' said the fierce policeman, losing patience. 'I tell you there is no one left upstairs.' The American sobbed, 'He isn't in the Annexe, I've already been to look and he isn't there!' Other desperate voices began clamouring to go back upstairs for colleagues they were sure were still up there.

'Okay,' the policeman said at last. 'Just you. Go and check. You – stand back!' He raised his gun threateningly and the press of people fell back.

Daz could hear the man's feet crunching rapidly on broken glass as he ran up the stairs. He watched the snagging of his torch-beam in the shadows. Then his voice came down the stairwell: 'There are wounded people up here! Ten more at least!'

It is what Daz thinks of most in the days that follow, after the Dutchman has told him his story. The dead child, and those ten forgotten people, lying wounded in the dark.

Chapter 21

I n her kitchen in End Point Bee makes toast and the shock carries to her on the air waves and makes time stand still, so that it fixes a stray moment of the wind upon the river – a red sail half unfurled – in her mind for ever. Time broken in half.

And then the long hours trying to pull information together.

The six o'clock news was clearer and gave more details. The Sudan Club had been attacked with tear gas and raked with machine gun fire but injuries there had been slight. In the Acropole, seven people had been killed: two Sudanese and five English. Not Charles. An English family, but not Maggie and Will. Twenty-one had been injured. There was a phone number, at last, for those who needed to ask after relatives. She left the children with Kay and went again to phone from the call box. Charles was not among the wounded. Her heart eased, as if only now could she begin to breathe again. Of Daz, she didn't think at all.

The night the Acropole was bombed Charles was sitting in a moonlit compound in Ban Gedeid. In one corner a camel walked sedately in endless circles, turning a creaking sesame press. The light from the hurricane lamp picked out the camel's shape in quirky shadows. Beneath the sound of the creaking press, the flat sound of the camel's broad feet padded softly in the sand.

Above them a giant moon glared blue-white, dwarfing the yellow glow of the lamp. It had been a long day. In a little while they would be on their way back to El Obeid but it was pleasant to sit for a while in the amicable dark, alongside the people he had been out with since early morning. The lamp, set on the ground between them, cast its warm soft light upwards on their dark faces while the moon gleamed coldly on the tops of their heads.

He sat, only half listening. The tight knot inside his chest was beginning to soften a little. It was good to be out, to be with simple people. If only life could always be like this. Did it have to be so messy?

He had gone to her house, the first day he was back in Khartoum. Sliding out of the office on some excuse, slipping along the few short streets. The house was, as usual, shuttered against the sun. She had answered the door to him herself.

How his desire and excitement must have shown in his eyes… His crude expectation exposing him. She had led him into the sitting room and he hadn't guessed what was coming but was watching her bum as she walked in front of him. Didn't guess until the moment when she turned to face him and he recognised with a shock that the tension in her eyes was embarrassment, not pleasure.

Strange how, in all the thinking he had done beforehand, he hadn't once considered refusal. The logic in his own life had overshadowed any doubt about the logic in hers. Was his ego really so big that he could get it this wrong? Well, he'd been roundly punished. What a fool he'd made of himself! Dave from Derby looked subtle, compared with this.

He hears her clear voice again in his head, forestalling him:

338

'Charles, this would be stupid. For you as well as for me. Will's landed the job in Accra after all – the confirmation came through two weeks ago. We're leaving in less than a month. It would be stupid to start something now. We'd only regret it afterwards.'

The night the Acropole is bombed Zahara hears nothing. She is sleeping the awkward, restless sleep of the drugged. Ibrahim, reading to his daughters while their mother sleeps at this strangely early hour, has explained to them that she is not well but she will be better soon. And when the bomb goes off, making the windows rattle and the neighbourhood dogs bark, he lifts his head and listens, but only for a moment. It's probably nothing, an explosion in the industrial area perhaps. It seems a minor disturbance, in the scale of things.

Chapter 22

Hers are the only white children on the plane. The plane is half empty and Khartoum airport is very quiet. The officials wave her through Customs. Is it her imagination or is there something wistful in their faces? She feels that they are looking at her and the children gratefully, that they should be coming back at such a time.

Charles has come to meet them and there is something wistful about him too. Something uncertain. Which is very strange, for Charles. They hold onto one another very tight without speaking.

Later, in the house Charles has borrowed from a colleague who is away on leave, they talk into the small hours. So much to talk about: the bomb at the Acropole, where they should have been staying tonight, the attack on the Sudan Club. The written warnings that have been handed out in the Unicef offices, telling them to check under their vehicles for car bombs, to report anything unusual. The suspects (members of the Abu Nidal terrorist group) will go on trial soon and reprisals are likely. The British are considered particular targets because of their history in Israel.

This unintended gesture of solidarity she has made, coming back – not active perhaps, but not passive either: she could have made it a reason to have stayed at home. She needed to be here, just as the children in their own unknowing ways

340

needed to come back. But the seven who died seem to shadow their every move as they go back down to El Obeid, especially the English family with the two small children. She had seen them in the hotel before they left in April. A family like theirs, eating at the corner table by the stairs. She had passed them in the street and thought they looked interesting. People she might meet another day. Who might become friends. They haunt her now. How could they have been marked out for such a fate? One minute they were living their lives, eating their evening meal, the next all their hopes and their dreams abruptly ended.

They had so often sat at that same table. There was no particular reason for it not to have been them. Only a matter of time and space. The terrorists had apparently been watching the Acropole for the last five months from the Sahara Hotel opposite.

Had they not guessed that they were special, that family? That they were marked out? Had their days not been heavy with it? They looked serene when she saw them, a family newly arrived in Khartoum, waiting to go to their posting, about to start a new life.

They go back to El Obeid the next morning. Charles disappears, as usual, to the office. Life resumes.

∽

'You mustn't let it get to you,' Josie said.

'I know. I do know.'

They sat at either end of the sofa. To Zahara it seemed as if they were two near-strangers, washed up together in an uncertain place, about to be separated, perhaps for ever. How is it that one person dying can make the whole world seem broken? Even the past is not immune. The familiar turning inside out.

'I'm only saying it for your sake,' Josie said. 'I don't want to sound hard. But if you let go now it will all unravel around you. And I'm worrying about how you'll cope when I'm gone.'

She looked up at Josie but it was as if her eyes weren't really working. The whole of the inside of her head is taken up with horrible images, obliterating everything. Fire, and burning flesh. It's as if the smell is inside her own nostrils, the sound of screaming is buried deep in her ear drums. She cannot imagine what Jamil is going through. He has fled back to Ed Damazeen like an animal bolting into its burrow. Abu, too, has retreated, into his house. And in their flat, Ibrahim tiptoes round her and the girls watch her warily from a hurt distance. Nobody seems close enough to reach out to her, and now Josie is sitting at the far end of the sofa and they are talking like people who do not really know one another.

'Come back to school, Zahara.'

She looks up, startled by the sudden urgency in Josie's voice. Josie's eyes fix hers. They do not let her slide away. 'You are needed, Zahara. We all need you, but especially your girls do. Come back to school. Try to make things a little bit normal again. Please, come back to us.'

She knows Josie is trying to be kind but a little voice inside her head tells her it is out of guilt, not kindness, that she is urging her back. Josie's ticket to the States is booked for two weeks time, and although they have found a woman to take her place, Zahara does not much like her.

Chapter 23

They formed the usual queue beside the flowering bushes, and the men in white turbans and *jelabiyas* handed in their daggers before boarding the plane. Bee watched the men in front of her warily. This trip to Port Sudan on the Sudan Air Boeing blotted out the future and the past with its shadow. She wanted it to be over and to be safely back in El Obeid, getting on with their last five months.

Charles looked over her shoulder at the men ahead of them in the queue. The stewardess was carrying a plastic box along the line and it was already half-full of knives and daggers, and one highly polished revolver. He could guess what Bee was thinking: they were only giving up their weapons to be polite. No one would be any the wiser if they did not, and now must be a peak-risk time for hijacking. The Acropole bombers were on trial somewhere in the city and not all of them had been caught. He lifted Catrin up onto his shoulders so that she could look over the hedge.

'Have you packed your mask and flippers?' he asked Kit, but only to catch his attention. Kit had been wearing his mask and flippers round the house every evening since coming back from the UK. He would have worn them to bed if they'd let him. Adam had a pair of flippers too, and a little mask of his own. He was standing with his teddy tucked nonchalantly under one arm, listening gravely while Danny read aloud to him from his National Geographic. Charles smiled. He couldn't imagine what Adam was making of the fishing practices of the Inuit.

'Daddy, a man gave that lady a gun,' Kit said urgently, digging him suddenly in the ribs. 'I saw it, in the box! All brown and shiny.'

'Yes, I saw it too.'

'Will she keep it, now? Will it be like when the teacher took my purple ruler?'

'*He* wasn't whacking anybody with it, so when we get off the plane she'll probably give it back.'

Kit gazed up at him, then hunched his shoulders with an apologetic little grin.

She listened, not turning her head. He sounded so calm. Did he not even think about the risks of travelling unnecessarily at such a time? And for what? Everyone they had talked to about Port Sudan had said the same thing: no one goes there after the end of May, it's so hot and humid, and the sea level is low and no good for swimming. And here they were, going (in July) on what Charles so transparently called 'a kind of holiday'.

She closed down her senses like a tortoise withdrawing its limbs.

But the plane did not fall out of the sky, and nobody showed any sign of wanting to hijack it. As they began the descent she looked out of the cabin window, intrigued in spite of herself to see what the Sudan did when it finally got to the seaside.

She laughed suddenly. He leaned over to see what was amusing. Below them, the edge of the land made a jagged brown edge against the turquoise sea.

'I thought there would be a fringe of green! Palm trees, or

344

something. But it just marches up right to the edge and falls into the sea.'

He knew what she meant. He too had thought the coast would look different from all the rest. The plane swung round, catching the light on its rising wing, and began the slow descent above the sea. 'I forgot to tell you,' he said, 'Simeon said the hotel isn't very good. He's offered us a colleague's house to stay in – a Sudanese colleague who's taken his family to a new post in Kuwait. I told him we'd be glad to take him up on it. Should be interesting.'

She looked at him. 'Why does my heart always sink when you say that word?'

'What? Interesting?' He looked perplexed for a moment, then grinned and shrugged. He looked just like Kit when he did that.

They took a taxi to the Unicef office, housed in an old Turkish building on a flat promontory surrounded by the sea. The breeze off the sea was pleasant. The water sparkled playfully in the sun. He saw her smiling as she stood looking at the view and his spirits lifted. Beyond, in the port, great ships and tankers were lined up in the docks. This was a world away from the Sudan they knew. It was going to be fun.

He led them inside and introduced them to Simeon, the tall Kenyan in charge of the Port Sudan office. Simeon invited them to supper. He gave them the keys to the house they were to borrow and said he would call by there and pick them up at six.

They got back into the waiting taxi and went to the Red Sea Club for brunch. They were the only people there. Bee stood by the pool looking down at the water. The pool was filled with seawater twice a week, they were told. A murky haze lingered at the deep end. She straightened and looked out at the tankers and ships just beyond the gardens in the port. His heart sank. He knew what she would be thinking: she wouldn't let the children swim in the port so how could she let them swim in the same water in this pool?

They would be so cross! He turned away and busied himself studying the buildings. He had been here before but he didn't remember the toilets smelling, and he'd forgotten how saline the Pepsi tasted. But they were thirsty and they would soon get used to it. Behind him, Bee was arguing with Danny, who wanted to swim. He sighed. It was not what he might have hoped for, but there were swings and a slide in the playground and the kids would soon settle down to play. She would cope – women were better at this sort of thing than men. He would make up for it later. 'I must love you and leave you,' he said, and kissed her.

That's right, she thought. Scuttle back to the office.

The house had been shut up for some time. Crowded with dusty beds, it still managed to feel strangely empty.

'Isn't this fun,' he said, but nobody answered.

Bee sat down suddenly on one of the beds and a cloud of dust enveloped her like smoke. Catrin climbed up to snuggle into her lap.

'It's very grubby, Daddy,' Adam said uncertainly. He and Kit were sitting side by side on one of the beds with their feet up, out of the way of the giant ants that tracked this way and that across the dusty floor.

'We'd better give it a clean then,' he said. He went in search of a broom. The kitchen was empty (four walls and a tap – there wasn't even a sink, dammit). The bathroom was decidedly dodgy, certainly nothing in there to clean with. Outside in the yard he spotted an old palm fibre broom thrown up onto the roof of the lean-to. He retrieved the broom, watched hopefully by the hungry goats in the next compound, who were bleating endlessly to be fed, and went back into the living room. Bee was silent, avoiding his eye. Even Danny, who had been hassling endlessly to go snorkelling, was quiet.

He looked at her, sitting there so very still and dignified, so resolutely not looking at him. He said encouragingly, 'We just need to give it a little sweep,' and began a pantomime routine of sweeping until the children started to laugh. But still she did not say anything. She didn't turn her head, just went on stroking Catrin's hair. She didn't mention (but he knew she would have observed) that there was no bedding, and they had brought none with them. The cotton mattresses and pillows did not look very appetising.

Simeon came to pick them up for supper. He walked in, tall and stately in his immaculate white safari suit, and looked round in horror. 'You can't stay here!' he said.

Rescued in the Nicholas of time, thought Charles.

Simeon took them back to his flat. His family had gone back to Kenya on leave, ahead of him. 'Please,' he said to Bee with a courteous little bow, 'Please, be my guests. Make yourself at home. It will be no trouble to me – I will be out on a field trip for the rest of the week.'

By seven in the morning she was alone in Simeon's flat with the children. She sat under the ceiling fan while the sweat trickled uncomfortably down her flesh. The day passed in a different pattern of sunlight through the high windows, and the children baulked over their school books in the same old way as usual. The hours melted slowly, one by one in the heat, until it was time for Charles to return from the office at three.

He came in like a rush of air. He was grinning. He kissed her on one ear and asked, cheerfully, 'Had a good morning?'

'They got a lot of schoolwork done,' she said, carefully oblique.

'Right then, kids,' he said rubbing his hands together. 'Get your cozzies on. I've borrowed the office pick-up – it's high time we found that place that's supposed to be good for swimming.'

Three days later and they still hadn't found it. The places they went to were so shallow that the water barely covered the reef. 'It's the time of year,' a man in the Red Sea Club said, helpfully. So they couldn't swim, only paddle and splash in the turbid water where small black fish nibbled their shins and made them squeal. Danny found a brown octopus languidly doing umbrella-stunts in the shallow water. Then he found a large turkey fish, hovering in its private haze of black and white speckled spines in two feet of water beside a coral overhang. His voice went squeaky with excitement – he knew all about turkey fish from his National Geographic. And so, from the same article, did she: the sting from one of those long waving spines would have killed them, if any of them had brushed against it. She made the children come out of the water at once. Only Danny minded.

She sat on the sand. Charles tried to persuade her that it was safe to paddle – they had seen the turkey fish easily after all – but she ignored him. Danny glowered at her with a hatred that was harder to ignore. She withdrew into herself, watching with fierce concentration the antics of the hermit crabs scuttling on the shore, while fish flipped lazily, over and over, in the viscous sea.

348

He'd had it so clear in his head how it would be: she would be surprised into liking Port Sudan and the children would love it. And then he could slip in the possibility of extending his contract and she would find it easier to say yes.

He'd been here once before but in the winter. He hadn't realised it would be so different in July. He'd really blown it. Worse than if he'd popped his question in El Obeid without bringing her here. She was never going to listen to him properly now, poor girl, after nearly a week trapped with the children in a stranger's flat and even less to do than there was at home in El Obeid. They hadn't even had a proper swim yet. It was such a nightmare it made him almost want to laugh — one thing going wrong after another. Even Suakim. The deserted town was just as magical as in the photographs, the ruins of the houses built of coral standing on an island surrounded by a sea so calm and clear that the brightly coloured fishes crowding round the deep coral shelf of the natural harbour glowed and flashed like electric lights. But even he could see that there was something mournful about the crumbling buildings. In the hot, hazy light they looked dissolved, as if an earthquake had shattered them. But it wasn't an earthquake, it was just time and the sea air that had done it. He'd thought she might want to sketch here but she said she had no energy for it. She seemed drained and depressed, sitting miserably on a rock at a little distance while he squatted with the children at the water's edge looking at the fish and holding on to Catrin by the straps of her dungarees. Better not let her fall in — that really would be the last straw! he thought grimly. But the fish were magical and he soon forgot to feel despondent: all this barren land and then under the sea a rainbow garden of fishes! If only she would throw off her misery long enough just to come and look she would see it too.

Zahara and the girls took Josie to the airport to see her onto her flight. Zahara was nervous about it. Josie had not been to the airport for years, had not been on a plane for even longer. She hadn't had a visa or proper papers – no passport, even – for so long, yet now, mysteriously, she had a brand new passport. How could she have managed that? Zahara imagined that Paul must still have influence in high places, but she wondered what was going to happen when Josie got to the desk and had to show her passport. Josie joked about them not letting her out of the Sudan but there were beads of perspiration on her forehead. The authorities are so jumpy now, Zahara thought. What if they decide she's a spy!

She looked at Josie. She didn't look like a spy. She looked like just what she was – a fading woman, overweight and plain, her long grey hair hanging lank down her back, her near-hippy clothes worn for comfort, coolness and modesty, not for fashion. Her feet, which had spread after many years of wearing sandals so that she found shoes uncomfortable now, were dark brown and hard-looking, but her face was pale because she always wore a hat in the sun. She was leaving her hat behind. An old, battered straw thing that she said had come from Ghana many years ago when she was still a travelling woman. She had given it to Faatma. 'Hang it on your wall,' she said, 'and think of me sometimes.' And when Faatma burst into tears, she added, 'Don't cry, sweetheart. I'll come back for it one day.'

But Zahara thought, as they waited patiently in the queue for the check-in desk, She will not be back. Now that she had severed the ties – with Paul, with her and the girls and Ibrahim, with the school – what would there be to come back

350

for? As they chatted idly about nothing very much she wondered what sort of goodbyes there had been in Josie's house, before she and the girls had drawn up outside and tooted half an hour ago. There had been no sign of Paul. Josie had come out, locked the front door and pushed the key back under it, so presumably Paul hadn't been there. She looked at her now and wondered at it: how could Josie have spent all of her adult life here, and most of it with a man she was now leaving, and show so little outward sign of upheaval?

She sighed, unconsciously, and Josie's hand found hers and squeezed it. She squeezed back. No, she could not imagine that Josie would ever be coming back. As if she felt her thinking it, Josie said in a low voice meant only for her, 'Pity I didn't make the full thirty years! But I'm just too tired, Zahara. I've been here long enough, it's time to go.'

'When will we see you again, Aunty?' Aasha asked, holding onto Josie's smock and squinting up at her worriedly.

'Maybe next time I see you it will be in England. Your grandma's invited me to go see her in Cardiff.' Aasha looked unconvinced. Yasmina asked Josie what she was going to eat for her first meal back in the States. Jamila said that anyway Cardiff wasn't in England, it was in Wales. Zahara let her mind wander. It was like saying goodbye to her mother all over again, that first time when they were children, and Jamil so small and lost, and how grown up she had tried to be and not let her real feelings show, just as she was doing now. She turned her head and studied the notices on the wall to their right, trying to stop the tears from spilling and running down. She felt like one of those advent calendars Aunty Audrey used to send at Christmas but the wrong way round: all the doors closing, one by one.

351

How could he have let things get into such a pickle? As they travel back to El Obeid for what he knows (but she still does not) is to be his last six weeks there of tying up loose ends before moving to the Port Sudan office, he cannot imagine how he could have arrived at this point, though each step along the way – when he takes it out of his head and looks at it – is logical and obvious. It is the fact as a whole that has jumped out of his grasp, awkward and unruly and looking different now as the sum of its parts.

He considers the arguments he will use, when the time is right. He will admit the personal: he will tell her just how depressed he is at the prospect of going back to the university. That is necessary – he needs her to know the extent of the compromises he will be willing to make for her sake in the future, if only they might defer going back for two more years now. (Well yes, he knows it will be two and a half years and she'll observe that fact immediately, but there's no point overstating at this stage.) In exchange he will point out the benefit to *her* interests of accumulating more capital before they try to buy her longed-for cottage. This she will surely be able to see.

This is the history of their marriage, he thinks. She is more conservative than he is, more resistant to change. Given time to think it through she usually accepts his point of view and embraces it. This is where the success of their relationship lies – the balance between his initiative, and her practical good sense honing it into something workable. It was true when he got the job in Norwich and she wanted to buy a cottage in the Suffolk countryside rather than live in the city: he managed to persuade her then of the sense in his suggestion that they should live in the town while he consolidated his position in the department and – more importantly – until they could

352

afford somewhere they really wanted in the countryside. He had persuaded her too about taking on this secondment in El Obeid. And they *had* had a good time, for all the difficulties. They had all benefited from the challenge. She wasn't finding it easy but she would be glad of the experience one day, when she looked back on this episode in their family history. He knew her well enough to know that.

He had needed no other argument than this, he realises gloomily, sitting in the cramped seat beside her and looking down through the small port-hole of the Twin Otter at El Obeid coming closer. He had had the moral high ground, he hadn't challenged her over Daz. (She never need know the other stuff about Maggie, thank God.) He still would have the moral high ground now, if only he had told her sooner about the contract. But when he got back from leave Calvin had started putting pressure on him: the Port Sudan job would not be on offer for ever, the powers that be needed a decision, and she was at End Point and unreachable by phone. And then the Acropole bomb. After that he knew that he had to stay, that really he had no choice. Poor old Sudan. This country needed people like him. People with energy and knowledge and commitment. He couldn't run away. And he knew she would feel the same (and indeed she has told him since that she *did* feel that, when the bomb happened). So he had radioed Calvin with his answer while she was still out of reach at End Point. Thinking, I can always say no later, if she really does want me to back out. And then he had signed the contract, still thinking that. But he had not written of it in his letters to her. It is something he needs to tell her face to face. Except that he just hasn't.

He pulls Catrin from Bee's lap onto his own for landing, holding her small body safe in the tense circle of his arms. He looks down at her fluffy head. Signing the contract, not telling

Bee yet – these aren't the real cock-ups. Where he has really fucked up is taking her to Port Sudan in July thinking he would win her over before he said anything about the job. Or if not her, Danny. The kids. All that seaside, he had thought. He might have got away with it too, if she'd been less resistant. If only he hadn't taken her there at such a stupid time of year!

The worst thing about it, he thinks as they bump down on the runway and Catrin gives her usual little yelp, is that now that he's spent time in the office in Port Sudan he so much wants that job! He likes the people that he's met, he likes the dynamic, mercantile nature of the place, the sharp, dramatic outlines of the Red Sea Hills and the fierce Beja tribes-people that inhabit them. He has so much to offer and it would be wrong not to try.

He thinks of Norwich and the suburban streets, of asphalt warming dully in the sun, daisies and dog-shit littering the verges, and ice-cream vans that jingle emptily on summer afternoons. He thinks of traffic jams at eight a.m. and centrally heated offices in winter, full of chipboard furniture and the smell of cheap, synthetic carpeting. Of students clamouring for attention, of dull essays, and the endless details of other people's unexciting lives paraded in front of him. And he knows he cannot go back.

Chapter 24

Zahara was listing all the reasons why she did not want to live in England: the weather, the drab grey skies; the hard faces of people in the street and the way they only ever talked about themselves, beginning with 'I' and ending with 'me'; the care with which they remind you that you are a foreigner, an outsider; the difficulty, as a foreigner, of finding a job; the resentment sometimes shown you when you do, because you, an outsider, have one and some of them do not. She thought of the faceless queues at supermarket tills and bored women behind counters, their glazed eyes skidding over the outside of your features, not engaging. She remembered the rented rooms they lived in when Ibrahim was still a student, and two years later the cramped square box of a house on a faceless estate in north London that they had lived in for ten months when Faatma was a baby, where they never knew the names of their next-door neighbours. No, she concluded, standing patiently in the long queue outside the Lebanese shop as she waited to buy powdered milk, apart from Ibrahim's career there were no compelling reasons for wanting to go back there to live, except for seeing more of her mother and of Nazmul, and her feelings about her mother were still ambivalent.

But when she listed the reasons for staying they crumbled away as her thoughts touched them. No Mastura, and her brief baby gone with her. No Jamil, now that he had stopped coming up to Khartoum. She worried about him, but worrying didn't bring him closer. 'I have to bury myself in work,' he had said. But she was afraid it might be alcohol he was burying himself in. He did not answer her letters. Perhaps he would never come back. His brief identity as a married man seemed pitifully transient now. She wondered where his untransient life would turn out to be. Perhaps he would marry a local woman and stay forever in the east, a long way from Khartoum. She could not force her comfort on him but her heart bled, eating out a hollow around his absence that she would cauterise if she could.

The queue moved forward a few steps and came to a halt again. The woman at the front was arguing shrilly with Hussein, who was rationing the three-kilo tins to two per household. Zahara sighed. She wondered if Hussein would allow her four tins so that she could keep two and take two to her father?

It was the holidays but she was working every day with the Australian woman who had taken Josie's place. They had another woman too, an Eritrean teacher who was clever and full of ideas. It was a busy time, getting ready for the new school year. Zahara listened to their enthusiasm – their ambitious enthusiasm, it seemed to her – and it made her feel tired. Like Josie, though she was twenty years younger, she just felt tired. I need a change, she thought. Ibrahim needs one even more!

She looked up at the dull sky, as brown as the city. How can I possibly think of going away and leaving Abu all alone? The same old circle of her thoughts. But Abu has become remote. She cannot tell if he is grieving over Mastura or simply retreating into his own inner world. He does not reveal himself to her. He is affectionate, but he is distant. She looks into his eyes and she cannot read them.

356

Could I ever? she wondered.

His books seem to have become more real to him than his own family, she thought crossly as the queue inched forwards again. When they went there now his house felt painfully empty without Jamil and Mastura. No, worse than empty, because Nura seemed to always be there. Mastura is dead and I am worrying about Nura! she chided herself. But even when she didn't see Nura face to face she could feel her flitting in the shadows, just out of sight, her presence like a living ghost. More real a ghost than any Mastura has left behind, she thought sadly as the queue shifted forwards again.

She wondered how Abu would feel about Ibrahim contacting the journal in London again. When they had offered him the post in their Africa Department before, two years ago, the elections were about to be held in the Sudan. How full of hope he had been then, how excited at the prospect of democracy! He had turned down the job: how could he not stay to share his country's new future? It seems so innocently hopeful now, when that fragile democracy is threatening to disintegrate. If the government falls, the Muslim Brothers might head a reaction in its wake. Or there might be a coup, and a slide into extremism. Khartoum is rife with rumours. Not just internal politics either. An exiled Iraqi minister was gunned down in broad daylight in the lobby of the Hilton Hotel on the banks of the Nile. It is said that radioactive waste from Iraq is being smuggled through Khartoum airport and left standing in old oil drums on the tarmac. Conspiracy theories multiply at every level and nothing feels safe or innocent any more. They talk about these things late at night, in the privacy of their double bed.

'How much do you feel you must stay for your father's sake?' Ibrahim had asked, not once but twice. He had already

357

been given his parents' blessing, if he ever chose to go. Each time he asked it there was less conviction in her reply.

She came to the front of the queue. She asked for four tins, for two households, and Hussein hesitated, looking over her shoulder at the long queue behind her standing hopefully in the sun. Unexpectedly (if grudgingly) he compromised: she could have three. She thanked him hastily before he could change his mind and handed over the money.

As she came away she looked at her watch. One hour and forty minutes she'd been waiting. At least you don't have to queue for milk in England – fresh milk is delivered to your doorstep every day.

No, apart from Ibrahim's career she could think of few good reasons for going but fewer still for staying. But it was so unlikely the journal would consider employing him now, after all this time – it really was not worth worrying about, and certainly she should not say anything to Abu yet, just as they had not said anything to the girls.

She walked across the vacant lot where the new supermarket had never been built, disturbing the skinny goat which was foraging under one of the *mesquite* bushes, to where she had left the car outside the pharmacist's. Her father had asked her to get him some drugs but when she went in to buy them the pharmacist said they were out of stock. She asked what the drug was, not recognising the trade name. Iron pills, he said.

She drove out of town towards the Nile house, wondering that her father should be suffering from anaemia. She had always thought it a female complaint. But it would explain why he had not been himself lately.

Silly! *That* did not need explaining. Mastura was dead: they were none of them themselves.

She missed Jamil, suddenly and acutely. I could go and see

him, she thought. But Ed Damazin was too far. There was no way she could go there alone and it would be missing the point if she went with Ibrahim, even if it were a reasonable thing to ask of him. Besides, just at the moment she thought Jamil would probably not want to see her there. And not for many moments to come, perhaps.

If we went to London just for two years, when we came back it all could be the same again. She turned into the drive of her father's house. Or as much the same as it could ever be, with Mastura gone. (She still could not believe it; she had to practise thinking it to make it real.) In two years time Jamil would be feeling more himself again and Abu would not yet be really old.

She drove slowly down the track, trying to avoid the pot-holes. It was a dull day, the heat very solid, threatening rain. Everything seemed colourless, even the trees. How drab it all looked in this light, a little forlorn. She tooted as she drew up outside the house, careful to warn her father of her arrival, not wanting any embarrassment. I'm obsessed with Nura! she reprimanded herself. Though she had hardly set eyes on the girl for weeks now. It was only her broken shoes by the front door and her *thobe*, smelling of sweat and neatly folded on a chair in the kitchen, which confirmed each time she came that Nura was indeed somewhere about.

She went into the house. The lounge was empty. The windows were closed and the air stifling. She threw them open and breathed in the soft river breeze. This was a part of her private ritual, coming home: breathing in the green river smell from the shade of this familiar room. She hated the thought of leaving it all behind. But then, she reminded herself, it will not go anywhere. In two years time it will all still be here when we came back.

She went into the kitchen but it was empty. Quite tidy, except for a plate in the sink. She put the tin of milk in the store cupboard and out of habit washed and dried the dirty plate and put it away. She went into the study.

Hassan sat in his armchair, asleep. His head lolled on the back of the chair and his mouth was open, his false teeth askew. A book lay on his lap. Gently she took it out of his loose grasp and placed it on the table. She lifted his precious glasses carefully off his nose and folded them and put them on top of the book. He stirred and sighed, murmuring something softly without waking. She looked at him, wondering who was there with him in his sleep.

She went back through the kitchen and out of the house. Outside, on a bench in the shade, Nura sat sprawling against the wall. When she caught sight of Zahara she got up hastily. In that brief moment Zahara saw what had been carefully hidden before. Straining against the shiny material of Nura's dress: the unmistakeable bulk of pregnancy.

She did not say a word, standing there stock still while Nura rushed off in the direction of the kitchen. Mastura is dead. Jamil's child died with her. But Nura – Nura the insolent, Nura the lascivious, Nura the enemy – Nura is with child.

Abu's child? she wondered, shocked into directness. Her own half-brother or sister? Claiming blood?

She shrank into herself, scudding like a wraith round the outside of the house, climbing into the car. Crashing the gears. Halfway up to the road she was forced to stop. She got out hurriedly and was sick, there in the dust beside the car.

It rained everywhere except in El Obeid. Charles, flying down to Muglad, saw sheets of water shining white on the ground just to the south of El Obeid. The flight was terrible, bumping through storms.

There will be visits every week now, these final weeks in El Obeid. To Muglad, or to Mieram or Abiyei. To check on the feeding programmes which are struggling to keep pace with the influx of Dinka. The old annual cycle of rain, of war and of displacement, but this year it is worse. He is seeing things so heartrending that he can't talk about them when he comes home. He cannot talk of anything much: his children seem suddenly precious and vulnerable, their lives hanging on delicate threads. In the camps the starving children are shrunken and withered so that they look like old men with trembling overgrown heads and huge eyes. They haunt his dreams. Sometimes when Catrin comes running to clamber onto his lap on his return, or when Kit leans with innocent ease against his shoulder as he sits in his chair, it feels as if some grim shadow is hanging over them, a feeling of threatened loss so profound that it is like an aura hanging over them all.

It'll be a relief to be in Port Sudan, he kept thinking. But he still hadn't said anything to Bee.

The new school term wasn't due to begin for several weeks yet. At home, the routine of English schoolwork went doggedly on. There had to be something to fill some of the empty hours, and in four months time, when they go back to England, they need not have fallen too far behind. When we go back home. They say it so often. 'Will I have wellies of my own when we go back home?' asks Catrin. 'I will go to big school when we go back home,' Adam says proudly. But the thought does not spur him on to greater efforts with his English schoolwork.

361

Kit dawdled over his so painfully that in the end, when he promised he would do it after lunch 'with no fuss', she let him put it off. But after lunch he sat endlessly at the table not doing his sums, while she sat beside him and the ants ran over her bare feet and up between her toes. Adam had done his sums in the morning so he was free to play now, and Kit was indignant. He sighed, and dropped his pencil for the umpteenth time.

'Pick it up,' she repeated, yet again. The endless stoicism of patience.

'I should have done it this morning,' he said, and she replied, 'Yes – tomorrow you'll *have* to do it in the morning.'

'I didn't know I had a choice!' he shouted suddenly, hurling his pencil across the room. She retreated to the kitchen, afraid she might hit him if she stayed.

How the days dawdle. Storms hover and do not break. The day wants to rain, Fatouma says. Summer stretches ahead of them forever. They have to last out until Christmas but it seems impossible that Christmas will ever come. She closes her eyes and endures.

'Uncle's truck! Uncle's truck is there, Mummy!'

She had seen it too, the moment before Yasmina shouted out, as she turned the car into his street on the way back to their flat. His dusty, battered old pick-up, stained with distant mud, parked outside his flat as if the old days had come back again.

She parked hurriedly, her heart fluttering with excitement and with fear. The girls were already leaping out and running along the road towards the block where Jamil and Mastura had their ground-floor flat. Jamil and Mastura: she still thought of them as a couple, she still called it 'their flat' in her head.

Yasmina was in front, already running up the path, her plaits swinging from side to side. Jamila was close on her heels. Behind them, Aasha panting. Faatma bringing up the rear with her, walking quietly as if she too had realised that this was complicated. Have they forgotten Mastura will not be there? 'Girls!' she called out warningly, but Yasmina was already knocking on the front door.

Jamil opened the door. But not the Jamil they knew. Faatma saw it too, she heard it in the sharp little intake of breath at her side. But the girls were throwing themselves at him just as usual. She went towards him warily, seeking out his eyes. He looked back into hers grimly. There was no light in his eyes at all.

He had always been such a bonny man. Bonny – her mother's word. Like her own father, her mother said. A tall man, well-fleshed, his short hair black and velvety. Now he was gaunt and his hair was cropped so close to his skull that he almost looked shaved, and she noticed for the first-time how his hairline was receding. The flesh had faded off him, so that he seemed to have shrunk. And his once honey-coloured skin had darkened, as if all the colour in it had intensified with the diminishment in flesh. He must have been working out in the fields, she thought as she followed him indoors. She could see the line on his neck where his shirt had kept off the sun. She longed to touch him, to gentle him, but he had held himself away from her on greeting, discouraging any embrace. Now Yasmina was hanging on his arm but he seemed unconscious of her, and it was clear he wasn't hearing a word any of them said to him.

'We have so missed you,' she said quietly when he turned towards her in the living room. 'We have looked for you every Thursday and Friday, and now it isn't even a Friday – it's a Tuesday!'

363

'I shouldn't be here. I'm clearing out the flat – Mohammed Abdul Bashir was going to do it for me but he did not have the time so I have had to come and do it myself.'

Mohammed Abdul Bashir? A knife seemed to turn in her guts. He had kept them out, but he was letting Mastura's family in.

He saw her expression. 'Not that Mohammed Abdul Bashir,' he said. 'Mohammed Abdul Bashir who is my foreman.'

'Oh,' she said, the wound closing up again. 'But I don't understand. Why are you clearing the flat?'

'I gave the landlord notice for the end of this month. It's very awkward to come now when we're so busy on the farm but it has to be done.'

She stood helplessly looking at him. He had not felt he could ask them to do it. How could that be? And how could he be leaving the flat anyway? It would be leaving them. They didn't have the space for him to stay with them when he came to Khartoum, unless he had their small living room as his bedroom. He could, of course, go back to staying with Abu, as he used to before his marriage. She thought of Nura, and instantly thought – No, he must not know about that! It would be too painful if he were to know about Nura now. It would feel like mockery. A most awful mockery, if his thoughts ran the same way hers did. Ibrahim still thought she was wrong. But she could think of no other explanation for all the oddities.

Then she thought, Perhaps he has seen it himself already. Perhaps that explains his grimness now. 'Have you seen Abu?'

He shook his head impatiently. 'I won't have time. I'll be writing to him about farm business. I'll tell him then.'

He grimaced as Yasmina climbed on the sofa behind him and tried to launch herself onto his back for the usual piggy-back.

Yasmina was looking up at him anxiously. 'Are you moving, Uncle? Will we see you in your new flat? Will it—'

'Girls,' she interrupted in her brightest, most not-to-be-questioned voice, 'run home and tell your father that Uncle is here. He will want to come and see him.'

Protesting, but only mildly, they turned obediently to go. 'You too, Faatma,' she added, seeing that Faatma was hesitating.

Jamil had turned away from her and was putting things into boxes. He hadn't offered them anything to drink. He seemed not to want them to linger. 'Ibrahim will want to see you,' she said, as if sending the girls off needed apology. 'But I wanted a moment with you alone.'

He turned and looked at her. His eyes, too, seemed to have gone very dark. She looked into them and she could not see the old Jamil anywhere.

'They have forgotten her already,' he said. He sounded more bitter than sad.

'Jamil! They have not forgotten! But thirteen weeks is a long time when you are small. A long, long time.' He grunted, and went back to his packing. She said to his back, 'How *could* they forget Mast—'

He turned on her, fast as a whiplash. 'Don't say her name!' His voice was harsh. 'Don't say it. I do not want to hear it.'

She went to him and put her hand on his arm. She felt the flesh tense away from her, the muscle all hard and rigid against her hand. 'Jamil!'

He turned his head away. 'I never want to hear her name again. All that is past. Finished. It can never come back and my life is finished with it. It is all endurance now, nothing more.'

'Jamil,' she said so softly that he might not even hear her. 'Don't turn away from us. We are your family. It isn't our culture to mourn alone.'

'Isn't it? We have no culture, you and me. We can do what we will.'

She tried again. Patiently. 'Jamil, you should not be alone. It isn't healthy to be alone.' His eyes said, I am not alone. And she knew that it was true, but it was not what she meant. He should have people around him who were his equals, not servants and employees who could not push him back into health when he wanted to stay sick in his mind. She tried a different tack. 'It won't be like this for ever. One day you will learn to be happy again.'

'What do you know about it?' he said harshly. 'What can you know? You are not me, you were not married to her. You know nothing of my life. Not now.'

She did not dare to touch him again. She folded her arms to keep her hands away. 'I want to know your life, Jamil. As it is now. I want you to tell it to me. I want to understand.'

'Pah!'

'I loved her too, Jamil,' she said, stung. 'Even if it was different. You are not suffering entirely on your own. And Abu loved her. And the girls – especially the girls. Of course it isn't the same for us as it is for you. But perhaps we could understand a little, if you would let us.' He had turned his back on her and she could not see his face. She pushed a little harder. 'We have missed her terribly. But we have missed you too, Jamil. We have missed you badly.'

'There is nothing of me left to miss.'

'And we've *all* been so worried about you. Mummy was asking if she should come over…'

He rounded on her with such fury that the words dried in her mouth. 'And what could *she* do? *She* knows least of all. She has no right to think *she* can help *me*!'

She looked at him helplessly. She remembered suddenly the

little boy he had been at five years old, uncomprehending in their mother's desperate embrace at the airport. That day more than twenty years ago. He had the same baffled, angry look in his eyes now that he'd had then. But now she too was somehow on the wrong side. He would not let her go to him now and take his hand as she had taken it that day. He could not stand in the safety of Abu's shadow, nor go home to find Old Faatma had cooked his favourite pastries to comfort him. This time, for her, there will be no years of standing over him protectively, tending his wounds when he falls, comforting him when he wakes crying in the night, as if he is her son rather than her little brother. The house on the Nile will never feel like his home again. Perhaps nowhere else will either.

Jonathon came down from Khartoum. His visit, at least, promised a few days of stimulus, like an island in the Dead Sea.

Charles wasn't there: he got on to the plane as Jonathon got off it, to go down to Abiyei with François. Bee made Jonathon breakfast of coffee, grapefruit and bread and jam. He sat across the table from her, his familiar sharp, humorous self.

'So how are you looking forward to Port Sudan?' he asked.

'We've already been. Just about everything went wrong. We didn't even get to swim.'

'Oh well,' he said, 'there'll be plenty of opportunity for swimming when you move there permanently. June and July are rotten times for swimming there anyway.'

'Pardon?'

'The summer's no good for swimming. Sea level's too low. There's sometimes more mud than sand.'

She said carefully, a sudden intimation chilling her so that she spoke very slowly and distinctly, 'What did you say about *moving* there?'

He stared at her. 'Oh shit.' He rubbed his jaw uncertainly. 'You can't mean you don't know?'

There was a silence in which she simply looked at him, saying nothing.

'I've obviously spoken way out of turn. But I can't believe he hasn't told you? I mean, everyone in Khartoum thinks he's moving to Port Sudan at the end of this month. How come he hasn't told you?'

'There's never been any question of us moving to Port Sudan,' she said evenly, too proud to let her surprise show. 'His contract ends at Christmas. There wouldn't be any point in us going anywhere else, would there? Not for four months. There must have been some kind of misunderstanding if anyone thinks he's moving.'

'Jesus! I really have put my foot in it, haven't I!' He looked at her, frowning. 'Excuse me for saying this, Bee. I've always thought – well, it isn't easy to say this but I've always thought Charles is – well, he can be – a bit of a slippery bastard. I mean, he's a great guy, don't get me wrong. But are you sure you know what he's up to? I mean, *I know* I haven't got it wrong. So how come he hasn't told you?'

She drew herself up with painful dignity, sitting very erect at the other side of the table. 'What are you saying? That I don't know my own husband? That he's underhand in some way? There's obviously just been some confusion. Please stop this. I've got quite enough to cope with without you adding unnecessary complications.'

Under the table her hands were trembling in her lap. She turned her face away, not wanting to see the look of concern – of pity, even – in his eyes. She wanted him just to go, to leave her in peace. In a few minutes he did, bending to kiss her cheek as he went. He didn't come back that evening, nor did she see him again the following day, and, since he left for Khartoum on the same flight that brought Charles back from Abiyei, she didn't see him again before Charles got back.

'You bastard!'

Hissed, it was far worse than loud anger, like a snake, lashing out at him from the grass. He hadn't thought of Jonathon coming to see Bee, but he had known that this hour must come. It was almost a relief. They'd get through this next bit, he'd do a bit of penance, and then they would move on. 'I am so sorry, love. I was going to tell you.'

'Tell me what? That you'd forgotten to mention the fact that you were going to suddenly cart us off to Port Sudan for the last four months of your contract without even a by your leave? Christ, what do you think I am? A bloody suitcase?'

So she hadn't realised yet about the extended contract. His heart sank yet further as he realised that he was still going to have to tell her that bit. 'It wasn't like that,' he said. (Thinking, One step at a time!) 'Of course I was going to tell you! It's just... there never seemed to be a good moment, and it was so difficult to tell you after we went up there because I thought you'd be prejudiced after that.'

'Prejudiced?' she queried scornfully. 'Prejudiced? You mean, the fact that we had a bloody awful time there was just me being prejudiced?'

'Of course not—'

'How dare you! How dare you make decisions that involve me and not even tell me! And then imply afterwards that it's my fault for not making it easier for you to tell me! I can't believe this, I really can't. How could you do this? How *could* you!'

He blinked. He'd expected her to be cross but she hadn't

really got a leg to stand on after what she'd put him through this summer.

Unless… had he got the wrong end of that particular stick? A sudden hopeful uncertainty gripped him and he peered into her face. Yes, she was very, *very* angry. He must have got it completely wrong – she hadn't slept with that junkie! But it wouldn't do to look too pleased about it at this particular moment in time. He composed his voice carefully and said 'I'm sorry, Bee, darling – I'm really sorry. I know I've done it all wrong, I can't think how I've been so stupid. I just kept hoping it would somehow get more straightforward and I could tell you and instead it's got more and more difficult. But I *was* going to tell you, of course I was! Tonight, as it happens, though I know you won't believe me now. I really was – I knew I couldn't leave it any longer.' He went to her and stroked her bare arm. 'And it's not really *so very* bad, is it? Not *really*, not in the scale of possible sins?' He peered into her face hopefully. 'Around about a five, wouldn't you think, on the sin scale? And I am really, really sorry I didn't talk to you about it before I agreed, but you were in End Point and I couldn't phone you, and they were putting pressure on me in Khartoum to make a decision, and of course after I'd actually said yes I knew you'd be cross, so then it was really hard to find the right moment to tell you. Besides, we don't have to go, not if you really don't want to. I always knew I could back out if you wanted me to.'

She stood watching him, as if rooted to the spot she had been standing on when he came in from the airport. She was quivering with rage, quite literally – her shoulders were shaking. 'Well you'd better do just that!' she snapped. 'What were you thinking of? There is no point at all packing up everything here and trotting off to Port Sudan just for four months! Do you have the least idea how much that would involve? What about the children? We'd

370

have to take them out of school all together, not to mention the unsettling effect of suddenly going off somewhere else just when they're looking forward to going back home.'

He ticked her points off in his head. The packing up of the house would have to be done in December if it wasn't done now. Tick. Four months off school was not so bad, they probably learned more at home anyway. Tick. The kids would adapt once they got used to the idea, as she would too. Tick, tick. None of it seemed important, compared with the load that had lifted off his heart.

She said icily, 'You'd better get over to the office and radio Khartoum. There's no need to let *them* go on in ignorance, even if you found yourself able to do that to me. How could you make me look such a fool?' she added, getting fierce again. 'Go on – go and tell them straight away.'

'I can't,' he said uncomfortably. 'There's no radio contact now till Saturday.'

'Huh!' she said derisively, and turning away from him she stalked into the kitchen.

He hovered for a while, not knowing whether to follow her or to leave her alone until she'd cooled down. She was bound to be cross at first, but she would come round. Conciliatory patience, that was what was required of him. He still couldn't believe that he'd made such a pig's breakfast of everything but he'd been rushed off his feet since they got back from Port Sudan and there had never been a right moment to broach the subject. Blimey, he thought she's this angry and it's only at the thought of moving to Port Sudan for four months! What's she going to say when I tell her about extending my contract? He didn't know what to do, so he went into the sitting room where the children were playing and surprised them by joining in the game. They couldn't believe their luck.

In the bedroom she weeps silently into the hard cotton pillow with the light switched off. There is nowhere she can go except here, where he might come and find her at any moment.

She can't believe that he has reduced her to this. They used to be equals but now, it seems, he can manipulate their lives without reference to any of them. She does not want to go to Port Sudan. She does not want to pack up this house only to have to pack up another in a few months time. She doesn't want the dislocation of starting again somewhere new, even for only a few months. Why couldn't he just let her slide through these last months with her head down and get through it blindly and as quickly as possible? Did he have to force her to expose herself and her cowardice at the eleventh hour, too weak and too useless to cry 'Yes!' and race off with him to Port Sudan with girl-guide vigour?

That look on his face – she'd seen that look.

Her feelings suddenly somersault at the memory of it. The clean flame of fury flickers out as she realises that he *does* know about Daz. He has known all along and he's never said a word.

She lies very still. He can't know! How could he know and not say anything?

Too soon, before she is ready, she hears his bare feet padding into the room and feels him standing looking down at her. His solicitous voice says tenderly, 'Bee, darling – I am sorry, I am *so* sorry!'

There is a silence as though he is waiting for her to speak. There isn't much point fighting him. Not now. She turns towards him and offers, 'I suppose the children and I could go home a bit earlier than we planned and you could go to Port Sudan on your own for the last four months…'

He kneels beside the bed in the half-dark, barred by the shadows where the electric light on the verandah filters through the shutters, and puts his arm across her shoulders as if he might be about to accept this compromise. A compromise that is already making her feelings sit up and feel brighter, in spite of the muddle they are in. But what he says is, 'I'm afraid it isn't quite that simple. They want me to extend my contract.'

She stiffens. She stops breathing to listen. 'How long for?' she asks suspiciously.

'Two years.'

He has her trapped like a mouse fallen in a bucket. He does know! He is trading *that* for *this*. The inside of her head goes very quiet.

He starts to speak but she interrupts him. 'As far as I'm concerned,' she says, icily calm, 'you can sign up for hell if you like. And forever, if you want to. But the children and I would not be coming with you. Not to hell, obviously.'

'Bee,' he says reprovingly, 'don't! It doesn't make it any easier.'

'I am absolutely sick of other people telling me what makes things easier. You bastard! You bloody, bloody bastard.'

He sighs, sitting on the bed beside her angry form, which is tensed away from him. He pats her on the shoulder like a parent comforting a child. And then, he goes away and leaves her alone.

All evening she cries, and broods, and cries again, lying in the dark like a naughty child banished from the light and easy family world which carries on without her – voices on the back verandah, children in the bathroom, sleepy good-nights from their bedroom, and only once her absence alluded to – Catrin complaining loudly, 'Mummy hasn't kissed me!' and the quiet rumble of Charles's inaudible reply, dignified, adult, while she lies exiled in the parental bed. For all her anger there is something rotten here. She does know that she owes him. In that brief, crazy episode that she has wished undone ever since, she sold her impoverished soul.

He woke at five-thirty as usual, although it was a Friday and his weekend. For a moment or two he lay in the half-light, disoriented to be waking on the *angareb* under the sitting room windows instead of in their double bed, to blue walls instead of pink, and no warm, voluptuous body beside him. Then he remembered.

He got up and took his briefcase to the back verandah. He made himself tea and sat at the table over his paperwork. Memos, supply call forwards, cash call forwards – the tedious detail of a highly constructed bureaucracy, which half drove him wild and half affirmed his place within the Unicef family. Under the pressure of the relief work in the south and his own impending move to Port Sudan he had hardly had a moment to keep abreast of the administrative demands. He wondered what the Khartoum office was doing about his replacement in El Obeid. They were eager for him to take up his new post in the Red Sea Hills but so far it was unclear what would happen here in his wake. The usual muddle threatened. It was, he thought gloomily, not so very different from his domestic muddle, but without the burden of personal guilt.

The sun was well up and the heat was rising when he took her a mug of tea in bed. She lay in glorious oblivion, sprawled at an angle across the bed under the veil of the mosquito net, the sheet pushed off in the heat. But her face, when she lifted her head off the pillow to peer up at him blearily, was crumpled and blotchy. She turned over, her heavy breasts shuddering, and took the mug from him without meeting his eye. He knew he was not to be forgiven in a hurry. It was

374

strange to stand there beside her, a fully clothed man in the presence of a naked, angry woman. He waited for a moment in case she had anything to say and then went back to his papers. In the next room, the chirrupy sounds of waking children sounded like the tentative chatter of young birds.

She lies on the pink sheet and watches him go out of the room. If she is supposed to do the talking, she has nothing to say — not without some wooing first, not without a little mollifying. Her whole self has risen up in rebellion at the betrayal. His betrayal. Which she cannot help feeling over-balances her own. She made a mistake, which she bitterly regrets, and this, it seems, is going to be the price. He has manipulated her weakness to his own advantage.

In any case, although he says the contract can be undone, if she were to make him do that she would be pitching her needs head-on against his, refusing like a horse at a fence. He has compromised her response before she even knew there was one to be made, boxing her in so that she feels like a package ready for posting.

She lies on the bed, robbed of the last shreds of her dignity, too miserable to drink the tea, or to get up and face him. How can she assert 'I' in the face of his 'me' and claim precedence for her wishes over his? He wants to make the world a better place, she merely wants to protect herself. She is trapped. Her only pride lies in behaving as well as she can with what is left of her feeble integrity.

Chapter 25

Hassan phoned. 'Don't come on Friday,' he said.

'But Abu—!'

'I will be away on Friday. On a visit to my cousins.'

She didn't believe him. He had never done such a thing before. Why now? 'I'll come when you get back,' she said, but he replied, 'I don't know when that will be.' 'Well, the Friday after then, if I haven't heard from you before.' But he was evasive, saying he might stay away longer than that. It was very strange. She put the phone down, mortally wounded. Another door closing in her face. All the silences like obstructions. And she didn't believe a word of it. She thought that if she went there, she would find him. And Nura, too.

Friday came round again, and nothing resolved. He had tiptoed round her for days but now he was more like his usual confident self and it was almost a relief. Charles uncertain was Charles unfamiliar. But as he grew substantial again she felt even more like his shadow. 'Let's go to Jebel Darju when it gets cooler and fly Danny's new kite,' he suggested energetically at lunchtime. She said yes but she could not simulate enthusiasm. *Does he just think I'm sulking?* she wondered.

The sun was sinking gently as they got out of the truck at the foot of the hill and began to walk through the yellow grasses towards the rocky slopes. The children ran ahead to examine the camel carcass that lay in the dry gully among the thorn bushes. The skin had dried to parchment, stretched over the picked white bones of the rib-cage. The skull was exposed now – the wind and sand had cleaned off what the dogs and wild animals had left. The first time they saw it Kit had believed this must be Daz's camel. Now they liked to pretend that it really was. And as if they were visiting a grave, they always talked reverently of Daz when they saw it, wondering what he was doing now.

She walked behind Kit and Adam, holding Catrin's hand, her mind elsewhere, not listening. Ahead of them, Danny's tee-shirt made a brilliant red oblong in the orange light of the sun as he clambered up the rocks with his kite. Thorny burrs from the grasses caught in their clothes and their shoes and Catrin, as usual, was complaining loudly that she hated *jebels*. Charles was a long way ahead, already on the summit. Kit and Adam toiled up the steep slope on their short legs, Kit's so skinny, Adam's solid.

'Hush!' she said to Catrin, who took no notice. She paused to let Catrin rest, turning her mind away to the great expanse which lay before her. The town looked small and insignificant, obscured by trees – surprisingly so in a place which always seemed so bare. Here and there a two-storey building stood proud of the green canopy. In the foreground, a steady file of boys and donkeys tracked to and fro, carrying water from the diesel-powered bore-hole on the edge of the town to the village on the far side of the *jebel*. At the base of the slope three women sat on the ground scooping out red clay to make pots, and far away a lorry ambled out of the town across the bush, a plume of dust rising gaily in it wake. It was like looking at a vast painting. Such a self-sufficient world, so sure of itself. Who was she to question anything?

It isn't only a question of the bad things she has done, she realises. Charles has changed. It is difficult for him, immersed as he is in this culture which doesn't expect her to voice an opinion, to remember to give her the space for one. She has changed, too – had already changed, before Daz – becoming hesitant. She is too unsure of herself now to push against his certainties.

Several days ago Danny realised what they were talking about. His excitement was immediate and vocal. Port Sudan was his idea of heaven. He could get a proper mask and snorkel, and new flippers. They could go to the places they'd been told so much about where it was possible to swim over the reef in deep water and explore the coral cliffs and overhangs. He would see octopus, another turkey fish. Dolphins even. He knew about the Red Sea from his National Geographics. They could buy a boat…

She couldn't bear to look at Charles's expression. She was sure it would be smug. She watched Danny's animated face as she listened to him running away and leaving her behind. 'But what about school?' she argued helplessly. Another two years of secondary school missed – how would Danny ever catch up in time for GCSEs? 'Don't be silly Mum,' he said, 'I'm learning so many different things here!' And Charles merely nodded. Danny had just made his argument for him. Kit, it went without saying, would not want to stay in the Sudan any longer than they had to: homesickness was at the root of a lot of his difficult behaviour. Adam, too, talked wistfully and often about going home. But Catrin would accept going to live in Port Sudan as easily as going back to England: for her either decision meant dislocation.

She'd stopped arguing. What could she say? She hadn't made Charles go to the office to radio Khartoum with his refusal. How could she? In the end the decision made itself, just as she was trailing now up the slopes of Jebel Darju: there was nothing else she could reasonably do.

She turned and saw Charles above her, profiled against the intense blue of the sky. The hot wind was blowing his hair back, his shirt billowed out behind him. From somewhere out of sight on the other side of the big boulders on the top of the hill Danny's kite climbed unsteadily into the wind. Kit paused to point it out to her excitedly before he scrambled hurriedly up the scree to the top. Even from here she could hear him shouting 'Can I have a turn? Can I have a turn!'

She watches them, her family strung out along a hill like lice on the back of a dead dinosaur. All their world poised here, as fragile as water, and all their hopes.

∾

Ever since the letter from the jounal came yesterday they have been talking. Barely sleeping last night. And today, because it is a Friday and they are not allowed to go to Abu's, they have talked all morning and all afternoon, so that coming out to walk along the Nile opposite Tutti Island – along with half of Khartoum, it seems – they are both of them exhausted as if they have walked a long way, although they are only idly strolling.

It'll be that girl's baby, that's why he didn't want us to go, she thought, her mind slipping back to Abu. It's probably been born by now. But she had not told Ibrahim what she'd seen at Abu's house so she couldn't say anything. She was sure Abu was really at home and the thought made walking in the wrong place along the Nile feel a strangely lost and sad thing to be doing. Perhaps it was just as well the journal had offered Ibrahim the job again, perhaps it was their fate after all.

She stopped to look out across the river at the muddy bank of Tutti Island where the *shadufs* were being worked, Friday or no, to keep the crops watered. Sinewy men laboured in the late afternoon sun, their skin shining with water as they lifted and plunged, lifted and plunged. You read this in history books about ancient times and then you come here and see it still happening. She looked at Ibrahim. His face was very still as he too looked at the island and the shimmering green of the crops on the far bank. How proud he must be that the journal had thought him worthy, even after all this time! But he still looked troubled. London. It was such a big decision. They turned and strolled on. This bank of the river was bare, trodden by many feet. They passed families and groups of young men walking in the opposite direction: long streams of Friday people ambling along in the river breeze in their shining best clothes. Ahead of them the girls were chattering eagerly about the possibility of going to London. They were so excited. Was it only she who was not?

What to do, what to do?

They passed two giggling young men, walking with their little fingers linked. Ibrahim said suddenly in a low voice, 'If we were in London I could hold *your* hand.'

She stopped, startled.

He stopped too, turning towards her but his eyes were on the river behind her. 'Will you not do it for me, Zahara? Will you not choose for me instead of for your father and Jamil?'

He had never said such a thing before. He looked so sad! She stepped close to him, not touching because they were in a public place. She looked unseeingly over his shoulder at the Hilton Hotel towering behind him. How could he not know what seemed to her to be so obvious? 'Ibrahim, I love you best

380

in all the world. I know we should be glad to go. It isn't that I cannot choose, it is only that it is hard to let go here.'

He looked into her eyes as if trying to read her meaning. 'Are you saying you think that we *should* go?' he asked uncertainly.

She nodded, holding his gaze. She could feel his intensity like a vibration all down the length of her body, warm and electric, as he stood there so close but not touching. She sent her own intensity back, shocked that he should have been so unsure of her. 'I love you Ibrahim. You are my life.'

He was like the sun coming out: his face lit up, his eyes sparkled. 'And we will go to London?' She nodded. 'Are you sure? Do you really mean it?'

'Ibrahim, of course I mean it. Of course we should go! And in London, I will hold your hand in the street whenever you want me to,.'

He looked round him, breathing deeply as if he were trying to hold the memory and fix it. The gleaming green of Tutti Island, the sun on the Nile, the bright clothes of the people all round them, processing under the *peepul* trees, and across the road the ugly rectangles of the modern buildings towering against the sky. 'Do you know, I think this calls for a celebration!'

She laughed, thinking he meant the Ice-Cream Parlour.

'I have never been in there,' he said, pointing to the Hilton. 'We shall go in, just once in our lives, and ask for tea. In silver pots. On a white table cloth.'

'Oh Ibrahim, it will be so very expensive!'

'Just this once I will take my family to the most expensive hotel in my country and I will buy them tea. And, maybe, one small cake each?'

Late in August Charles made his last trip down to Abiyei. He said his farewells at numerous dinners in his honour. The veterinary department presented him with a thirteen-foot python skin as a memento. He promised he would come back to visit them all.

In the house, she was packing. There was no sense of achievement in it of a target successfully reached, only a dutiful weariness. They sold the local furniture and packed up the valuables they were taking with them (the washing machine, the computer, the freezer), to be shipped up to Khartoum on the plane and stored in the Unicef hangar until they had found somewhere to live in Port Sudan. Clothes and some toys, books and other things that they needed for their immediate use, went into the suitcases. As fast as she packed suitcases Catrin seemed to unpack them.

The weather was heavy, threatening rain that did not fall. The humidity sapped her energy like a thick sponge, but Charles was cheerful and in high spirits, full of excitement about his new post, already half embroiled in it even as he disengaged from the present one. She felt the concern in his eyes when he looked at her, worrying that he might have pushed her too far; she felt the cold rush of unawareness in its wake as he turned his attention to other things. She'd said she would go, she had given in. But what she had agreed to three weeks ago in drained self-despair was no longer quite what she felt in the dogged grind of putting the decision into action. She kept thinking, Why? Why am I doing this? Do I owe so much?

She used the East Anglian newspapers – which Kay had been sending them for the property pages – to pack up the crockery, refusing to let herself look at them. She wrote to the estate

382

agents to say they were postponing their plans for the time being and not to send any more details. Her paints and brushes, scarcely used since their return, she packed away in the suitcase without hope or ambition. Two more years. It would pass. It already had, once. And when it was over they would go home as they had planned, there could be no arguing then. She would surely, by then, have done enough penance. She would have earned the right to hold out for what she wanted, what she believed was best for the children as well as her.

Except that for Charles it would never get easier, going back, only more difficult. And within the dark and silent privacy of their marriage, did acquiescence now make her future rights more certain, or less? Was she not giving in now in a way which would plump up like a fattening bird and return to haunt her? She saw it in his eyes: his logic prevailing, the confidence that his good sense took priority over her emotional and short-term objections. That if he pushed the point confidently enough she would always give in.

She dared not look at him properly, afraid that if she did she might find she could no longer love him. As if he had asked too much of her and, pushed beyond herself, she was shrivelling, first into acquiescence, then into inability to respond at all. She fulfilled expectations but had none.

On the penultimate day of August they left El Obeid for the last time, flying to Khartoum through turbulent skies. Installed in yet another borrowed house – a German family this time, people she had only met once – she settled the children to wait while Charles went up to Port Sudan and found them a house. This at least they had agreed on: she and the children would stay in the comfort of Hans and Monika's well-appointed house in Khartoum until there was a new home in Port Sudan for them to go to. Charles, as ever, was optimistic that it would not be long.

She wandered round Monika's house, listless and ill at ease. All the books and magazines were in German. There was nothing to do, no domestic projects to while away the hours. But the children were happy enough: here was a whole playroom of someone else's toys.

Chapter 26

In the early days of September it rained heavily in the upper reaches of the Nile, a long way to the south of Khartoum, and the river began to rise.

Days later, miles downstream, where it had not rained at all, the swollen river began tugging at the tops of banks, spilling over here and there and lapping into the low-lying areas of the sprawling twin cities of Khartoum and Omdurman. Heavy storm clouds wrapped the streets like a mantle of rubber, holding in the heat. The electricity supply was intermittent, the water in the taps filthy.

In her borrowed house, Bee sat like a trapped bird. Movement created heat, so she sat motionless through the long monochrome hours, letting the sweat roll down, hardly even brushing away the persistent flies. The children wilted listlessly at her feet, too hot to play, querulous with boredom. Before he left, Charles had arranged for some large containers of clean drinking water to be delivered but there wasn't much left now, and no one had come to bring her more from the Unicef office as had been promised. Without electricity the house was like a cooking box, holding in the heat. Without the electric pump, the water pressure was too weak to fill the tank on the roof, or to run the shower, or fill the toilet cistern. There was merely a half-hearted muddy trickle in the kitchen tap. The thick air pressed down like a weight. Few people passed in the street outside, except for an occasional car carefully negotiating the pot-holes. Everyone, it seemed, was lying low like them. They might have been the only people left in the city, along with Mussa the elderly *gafir*. Of the people they knew, Carlo and his young wife were the only ones not away on leave. Greta was heavily pregnant and expecting twins. They lived in the next street.

She gets up every morning thinking *today* she will go and visit Greta, but it is too much effort, too much of an imposition with four cross children in tow. Too hot to go out in search of a taxi, so nowhere else to go. Nobody calls. Probably no one remembers they are here, washed up in Khartoum, a part of Charles's baggage, stored in transit. She thinks that they might as well have been packed up with the washing machine and left in the hangar.

The clouds mass heavily, trapping the heat and the sour stink of rubbish.

A terrible anger is spreading through her like ice. What is she doing here? She feels not like a trapped bird but like a rat in a hole, cornered.

And then it rained. The skies broke as dusk fell, crumbling away like silt and emptying into the streets. Dissolving the heat. The power went off, the lightning was vicious. And the children were terrified. Even Danny. The deafening roar of the rain on the flat roof of the house and the pitch darkness beyond the fragile flickering light of their single candle dwarfed them all. The children huddled against her, shivering. The temperature had plummeted.

She awoke out of her body like a snake sloughing off its skin, the cold air lifting the iron lid off the top of her mind. She must go up on the roof and put out all the bowls and buckets she could find to collect water so they could have something to drink, and for washing. Kit clung to her and Catrin cried. She disengaged them gently, telling Danny to look after them, she wouldn't be long.

On the roof, perilously close to the exploding sky, she ran about filling jerry cans from bowls which filled to overflowing almost as fast as she could set them out. As she poured water clumsily by the feeble light of a torch the wind seized her terror and flung it away. The sky was enormous and she was such a tiny, meaningless figure in the bottom corner of the canvas. A fierce energy flooded her, along with the rain. She threw back her head and screamed into the roar of the storm. No words, just jubilant sounds – 'Aiee! Aaaieee!' The wind whipped her voice away and swallowed it whole.

By dawn the storm had spent itself and one by one they fell asleep huddled together in the big double bed, with all the sheets from the cupboard tucked over them to keep warm. Hours later they woke to find the street outside flooded. The house was marooned in a brown sea.

No one was spared. In the garage of his expensive European house, Carlo had spent hours struggling by torchlight, in water up to his knees, trying to get his Porsche up on bricks. In the house his heavily pregnant wife, the house-maid, the two Irish setters and their eight pups, spent the night on top of one bed balanced precariously on top of another. Elsewhere latrines collapsed and mud-brick walls fell down, drains were flooded and whole shanty settlements were flattened. Rubbish floated away, along with the carcasses of drowned cats, dogs, rats, and the occasional goat. The city stank.

By ten in the morning it was raining again.

In Souk Two, Zahara and Ibrahim, like so many others, sat with their girls, high and dry in their first floor flat above the flooded streets, living frugally, as they waited for the waters to subside. They were patient: they had seen it all before. They no longer knew if they would be here to see it all again. They worried about Abu in his house beside the Nile, but the house was built for floods. He too had seen it all before.

It would take days and days before the power was restored, by which time countless quantities of vaccines and food stocks would have perished. The homeless in the refugee camps had been made homeless again, their tents washed away, their numbers swollen by thousands of locals who had lost their houses. Khartoum itself was in need of emergency supplies.

Almost immediately, international flights began lumbering in with emergency relief, taxiing down a runway where shallow water rose in a spray of rainbows instead of the usual dust behind the heavy planes.

Safe and dry in Port Sudan, Charles heard the reports coming in: the pivot of attention had switched abruptly from the south: now that cholera and typhoid were immediate risks in Khartoum vaccines would need to be flown in. The homeless would need grain, too, and blankets. The sick would need dehydration salts and drugs. He wondered how Bee and the children were managing, and if they should come to Port Sudan by road immediately. The hotel where he was staying was crude and none too clean but it would be better than a flooded house in Khartoum.

It rained heavily all day. Not the spectacular storms of the night but a steady, dark downpour. The children spent hours watching at the window. They laughed as a dead cat floated slowly past along the flooded street, swollen like a balloon, its paws in the air. Like a fat cartoon cat asleep on its back.

She did the same few jigsaw puzzles over and over with Catrin, and worried helplessly about all their precious electrical goods, which were stacked on the floor of the Unicef hangar at the airport. The boys were still happy enough playing with the unfamiliar toys, scooting loudly round the noisy floors on a tricycle until she had to ask them to stop. There was a temporary excess of food: no power at all for twenty-four hours and the freezer had already defrosted. All its contents would have to be eaten or thrown away. But she was worried how much cooking gas was left in the two cylinders. They both felt ominously light.

At lunchtime she took a plate of food out to the old *gafir* in his quarters at the back of the house. Mussa could only accept the bread and the vegetables since she didn't know whether or not the meat was *halal*. He came to the door of his bare little room huddled in his blanket and stared out at the rain with dismal, rheumy eyes before retreating.

The water was still rising. Little wavelets ran up against the lower step at the front door of the house and splashed on to the second. If it went on like this it would be in over the top by nightfall. The stench was powerful.

The rain stopped, then it started again. By dusk it was little more than a drizzle.

Before she went to bed she took her candle to look through the front door. The flame glinted on the water, which tapped gently a few inches below the top step. It had stopped raining. Above her, ragged clouds scudded over a scattering of stars.

The children were as desperate as she was to get out of the claustrophobic house and she was forced to tell them why they

389

couldn't come with her in such detail (the dangers of paddling in such filthy water, the hidden open drains which they might fall into, the nasty diseases they might catch) that then they were scared that she was going, but go she must. A message might have come from Charles: maybe they could go to Port Sudan by road, even though it was too soon for him to have found them anywhere to live yet.

She hated leaving the weight of their fear on Danny's shoulders. He hustled them back into the house, suddenly seeming far older than his twelve years. They wouldn't be alone (Mussa was in his room at the back) but it hurt to leave them.

She hesitated on the edge of the front step before braving the muddy water with one tentative foot. Warm water filled her canvas shoes as she stepped in up to her knees. She waded cautiously along the front of the house and down the short drive to the gate, clutching her dress up out of the water. Unseen things bumped into her legs below the surface: bloated things, and once the scratchy spikes of a submerged plant. She waded out into the road, trying to remember where the open drains ran. She wasn't alone. There were a few men about, splashing valiantly along the flooded streets. The sun broke through the cloud and instantly it was steamy, like jungle heat. She crossed the road cautiously at the corner and nearly lost her footing as she stepped on the edge of a hidden pot-hole.

On the far side of the main road the cemetery wall beckoned, a long snaking line standing proud of the water, on which she could walk the rest of the way to the office. As she stepped up a plastic bag floating under the surface wrapped itself round her other leg in a slimy embrace. She gave a little shriek and scrambled hurriedly on to the wall. In the flooded cemetery the bodies lie graveyard quiet. She thinks of the loose soil shifting under the tug and push of the water. Of rotting

390

winding sheets dissolving, and bones clanking gently like the rigging of boats.

Do old bones float? She snaps her mind tight shut, not looking.

The Unicef office was in chaos. People rushed in and out, sorting out supplies, arranging emergency supplies. The big generator roared in the street outside and the air-conditioning stirred the dull air, slicing across the corridors in chilly gusts from each open doorway.

She sat in the reception area, dazed and overlooked. A message had been sent up to personnel but obviously in the confusion she had been forgotten. She huddled into herself, trying to clamp down the rising panic. Her hands in her lap were white-knuckled. But she was a robust-looking woman with a calm face and nobody noticed her tension. Nobody noticed her at all.

Martha, the pretty Egyptian receptionist, was surprised to see her still there when she came back to her desk. She suggested Bee should go up to Osman Nigeria's room: if any news had come from Charles, he would have it. She rose, feeling cruelly exposed, and made her way cautiously up the hot stairwell.

Osman Nigeria was haughty, especially with women. He particularly did not like it when his authority was questioned and she'd had a run-in with him once before when she'd come to complain in person that their duty free card had lain so long on his desk that they had been unable to use the shop facilities for nearly a year after their arrival. She saw his eyes narrow as she came in, but when she asked if there had been any message from Charles he hunted through the papers on his desk without comment. He found a sheet of paper and handed it to her.

It was a radio message from Charles, dated the previous day. Most of the message was about vaccines but the last sentence read 'Is my family...?' That was all there had been time for before the radio link had been lost.

She stands across the desk reading it. Her eyes are scalding hot but her heart is cold. She feels as if the five of them are a bolt-on extra, functional as the beading on a lampshade, the nodding dog in the back of a passing car. Who really cares if they are happy? Who cares at all if they are busy?

She stands stock still as her heart contracts. She knows quite suddenly what she is going to do. It is so clear and precise an idea that it rises fully formed as if long planned, though she hadn't thought of it consciously until this minute. It is as if something in her head has slipped and light has come rushing in.

She looks up at Osman Nigeria, shuffling papers while he waits for her to leave.

'Is the airport open?'

'For international flights, as of this morning, yes. Internal flights are in confusion.'

'I meant international. How soon could you get tickets to London for me and my four children?'

His eyes narrowed. 'London? I don't understand. If you are having problems because of the floods surely you should go to Port Sudan?' The question sounded like a statement.

'I want to go to London.'

'You cannot go to *London*! There is no authorisation.'

'Bugger the authorisation!' she snapped, suddenly angry. She added coldly, 'We have very little water in the house and soon there'll be no food either. The street is an open sewer. The mosquitoes are multiplying. You said yourself there are no internal flights—'

He interrupted her sharply: 'If you have no water, that can be arranged. For food, the shops in Souk Two are open. There is no problem. The Unicef plane will be flying to Port Sudan in a few days. It would be better if you went there. Your husband is expecting you.'

'You don't understand: I do not want to go to Port Sudan, I no longer intend to go to Port Sudan. I am going home, and as soon as possible.'

'But your husband—'

'Bugger my husband!'

She saw him blink and knew instinctively that she had him in retreat.

'But I have no authorisation! I cannot issue tickets without authorisation. There has been no cash call forward… '

He drew back nervously as she lurched forwards across the desk and slammed her fist down on his papers with such force that she remembered it afterwards because of the bruising.

'Bugger your bloody cash call forwards! You can't keep us here against our will and we want to go back to the UK. If you don't have the authority to issue tickets then find me someone who has!'

'But they are in an emergency meeting!'

She drew herself very upright and said firmly, 'If you don't go and get someone right now I shall stand here waiting until you do and I may scream.'

It is quite satisfying, the speed with which he leaves the room. A sneaking part of her feels sorry for him. After all it is not his fault. She is breathing hard and in the pause while she waits for someone to be sent to her she realises she must have been shouting. She is aware of curious glances through the open door as people hurry past outside. She hopes that someone more senior will come quickly before the courage of her anger leaves her.

A woman comes in. A smartly dressed blonde with impeccable make-up. She says in an American accent, 'Hi, I'm Laura Golding. I'm acting head of personnel while Jeremy is on leave.' She looks at Bee, a piercing quizzical look, not unsympathetic, and closes the door carefully behind her. Bee is too upset to notice the proffered hand, so Laura pats her on the shoulder instead and invites her to sit, not at the desk but in one of the plastic-covered armchairs by the air conditioner, which isn't working properly.

Laura says, 'I gather from Osman that you are anxious to return to London? I guess you realise this puts us in a bit of a quandary.'

She sits silent, feeling like a schoolgirl who has been called in by a kindly headmistress to be told that her demands are unreasonable.

'I guess you're probably in very difficult circumstances because of the floods? We're all in much the same boat, no pun intended. The problem is, before we can purchase international tickets we need authorisation from above. Normally such matters are outside the remit of the national office.' She looks at Bee closely: 'I'd understood that you were on your way to join Charles. Has some emergency arisen that requires you to go back to England?'

She hesitates on the balance of a lie. It wouldn't be difficult to fabricate some family calamity at home that necessitates her return, but she is afraid that if she makes up some story it will only catch her out later. She is tempted to confide in Laura, who surely will understand, and Laura is smiling at her with patient sympathy. She begins to explain.

It is nearly an hour before they come out of Osman Nigeria's office and permit him the use of it again. She is very anxious

394

that she has been away too long and the children will be frantic with worry, but a burden has been lifted off her back so that she feels taller as she walks to the door of the building with Laura. They shake hands warmly on the step. Laura has promised the tickets, as soon as it can be arranged, but she makes no promises when that might be. And she is anxious that Bee, in return, will keep her options open.

Afterwards Bee suspects she has been accommodated in a strategic gamble: if Unicef makes it possible for her to return to the UK now, on compassionate leave, she will be less trouble to them in the short-term and they will be hoping she will return as soon as conditions here are easier, because her presence in the Sudan secures Charles, whom they obviously value highly. It is unclear how far Laura has been outlining strategy on Bee's behalf, and how far on Unicef's. Either way, they are to go home on an open ticket in expectation of their return.

Back at the house the children are emotional.

'I fought you'd drownded,' Catrin said in her ear, clinging tightly round her neck.

For a moment before she told them she was afraid to admit what she had done. But they had been so cooped up, so unsure of what was happening or where they were going, that instantly she told them they were in a frenzy to be gone. It was difficult then to admit that she didn't know when that would be.

A little while later she found Danny brooding quietly at the table. His book was open in front of him but he was leaning on his arms looking out of the window. She put her hand on his shoulder and he peered anxiously at her through his glasses, which had slipped down his nose.

'Does this mean we aren't going to join Dad in Port Sudan?'

She drew up a chair beside him. 'They're getting us return

tickets. It's seen as compassionate leave. We can come back if we want to.'

'But you don't want to, do you?'

She looked into his blue eyes, so like his father's, and she didn't know what to say.

'What about Dad?' he said.

She hesitated. 'Dad arranged to stay on without even asking me. That's a terrible thing to do to someone, Danny. Dad and I are supposed to be partners. We're supposed to be equals. He never even asked me what I thought about it.'

'He said he could cancel it if you didn't want to go to Port Sudan.'

'Yes, but he'd already left it much too late. Besides, that's not really the point. He shouldn't have arranged something so important without talking to me first.'

'I wanted to go.'

'I know you did, pet,' she said, pushing his hair off his sweaty forehead. 'But imagine how it would have felt if you *hadn't* wanted to.'

He looked at her searchingly. 'And you didn't.' It was a statement. He didn't sound accusing.

She shook her head. 'No, I didn't. I tried to want to. I *wanted* to want to. But really I just want to go home, like Kit does, and Adam. We said we'd come for two and a half years and that's what we've done, and it isn't fair to change it now, not unless we all agreed we wanted to stay.'

'But Mum, does this mean you and Dad are splitting up?'

She wished she could give him some certainty. She knew she should never have let Charles bully her into agreeing to go to Port Sudan. She knew she should have been clear about what she needed from the beginning. But she didn't know what impact her tardy decision would have now. She felt as if she had been trapped and that the very act of jumping would unleash unknown repercussions.

'I don't know what it means,' she said at last, feeling she must be truthful. 'I feel as if Dad's pushed me into a corner and this is the only way I can get out of it but it isn't the way I want it to be and I don't know what will happen. It's up to Dad, really. We'll only be doing what we'd planned to do all along. It's up to him whether he comes back to us or whether he doesn't.'

Danny looked at her. 'I think Dad will want to stay. I think his job is more important than we are.' Suddenly he burst into tears. She pulled him to her and he took off his glasses and sobbed like a little child, gruff and nearly adolescent as he was. She rubbed her face in the coarse, bouncy tickle of his hair and wished she could cry too, but no tears came.

All day the children squabbled and played, fractious and impatient, but the tenor of the endless hours had changed: they knew now what they were waiting for. Excitement ran high. Kit was like a buzzing fly caught in a web. They hung very close about her. When are we going? Why don't you know? When will we see Daddy again? Are we going to our house in Norwich? 'I want to go to our house in El Obeid,' wept Catrin. 'That's not our house any more, stupid,' Kit said callously. But Bee recognised Catrin's anguish. She too felt suddenly and illogically homesick for the familiar house in El Obeid, with its dusty blue walls, and its green walls, and its pink bedroom. It was the past she was missing, even before they were out of Khartoum. Not with the pain of wanting something which had ended to go on, but with the pain of regret for something within it which might be ending: a significant part of her children's childhood that could never to be recaptured. Her marriage, perhaps.

She couldn't bear to think how Charles would feel when he knew. She only knew she could do nothing else. She should never have let it get to this. She was letting him down.

But another part of her is bitter with a strange, twisting anger. For two years she has looked forward to going home as a reward hard-earned and well-deserved but instead she is in retreat, letting people down, backing out of decisions, running away like a coward. He has robbed her of the experience she had once looked forward to. She feels as if she has paid in blood and is being repaid in dust.

She will be known for it now in Unicef. The woman who ran home when things got tough. Who left her husband in the lurch. Who let Charles down, that poor, hard-done-by, dedicated man.

By the following morning the flood waters had sunk away, leaving behind a deep silt and a powerful faecal odour. Greta called by on her way to the Unicef office, picking her way delicately through the mud, her arms folded protectively across her hugely swollen belly. They sat on Hans and Monika's big leather sofas and drank coffee, and Greta made her laugh with her stories of the night of the storm. 'I too would go home now if I could,' she said suddenly. 'But I am too pregnant, they won't let me fly now.' She looked very young, suddenly, and rather lost. But at that moment Catrin emerged from the depths of the toy box with a shaggy black wig perched on her head and Greta laughed and stopped looking sad.

'Come and see me,' she said as she left, 'I will be very glad to have a visit.' And Bee promised that she would, but that same afternoon Laura came bearing plane tickets. A Unicef car would come at midnight tomorrow to take them to the airport, she said, looking at Bee carefully like a doctor assessing a patient. She had argued their case with New York on health grounds, pointing out that the sooner Bee got the children out of Khartoum the better, in the present circumstances. And as there would be no internal flights for a while – and all the Unicef vehicles were engaged on relief work, so none could be spared to drive her and the children to Port Sudan by road – going back to the UK was probably, on balance, the best solution. On open tickets, naturally, so they could return when things got back to normal.

She could feel herself being coolly measured. Was she to be judged the worse if she seemed to be on the brink of nervous collapse, or – if she appeared self-possessed – would her exodus seem fraudulent? She shrank back, careful to give nothing away, a taut-faced woman surrounded by demanding young children. She wrote out a message for Laura to telegram to Kay in London with details of the flight.

After Laura had gone, she realised she hadn't asked whether Charles had been notified. She hoped not. Surely Laura, so supportive and understanding, would have mentioned it if he had been? He should hear the news from her and from her alone. But she had started a letter several times and trailed off each time, not knowing what she wanted to say to him. It all seemed suddenly so ordinary. So much of their lives here, however extraordinary, had been lived out in banal details.

Kit's voice rose petulantly, fighting with Catrin over a car she had taken. Danny lay on his back on the floor endlessly pushing the tricycle backwards and forwards, backwards and forwards, with his foot. There was nothing between her and leaving but thirty-six long hours of meals and washing up, of tidying away toys and playing with listless children, and reading the same well-worn stories over and over.

What if Charles should turn up unexpectedly? What would

she say? Would she be able to stand her ground? She was terrified that, face to face with the smooth assurances and utter confidence of his persuasion, she would forget why it was so important to go home.

But nothing happened. She threw out the last of the food from the freezer and found some tins in the store cupboard, indecipherable since she didn't speak German. She was using up Monika's precious supplies but she was beyond caring. She resisted going out to one of the little corner shops in search of bread, like an animal lying up in the nettles waiting for night. She fed the children but ate nothing herself.

In the morning she packed their cases, though their flight was not till after two a.m. that night and they wouldn't need to leave the house until midnight. Mussa came in to sweep, and to talk. She realised he was lonely, shut away by himself in such strange times. She had hardly thought of him at all till then. He talked of his wife, long dead, and his son who was a porter in the Hilton. They were like two sea animals, him and her, revealed by the retreating tide, sitting haphazardly on a mud-bank. She felt curiously, temporarily, attached to him and guessed when he lingered, amused by the children's antics, that the feeling was mutual.

By seven in the evening it was fully dark and the night stretched long and empty until it would be time to go. Adam complained he was hungry again. Kit was already planning his in-flight meals. She insisted that they went to bed as usual, not wanting to have to cope with over-exhausted children later. A car passed along the street, a strange sound through the mud and puddles. She sat very still, listening. The sound of its passing faded safely away.

She went to bed and tried to get a few hours sleep. Minute by slow minute the time trickled downwards like sand through

400

an hour-glass. She couldn't read. She felt sick with nerves. She was desperately weary but when she lay down she could not sleep. She watched the clock by the light of the candle, blocking out all the demanding unanswered questions of where they would go, what they would do, once they were back in London. To get out was all.

At twenty to twelve she dressed, then woke the children and got them to calm down and concentrate long enough to get into their clothes. Catrin was big-eyed and dazed with exhaustion, sitting on the bed with her thumb in her mouth and her hair all fuzzed, too sleepy to dress herself.

By ten past twelve, when the promised car still had not come, she realised it might not come at all. Quickly she told Danny to take charge while she was gone – she would have to run to the Unicef office and wake one of the drivers. She wouldn't be long. Catrin let out a long mournful wail and clutched at her skirts.

There were no lights anywhere and at first the street seemed pitch black. But the moon was full, sailing serenely at the apex of a bright starry sky. After a moment her eyes adjusted. Now the street was full of moon-shadows instead. She stepped out gingerly, squelching into the mud. There was a cool breeze and the dark shadows of small garden trees tossed and shook. She walked down the middle of the rutted street in the moonlight. She might have been the only person left in the whole city, but still she felt exposed.

When she came to the cemetery her heart began to thump. Under the sailing moon the graveyard stretched so wide and empty. The shallow humps of the graves were visible, standing proud of lingering pools of water. She began to run, slipping on the half-dried mud.

At the corner of the cemetery a taxi stood sleeping like a washed-up cockroach at the side of the road. She paused uncertainly. There was a man asleep in the driving seat, slumped up against the window. Perhaps it would be wiser to seize this chance than to risk going on to the office and maybe finding no one? She tapped cautiously on the driver's window. He didn't stir. For a moment she wondered fearfully if he was dead. She tapped again, harder. He woke with a jump.

She told him quickly in her stunted Arabic what she wanted. With a lazy, knowing grin he signalled to her to get in. He started up the engine. In the glow from the headlights she could see the whites of his eyes in the driving mirror as he kept looking at her reflection. What was she doing, out alone at this time of night? Where was her husband? Her father, her brother? She knew she deserved no better, in his eyes, than any insolence he cared to show her. Any at all.

She was seized with sudden panic. What if he didn't do as she'd asked? He was physically between her and her children! She sat with one hand clutching the door handle, ready to throw herself out if need be at the next corner. But he drove off calmly, back the way that she had just come and down the street towards the house, taking the pot-holes slowly.

She ran to the door and found the children waiting anxiously just the other side of it. They were late now. Danny had dragged the suitcases into the hallway ready. She blew out the candle, locked the door from the outside and slid the key back under it as if she were sealing her past.

The airport was an island of light in the dark city, powered by its own generators. An odd suggestion of normality, but it was almost deserted. When she got to the check-in desk the clerk said there was a delay: take-off time was postponed until four a.m. He gave no reason and she asked for none. She could not bear to consider that they might not leave tonight after all.

She looked for a bench in a less central part of the hall. Fear of some last minute crisis haunted her like a shadowy phantom, influencing her every move.

Kit was being difficult. He was terribly over-wrought and there was an edge of hysteria to his excitement that they were going home. He couldn't leave the others alone, trying to provoke a reaction out of Adam, who was sitting quietly leaning against Bee and clutching his beloved old teddy to his chest. Even Catrin, heavily asleep across Bee's lap, wasn't spared his relentless attention. Every thing Bee said to him he refused, denied or contradicted.

At last, they were called forward into the Departure Lounge. She breathed a sigh of relief as they passed through Passport Control and Customs. The customs officials were unusually gentle with her and didn't search her luggage with the usual diligence. They waved her through, smiling benignly at a lone woman struggling with four young children. She was carrying Catrin, draped over one shoulder, and a heavy bag over the other, another bag in her free hand. Danny struggled valiantly with the rest of their hand-luggage. Kit defiantly carried nothing except his Superman. Adam dawdled and kept getting left behind. They shuffled through into the bare, uncomfortable departure lounge and found a seat. Even if the flight were not further delayed it would be a long wait.

All my life waiting, she thought.

It was after 4.30 when a garbled message on the tannoy announced that their flight was boarding. She jumped up, her spirits lifting. As she turned to help Adam with his bag she saw Charles striding down the hall towards them.

403

Chapter 27

He had been out on a two-day field trip in the Red Sea Hills but on the way back into town he asked Rashid, the driver, to call in at the office in case a radio message had come through from Bee. Instead there was one from Laura saying that Bee and the children were leaving for England.

He stood in the middle of the office reading yesterday's message over and over, uncomprehending. *England?* Why? There was no indication that any of them were ill, nor any other reason. Then he registered the date of the flight. Tomorrow!

It was midday. The international flights generally left in the early hours, so that would mean tonight, in effect. The journey to Khartoum by road could take twelve hours even in normal conditions and he had no idea how widespread the impact of the flooding was, or what conditions in Khartoum were like now. But he might just make it. God willing, he might.

Within ten minutes he was back in the Land Rover with Rashid and they were speeding out on the tarmac road, which switch-backed along the coastal plain at the foot of the sharp escarpment of the Red Sea Hills. Away to their left the sea glittered blindingly in the afternoon sun. They passed Kilo 16 where the turkey fish had been. The tarmac road was good all the way to the capital but traffic was heavy and it was a dangerous route. Rashid drove fast, overtaking precariously. The dips and summits obscured oncoming traffic. There were so many accidents on this road.

They came up behind a truck of Rashaida women. The women sat in the back, patient as cattle. Eight pairs of eyes stared out at them from the depths of their black veils and laughed mischievously. Rashid clicked his tongue in disapproval and overtook the truck.

The road stretched endlessly, snaking through the glaring afternoon as it climbed steadily into the hills. The dirt roads which led out of Khartoum towards El Obeid were littered with the bleached bones of cattle and camels picked clean by vultures but on this metalled road to the coast the corpses were all trucks and lorries, lying in tangled wrecks at the sides of the road, picked clean by small boys. Overladen lorries roared along the highway. Charles closed his eyes as Rashid weaved in and out of the heavy traffic, praying they would get to Khartoum in one piece.

He took turns at the wheel but he drove less daringly than Rashid and they made slower progress. They stopped once for a plate of beans and a glass of tea at a road-side stall before pressing on again into the late afternoon. They had been out on the road, on and off, since six that morning. Rashid had not even questioned the sudden decision to go to Khartoum. All part of the job, for him. Charles pondered Rashid's stoical acceptance of complexities beyond his jurisdiction. But when he asked him if he minded the unscheduled trip, Rashid said his son worked in Khartoum and he hadn't seen him for six months. 'It is God's will,' he said.

He told Rashid why they were going. Rashid was shocked. A wife leaving without her husband's permission? No Sudanese woman could leave the country without a letter from her husband authorising it, even if she was on her way to join him abroad, so how could a *khawaja* wife? He didn't say, but Charles guessed he was thinking, How is it these *khawajas* do not control

405

their women better? Realising the urgency, Rashid drove even faster. Charles had to avert his eyes from the road ahead.

The landscape around them mutated grandly as they passed up and into the necklace of dry coastal hills and down onto the plains beyond. Dusk fell. Kassala, Gedaref – the names of the towns meant nothing in the night. It was well after midnight when they reached Wad Medani. The town lay in darkness, the power was still out all along the Nile and besides it was late. Here and there the soft orange glow of a fire or a lamp was the only sign of life. The sky was enormous, full of moonlight which glinted on the zinc roofs of the settlements they passed. As they moved through the rich alluvial plains of the Gezira the irrigated fields were clearly visible, as neat and orderly as East Anglian fenland, bled colourless by the moon.

It was a strangely inhuman night, only the busy trucks and lorries and an occasional car to remind him they were not alone on the face of the earth. Some of the lorries drove without lights. thundering black shadows that loomed up in the arc of their headlamps and out again just as suddenly.

It was after three a.m. when they reached Hans and Monika's house. The house was in darkness. He banged on the door but he sensed already the deathly stillness of absence. He went round to the back and knocked on Mussa's door. The old man called out fearfully, 'Who's there?' As soon as he knew it was Charles Mussa unlocked the door. *Ya Sitt* and *awlad* left at midnight, he said uncertainly.

He could have wept, standing there. To come so far and miss her by so little! Three hours was all that lay between them.

He was utterly exhausted but he couldn't think of sleeping. Wearily he told Rashid to drive him to the airport, more as something to do than in hope. They would have been airborne for an hour or more by now.

406

There was still a clerk on the KLM desk, packing up. Charles asked gloomily what time the flight had left.

In a moment he was running, galvanised awake. The official on the gate barred his way, shaking his head at Charles's proffered diplomatic pass. 'My wife has taken my children without my consent!' he said urgently. 'They are about to board that plane!' At once the official stood aside and ushered him through, shouting to his colleague on the passport desk beyond to let Charles pass. He ran past the desk and through into the customs hall, which was almost deserted. Hurriedly he repeated what he'd told the first official and the customs officer shooed him through into the departure lounge. As he came through the doorway he saw Bee and four sleepy children just standing up to go to the boarding gate.

'Daddy! I knew you'd come!' yells Kit, hurling himself forwards to hug him tightly round the legs. Adam, grinning in delight, is coming towards him. Danny is laden down with bags but he too looks overjoyed. It is the look of fear on Bee's face that brings him up short. He stops a few feet away, aware of curious eyes watching his back from the entrance behind him.

'What's going on, Bee? What are you doing!'

Everything is still. He is aware of nothing but her frightened eyes staring back at him.

'We're going home.' Her voice is quiet – so quiet he can scarcely hear the words. Catrin turns sleepily off her mother's shoulder and grins at him past her thumb. 'Daddy's comed!'

'But why? Why are you going? What's wrong?'

Her instinct is to say nothing. If she gets drawn into discussion she might lose her own conviction. He will try to compel, she knows, with moral arguments, knowing her weak spots. With his high moral sense of public good and his ill-developed sense of his own family's welfare. 'Don't confuse the children by trying to stop us now,' she said.

'Who's doing the confusing?'

She was silent, retreating into herself.

'You are *my wife*,' he said. 'I *don't want* you to go!'

Goaded, she snapped back 'Your *English* wife! Your equal. Remember?'

He stepped forwards to touch her but she stepped smartly back. The children were watching them, looking from one to the other with big, bewildered eyes. Kit began to cry, clinging to Charles. 'Come with us Daddy! We want to go home. Come with us.'

He looked down at Kit with unseeing eyes. He said to Bee, 'Okay, go home for now if you really feel you have to. But when you've had a break you can come back. I'll find us somewhere to live in Port Sudan soon. You can get Danny a proper snorkel and some flippers. I've found a really good place to swim. You'll enjoy it, honestly you will. When we've settled there.' His eyes filled with tears. 'Please come back, darling. Please don't leave me! *Are* you leaving me?'

It seemed to her that it was him who had done the leaving. She didn't know where he was any more but it wasn't anywhere close to her. 'You don't have to stay here, Charles. If you cancel the contract you could come back for good at Christmas, just as we always planned.'

'But I thought we'd agreed all this! I thought we agreed that as long as I have something to offer we should stay. That it's our duty to stay. Good God, Bee, isn't it obvious? People are starving here. Their children are dying of preventable diseases. We *can* make a difference! Surely you see that?'

408

She looked at him wearily. The old familiar argument. And he always argued longest and therefore always believed he'd won. 'You might make a difference, but what about me? What difference do I make?'

'You make a difference to me! You keep me going, you make life worthwhile. Of course you're a part of it.'

To service you? she thought. He hadn't, she noticed, said because I love you. The same old thought was in her head: this isn't our world, these are not our people. We are intruders here, and our moral framework is dubious. She would not voice it. She knew he would deny it. '*You* can come back to us,' she repeated. 'It is your choice, Charles.'

For a moment she feels pity. He looks so shrunken, standing there helplessly. A crackling voice over the tannoy calls their flight again. She is calm now, no longer frightened of him. But she dare not kiss him, for fear her resolve would crumble. She holds herself away. 'I'll write. As soon as I get back to London.'

He nods, too emotional to speak. The tears in his eyes threaten to spill as he stoops to kiss the children and clasp them to him tightly.

'We've got to go. Say goodbye to Daddy, we have to go now and get on the plane.'

Reluctantly the children disengage themselves. She picks Catrin up again and awkwardly takes Adam's hand as well as the heavy bag. As she turns to go she feels Charles touch her shoulder fleetingly in farewell.

All four children are crying as they go through the gate to where the great jet crouches on the tarmac just outside, shimmering white under the lights. She ignores the concerned gazes of the cabin crew as she leads the children up the steps and inside the plane. She does not look back once.

Chapter 28

The lights took forever to turn red. She waited disconsolately under her umbrella, standing back from the kerb to avoid being splashed. Why do the big red buses never look cheerful? Is it simply that nothing can, in this eternal rain?

She tried not to think of the blue skies and brisk, sunny winds of home. Instead she concentrated on the job in hand. She must take Ibrahim's books back to the public library first, because they were heavy and slowing her down. Second, she would go to the agency to see if any jobs had come in, even though they would surely have phoned if any had. Then she would try the estate agents again: they'd hoped to have some more properties available to rent this week. Lastly, a careful trip round the supermarket, trying to make their limited housekeeping stretch over all the things they seemed to need. If she didn't manage to find some work soon she wasn't sure how they would manage. She had already stopped hoping for supply teaching: there seemed to be too many others in the same position as her, chasing too few jobs. But she might well get somewhere with her Italian, rusty as it was. There was hope of some evening classes teaching Italian.

Ibrahim was enjoying his new job. She could see how much by his face, by his re-awakened energy. Though the pay was inadequate. In Khartoum it had sounded generous. The escalation in prices since they were last in London had taken them aback. But he too found people distant and reserved, as cold as the weather. The girls were happy. They were settling well at school but that posed a problem too. It limited their flat-hunting to an even smaller radius in this dismal suburb.

She had forgotten London was quite so ugly! From Khartoum London always seemed so elegant and sophisticated but its wet reality was as drab as Khartoum was in its hot dustiness. Nothing is ever as good as you might hope for. It is always better to expect little and make the best of what comes.

Her mother had come down at the weekend. *This isn't good enough*, her face seemed to say as she looked round the temporary flat, but all she said was, 'You'd get more for your money in Cardiff.' Nazmul was working as a surgeon in Newport now, on a very good salary, which – along with his nice house – Doris mentioned quite a lot. 'You will come there for Christmas?' Doris asked, but it sounded more like a statement. 'We will like that,' Zahara replied, and meant it. How like Grandma Pugh she is getting, she thought, looking at her mother's legs planted square on the carpet while Doris talked about Khartoum with that familiar, faintly dismissive edge to her voice. But Zahara has her stories tucked safe inside her head, her mother cannot diminish them now. The truce between them will hold.

So many thoughts she is forced to pack away inside her head, along with the thoughts about Mastura burning to a bundle of black sticks, her skin on fire. Thoughts of Abu, alone in his house. Suspicious thoughts about Nura, and Nura's baby.

The baby. It would certainly be born by now. Her father might, at this very moment, be crooning as he held it in his arms in his study overlooking the Blue Nile, hooking his finger in its tiny palm, loving this new child with all the pent-up love of his abandoned old age. It was her guilt, too, for abandoning him. What could she expect, except that he would find solace where he could?

She had told no one about the baby. Not Jamil in her letters to him, not even Ibrahim. Some secrets run too deep for telling.

Motionless at the window, watching the river slide away on its eternal life-giving journey, Hassan stood musing. The Nile was truly blue now as the weather turned and winter began to settle in. He was alone, as he had known for a long time he must, in the end, be alone. They had all gone in the end, one by one, even Zahara, though she had taken some pushing. And Jamil, the last one left, was as good as gone, though he had not gone in the manner Hassan would have chosen.

Behind him he could hear the comforting swish-swish of Nura's broom, sweeping the kitchen. She was a good girl, though she had her faults. He hoped she would not leave now that the baby was born, but it would be a hard time for her. It is one thing to keep a pregnancy hidden, quite another a baby.

There had been difficult moments, when her father and her brothers had come looking for her, rightly suspecting the young Khababish tribesman. But they came too late: Amir had already made himself scarce by then. Hassan knew that if they found her they would kill her too, so he told them she had stopped coming to work and he had no idea where she'd gone.

After that, of course, she was stuck. If she were to show her face outside the house word would quickly get back to her family. Baby or no baby, she was in too much trouble to get out of it now, even if once the baby was born it were spirited away. He could arrange that, just as he could have organised an abortion for her, had she wanted one. There had been time for that, too. But it was already too late for her, in the world she lived in, even back then at the beginning. As soon as she was suspected, it was too late.

It had been a strange summer since Mastura's death. Like shrapnel flying through the air, the repercussions had spread wide, far beyond lovely Mastura's own life. The shrapnel of sorrow, the pain of loss, pressing wicked fingers into the secret places in everybody's lives. He had lost his sense of purpose for a while, had only a pained conviction that he must make his own small gestures in protest. There had been no decisions, just a vague mutual drifting, the girl's and his own, through a series of non-decisions. He had not foreseen the consequences.

Well, all that is behind him now. They have all gone, as go they must and make their lives where they can. But Nura is still here, singing sweetly as she sets up the charcoal iron. And he has decided at last what he will do. He will rent out the house; Mohammed al'Mahdi will take it. Maybe Jamil will take it back one day. For himself, he will rent a house in Shendi, or in Dongola perhaps – some other place beside the Nile. Somewhere where the girl knows no one. She can continue to work for him, and keep the child if that is what she wants. No one will know that she is not a young widow, if she says that she is, and he will ensure that there is some money put by for her, in case she does not find a husband before he dies.

If he is here or if he is somewhere else, what difference does it make, now that his family has gone? His needs are few and easily supplied, whether by Nura or by another servant. So long as he has his books and a view over the river he cares little where he lives.

In the middle of the village there was a broad shade tree, and beneath it a solitary *angareb*. Hamid and Mustafa went off to look for the village headman leaving Charles for a few moments alone, sitting on the *angareb* under the tree.

A young boy stood nearby with his little sister, watching him. He spoke to the boy in Arabic but the child didn't understand him. His head seemed too big for his malnourished body but the little girl was surprisingly plump in her ragged pink dress. He guessed, from the protective, caressing gestures of the older child, that the little girl was the indulged baby of the family.

The region was very poor. The resident Beni Amer population had accumulated many displaced relatives from over the Ethiopian border thirty miles away, and the Eritrean People's Liberation Front tended to use this area as a base from which to wage their war back over the border, against the Ethiopian government.

Everyone else was out in the fields. He was glad of the few moments of peace while he waited for them to come to the meeting. He smiled at the two kids and slipped back into his private thoughts. Somewhere far away his own round-limbed little daughter was living in an utterly different world. His boys, noisy, self-confident, engaging, might be chasing a football in a cold school playground at this very moment.

And his wife? What was she doing?

She seemed as foreign as the idea of his kids running about in the cold. *I have no wife, he thought gloomily.*

Alone, there is a certain freedom. He tilted back his head and stared up through the dense canopy of the *mesquite* tree with its finely-toothed evergreen foliage. Shall he go home at Christmas? Has he still got a home in England to go back to?

Voices. Hamid and Mustafa were coming towards him, with

an ancient man in a tattered shirt. Charles stood up and went to greet them. It was too hot to hold a meeting out in the sun; the old man said they could use the school, gesturing to a long, low building with a zinc roof that stood a little apart from the thatch-walled huts. They went into the classroom and sat waiting for the villagers to come. Through the windows he could see them walking in ones and twos towards the school, glancing curiously at the Unicef Land Cruiser parked in the middle of the village. He sat on the solitary chair, the villagers sat down on the floor as they came in, Mustafa stood by the wall talking to the old man.

He wondered what these villagers could find to talk about so busily when they saw one another day in, day out, all their lives. His mind wandered off, thinking about Bee. About himself as a father. About his work here. The perpetual argument he had with himself: which way would he jump, after all?

He noticed the boy and the little girl again. They had wormed their way through the press of people to sit by the wall not far away, still watching him. The little one was kneeling in the protective space between her brother's knees. He smiled at them. The boy smiled back, the little girl's eyes widened. He still hadn't heard her say a single word. Mustafa clapped his hands for silence. The sun beat steadily on the tin roof and hardly a breath of air came in through the windows. Mustafa outlined Unicef's proposals for a vaccination programme. It was the same speech he had already given twice that day in other villages. Charles stopped listening. *Shall I? /Shan't I?* The continual refrain through his head. If I leave, he thought, I will be turning my back on all the good I could do here. If I don't leave, will I be failing as a husband? As a father, even? Which of these failures is the greater wrong? Mustafa talked

415

expansively. The familiar phrases turned like a litany, comfortable, reassuring. A vaccinated child is a safer child.

He thinks, Perhaps I am just no good. I know what I want. It's knowing what I ought to do that is the problem.

Mustafa points to simple pictures on the flip-chart: the cycle of the amoeba.

I can't, he thinks—

But they are interrupted by the sudden heavy beat of aircraft engines. The plane sweeps in abruptly from behind the encircling hills. For a moment there is a tense, listening silence. Mustafa has stopped speaking, turning like everyone else to look through the windows to where the aircraft is visible, flying low in a circle above the village, a sinister metal lozenge. At that moment the room breaks into uproar. The plane is Ethiopian and there are bombs slung from the underside of its wings.

The headman seizes him by the shoulder and shouts over the roar of the plane's engines: 'Quick! It isn't safe here! Follow me!' The villagers have leaped to their feet and are squeezing through the narrow doorway and rushing in panic towards the huts.

In the nearest hut he is pushed underneath one of the rickety *angarebs* which stand against the matting wall. Mustafa squeezes in after him. The old man and Hamid are struggling under another. An elderly woman sits in the corner crying and rocking, muttering something which sounds like a prayer. The throbbing engines are screaming closer again, the air is pounding with their beat. Half-suffocated, the rough thatch of the wall scraping painfully into his back, he peers over Mustafa's head towards the doorway. The engines pass overhead in a roar.

There is a strange moment like a pause when through the throbbing din he hears the faint whistle of the bomb descending. Then the deafening thud suck and shatter of explosion, very close. Almost immediately there is another. The sound of the engines swings away, masked by the heavy sounds of rubble raining down on the roof of the hut and the ground outside. Through the doorway, as the plane circles, he sees more bombs detach and fall, and moments after he hears the dirty crunching roar of three more explosions somewhere beyond the village.

At that moment the little girl runs across his line of vision, screaming in terror. Her brother appears in her wake, desperately calling her back. Then the plane is roaring overhead and the awful suck and crunch comes again, once, twice, so that he cannot help but close his eyes and the ground shudders and the hut shakes and stones rattle down on the thatch. When he opens his eyes, sand has filled the air like fog and Mustafa has shifted, so that he can't see out.

He turns his head. Through the tattered rope of the old *angareb* he can see up into the roof. His eye calmly observes the scrawny chicken carcasses, strung up on a rope to dry, swinging gently. Blue sky is visible through the apex hole. The strangely ordinary glare of sunshine pierces the holes in the old thatch, through which sand sifts steadily and falls in his eyes. By these things he knows he is not dead.

It takes him a moment to recognise the silence.

The smoke from the abandoned cooking fires coiled calmly upwards. Dogs were creeping back out of the bush. The school building stood in smoking ruins, two of its walls blown outwards, the tin roof buckled and twisted where it had collapsed. The first two bombs had been direct hits. The last two had hit the well. On the sand near the well, the little girl in her shabby pink dress lay spread-eagled on the ground. Not far away her brother, covered with blood, gasped and spluttered in the arms of a distraught woman.

He didn't have to ask if the little one was dead. An old man hovered over her, his face in his hands, rocking and keening. 'Her grandfather,' Mustafa said. But the boy was alive. They must take him with them to the hospital in Tokar, if the Land Cruiser hadn't been damaged.

There were other casualties but miraculously none of them serious. The ground was littered with rubble and straw and broken timbers from the shattered buildings. Two huts and an old granary had collapsed under the shower of debris.

In the middle of the village the Land Cruiser stood unharmed. It was the vehicle which had drawn the attack, the villagers said. The Ethiopian military apparently assuming that the Eritrean People's Liberation Front must be holding a meeting in the school, although the village was thirty miles inside Sudanese territory.

They took the boy with them when they left. He was bleeding heavily from a wound on his head. Splinters of bone gleamed white against the raw pink mess in his hair. His grandfather travelled with him, cradling the boy silently, staring into the distance with unseeing eyes.

Horror and shock, outrage and guilt: Charles's emotions were all over the place. It was their vehicle that had drawn the attack, yet they had come promoting survival. Was it a genuine error on the part of the Ethiopians? Had they themselves made a mistake, going there?

They dropped the old man and the motionless child at the hospital in Tokar. Afterwards, driving back fast towards Port Sudan along the tarmac road, Hamid and Mustafa talked loudly and excitedly with the elation of survival, but he was silent. All the way back to Port Sudan he was composing letters

418

in his head: to the Governor, to Unicef in Khartoum. To the highest authorities in Unicef abroad. He would not let this rest, he was thinking angrily.

Back in his flat in Port Sudan he poured himself a glass of contraband whisky and went out onto the balcony. The night air was gentle, cool off the sea and fragrant with salt. The lights of the distant port winked and bobbed on the water. He could hear the wavelets running up into the creek below.

Behind him, the brightly lit flat looked comfortable and inviting. Their boxes had arrived at last, not too damaged by the floods. He had bought more furniture in the local *souk* and had had leather cushions made. On the balcony, large pots held carefully tended young plants. His space, his kingdom: a novelty, this.

It was hard to admit how much he'd enjoyed furnishing this place. Things he had always deferred to Bee now in his own hands. He had wanted it to be otherwise. But maybe, like a bower bird, he might woo her yet. The image had occurred to him as he watered his new plants that morning, making him smile. Strutting my stuff, he thought.

There are vacant bedrooms furnished with beds for the children. Their toys are stacked in new cupboards, waiting. In his bedroom, he sleeps at an angle across the new, imported double bed. Her books are on the shelves, next to his. The clothes she did not have with her when she left hang beside his in the wardrobe. They are not here, his family, but their presence is like a gesture, a pencilled date upon a calendar. And in the meantime there are projects he would like to set up and journeys he wants to go on. He knows an Englishman who has promised to take him deep into the Red Sea Hills by camel. And he wants to explore the coast from the sea: he has

419

met a bluff, friendly Cornishman working for the EC who says he will take him out on his boat. None of these things could he contemplate if Bee were here. If she were here he would feel her eyes upon him, claiming him. He would be struggling to temper his energy and activity to her obscure needs. But now he is free. He can go and come as he likes and if he is sometimes lonely there is always somebody he can visit. And if not that, he can sink himself in the book he is writing. *Aid: The Politics of Need*, he has called it.

He sits at his desk and begins to write. He writes for most of the night: five letters. The first three are to the Regional Governor, to Unicef in Khartoum, and to Unicef in New York, to notify them of the day's events. The fourth is to the University of East Anglia, handing in his notice. The last is to his wife, but it is late. The muezzin, from the loud-speaker on top of a nearby minaret, breaks the night in two with its crackling, mournful fall. He leaves the letter unfinished and goes to bed.

Chapter 29

There is something strange about Bee, an air of closure, which haunts Kay. Her sister laughs at the same things she has always laughed at but the laughter has no ring to it and her eyes stay distant. And if it is not surprising at first that Bee doesn't intend to return to the Sudan (after all, it is hardly worth the upheaval, given their contract is due to end at Christmas), it is very disturbing when it becomes clear that Charles intends to stay for another two years. As the story has unfolded, in the days and weeks since her sudden return with the children, it somehow never quite fits the hollowness in Bee's eyes. Kay finds herself thinking, And is that all? Has she done the right thing, coming home? And immediately it feels like a betrayal to even be thinking it. She asks, 'Are you separating, then?' And Bee just shrugs.

Kay is shocked by this. Chasing babies, chasing men, through the last frantic months of her twenties, she cannot quite believe that a whole marriage could be relinquished with such apparent ease. Surely it was worth a greater fight? And if Charles was bull-headed and egotistic (and Kay had never perceived him to be otherwise), if Bee must resign herself to the greater compromise, surely their marriage was worth it?

She considers these things with the practical good sense of someone looking in from the fresh air outside. But she knows she is not like Bee. When she thinks something she says it. Bee has always absorbed inwards, saying little about her inner self. Kay is frightened for her now. There is something there that was never apparent before, a haunted look. Self-doubt where once there was quiet self-esteem. It's as if Bee's inner confidence has been fatally sapped. On the surface she is normal, rushing about getting the children into schools, sorting out their house in Norwich, getting their furniture out of store. But none of it *sounds* quite right. The words are slightly wrong, the tone is too carefully cheerful. This is a facade to placate others. She cannot feel where Bee is any more.

She goes up to Norwich every weekend. Making up for lost time, she says. Bee has been lucky: the tenants had already given in their notice so she isn't homeless. Kay loves the children dearly, and in some ways she and Bee have as good a time together as ever they did, taking the children out during the day, sitting over a bottle of wine and sisterly gossip by night. But she notices that Bee no longer talks of buying her dream cottage and she avoids the issue when Kay tries to talk about it. Nor does she seem to be doing any painting. When Kay asks her, she is evasive about that too.

In October Kay announced that she was going to come and stay in the house for a week and look after the children while Bee went off for a holiday by herself. Kay was adamant. It was obvious, she said, that Bee needed to be alone for a bit, to have some time and space to herself. She needed a chance to paint without childish interruption. Well didn't she? Kay looked her sternly in the eye, challenging her.

Bee looked down at her hands, considering. She knew where she wanted to be, and she longed for solitude the same way a drowning woman longs for air. But she was frightened of the prospect of it, now that it was suddenly within reach.

She climbed the steps and turned the key in the lock. As the shabby door swung open she sniffed the air cautiously. The house exhaled its stale breath over her, smelling of damp. The wind whipped underneath the house, among the stilts, around the corpses of old canoes which were stored there. She shivered.

It was strange to enter alone, this house of transient people, of the noisy joy of return, and of tears on leaving. She walked round the familiar rooms feeling like a pale and insubstantial shadow. She couldn't compete with the vitality of the ghosts who moved before her.

The place felt neglected and rather mournful. Salt stains fogged the windows. A long finger of mildew crept down the studio wall at the corner where the tin roof was loose and they only remembered when it was too windy or too dark to sort it out. In the kitchen the various notes written by one branch of the family to another have yellowed a little more since her last visit, collected a little more grease, a few more scuffs at the edges. The house is tidy but it feels dead. It always feels like this on arrival, but on her own it will take longer to wake it up.

She unpacks the car and takes her suitcase upstairs. The bed will be damp. She must remember to switch on the electric blanket early. She puts her clothes in the old chest of drawers. When she was a child, her parents put their clothes in here. She thinks of them and cannot imagine that they ever existed without the complex weight of old age they carry now, blocking out horizons, impeding vision. Was it possible that they once filled these drawers with their clothes while thinking about frivolous games on the beach with young children, or an argument that they hadn't been through many times before, or even the prospect of making love later, in this same bed?

In the sitting room she lays out her painting things carefully and puts her books in a pile on the table by the window. There is a new picture hanging over the bookcase, a sentimental scene she doesn't recognise and does not like. A purchase of her cousin Emily, probably, it has her stamp on it. On the bookcase a child's drawing stands propped against the wall. She takes it down to look at it. It is a strong, quirky picture of a dog. It has an unconscious perfection, a flow of shape and form. Turning it over she sees Kit's name, in her own writing, and the date: May 11th 1988. This is disturbing and dislocating. How could she have forgotten? It is less than six months ago! She feels as if she has just been thumped between the eyes.

Later, finding she had forgotten to bring coffee, she went out to buy some from the village shop. The grassy space between the old wooden shacks and the village was filling up with cars as late tourists came out to enjoy the autumn sun. The river ran slack between its shored-up banks. A sailing dinghy was heading out towards the sea.

On the village green, the Old Pottery was full of people browsing. She felt lost without the children, she wanted human company. She went into the café at the back of the gift shop and ordered coffee. It was warm and homely in the little tea-room, the familiar clutter of fishing nets and glass balls decorating the walls, the same old photographs. The room was crowded and noisy. 'And it was a lovely Marks and Spencers dinner I gave him. Four pounds ninety-nine, that dinner cost, but all wasted. I gave it to the dog after.' She listened. Like the play-group where she took Catrin, like the mothers waiting

424

outside school – everyone so self-absorbed in tiny unimportant detail: I couldn't get him trainers because they hadn't any size four; he doesn't like cornflakes so I only get him Weetabix; this rain, it's getting on my nerves. Not seeing the world out there, only the world within. She heard it, but she hated herself for observing it. She felt like a stranger who talks a different language and shares no common tongue. You see things, and then you are different. And perhaps it will never be the same again. Not until you forget.

She listened to the soft Suffolk lilt in the voices at the next table. People who belonged here as she never would. Wherever she went she was an outsider, thinking different thoughts. She didn't have to go all the way to Africa to experience that.

Abruptly she got up from the table and went to pay her bill.

'Is there a loo here?' she asked.

'Up the stairs, first door on your left. Are you just here for the weekend or will we be seeing you later in the week?'

The question startled her. 'Probably. Yes.'

The bathroom window looked out over a network of small gardens enclosed by flint walls and crooked, red-tiled roofs. A flock of glossy starlings was marauding the heavily laden apple tree that hung over the garden wall. It made a brilliant picture in the sunshine, the starlings so gaudy, the apples flushed with crimson, the roof tiles rust-red against the sharp pallor of the flint walls. Captivated, she stood looking down. This was the sort of garden she would like. A view from a bathroom of mellow buildings and comical birds.

The thought brings her up short. She doesn't know if she is in the business of looking for houses any more, just as she doesn't know if she is separated or still married.

How can she know what she is doing if she doesn't know *that*?

425

How can she know it on her own?

He is a long way away. His letters come but they don't tell her much. He talks of the people he meets, the changes in the office, the things he has bought for the flat. But he hasn't mentioned Christmas. He doesn't talk of what he feels, and he does not talk about their marriage, apart from saying how sorry he is for having hurt her, and how he hopes she will forgive him and feel less badly about it in a little while.

All this says that they are connected, but she doesn't feel it. Sometimes she thinks she is going mad with the emptiness inside. She doesn't know who she is any more.

In the afternoon she forced herself to take her painting things and her little folding stool out on to the marshes. It was bright and windy but out of the wind the sun was still warm. She walked out of the village briskly and turned onto the path past the old barn with the broken back, which she had so often sketched or painted. The grass in the fields on either side was bright with late growth but the trees were on the turn and the marshes were already acquiring their brittle, faded winter look.

In the marshes, the reed beds stood tall and even. They towered over the path, which wound its way along the edge of the tidal creek. She paused and looked back. The wind was susurrating in the reeds like a thousand sighing voices. All around her the horizons were wide and shallow, from the distant rise of trees inland, from side to side of the wide, flat-bottomed valley, to the whispering bank of shingle which shielded the marshes from the sea.

She shivered. Less from the cold wind than from a feeling of dislocation. Inland, dead trees, bleached and shining in the sun, stood out above scrub chestnut and stunted oak. All around her, echoes. Discomfiting echoes: the stunted trees; the

426

pale reeds like farmed sorghum; the delicate shades of yellow and grey-blue; the pale bright light. And out of the wind, even a pale reflection of the heat of the sun. She shook her head, dislodging unquiet confusions. Hurried on along the edge of the creek.

The old windmill. She remembered it from childhood, when it had still had a wooden top and broken sails. Now it stands truncated. Carefully she chose a place to set her stool to catch the light on the mellow brick just so above the pale straight line of the reeds. How ironic, she thought as she organised her brushes and pulled her hat down lower to stop the wind blowing her hair in her eyes: the same preoccupation with water but to opposite effect: this wind-pump, like a *shaduf*, was about the lifting of water but for drainage not irrigation. The thought buffeted her, the connection of place with place suddenly obvious and conscious.

Brush in hand, block of paper vacant before her, she shivered slightly in the wind. Once she would have been invigorated by the cold, and inspired by the scene in front of her to try to capture the subtle shades and shapes. But something in her head has slipped. She looks, but she no longer sees an innocent Suffolk landscape. Everything she looks at echoes. She sees not wild reeds but cultivated sorghum, not thorn and oak but acacia scrub. Not cold but heat. Not the chill glare of a wintry sun on marsh and hidden water, but the hot sharp glare of sun on sand and rock.

It is like a scar where the flesh has grown over hidden grit: it moves with her until, roused by unexpected echoes, it shoots her with a stabbing pain.

The brush hovered. Her hand was tense – the brush was quivering. *What's wrong with me?* She whimpered out loud, and the sound made her afraid.

Not the right place, not today. Try somewhere else. Somewhere firmly itself, beyond alien association. Hurriedly she put her things back in her bag and picked up the folding stool. She walked quickly on. The path dipped and swung alongside the sheer, flat face of the reed-beds. It was muddy underfoot and at times she slipped and stumbled. The sun was in her eyes, hard and edgy. She walked faster. On, across the white light of the shallow valley. Up into the shadow of a wood. Stumbling, panicky.

She stopped. Light filtered down through the trees on to the bare floor of the copse. Smooth slender boles of sycamore trees crowded round her. The wind creaked in the swaying branches overhead. Here, even here, it was with her. She was not in Suffolk. It was not cold. She was in a brittle, hot wood in Northern Kordofan. She could feel it all around her, in the dead crunch of the leaves underfoot, in the birdless silence. In the way the sun glanced through naked branches. She began to run.

A sandy road stretching before her, shining white in the sun. The crooked thorns on either side slanting to the land, remembering the sea.

The faint saline smell came to her like an anchor. She ran on clumsily, wanting the reassurance of water, the forgetfulness of the ocean. It wasn't far away. At the end of this track perhaps, there would be a path down to the shore. Then a sudden smell slapped her between the eyes and stopped her in her tracks. Camel dung. Abrupt and pungent in her flared, anxious nostrils. She sniffed cautiously. It was there. Definite. Real. Now she knew for certain she was going mad. She crumpled abruptly in a heap on the sandy turf. Dry sobs rise like ugly fish. She hears them and knows it must be true: she is going mad. She is never to be free.

She sat for a long time. The silence absorbed her sobs and offered back emptiness. She stopped, her head on her knees, listening in terror to the silence. A few dry leaves rattled in the hawthorn hedge in the sharp breeze. Memory goes with you like a bad smell. Or the reverberations of a bad marriage. A taint on the skin, a film across the eye. You absorb or you reject, but you cannot escape. She sat with her face still buried in her arms, listening. The wind creaked and rattled, a single bird sang. But, far away, she could just make out the anchoring whisper of the sea.

A creaky calm began to seep in, like the damp which was creeping up through her jeans from the rabbit-bitten turf. She got up, cautiously sniffing the air. The smell of camel *was* there. She hadn't been imagining it.

Beyond the thorn hedge, a dung heap was steaming gently in the sun.

She stared at it. She was cold. The wind crept inside her jacket. She bent down and picked up her stool, her bag, her discarded hat. Straightening, she snuffed the air, placing the smell carefully like a blind woman.

This is not heat but cold.

This is not sorghum but reeds.

This is not acacia but hawthorn.

Not camel dung but ordinary, unsurprising cattle manure from a Friesian herd on a dairy farm on the Suffolk coast.

I am not mad, merely a little displaced.

I can embrace my past, and embrace my life. Or I can run away.

Charles was in it, too. Perhaps he was all of it. She was so tired. Always so tired, fatigue like an amoeba dragging down her limbs. Stop running. Stand and face the questions. Look them in the eye. It was time she did.

429

She walked quietly, along the track towards the sounding sea.

It is dark. She is in the pub. She reads a novel as she eats her meal. There is a certain calm, here in the shelter of the old settle beside a roaring log fire. Alone in the saloon bar but the sound of cheerful voices in other rooms.

It hasn't been a bad day, after all. When she got back to the house, walking along the ripped edge of the sea, she had settled down to draw and to her surprise it had gone quite well. A charcoal drawing of the flowering reeds she had brought back from her walk. Tomorrow she would paint them, a study in subtle fawns and greys.

The panic attack still haunts her. She is all right, but she so nearly wasn't. It is good to be in the bustle of the pub. Nobody takes any notice of her as she sits in her corner, shielded by the high backs of the two settles. Now and then the outside door opens with a rush of wind and footsteps leave or enter. The other bar is filling.

A noisy group comes in. Feet pass, the creak of leather jackets, a confusion of boisterous laughter. Over the back of the settle she glimpses a green and orange Mohican passing down the worn old passage between the settle and the wall and thinks inadvertently, inevitably, of Daz. Where is he now? Muddy feelings of regret, of guilt and shame, tarnish the thought of him and she pushes the memory away. The leather-clad bikers are hustling into the darts room next to the bar and stripping off their creaking gear. She can't see them but she hears snatches of their raucous conversation, the local cast of their voices, not taking much notice as she goes back to her book.

That is Daz's voice. She hears him quite clearly. Teasing one of the girls, out of sight in the cramped little room by the bar. The girl's voice comes back, slightly plaintive.

Oh God! She thought he was still safely in the Sudan, and besides, he didn't get on with his father and hadn't visited since his mother died last year. Perhaps it wasn't him, but she must leave immediately, just in case.

She had to go to the bar to pay her bill. She went to the far end, away from the darts room. She was sure now that it was Daz. She could hear him laughing. The barmaid totted up her bill distractedly. There wasn't enough change in the till. The girl grinned at her with an apologetic shrug and went to fetch some. At that moment the green and orange punk came out of the darts room and squeezed past her towards the Gents.

She felt him stop behind her. She could feel him looking down at the back of her head. His familiar voice, sounding astonished, said her name. She turned towards him and tried to look surprised.

His greeting was unambiguous. He seized her in a great bear hug. Then he held her away to look into her face before pulling her close again and giving her a smacking kiss on each cheek and then a great boisterous kiss on the mouth. I suppose we must look a funny pair, she thought, seeing the barmaid's expression. She put her hand out to receive her change. He still had his arm round her shoulders. He kept saying 'Wow!'

'Is Charles here? Where are the kids?'

'I'm on my own. Just for the week.'

'Let me get you a drink! What are you drinking?'

'No really, I was just going.'

He looked down at her. That penetrating gaze. All that noise, and then that silent intensity as if he was looking right inside her head. Familiar, but until that moment she had forgotten it.

'Surely you've got time for a quick drink with me first?' He sounded disappointed.

'I'm not...'

'Just you and me,' he said quickly. He jerked his head towards the doorway of the darts room from which came loud guffaws. 'You don't have to cope with that lot. We've been out for the day on the bikes. They're a bit pissed, to tell the truth.'

She looked up at him. As he talked, his bright plume of hair seemed to bristle. His scalp was shiny. She'd forgotten how ugly he was, even without the Mohican. But he didn't look pissed. He looked older than she remembered. Serious too, in spite of his hair. He held her gaze and raised his eyebrows quizzically.

'All right,' she said reluctantly. She didn't want to talk about the Sudan, not tonight. And Charles – she wasn't sure she *could* talk about him, even if she wanted to. What was there to say? Too much, and nothing at all. 'Fisherman's Ale – just a half,' she said to the barmaid. 'What'll you have?' she asked Daz.

'No, this one's on me,' he said. 'A small thank you for all you've done for me. Pint of Guinness, Betony,' he said to the girl.

They took their drinks and went back to where she'd been sitting by the fire. He sat across the table from her, his eyes watching her over the top of his pint. She looked back, still surprised at the flesh and blood reality of him. He was as skinny as ever, as unprepossessing in his faded tee-shirt and worn leathers as he had been in a *jelabiya*. But he was more substantial than in her memory. Warm-blooded, indefinably himself. She had, she realised as she watched him, made him otherwise, in her thoughts. A pale shadow. Her victim.

He didn't look the tiniest fraction her victim now. He grinned his crooked grin. 'Well this is one big surprise! I thought you weren't coming back until Christmas.'

'I thought you were still in Babanusa.'

'I left there in July – spent two months in Omdurman

432

working in a refugee camp. I would've stayed longer only I had to come back 'cos my dad was taken ill.'

'Oh. I'm sorry.'

'So am I. He died two weeks ago. I miss him, you know, now he's gone. I never expected to. I told you we didn't get on, didn't I? Well, he didn't relent. Right up to the very end he didn't. But now he's gone I miss him. It's like it's sort of *draughty*, you know? Like he was blocking out the wind and the rain and now he in't there any more. Anyway, that's enough about me. How're the kids?'

She told him they were well, that Danny had taken to secondary school like a duck to water. That Kit and Adam were loving primary school, and Catrin was at play-group and would be starting nursery next term. She wondered, as she told him these banal scraps, if she was perhaps a disappointment without the children. The warmth in his voice as he asked after them made his affection for them obvious. It re-aroused hers for him. The punk hair-style became less dominating, his eyes became more so. He kept looking at her, that piercing look. She half wanted to run away from it and it half drew her back.

'I was in the Acropole the night it was bombed,' he said suddenly. 'We weren't there when the bomb went off, we went in after – they needed medics and I was with a crowd of nurses and doctors. I was shit scared I was going to find you in there. And when they said some little English kids had been killed, you can imagine how that felt. Until I saw it wasn't your kids. And then I felt terrible for being relieved. I still have nightmares about it.'

She stared at him in surprise. The bombing had had such an impact on her and she hadn't even been there. She hadn't once thought of it having any significance for him. Her resistances crumbled a little. As if he sensed it, he asked again

433

after Charles. He was watching her intently. She wanted to be evasive. And then suddenly she wanted not to be.

'He's in Port Sudan. For two more years. He signed the contract without telling me.' She heard his sharp intake of breath and knew she didn't have to explain. 'He's supposed to be making his mind up whether to back out of the contract and come home at Christmas after all. I have a horrible suspicion he's not going to. I have a suspicion he's going to give in his notice at the university here.' He put out his hands and covered hers where they lay on the table. His hands were warm and calloused. Rough, strong, disarmingly simple hands. She looked down at them distractedly. 'I don't know whether we're a couple any more. I don't know whether I'm still married. I've told him I'm not going back, but I think he thinks that he can have it both ways at once. I think he supposes that in a while, when I've had time to stop being cross with him, I'll be quite happy to fly out there with the children for the school holidays. I think he hopes that snorkelling and swimming and a few weeks of sunshine by the sea two or three times a year will be enough to persuade me, and then he can keep his job and pursue it without any awkward distractions like wife and children, and have us as well, part-time. And come home once a year on leave and play happy families in England.'

She stopped. She hadn't said this much to anyone, not to her best friend Elizabeth, not even to Kay. Why did he have this effect on her, drawing her out in spite of herself? He was looking at her understandingly. Damn him. In a minute she'd be thinking about letting him come home with her to bed. Sympathy is a very crude form of seduction. She took her hands back and stared crossly into her glass.

'And you? What d'you feel about all of that?' he said.

She wasn't going to reply. But she had told nobody this, and

434

she did need desperately to tell. 'I don't know what I feel. I know I don't want to live in the Sudan again. I know I feel betrayed by him making decisions without me – and I was so angry that he took us all to live there in the first place. But I know that if I see him he'll persuade me it's all a good idea.' She looked up and he nodded. The girl behind the bar was wielding a tea towel slowly and watching the TV that was audible from the other bar. 'He is very persuasive, you know. He can tell me black is white and I know it isn't but after a while I'm not very sure about it any more and I say yes to things when I should say no because I can't remember why I should stick to saying no. He tells me it would be selfish to put my own feelings before the lives of other people and after a while I haven't got any arguments left which sound reasonable, even to me. So I say yes and afterwards I wish I hadn't. And then I feel terribly angry – with him, but with myself as well because I'm not even very good at that sort of life. Trouble is, I don't feel any good at this sort of life either, not any more.'

'But why don't you feel you're any good?' He peered into her face. 'You seem pretty wonderful to me! And it's not *a fault*, not being able to thrive out there. Not many people do, even without four kids in tow. It's not exactly a sin!'

She wanted to say, And now I can't even seem to paint any more, I'm good at nothing and good for nothing. But it sounded too plaintive. She changed the subject and asked him about himself.

He told her about the camps in Omdurman. He talked easily, with a confidence she didn't remember. She listened, her inner thoughts running in a tangle underneath. She had not succeeded in making her own commitment. She hadn't taken on her own share of the weight. She had run away, but her absence wasn't significant. Even Charles didn't seem to care enough about her absence to come after her. She felt as if she would be haunted by the failure for ever. As if inside her head she was homeless.

He started asking her questions, taking hold of her attention and squeezing it, pulling her unwillingly into the space between them. When had they left El Obeid? Did she get caught in the floods as well? He'd been there too, he'd been in Omdurman by then. Christ, hadn't it been awful! And such a stink, afterwards. He said that the final time he'd passed through El Obeid on the way up from Babanusa he'd sneaked past their house and seen it all shut up and thought they must have gone to Khartoum for a meeting. The *frangipani* tree at the front of the house had been in full flower and he'd remembered how Catrin liked to collect the flowers off the ground and wear them behind her ears. She laughed. A small feeling of affection for the place suddenly welled up, like a bubble rising out of mud to the surface of the pond.

Once, in El Obeid, talking of home, he had done the same thing for her in reverse, anchoring her to her own memory.

How warm and human he was, under that forbidding hair and shaved scalp. As one hour passed, and then another, she realised with surprise that she could, if she chose to, see him again – tomorrow, or the next day. Or the day after, if he wasn't rushing off somewhere. She asked him coolly how long he planned to be around.

He said, with an amused look, that he was staying in his dad's cottage until he'd decided what to do with it. He didn't know whether it mightn't be best to sell it. When he went back to work in Omdurman again the money would be useful. There was a lot he could do in Omdurman with funds like that. 'Or maybe I'll go somewhere else all together,' he said.

'The world's a big place. Get myself some proper training first though. As a paramedic, perhaps?'

His friends were coming out of the darts room. They came over on their way to the door, staring at her with open curiosity. He introduced her as a friend from the Sudan. The only girl in the group, a young pale slip of a thing with long brown hair and a pretty face, stared at her and turned away. There was an unmistakeably jealous edge to that look. She was surprised. Then she felt guilty. Daz should go off with them, these were his friends. But he was telling them to go without him, that he'd make his own way back. And suddenly she was glad.

The pub was closing. Last orders had been served and the lights switched on and off a few times. They got up and made their way out into the chill night air. The salt smell of the sea made a sharp edge to the dark wind.

'Goodnight,' she said.

'Come on, I'll take you home.'

'I can walk.'

'I'm sure you can, but you could come on Sammy instead.'

'Sammy?'

'This is Sammy,' he said, patting the large black and silver motorbike parked just in front of the pub. 'Sammy, meet Bee. Bee, Sammy. Much less trouble than a camel but same evil temper. 'Cept that this Sammy is a she. Come on, give you a quick burn up!'

He strapped on his helmet and climbed on to the bike. She hesitated.

'Come on,' he said, patting the seat behind him. 'It's one of them wooden houses, in't it? Down by the river? You don't need a helmet just to go down there. Nobody'll be none the wiser.' He laughed at her suddenly as she hesitated. 'Come on, Bee! Let go for once – be daring!'

Stung, she had a good mind to walk home just to spite him. Daring, indeed! She'd been travelling illicitly on boyfriend's motorbikes when he was still on stabilisers.

He bounced up and down and the powerful bike creaked on its springs. He looked ridiculous straddled there, disguised in his helmet, bouncing like a baby. She couldn't help but laugh. She climbed on behind him. Tentatively she put her arms round his waist. He patted her clasped hands fondly with one gloved paw and kicked the bike into life. The echo roared back at them from the silent walls of the cottages. It was late, and very dark.

Down the straight road, away from the village towards the river, they sped. The cold wind swept over them. The headlamp framed the road and the dark huddled shapes of the wooden houses beside the river. She seemed to be the only person in residence this weekend and she hadn't left any lights on. At the river they swung to the right and drove slowly along the narrow stony track between the cluster of black buildings. She was glad she wasn't coming back alone, though perhaps it was only the light of the bike that made it seem sinister. There was no moon and the sky was dull. Beyond the sea-wall that surrounded the village the clouds soaked up the light from the street-lamps like a sponge.

'Which one?' he shouted over his shoulder.

'The end one,' she shouted back.

He swept round the corner of the house, spitting gravel. As she climbed off he cut the engine. In the sudden silence she could hear the pounding sigh of the sea, rhythmical as a languorous heartbeat. She was cold, even after so short a ride. Standing shivering beside the handlebars she said, 'Do you want some coffee?'

He laughed. 'I was afraid you weren't going to ask.'

He got off the bike and pushed it on to its stand. Easing off his helmet, he plumped up his Mohican and followed her up the concrete steps. She could feel him just behind her, as if he might put his hands upon her at any moment. But he didn't and she pushed the thought away. Probably he just wanted to talk. Like he said, there was nobody you could tell about so much of it, and there was so much to tell.

She unlocked the shabby old door and felt inside for the switch.

How glad she was not to be coming in alone. She was humming as she went off to the kitchen to boil the kettle. When she came back to the sitting room he was examining her drawing on the table. He looked at it seriously, and then he looked at her. She had that sudden feeling she'd had before: he had looked at her in that same serious, penetrating way when he examined her watercolours in El Obeid. She realised she had no idea whether he'd been to college or not, or what he was interested in, beyond everything and everyone.

He nodded at her as he put the drawing down, as if she had passed muster. A little feeling of pleasure curled upwards like smoke inside her. He prowled round the room, looking at everything. Kit's drawing of the dog made him grin. Emily's purchase on the wall made him frown. She went off to make the coffee and caught herself smiling.

Daz poked his head round the kitchen door. 'Wow! This is quite some place!'

'It's a lovely place. A much loved place,' she said contentedly, spooning coffee into a jug. He was standing behind her. Then he was putting his arms around her and pulling her back against him. She was startled to feel him hard and erect in the small of her back. 'Oh!' she exclaimed softly.

'My most favourite woman. You don't know how much I've

thought about you!' he whispered into her hair. 'Can we forget about the coffee? Can't I take you to bed instead?'

Not in the room at the top of the stairs to the left (where the empty bunk-beds stand against the walls and no child's breath stirs the air) but in the room to the right – in the bed her parents used to sleep in on family holidays, where she herself was conceived (though she does not know it), where she has lain a thousand times with Charles (loving or indifferent, intent or vacant) – she lies now in the arms of her lover. The room is filled with a dry ebb and flow, the tidal whisperings of her perennial ghosts.

'I lost my virginity in this room,' she muses out loud.

'*Lost* it? Weren't he that nice, then?'

She considers. 'He was nice. But I never seemed to get anything right. Not even kissing. He said I made too much noise.'

He lifts his head to peer down at her. 'Nothing wrong with *your* kissing! Was it Charles then?'

She catches the inference and laughs. 'No, it wasn't Charles.'

They lie quietly, thinking about different things. She turns her head to look at him. Runs her palm over the bristle of his hair. It bends and bounces under her hand like a brush. His head where it is shaved is growing a gingery stubble, like his chin. And the orange and green is growing out of his plume: the roots show dark underneath.

'You've got your name back, anyhow.'

'Me?' He sounds confused. 'Daz? Oh, you mean my hair? No, I was always called Daz. Since I was about five, anyhow. David Anthony Zimmerman, unavoidably DAZ.'

'Zimmerman?'

'Yep. My dad was German – didn't I ever tell you? A prisoner of war. Stayed on afterwards and married a local girl.

Or at least he did when he finally got round to making an honest woman of her.'

Rolling over onto her stomach she lifts herself to look down on him where he lies on his back.

'How old are you then?'

He groans. 'Don't ask. Too old! I'll be thirty next month.'

Another misconception bites the dust. Thirty? Next month! Four years younger than her. Not a baby at all, then. Just a great boy. Her mental picture of him goes through several convulsions. Then her mental picture of herself goes through another. She laughs out loud. What a fool she's been! How blind. Not a boy, a man. It's obvious really, now that she looks to see. The little lines around his eyes, his mouth. A great boy-man. Why had she ever thought otherwise? Mere self-flagellation? A hook on which to hang her guilt? He was old enough to look after himself all the time. He had been, after all, always her equal. And she has not seduced him. Hasn't even taken advantage of him. Not really.

He squinted up at her. 'What?'

She shook her head and just smiled. He leaned over to where her heavy breasts scooped downwards towards the bed. The wind moaned, banging a loose bit of tin on the roof. He placed the tip of his tongue on the delicate place between her armpit and one swinging breast.

'D'you know, I fancied you right from the moment I first set eyes on you in the *souk* in El Obeid,' he said. She looked down at him.

'I felt terribly bad that I'd seduced you,' he added. 'Thought I'd taken advantage of all your warm nursey feelings.'

Her eyes widened in astonishment.

'I'm not very good at relationships. I get up close and then I don't really know what to do with the feelings.' He avoided her eye, studying her breasts. Under his scrutiny she felt her nipples stiffen. 'So I haven't got much to offer. Even my friendship isn't much cop – I'm not exactly reliable.' He looked up at her. 'But if you wanted me, I would try really hard to be a good friend.'

She looked down at him squinting up at her and raised her eyebrows, saying nothing.

'Okay, your lover then. *And* your friend.'

'Is it possible to be both?'

'I dunno. I hope so! You do it like this,' he said, suddenly rolling her over and noisily kissing one breast. 'And like this.' He kissed the other. Then he kissed her soundly on the mouth and silenced her reply.

The bed was warm but there was cold at her back as she turned towards him. The world changes and that which was dark becomes light. The spectrum of the light shifts and all the colours change. She looked at him as if she was seeing him for the first time.

Later she lies listening to the distant pebble-dash sigh of the sea and the soft sighing breath of the man who sleeps beside her. She thinks of her children, tucking them one by one into the safety of her thoughts.

And then there is Charles. There is no safety she can tuck him into and the old anxiety rises, but she listens carefully to the sea and quietens her breathing again to its steady pulse. He will make his choices, but she too can make hers. She can negotiate. They can create new balances between them, if they choose to.

She turns to look at Daz, his sleeping face gentled by the light of the lamp. A part of the past who has walked into her present, and who knows if he will be in her future? But she does have a future. She can see it now, and herself inhabiting it, a whole woman, alive in her own skin. Nobody's shadow.

Glossary

angareb – rope bed
awlad (plural of walad) – boys
bukra – tomorrow
fatur – main meal of the day, eaten late morning
gafir – watchman, caretaker
haboob – dust storm
hafir – reservoir
jelabiya – traditional male garment
jebel – hill
jir-jir – salad rocket
kerkedeh – hibiscus
khawaja – literally lord or master, used for white person
lá – no
limoon – lemon
madrassa – school
racuba – open thatched shelter on wooden posts
simsim – sesame
sitt – madam
souk – market
SPLA – Sundanese People's Liberation Army
thobe – long cloth worn by women, wrapped around over
their dresses
tibeldi – baobab tree
wadi – water course, usually dry
walad – boy

Acknowledgements

This novel is a work of fiction and all the characters in the story are imaginary. However the events that form the framework are real and the descriptions of them are as close to the first-hand accounts I was given at the time as memory allows. At times Unicef gets rather a hard press at the hands of one unhappy woman teetering on the edge of breakdown, but her experience is highly subjective and does not reflect on a massive organisation that delivers millions of pounds worth of benefit all over the world. The department at the University of East Anglia in which Charles worked is entirely fictional.

Many people have helped this book come to fruition but first and foremost I want to thank my children Tom, Owen and Penny, and my first husband Andrew (who is nothing like Charles!), because without the four of you there would be no book. I am also indebted to numerous people for their stories and experiences. In particular I would like to mention Rosamund Soheir Majid, cousin and friend, who sadly died before I could show her this book, and Ellen Ishmail. There are others whose names I do not remember but whose stories live on vividly in my head, like the Irish girl from CARE who described going into the Acropole Hotel just after the bombing, and Celia, who inadvertently gave me the title, one hot morning in Khartoum. I hope I have taken good care of the stories I have borrowed from you all. I would also like to thank the Pagoulatus family and all the staff at the Acropole Hotel who used to make our stays there such a pleasure, and also the staff of Unicef in Khartoum who looked after us rather better than might appear from this story. Thank you to Caroline Oakley for her editorial input, also Penny Thomas, and all the staff at Honno. I am especially grateful to all those friends and family members who have been hauled in to read work in progress: your wonderful support and encouragement has helped keep me going, especially my mother, Meg Evans, who has been supportive beyond the call of duty. Last, and most of all, thank you Nick for your loving enthusiasm and your stern wisdom. Without you, this book would still be languishing in a (very dusty) drawer.

About the Author

Hilary Shepherd spent two years in the Sudan with her young family during the 1980s, before returning to Wales to run an organic farm. She now earns her living as a wood-worker making windows, windows and kitchens, and lives with her husband Nick in an old house on a Welsh hillside and sometimes in Spain.

ABOUT HONNO

Honno Welsh Women's Press was set up in 1986 by a group of women who felt strongly that women in Wales needed wider opportunities to see their writing in print and to become involved in the publishing process. Our aim is to develop the writing talents of women in Wales, give them new and exciting opportunities to see their work published and often to give them their first 'break' as a writer.

Honno is registered as a community co-operative. Any profit that Honno makes is invested in the publishing programme. Women from Wales and around the world have expressed their support for Honno. Each supporter has a vote at the Annual General Meeting.

To receive further information about forthcoming publications, or become a supporter, please write to Honno at the address below, or visit our website:

www.honno.co.uk

Honno
Unit 14, Creative Units
Aberystwyth Arts Centre
Penglais Campus
Aberystwyth
Ceredigion
SY23 3GL

All Honno titles can be ordered online at
www.honno.co.uk
or by sending a cheque to Honno.
Free p&p to all UK addresses.